FORSAKEN

FORSAKEN

A Novel

Ross Howell Jr.

NewSouth Books
Montgomery

NewSouth Books
105 S. Court Street
Montgomery, AL 36104

Publisher's Cataloging-in-Publication data

Howell, Ross Jr.
Forsaken / Ross Howell Jr.
p. cm.

ISBN 978-1-58838-317-4 (hardcover)
ISBN 978-1-60306-396-8 (ebook)

1. United States—Virginia—Fiction. 2. Capital punishment—Virginia.
3. Christian, Virginia, 1895–1912. I. Title.

2015956099

Design by Randall Williams

Printed in the United States of America
by Bang Printing

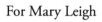

For Mary Leigh

Notice to the Reader

Charles Mears, Virginia Christian, Ida Belote, Dr. George Vanderslice, attorney George Washington Fields, and many other characters in this novel were real people, but the book itself is a work of fiction. References to real people, events, court records, articles, establishments, organizations, or locales are intended only to provide a sense of authenticity, and are used fictiously. All other characters, incidents, and dialogue are drawn from the author's imagination and are not to be construed as real. The language used in the book includes crude idioms and epithets that reflect the authentic language of the period. The author intends no offense, disparagement, or hurt.

— THE PUBLISHERS

Contents

FORSAKEN

August 16, 1912, the day after her seventeenth birthday, Virginia Christian died in the electric chair at the state penitentiary in Richmond, Virginia; she is the only female juvenile executed in the commonwealth's history. She had been found guilty of murdering fifty-one-year-old Ida Belote in a bedroom of the woman's Hampton home.

Times-Herald reporter Charles Mears covered the trial and interviewed the girl after she was sentenced. Though she confessed her guilt, Mears twice wrote William Hodges Mann, the last Confederate veteran to serve as governor, asking him to spare her life.

— THE AUTHOR

1.

My Testament

I was born Charles Gilbert Mears on August 21 in Southampton County, Virginia, during the financial panic of 1893. Mother told me the midwife moved her pallet onto the gallery to catch the breeze. She spread damp cloths over my mother and the two of them prayed for nightfall. The midwife sang, "Bend down, Jesus, bend down low!" I was born at twilight. Mother said from that evening on nothing was so restful to her as listening to the ratchet of katydids in the gloaming.

I never knew my father. In the tintypes he is a big man with a full beard. Mother looks slender as a lily next to him. The month before I was born, he traveled west to find work. The Southampton Bank & Trust failed and took his business with it. He never returned to my mother and me, but never did I hear her speak an ill word against him.

Before the panic my father had a thriving freight business with three heavy wagons, teamsters who were sober and reliable, and six pairs of mules. For a while he made ends meet by bartering to haul goods and equipment. Then even grain for the mules grew scarce. He sold the mules, but no one had money for the wagons. They were all that was left, abandoned in a field behind our house. I remember leaping from their sideboards to slay Yankee cavalrymen, the rusty wagon springs creaking. When the days grew hot, I rested in their shade, listening to cicadas in the trees. Beyond the wheel spokes the wide, barren fields shimmered in the sun.

The money from the mules my father gave to my mother. He kept enough to make passage to Provo, Utah. He was hired as a laborer to build a railroad spur from Salt Lake. My parents exchanged letters until after I was born. Then my mother's envelopes were returned. Rumor had it Father was killed in a brawl with an Irishman. I didn't know if that was true or if he simply abandoned us.

Mother insisted I should never take it as an omen, but on the night of August 21 in 1831, the slave Nat Turner led the Southampton insurrection. The old people where I grew up still remembered. Seventy Negroes marched from plantation to plantation, using knives, axes, and sickles to butcher white people. Under Turner's order, no firearms were used, since the reports would have alerted neighboring plantations. Turner himself carried a broadsword. Fifty-eight whites—men, women, and children—were slaughtered. Militias quelled the rebellion and the reprisals were brutal. Turner confessed to his crimes and was hanged by the neck. His body was drawn and quartered. It was said a plantation owner had a slave fashion a satchel with Turner's skin.

An old man lived alone in a shack near our land. He claimed when he was a boy my age he hid under the stone foundations of his house as the slaves of Turner's rebellion set it alight. They had murdered his parents inside. He said the slaves spoke in tongues he had never heard and their eyes gleamed red in the firelight. I listened, slapping at mosquitoes, breathless.

People said the old man was daft. He seemed to pass his hours in a world of dreams and phantasms, muttering to himself like a mad actor on the stage. People living nearby sometimes heard blood-curdling shrieks at night, and claimed he was a drunk, addled by bad whiskey. But never once did I see him imbibe, or smell spirits on his breath, or discover tell-tale jugs hidden in his hovel. Though he scared me, I loved to hear his talk. My mother never discouraged my visits. She would wrap a meal of cornbread and bacon for him, usually with beans or chickpeas.

The walk home after one of my visits was a torture of shadows and crickets and rustling marsh grass. Sometimes the old man would show me an artifact he kept wrapped with canvas and twine in his wood box. He said it was a leg bone from Nat Turner's skeleton, given him by a doctor said to have assembled it after the slave was mutilated. The old man let me touch it with my fingertips, gazing wide-eyed on it himself as if he held a relic from the holy land.

The bone might simply have been carried in by one of the old man's hounds. The story of it could have been imagined from beginning to end. But as he spun his tale, sitting on his haunches like a wild creature, his eyes gleaming, his unkempt beard flecked with spit, terror sprang up in the Southampton fields beyond his cabin walls. Rainwater in puddles after a storm was thick with blood. Birdsong echoed with the screams of dying women and children. Scythes and axe blades glinted in moonlit pastures. Or so it seemed to me as a boy.

Nat Turner could recite whole books of scripture from memory. His intelligence was a wonder to local white clergy and a miracle to the Negroes who heard him preach in the open fields. When he was executed, he claimed an angel had visited him. The angel had told Turner he would see a sign when it was God's will for him to massacre the people who enslaved him. The summer of the insurrection an eclipse blotted out the sun. After the rebellion colored people could not congregate to worship unless supervised by a white pastor. Laws prohibited teaching a slave to read or giving a slave a book, even the Bible, anywhere in Virginia.

Some evenings after supper Mother would sit with me in the parlor and read the scriptures.

"From the Gospel of Matthew, Charles," she said, her glasses perched at the tip of her nose. "'Lord, when saw we thee an hungred, and fed *thee*? or thirsty, and gave *thee* drink? When saw we thee a stranger, and took *thee* in? or naked, and clothed *thee*? Or when saw we thee sick, or in prison, and came unto thee? And the King shall answer and say unto them, Inasmuch as ye have done *it* unto one of the least of these my brethren, ye have done *it* unto me.'"

"Mother, what is 'an hungred?'" I asked.

"A person who's starving," she said.

"And 'the least of these'?"

"The helpless."

"I want to help," I said. I was six years old.

"You're a good boy, Charles," my mother said.

When I was ten she passed away. I was taken in by her maiden aunt. When I matriculated at the College of William & Mary, I was so pious the other boys called me "Preacher." I led Bible classes at the college chapter of the YMCA and a Temperance prayer group for young men on Saturday nights. Not one Sunday did I miss service at the Methodist church by campus. But in our yearbook my classmates named me "most likely to bum tobacco."

Often my friend Fitzhugh Scott and I would sit on the steps of our boarding house, gazing across the green to the old Colonial Governor's mansion, where Thomas Jefferson sometimes dined as a student. We liked to talk poetry or religion. Fitz leaned against the steps, legs akimbo, while I smoked.

"Well, you have a point, Preacher," he said, loosening his collar. His sunburned cowlick bristled through a coat of pomade. "Transcendentalism is not Christianity. But it's hardly *pagan*. Wouldn't you say Walt Whitman voiced Christian ideals? And lived them?"

"I suppose," I said.

Soon after, my friend died. Studies and devotions seemed trivial then. I felt Death was stalking me, staring at me from the pages of books. I left college, taking a job at a newspaper in Hampton.

In the daily tramp of events I believed I might rejoin the living.

That's how I came to report on the trial and execution of Virginia Christian. What follows is my account of what happened, then and after. I like to believe I'm telling the truth. But I've learned the truth hides somewhere in the shadows of what happens.

2.

Black Woman Held

Poindexter was a good man to talk to. He was the telegraph operator at the C&O depot. Say he helped somebody with a message, or noticed somebody come into town on the afternoon train, or overheard somebody talking on the platform—Poindexter would let you know if something was up.

Late afternoon March 18, 1912, I was heading for the depot. It was a Monday and all the news was from the mountains. The wires were humming with stories about the Allen gang. They'd killed a sitting judge, Commonwealth's attorney, sheriff, and a witness up at the Hillsville courthouse. Wanted posters were tacked up at the depot and the sheriff's office. The governor had called Baldwin-Felts detectives into Hillsville. They were manhunters. I thought I'd have a smoke with Poindexter, see if he'd heard anything, and walk back to the office.

A colored boy ran by me like the brick sidewalk was burning coals, grabbed an iron gate to stop himself at a stoop, and hollered up the steps.

"Jeff, come quick! Woman got killed over on Washington. Best come on, you want to see it!" Another boy dashed out the door and down the steps. The two of them ran up the street.

I set off at a trot and saw the two boys turn the corner. A little over a block away, white and colored people were congregating.

The address was 809 Washington Street. There was a trellis gate with climbing roses starting to bud. Standing just outside a group of colored women on the walk was a tall white man in a bowler. He was chewing a cigar stub.

"Sir, what happened here?"

"Widow woman got killed. Say her washwoman done it. Somebody at the C&O seen the girl coming and going from the house."

About fifty feet down the street was a sleek chestnut mare hooked to a buggy. I recognized her. She nibbled at a patch of new grass at the edge of a yard. One of the buggy wheels was up on the curb.

A tall man with thick brown hair parted in the middle and a Vandyke emerged from the house, heading for the street. He was carrying a small black bag. That was Dr. George Vanderslice, coroner for the city of Hampton, the owner of the mare. He walked to the trellis gate and stopped, casting his eyes about until he saw the buggy.

"Phoebe!" he called. The mare lifted her head and nickered, but didn't move. He opened the gate and started toward the buggy. The people on the sidewalk made a little room for him, but they still blocked my way.

"Dr. Vanderslice!" I shouted. "Can you give me any information?"

"Go to the sheriff's office, Charlie. Get a statement there."

"Has there been a homicide?" I asked.

"Yes," he said. "Go to the sheriff's."

"Who was the victim, Dr. Vanderslice? Was it a woman?"

"Mrs. Ida Belote, a widow," he said. "Now get going!"

The name was painted on the mailbox. I made a note of the spelling. The house stood a hundred yards from the C&O depot. I headed down Washington Street at a sprint. Sure enough, Poindexter was on the platform. His cap was askew and his eyes glistened with excitement.

"Did they tell you I seen the colored girl, Charlie, the one does the washing for the widow woman? Seen her walking fast toward Sam Howard's store about 11 o'clock this morning. Why I reckon this is the biggest thing ever happened in my life."

"No," I said. "I'll have to get your statement."

"Couple guys loafing on the mail carts this afternoon heard some boys hollering and said there must be trouble." He whistled. "This sure beats it, don't it? Neighbor lady brought the girls in."

"What girls?"

"The widow woman's girls. Two of them. They're sitting in there right now."

I pushed open the swinging doors into the depot. The sun hung just above the rooftops and the air was getting chill. It swirled at my ankles as the doors shut behind me. A woman I would guess to be in her fifties was sitting on the bench. She was wearing a straw bonnet, the kind you'd expect to see in summer. It sat too far back on her head and the ribbon was untied. A pale, thin girl was leaning her head on the woman's shoulder, and a younger girl was leaning hers on the pale girl's. The younger girl had a pink peppermint stick in her mouth.

The woman on the bench sat forward when she saw two sheriff's officers approaching from the platform. The girls raised their heads. The officer walking in front was a big man with sandy red hair and rosy cheeks. The other officer was smaller, wiry build, brown hair.

"Ma'am, I'm Deputy Leslie Curtis Jr.," the officer in front said. "This is Officer R. D. Hope. Are these your children?"

"No," she said. "These are Mrs. Belote's children. I'm Mrs. Belote's neighbor. This is her daughter Harriet," she indicated the pale girl beside her, "and this is her baby girl, Sadie. Sarah Elizabeth." She patted the knee of the younger girl. Harriet looked pretty calm. Sadie's eyes and nose were red from crying.

Sadie took the peppermint stick from her mouth. "Is Momma

all right?" she asked the deputy. "Did she get hurt?"

"She did, honey," the deputy said. "We'll just have to wait and see how bad. Do you girls remember your momma having trouble with anybody?"

"Uh-huh," Sadie said. "Momma was mad with Virgie about taking her skirt."

"Who's Virgie?"

"Virginia Christian," the older girl Harriet said. "She's the colored girl who washes clothes for my mother. My mother thought she'd stolen her best black skirt. But we found it." Harriet's face hardly moved as she spoke. She sat rigid as a feral cat. Her voice seemed to come from somewhere else. Her eyes looked black as ink.

"Do you know where this colored girl lives?"

"Wine Street," Harriet said. "Three hundred something."

"Ma'am, has any family come round?" the deputy asked the woman on the bench.

"Not yet," the woman said. "The girls have an older sister, Pauline Wright. She was married just this past year. Lives over in Newport News. I'm sure she'll get here soon as she hears the news. Then there's Mrs. Belote's brother in Norfolk, a businessman."

"I hate him," Harriet said.

"Goodness!" the woman said. "You shouldn't speak that way about your uncle."

"I want Pauline to come," Harriet said.

The woman nodded and stroked the girl's hair. "She will, dear. She will."

"Ma'am, could we ask you to look after the girls, then? Sheriff's office ain't really a fit place," the deputy said.

"Of course," the woman said.

"Well, R. D.," the deputy said, "let's tell Chas about this colored girl."

"All right, Junior," the other officer said. They tipped their hats to the woman on the bench. "We're much obliged, ma'am."

PASSERSBY HAD JOINED THE crowd on the street in front of the Belote house. A couple of saddle horses were tied to the fence. A freight wagon was parked in the street. The teamsters were smoking cigarettes with their boots propped up on the rail of the wagon. They were watching a pack of boys roll hoops in the street.

"You men get that rig moving!" the deputy hollered.

"All of you, move on!" the other officer said. No one did, except for the teamsters.

A hearse from Rees' Funeral Parlor was parked where Dr. Vanderslice's buggy had been. Two men filed out the back door of the house carrying a litter. A body was bound in a bed sheet. Dark splotches stained the sheet. Some of the women in the crowd gasped and put kerchiefs to their faces.

"Look yonder!" a white boy hollered. "That there's a *corpse!*" His hoop banged into the picket fence and a woman shrieked.

"You boys don't get on, I'll haul ever one of you to jail," the deputy said.

The white boy grabbed his hoop and dashed off.

The two officers from the depot entered the rear of the house. I stood outside on the little porch. Inside was Deputy Charles Curtis, the one the officers called "Chas." I recognized him from a story I'd covered, a domestic disturbance in a Negro house. He was a good investigator.

He looked up from where he was crouched. "Looks like we had us one hell of a catfight in here, boys," he said as the officers walked in. "Watch, Junior! Don't touch that wall." He pointed to a smear of blood at the door frame. Junior snatched his hand back.

"Sorry, Cousin," he said.

Chas continued to examine something on the floor. He sighed. Then he stood and hooked his thumbs in his holster belt. He was a big man with the same sandy hair and florid complexion as his cousin, but taller. "One of them won't be caterwauling no more, that's for sure. You interviewed anybody, Junior?"

"Neighbor lady and two girls over to the C&O," the deputy said. "The daughters. What they said, reckon we need to hunt up this colored girl on Wine Street does the washing."

"Girl name of Virgie, right?" Chas asked.

"That's right."

Chas rubbed his chin. "Yep, figures. Lady out front lives across the street claims she seen the colored girl leaving in a hurry this morning. Near as we can make out," he said, tapping a finger on his holster, "the daughters was the first ones in the house this afternoon. Doc V and me talked to them here. The little one's eight. She come home from school about noon. Walked into the kitchen and called for her momma, got no answer. So she put away her books, she said, and went to Mrs. Guy's, that's the neighbor lady next door, to see if her momma was there. Mrs. Guy fixed her something to eat. Then she goes outside to play with some of the neighborhood kids. Then the older daughter shows up. She said she's thirteen."

"Looks like a preacher's wife, don't she, Chas?"

"Reckon she does, Junior, now you say it. Real stiff-backed. Anyway, she's the second one in. Gets home from school right after three carrying loaves of bread she bought with the dime her momma give her in the morning. Puts the bread down on a stool in the kitchen. She calls for her momma, too. No answer. Goes to the front room to put away her books. Starts to feel uneasy. By the door she sees her momma's hair combs on the floor. Figures that's strange. Some of her momma's hair's in the combs, too. Long strands. Then she sees blood drops on the floor.

"So she runs back to the kitchen. Notices more blood drops and bloody water in a basin on the sink. Now she's good and scared. She runs out the front door to the gate and sees two boys in the street. Asks them will they come in the house and look around. She waits at the gate while the boys go inside.

"Them two boys, that's numbers three and four. Boys see the blood drops on the floor and get scared, too. So they scurry off to fetch help at the depot, leaving her at the gate. Pair of men on the platform hear the boys hollering, soon as they hear 'blood,' they roust the telegraph man Poindexter and tell him to send for the sheriff."

Chas unhooked his thumbs from the belt. "Junior, I'm gone take R. D. over to Wine Street with me. Can I get you to stay here, keep them people on the street out of the house, messing up the crime scene?"

"That'll be fine," the deputy said.

"Awful thing, them girls coming up on their momma like that," Chas said.

I stepped behind a porch post to make room for the officers to pass. When they were a ways down the sidewalk, I followed. The two colored boys who ran by me earlier fell in behind them. One of the boys hooted. The deputies turned and said something and the boys ran down the sidewalk away from them. The officers got in their car and drove down the street. The boys chased after the car as it turned the corner.

By the time I reached the front gate of 341 Wine Street, Chas and Officer Hope were walking a Negro girl out, one man holding each arm. That was the first time I saw Virginia Christian. She walked between the officers without raising her eyes. She was small, about five feet tall, and sturdy. Her color was very dark. She walked with a heavy stride. At the gate she looked up at each of the colored boys on the sidewalk. Then she looked at me. She looked angry. Then her face turned away. The deputies walked her past us. Chas opened the door to the vehicle. Officer Hope helped her onto the running board and eased her into the back seat. The officers stepped into the car and drove away. I shouted questions as they rode by but they didn't reply.

One of the colored boys whistled.

"You see that, Jeff? She stared her a hole plumb through us. Like she gone murder us, too."

"Hot dang!" the other boy said. "We got us our own murderer, right on this street."

A colored man came out of the house and started down the sidewalk.

"Sir, what's happened here?" I asked.

He didn't answer. He looked about him, befuddled, then turned and walked past the boys. I stepped in front of him.

"Sir, are you any relation to Virgie?"

"She my girl."

"What is your name, sir?"

"Henry Christian."

"Did the police arrest your daughter?"

"Yes," he said. He held a thick piece of paper he kept folding and refolding. His hands were shaking. He placed the paper in the pocket of his coat.

"Did they state the charge, sir?"

"Them deputies didn't say nothing. Nothing. Here, I got to get by. I got to see Mr. Fields."

"Thank you, sir," I said. He continued up the street until he came to the gate for a big clapboard two-story house at 124 Wine Street. A shingle by the gate was painted, "George W. Fields, Esq. Attorney at Law." I watched Mr. Christian pass through the gate and up the walk. He knocked at the door. When it opened he went inside.

I walked back to the Christian home. Black children were milling about the yard and in the street. I heard a woman sobbing inside the house. Through the front door I could see a colored woman reclined on a pallet. She was a big woman, with light skin. She leaned against thick pillows that held her torso upright.

"Oh, Lord! What they gone do with my Virgie?" she asked. The children in the yard began to wail.

I stuck my pencil and notes in my breast pocket. I wanted to smoke a cigarette. But I started to run as fast as I could toward the sheriff's office.

A couple of reporters already were there.

"Looks like you been doing some serious bird-dogging and all, Charlie." It was Charles Pace, my competitor at the *Daily Press*. Everybody called him Pace. We covered the same beats. I resented him because his instincts for the news were better than mine. He resented me because I'd had it easy, a college snob. He'd first come to Hampton as a bound boy, forced to work his keep on the docks.

My face was flushed from running and my eyeglasses had fogged up. I took a handkerchief from my trousers and wiped the lenses.

Pace was scanning the cork board at the front of the sheriff's office. I hooked the wire temples over my ears. Pace was tall. Peering around his shoulder, I could make out Dr. Vanderslice's signature. He must've posted the coroner's report.

"Hey, how about making some room?" I asked.

Pace didn't move. He made a couple more notes, then caught me with an elbow as he turned. He trotted out the door. I rubbed my ribs and started to read.

The body of the victim, Ida Virginia Belote, was lying face down in a back room on the right-hand side of her house. The deceased appeared to be about 50 years of age. Her upper and lower false teeth were lying on the floor of the room near her body. A bloody towel was rolled and stuffed tightly down her throat, pushing in locks of hair. The towel depressed the deceased's tongue and inverted her lower lip. She had finger marks and bruises about her neck and beneath her jaw. Her right eye was blackened, and her left eye was swollen shut. Just above the deceased's left ear was a three-inch long cut down to the bone. The head and face were bloody. At the throat of the deceased was a sailor's neck cloth. There was a dry abrasion on the elbow of the left arm. There was no visible sign of rape.

In the middle room, near the front door, were shards of brown crockery. A spittoon covered with blood lay on the floor, along with three small black hair combs. On a box behind the door of the middle room were blood stains. There were blood stains on the floor leading to the adjacent back room on the right. Blood stains were on the door facing leading into the room on the right, about two-and-a-half feet from the floor. Under a bureau between the window and door was a pool of blood, and smeared blood and bloody clothing on the floor. A white porcelain jar top was found shattered into many pieces. No money or purse was found.

I scribbled notes and ran for the *Times-Herald* office. I just made the deadline. The front-page headline read, "IDA BELOTE IS BRUTALLY MURDERED, BLACK WOMAN HELD."

I SAT OUT ON the porch of my rooms, smoking. We'd had a shower at nightfall. The wind was raw. I read the story for probably the twentieth time and folded the paper. When the wind stirred, water dripped from the trees onto the roof of the porch. My hands were freezing.

In the morning Tyler Hobgood, the editor at the paper, called me into his office. Mr. Hobgood usually looked like he'd spent the night away from home. When he'd hang his suit coat on the tree, his shirt was always rumpled, the collar askew, and his shirttail poked from the back of his vest.

"These coloreds," he muttered, and shook his head. "A white woman in her own house." He looked into my face. I had never noticed how sad his eyes were. His moustache needed a trim. "Stay on this one, Mears," he said. "Day or two, you might be reporting a lynching."

"Yes, sir."

"Whole lot more serious than college, ain't it?"

"Yes, sir."

He opened a desk drawer and took out a bottle. He poured a dram of whiskey into his coffee cup. He tilted the bottle toward me.

"Want a little hair of the dog?" he asked.

"No thank you, sir."

"Still teetotaling?"

"Yes, sir."

"In this line of work," he said, "you might want to change that, Mears."

"Yes, sir."

He drank down the whiskey and set the cup on his desk.

"Can you spare a cigarette?" he said.

"Yes, sir."

"Mayor Jones is worried about violence," he said. "Ordered the coroner to complete the inquest soon as he can. Lucky Strike. Good cigarette, Mears."

"Thank you, sir."

He struck a match. "Nobody wants a mob in the streets, Mears. Bad for business." He lit the cigarette, shook out the match, and blew a puff of smoke. "Anyway, get what you can at that inquest. They're convening at the sheriff's office. And don't forget I need something for the society section on the Ladies' Club meeting over in Phoebus."

By the time I made it to the courthouse, Dr. Vanderslice's mare was nibbling daffodils in front of the Elizabeth City County jail.

3.

Inquest

The night of the Belote murder Dr. Vanderslice swore in five men for the coroner's inquest. They had inspected the crime scene at the crack of dawn Tuesday morning and were drinking coffee in Sheriff Curtis' office when I opened the door. The sheriff had his boots up on the fender of the wood stove in the middle of the room. The heat felt good.

"You're getting an early start, Charlie," Dr. Vanderslice said. He was standing by the stove, warming his hands. "Come in and have a cup of coffee."

The sheriff sat up and pulled a chair away from the wall. "Chilly out there, ain't it, son?" Dr. Vanderslice handed me an enamel cup and a plaid cloth. I picked up the handle of the pot on the stove with the cloth and poured some coffee.

"Thank you," I said.

"Sit down," Sheriff Curtis said. I pulled the chair close to the stove.

"You're the first one in," Dr. Vanderslice said. He removed a folded document from his breast pocket and handed it to me. "I expect you'll be wanting to read this. Today we're interviewing more witnesses for the record." He nodded. "Go ahead."

I unfolded the paper.

Virginia, County of Elizabeth City, To wit: An inquisition taken
at the residence of Mrs. Ida V. Belote, 809 Washington Street,
Hampton, Virginia and continued at the jail office in the County of
Elizabeth City on the 18th day of March, continued March 19th,
1912, before G. K. Vanderslice, MD, a coroner of the said county,
upon the view of the body of Mrs. Ida V. Belote there lying dead.
The jurors, sworn to inquire how, when, and by what means the
said Mrs. Ida V. Belote came to her death upon their oaths, do say:
said Mrs. Ida V. Belote came to her death on March 18th, 1912,
from injuries, wounds and strangulation, received at the hands of
Virginia Christian, a deliberate murder. In testimony whereof the
said coroner and jurors have hereto set their hands.

"First-degree?" I asked.

"That'll be up to the Commonwealth's attorney, but the constable discovered the victim's purse on the girl's person after she was
arrested. Apparent motive is robbery. Appears the girl was lying in
wait for the widow. I don't see any way around it, do you, Sheriff?"
Dr. Vanderslice said. Sheriff Curtis shook his head.

"Especially when you take into account the violence of the act.
And the fact that the victim's children discovered her corpse," Dr.
Vanderslice said. "This'll be your first murder trial, won't it, Charlie?" He sipped at his coffee, then brushed the tips of his moustache
with the back of his forefinger.

"Yes, sir."

"Young fellow over at the *Daily Press* is about the only other
one paying much attention right now," one of the jurors said. I took
out my pencil and pad.

"Let me go ahead and get the jury names from this, Dr. V."

"Certainly."

I noted the names from the report and refolded it. Dr. Vanderslice put it back in his pocket.

"About that scarf at Mrs. Belote's neck in the posted statement," he said.

"Yes, sir?"

"Mrs. Belote took in a boarder a few months after her husband died, to help with the bills, I expect. Fellow's name is Cahill. We interviewed him. Took work at the shipyard after he left the navy. The Mrs. and the girls liked to wear his uniform blouse and scarf around the house. Seems like a nice enough fellow. Says he overheard the Mrs. giving the colored girl the what-for over something had gone missing. Said the Mrs. could lay it on pretty hot when she wanted to. Bet that little woman didn't weigh ninety pounds."

"Ever want you a jar full of piss and vinegar, just find you a small woman of a certain age, ain't that right, V?" Sheriff Curtis said. Dr. Vanderslice smiled and nodded.

"Thank you, sir," I said. "I'll follow up on that."

"I'm sure you'll do a good job, son."

"Sheriff Curtis, would it be all right if I saw the prisoner?" I set my cup on the floor by the stove.

"Sure, head on back, Charlie." He stood and picked up the keys hanging next to the lock of the steel door leading back to the jail. He unlocked the door and swung it open.

"I expect she's about finished her breakfast," he said.

The floor of the jail was stone and the air was cold. Virginia Christian sat huddled in a blanket on a spring cot behind the bars of her cell. Her eyes were open, downcast. She sat so still I didn't think she had heard me enter. She was staring at the stone wall beyond the bars. I cleared my throat.

"Virginia Christian?"

She raised her eyes. The dim light obscured her face. I could not make out the features. "Daddy gone come, fetch me out of here?" she asked.

"I don't know," I said. "I don't think so. My name's Charlie Mears."

"Why ain't my daddy gone come?" She blinked once and leaned forward. I could see her cheek now. Her hair was flattened on one side from lying on the cot. On the floor by the cot was a tray and cup. Nothing on the tray had been touched.

"Well," I said. "Mrs. Belote is dead."

"Humph," she said. She put her hand to her cheek. It glistened in the light. She shook her head slowly. "I knowed I never should gone back. I told my momma so, too."

"It's best not to talk," I said. "Not to anybody but your lawyer."

"I ain't been in jail before," she said. "I ain't got no lawyer."

"Your father's getting you one," I said.

"How come you know so much?" she said. "Maybe I ought not talk to you neither."

"I work at the newspaper, I reckon is how I know."

She studied my face. "You ain't nothing but a boy," she said. "I can tell a white boy's age, good as I can tell a colored's. Bet you eighteen years old."

"That's right," I said.

"Told you," she said.

"Well," I said, "I'd better get back out front." She sprang up and put a hand on the bars. The coils on the cot hummed.

"You see my daddy, you tell him come fetch me. I'm lonesome. Momma don't like it when I ain't home."

"If I do see your father, I'll tell him. I promise."

She raised her other hand to the bars.

"What you say your name is?"

"Charlie." I heard keys jangling.

"Charlie?" Sheriff Curtis called. "Come on out. Couple reporters heading up the street. They better not see, cause I ain't gone let them back there with the girl."

"They calls me Virgie," she said.

I heard the tumblers turn in the lock. "Charlie, you coming?" Sheriff Curtis called.

As the sheriff locked the jail door behind me, Constable J. D. Hicks came in the front door of the office. He was a big man with thick hands. The constable guarded the jail and served as bailiff during court sessions.

"Dr. V expects to call about a dozen witnesses," Sheriff Curtis said. "Let's move this table over." The sheriff and the constable moved a long table from against the wall out to the middle of the office.

"I'll fetch some chairs from the courthouse," Constable Hicks said. "Boys, do you mind?"

The five jurors followed the constable out the door. Newsmen started to file in.

"You fellers wait till we get things set up," the sheriff said. "Space is tight. Gone have to stand in the back, anyway."

I stepped outside with the others and lit a cigarette.

"Getting a poker game up this evening, Charlie," Pace said. "You interested?"

An older reporter next to Pace chuckled.

"Oh, that's right," Pace said. "That'd be against your high morals, wouldn't it, Charlie? Coroner ain't giving you any preferential treatment, is he? You being his pious little college boy and all?"

I could feel my face reddening. I held the cigarette in my lips and pulled out my handkerchief. I wiped my glasses and wrapped the frames back behind my ears. I saw the jurors coming out of the courthouse, each man carrying a chair under each arm. I trotted across the square into the courthouse and picked up a couple of chairs, too. Pace and the other newsmen followed. They each grabbed chairs. I held the door for Pace and the constable.

"That ought to do it, Charlie," the constable said. "Just pull that door to."

Witnesses began to arrive about 9:30. Poindexter was among the first to show up. He looked nervous. The sheriff offered him a chair but Poindexter refused and paced the back of the room. I smiled at him when he looked my way but he did not smile back. He had worn a big winter coat and he did not remove it, even though the room was warm. Sweat glistened on his forehead. Finally the sheriff had enough and told him to sit down. Poindexter complied. Then he stood up again, shucked off the big coat, and sat back down, piling the coat on his lap.

Dr. Vanderslice greeted the witnesses as they entered and showed each one to a seat. I recognized Mrs. Stewart, who lived upstairs at the C&O depot with her husband, Gus, the station manager. Other women I remembered seeing standing in front of the victim's house came in. The only person of color who entered was a woman wearing an apron and bandanna. A trim man with wavy brown hair and a thick moustache entered. Dr. Vanderslice nodded to him as he took a seat. The constable opened the stove firebox and jabbed at the coals with a poker. He added an armload of wood, shut the firebox, and turned down the draft. Then a small, pale woman entered the jail, the girl I recognized as Harriet flanking her on one side, and the younger girl, Sadie, on the other. Everyone in the office stood, some leaning one way or the other to get a view. These were Mrs. Belote's three daughters. Dr. Vanderslice took the woman's hand in both his for a moment and bent to speak to her. She pressed a white kerchief to her cheek. Dr. Vanderslice touched Harriet on the shoulder, Sadie on the head, then guided the three to their chairs with the other witnesses. Sheriff Curtis unlocked the iron door and went back in the jail. He returned with Virginia Christian. She stood, the sheriff holding an arm, by the door.

"Hello, Virgie," the little girl called from her chair.

The black girl smiled faintly and lowered her eyes.

Dr. Vanderslice beckoned the jurors, who took their seats behind the table. He immediately seated himself with them.

"Coroner's inquest, Virginia, County of Elizabeth City, here continued. I now call Miss Harriet Belote," he said.

When the girl stood, she wavered, and her older sister reached for her hand and held it a moment. The girl's black hair hung in a long braid down her back. Pace leaned forward. The room was silent, save for the crackling of the new wood in the fire and the wind sighing in the flue. The girl stepped forward and sat in the chair, erect, not touching the chair back.

"Harriet Belote, you told me you went to school yesterday?" Dr. Vanderslice asked.

"Yes, sir, I did."

"About what time did you leave home for school?"

"About a quarter after eight."

"Was everything all right when you left for school?"

"Yes, sir."

"Mr. Cahill, who boards at your house, had he gone to work?"

"Yes, sir."

"When you returned from school, was everything all right?"

"Everything was quiet. My little sister was out playing. I thought my mother was out."

She sat perfectly still, her back to us. Her voice was calm and musical, like the middle range of a piano. Dr. Vanderslice and the jurors never took their eyes from her face.

"Did you see anything unusual when you went in the kitchen yesterday?" Dr. Vanderslice asked.

"I noticed the bloody water in the basin."

"When you saw the bloody water what did you do, did you go in the room?"

"I looked at it and then started in the front room to get my lessons and something told me not to go into the room; I saw my mother's hair and combs lying on the floor, and I called my sister."

"Did you see any blood on the floor?"

"I saw two little splotches; I did not go into the room where it was."

"Why didn't you go into the room?"

"My heart just failed me, that's all."

"Where did you go then?"

"I ran out and called the Warriner and Richardson boys and told them to go in there."

"What did they do?"

"They went in there and saw the blood and they were frightened too, and they went down to the depot and called two men."

"What two men did they call?"

"Gus Stewart and another man. They work at the depot."

"You stated that your mother was all right when you left home that morning. Had your mother had any difficulty of any character, or any kind, at any time?"

"I know about the skirt."

"Well, what about that?"

"Sunday a week ago when my mother was getting ready to go over to my married sister's in Newport News, she missed her best black skirt."

"Had you missed any sort of articles before?"

"A gold cross and chain of mine, but I got that back, and another time a ring that was missing and she looked around and found it behind some things. And Momma missed a light apron and my little sister missed her gloves, and once a locket. Momma did not say anything about these but she said that she could not afford to lose a skirt."

"And Virgie once quit washing for your mother?"

"Yes, sir."

"Did your mother discharge her when she quit washing that time?"

"No, sir, she didn't discharge her. She stopped on her own accord, she said her mother was paralyzed, and she said she could not wash any longer."

"You always found her amicable, and of a pleasant disposition?"

"Yes, sir, she seemed to be pleasant; we did not miss anything the first time she washed for us, not a thing."

"Thank you, Miss Harriet; I have no further questions for you."

She stood and faced us, pale and rigid. I heard Pace breathe next to me and realized I had been holding my breath, too. She glanced quickly at Virginia Christian and sat down.

"I now call Miss Sadie Belote," Dr. Vanderslice said.

The girl popped from her chair like a jack-in-the-box and stepped lightly toward the table. Dr. Vanderslice chuckled and gestured toward the chair. She sat, looked once over her shoulder at the small woman, her sister, who nodded, and then back at the coroner.

"How old are you?" he asked.

"Eight years old."

"You know how to tell the truth, don't you?"

"Yes, sir."

"And you know what will happen if you don't tell it?"

"Yes, sir," the girl said, nodding solemnly. "Momma will tan my hide."

Dr. Vanderslice touched his moustache, hiding his reaction. A juror smiled, remembered himself, and coughed into his hand.

"And you will tell me the truth about everything I ask you, won't you?" Dr. Vanderslice asked.

"Yes, sir."

"Who is your mother?"

"Mrs. Belote."

"Mrs. Ida Belote?"

"Yes, sir."

"And Harriet Belote is your sister?"

"Yes, sir."

"Did you go to school yesterday?"

"Yes, sir."

"About what time did you get out of school?"

"A little after twelve."

"What did you do?"

"I went in the front room, put my books away, and called Momma."

"Did she answer?"

"No, sir."

"What did you then do?"

"I went next door to Mrs. Guy's looking for Momma."

"Was she there?"

"No, sir, Mrs. Guy served me dinner."

"After dinner what did you do?"

"I went to play with the neighbor boys until my big sister got home."

"Who does the washing for your mother?"

"Virgie."

"Virgie Christian?"

"Yes, sir."

"Did you see her yesterday?"

"I saw her standing on the corner when I was leaving school.",

"Did you speak to her?"

"No, sir, I was on the other side of the street when she called me."

"What did she say to you?"

"She told me to tell Momma that she can't come to wash today."

"Were you home when your mother missed her skirt?"

"Yes, sir."

"What happened then?"

"Momma sent me to fetch Virgie."

"Did Virgie agree to pay for the missing skirt?"

"Yes, sir. She said that she didn't have the skirt."

"Did Virgie quarrel with your mother?"

"No, sir."

"Thank you, Miss Sadie; I have no further questions for you. I now call Mrs. Pauline Wright."

The small woman stood. She helped Sadie take her seat next to Harriet, then sat in the witness chair.

"Mrs. Wright, have you heard your mother speak of losing a skirt?" Dr. Vanderslice asked.

"Yes, Momma was up to my house Sunday a week ago. She sent for Virgie about it."

"What did Virgie say about the skirt?"

"She promised to pay five dollars for it, but said she didn't have the skirt."

"Did your mother and Virgie quarrel over the lost skirt?"

"No, sir, when Virgie was called, she looked scared."

"Were you at your mother's last Sunday?"

"Yes, I was. Momma said she hoped Virgie would come tomorrow and pay for the skirt. If she didn't, she'd make trouble for her."

"Was the relationship between the woman and your mother pleasant?"

"So far as I know."

"Thank you, Mrs. Wright. I have no further questions. You and your sisters are free to go. There's no reason for us to keep you here." Dr. Vanderslice and the jurors stood as Mrs. Wright helped Sadie with her coat. It was easy to read the sadness written in her face and Harriet's. Virginia Christian kept her eyes lowered until the sisters left and the constable closed the front door behind them. The colored girl raised her eyes and looked at the door for a long time.

"I now call Mrs. Mary Stewart," Dr. Vanderslice said, taking his seat.

Mrs. Stewart, the wife of the C&O depot manager, testified to observing the comings and goings of Virginia Christian, Mrs. Ida Belote, and the girls, as did other witnesses. There were differing descriptions of the colored girl's dress and manner, whether she appeared agitated or calm, whether she was walking or running, but the testimony showed that she had in fact entered and left the house the day of the murder. Also called to testify was the black woman in the apron. She was Lucy White, who cooked for one of Mrs. Belote's neighbors. She also testified to seeing Virginia Christian enter the Belote house on the day of the murder.

"I now call Mr. Joseph Timothy Cahill to the stand," Dr. Vanderslice said. The trim young man with the bushy moustache stood and approached the inquest table. His gait was lithe and agile. He took the seat.

"Mr. Cahill, how long have you boarded at Mrs. Belote's?" Dr. Vanderslice asked.

"Since November of last year."

"About what time did you leave for work on yesterday morning?"

"About six to seven minutes after 6:00 a.m."

"Do you know of any problem that Mrs. Belote had with a servant?"

"Yes, she had a little argument about a skirt."

"What about the skirt?"

"I was there when she missed her skirt. She sent her little girl around for her. Mrs. Belote told her she wanted the skirt or five dollars. The girl seemed very cool."

"Was Mrs. Belote angry?"

"Yes, she was a woman of stern mind."

"Was Mrs. Belote abusive to her?"

"No, sir, just stern."

"How much do you pay for board at Mrs. Belote's?"

"Five dollars per week."

"When do you pay for board?"

"Each Saturday evening."

"How do you pay?"

"In cash, five one-dollar bills."

"What did she do with the money?"

"She would put it in her small change purse."

"Would you know this purse when you see it?"

"I think so."

"Was it like this?" Dr. Vanderslice held up a small, gray, leather purse.

"Yes, sir, that's it."

"Mr. Cahill, do you at any time wear your Navy uniform blouse?"

"No, I wear overalls."

"Would the young ladies there ever wear your uniform blouse with your name on it?"

"Yes, they would from time to time."

"Would they wear your neck kerchief?"

"Yes, they would."

"I have no further questions of you. I now call Mr. Poindexter."

Cahill nodded to Dr. Vanderslice and the jurors and walked back to his chair among the witnesses. Poindexter's big coat flopped on the floor when he stood, and a woman sitting next to him helped him arrange it on his seat. He stepped quickly to the witness chair.

"Mr. Poindexter, you are employed at the C&O depot?" Dr. Vanderslice asked.

"Yes, sir, I am a telegraph operator."

"Were you working yesterday?"

"Yes, I was."

"Do you know Mrs. Ida Belote when you see her?"

"Yes, sir."

"Did you see her yesterday?"

"No, I didn't see her yesterday."

"Do you know this girl who works for Mrs. Belote?" Dr. Vanderslice pointed to Virginia Christian. She raised her head and looked at Dr. Vanderslice, then up into the face of Sheriff Curtis, then down at the floor. Poindexter cleared his throat.

"Yes, I know her."

"Did you see her yesterday?"

"No, I did not."

Dr. Vanderslice furrowed his eyebrows and leaned forward. "Mr. Poindexter, when was the last time you saw her?"

"Oh, yes, it was yesterday, yesterday between 9:30 a.m. and 10:30 a.m." Poindexter cast a glance at Virginia Christian. He turned to the jurors and smiled nervously.

"I'm sorry," he said. "I get the fantods talking in front of people. I'm not used to it. I'm used to somebody handing me a slip of paper, I type in the message, give them the bill. That's what I'm used to."

"That's all right, Mr. Poindexter. Take your time. How was she dressed when you saw her?" Dr. Vanderslice asked.

"As well as I can remember, she had on a black skirt with I think a hole on the right side about a foot from the ground."

"Were you looking out the office window?"

"No, I was at the office door. I didn't notice the color of her shirtwaist."

"Was she wearing a hat?"

"No, I didn't see a hat."

"Did you speak with Virginia Christian?"

"No, she was not within one hundred yards of me."

"Thank you, Mr. Poindexter; I have nothing further. I now call Constable J. D. Hicks."

Poindexter pulled a handkerchief from his hip pocket and wiped his brow. Now that he was leaving center stage, he looked relaxed, like a boy leaving the proctor's office. He retook his seat among the witnesses.

Constable Hicks lumbered toward the witness chair. He was holding something with the big fingers of one hand. He had slicked his hair down with pomade. When he sat in front of the jurors, he looked like a man in a child's parlor chair.

"Constable Hicks, tell us what you know about this case?" Dr. Vanderslice asked.

"Virginia Christian was brought here yesterday. She was searched and turned in a small change purse. I asked her did she have anything else. She said no. I had her take off her shoes. I ran my hand around in her stockings looking for a knife. I told the sheriff that I had searched her. He instructed me to go back and give her another overhauling." Despite his bulk Constable Hicks had a high voice, near tenor in pitch. His features were heavy but he had a kind face.

"Did you give her an overhauling?"

"Yes, sir. I went back up and brought her out of her cell. 'Virgie,' I said, 'have you got anything on you?' She said, 'No, sir.' I then asked her when was the last time she had her monthly? She said, 'Yesterday. I've finished with them.' Sheriff R. K. Curtis came in. I then made Virginia Christian disrobe and I found on her sleeve, a good-size bloodstain. I then asked her if she had any more bloodstains on her. She said, 'No.' I found under her left arm a bloodstain. I asked her to explain this stain. She said her mother had a hemorrhage and she reached across to give her something to wipe with. A drop of blood must have gone through. I instructed her then and there to pull everything off. I found bloodstains on this garment."

He held up what looked to be an article of women's under-clothing.

"I found this instrument strapped around her waist; in it was a purse."

He held up a pouch, maybe made of canvas. The chair creaked when he leaned forward and handed the articles to Dr. Vanderslice.

"Constable Hicks, you say you found this thing tied around Virginia Christian's waist?" Dr. Vanderslice held up the pouch for the jurors to see. "And in it was a purse?"

"Yes, sir. It contained four one-dollar bills and a gold ring."

"Did you ask Virginia Christian about the purse?"

"Yes, she said the purse belonged to her mother and she was keeping it for her."

"How was this thing strapped to her body?" Dr. Vanderslice placed the pouch on the table beside the undergarment.

"It was strapped right next to her drawers," Constable Hicks said. He looked sheepishly at the coroner and the jurors. "The sheriff then sent around to her parents' and got a new set."

"Would you know the purse found on her?"

"I think so."

"Is this the purse?" Dr. Vanderslice held up the item he had shown Cahill.

"That's the purse, all right."

"Was she told for what she was arrested?"

"I think not."

"Did she volunteer any information to you about Mrs. Belote?"

"No, sir. She said that she had been washing all day."

"Where did you say you found the instrument or bag?"

"It was tied around her waist, tied with a necktie and string."

"Thank you. I have no further questions of you, sir." Again the chair creaked as Constable Hicks stood.

"I would like to thank all of those who testified today in this matter," Dr. Vanderslice said. "The inquest is now closed."

I looked to see the sheriff turn Virginia Christian toward her cell.

Witnesses had seen her enter the Belote house. Testimony established robbery as a motive. In custody she had lied to authorities and concealed evidence. Murder in the first degree. I burst out the front door of the sheriff's office, with Pace right behind. He easily outran me, heading in the direction of the *Daily Press* offices. At the corner I stopped and lit a cigarette. Everything pointed to the girl, but I wanted to ease my mind about the boarder. Tomorrow I'd see if I could find Cahill's employer.

The air had hardly warmed since morning. I set out for the office, wishing I had worn a scarf.

4.

Orphan Girls

On Thursday morning, March 21, at 11 o'clock, Ida Virginia Belote was to be laid to rest beside her husband in the St. John's Episcopal Church cemetery in Hampton. My rented rooms on the second floor of a brick carriage house near the trolley stop on Lincoln Street had a porch. From it I could see the entrance to the cemetery. The family had announced the interment would be a private ceremony, and Mayor Jones had instructed Sheriff Curtis to have deputies on duty early to keep gawkers at a distance. Mr. Rees, the undertaker, had hired a couple of big fellows from the docks to help out, too. When the men lifted their arms to hold their top hats against the wind, the suits Mr. Rees loaned them for the job looked like they might split at the seams.

I caught the trolley to the docks and walked to the entrance of the Newport News Shipbuilding and Dry Dock Company on the coal pier side. As I made my way across the C&O tracks, I could glimpse a section of the *Texas*. The prow of the dreadnought was hung with scaffolding. Her superstructure towered above the yards. Seagulls spun and screeched among the masts and guy wires. A guard at the gate remembered Cahill right away.

"Bandy little fellow with a moustache?"

"Yes, sir."

"Best damn rivet man in the shop. Heard about the trouble

over at his landlady's. I don't know where he's hanging his cap now. Wait here at the gate when the shift changes at five of the evening, you're sure to catch him."

"Thank you, sir. Do you keep records of the men's attendance?"

"Yes, they sign in and out here at the gate."

"Do you have this Monday's records?"

"I do. I turn the time sheets into the office of a Friday."

"May I ask you to check to see if Mr. Cahill was at work on Monday?"

"Oh, I'm sure he was. Supposed to launch that battleship in May, so they're working round the clock."

"I'm sorry to ask, sir, but do you mind checking?"

"All right," he said. "Just hold on." He went back into a little office where clipboards were hanging from pegs. He picked one up and began to leaf through the sheets.

"Monday, March 18. Signature: J. T. Cahill. Ingress: 6:45 a.m. Egress: 5:10 p.m."

"Thank you, sir. I'm grateful for your trouble."

Newspapers were piled high in the rubbish can by the entrance. I pulled out a few. Stories about the testimony in Dr. Vanderslice's inquest were all over the front pages—Hampton, Phoebus, Norfolk, Newport News, Portsmouth, Chesapeake, Suffolk. Reporters from the *Richmond Times-Dispatch* and the *Williamsburg Bee* had been at the sheriff's office, too. "NEGRESS STRANGLES WIDOW IN GRUESOME CRIME," read one headline. "INNOCENT CHILDREN DISCOVER SCENE OF HORROR," read another. "BASIN OF BLOOD TESTIMONY RIVETS JURORS," was the headline Mr. Hobgood gave my story in the *Times-Herald*.

Passions were running high. Some feared a race riot. Ministers of the black church congregations in Hampton and Newport News were alarmed. An article stated a colored preacher from the pulpit had called for the speedy execution of Virginia Christian. "Murder of Mrs. Belote Is Deplored by Negroes," read a headline in the *Daily Press*. For the story Pace had interviewed two colored preachers who said the crime was a real setback for relations between the races. They claimed their congregations were willing to hire private investigators to assist the sheriff's office in bringing the girl to justice.

For background to my story on Mrs. Belote's funeral, I decided to check the morgue at the *Daily Press*. The clip file about Hampton residents at Pace's paper was better than ours at the *Times-Herald*. I was smoking a cigarette outside when Pace came trotting up the steps. He stopped and grinned.

"Looking for a job, Charlie?" he asked.

"Yours," I said. He stepped by me, giving me the finger over his shoulder as he went inside.

Mrs. Belote's beloved husband, James Edward Wadsworth Belote, had died at their Washington Street home on June 6, 1911. The cause of death was throat cancer, according to the obituary. For some reason people called him Frank. His family was from Northampton County, North Carolina. He'd moved to Hampton about 1880. He worked as a bookkeeper for various firms in the yards. Except for the proprietor of a saloon by the docks, who remembered him as a man who liked to argue politics, nobody seemed to recall much about Mrs. Belote's husband.

One thing was certain, Frank Belote was prolific. At the time of his death he had five sons, all grown men. There was a marriage notice about Pauline, his oldest daughter. She'd married George Wright, a welder in Newport News, in 1909, when she was nineteen years old. According to the notice, her two younger sisters, Harriet and Sarah Elizabeth—Sadie—lived at home with their mother, Mrs. Ida Virginia Belote.

My hunch was the two girls would be staying with their older sister, at least for now. When I finished at the *Daily Press,* I located the Wrights' address in Newport News. Too bad I hadn't thought to check before I went to the shipyards earlier. The address was near the point where the James River runs into Hampton Roads. I caught the trolley as far as I could. The place was a white cottage with big azaleas planted at the foundations. Fat buds were scattered among the branches, but none of the blossoms had opened. The sun was bright and a breeze blew cold off the Roads. Sadie was sitting by herself on the stoop. Her hair was the color of honey and drooped in thick ringlets below her shoulders. She was holding a big doll with a frilly bonnet. Her nose was running and she wiped it on the hem of the doll's dress.

A petite woman wearing a black skirt and black shirtwaist came out on the stoop. I recognized her from the inquest.

"Sadie," she said. "It's too cold! Come inside the house and shut that door. Goodness!"

"Mrs. Wright?" I said.

"Yes?"

"My name's Charlie Mears. I work for the *Times-Herald*. I'm sorry to trouble you at such a difficult time, but may I ask you some questions?"

She bit her lip and studied me. "My husband's not at home," she said. "It would be better if you came back later."

"I'll only take a moment of your time, ma'am."

"Oh, all right, come inside. Sadie, for goodness' sake, stand up and get inside this house before we both catch our death."

I stepped quickly up the walk. There were purple crocuses barely open by the stoop. Mrs. Wright held the door.

"I'm sorry, Mr. . . . ?"

"Mears," I said.

"Come in, Mr. Mears. Sadie, take Mr. Mears' cap."

She shut the door behind me. There was a coal firebox in the fireplace and the room was toasty. I handed Sadie my cap. My glasses began to fog. I removed them and wiped the lenses with my handkerchief. When I put them back on, I saw Harriet Belote standing by the fireplace mantel. She was pale as a lily. Her long, jet-black hair fell down her back. Her eyes were very bright. In one hand she held a book, a finger keeping her place. Though I had seen her twice, first at the depot and then at the sheriff's office, I had not noticed how pretty she was. Like her older sister, she was dressed in black.

"You have a cowlick."

"Sadie!" Mrs. Wright said.

I looked down. Sadie was gazing up at me, clutching her doll.

I brushed at my hair with my hand. "The cap," I said. "It seems to do it."

She nodded. "I know," she said. "Dolly's will, too, if she sleeps on it funny. See?" She held the doll up and pointed to its forehead.

"Yes," I said. "I see."

"Harriet, why don't you take Sadie in the bedroom so Mr. Mears and I can talk," Mrs. Wright said.

Harriet nodded and moved toward the door. She waited until Sadie joined her, then took her by the shoulders and guided her from the room.

Mrs. Wright sat in the Morris chair by the fire and folded her hands on her lap. I sat in a ladder-back chair facing her. "I'm worried sick, Mr. Mears," she said. "Sadie's all right. I don't think she grasps what has happened. But Harriet hasn't spoken a word since yesterday. She won't eat a bite. Nothing."

"Yes, ma'am," I said. "It must be terrifying to lose her mother this way. Maybe a person of faith?"

"The minister at St. John's is stopping by this afternoon. He delivered a lovely eulogy for Momma." Mrs. Wright's hands were clutching the fabric of her skirt. "She wants to live here, Mr. Mears. I'm their sister and I love the girls dearly, but it's just not possible." She lifted her hands. "The house is so small. We're just starting out. It wouldn't be fair to George." Her chin trembled. She pulled a kerchief from the wrist of her shirtwaist and touched it to her eyes. She folded it in her hands on her lap.

"Is there anyone else?" I asked.

"Oh, Harriet's named for her grandmother, and they've always been close. Grandmother has a beautiful place on King Street, not far from where she and Grandfather ran the grocery, but Grandfather's gone now and she's in her eighties. She's done everything she could. She even purchased the house on Washington Street for Momma and Daddy, gave it to them. She's done everything you could expect. If Harriet asked, she would take the girls in an instant, because she loves them so, but she's not well, Mr. Mears. Even with servants, she couldn't manage two young girls. I don't know why Harriet won't listen to reason."

She paused.

"Daddy was not the best of fathers, Mr. Mears. His drinking made everything difficult. For everyone."

"I understand, Mrs. Wright. In college I was a member of the Temperance Club. I've kept my pledge."

"God bless you, Mr. Mears." She looked up at the daguerreotypes on the mantel. "Our uncle Lewter is a wealthy man. He has a successful business in Norfolk," she said. "You probably know it. They sell big machines to the shipyards. I don't understand it, but George, my husband, could explain it for you. Uncle Lewter and Mary have a family themselves. A little boy, Floyd, and a girl, Maggie, who's almost exactly Harriet's age. It will be the best situation."

I nodded. "Ma'am, do you believe that Virginia Christian is responsible for your mother's death?"

"No," she said. "I just don't see how that could happen. Momma visited with us Sunday a week ago. She told me about a missing skirt, that she expected Virgie to pay her for it. Momma was always missing things. She had too much on her shoulders. Alone, with two young girls to raise. She wore herself out. I'm sure she just misplaced things. Whenever she thought something'd been stolen, it would show up somewhere. But she was cross all the time, and no wonder."

"You said your mother never quarreled with Virgie?"

"Oh, my word, no. Whenever Momma confronted her about something, Virgie looked scared more than anything. I think Momma frightened her to death. She'd cringe at the sound of Momma's voice. Virgie never said anything back to her, no matter how hateful Momma was. And she always was sweet with us girls. Virgie's just a girl herself. I remember her talking about school, how she liked it. But she had to quit when her mother got sick. I don't think she could really read or write a word.

"It was funny how she had to have things arranged just so when she was working. Ironing board right-to-left. Clothes basket to the left of the ironing board. White things on top. Colored things on the bottom. Two irons on the stove, one on the stand. Once I borrowed an iron from the stove to touch up a skirt hem and you'd have thought the house was afire, the commotion Virgie made when she missed it. But she was a worker. Lord knows she earned every penny Momma paid her."

"Did you ever have occasion to speak with Mr. Cahill? The boarder?"

"Oh, I think a couple of Sundays, when I visited Momma," Mrs. Wright said. "Sometimes he'd bring fresh fish or oysters from the docks, and Momma would cook everyone a nice Sunday dinner. He was very pleasant. Always a gentleman."

"Was there ever any problem with his payments?"

"Oh, no. I'm sure Momma would've told me."

"He's quite a handsome man."

"Harriet certainly thinks so," she said. "And Momma, too, for that matter." She smiled, and looked down at her hands. "At least, she *did* think so."

"Mrs. Wright, you've been very generous with your time. I'd better go. I'm very sorry for your family's loss. I will remember your mother in my prayers."

"Thank you, Mr. Mears."

I stood to leave. She offered her hand, and I shook it.

"Ma'am, does Harriet like to read verse?"

"Why, yes, ever since she was a little girl."

"I'll see if can find a volume for her. Maybe it will help her pass the time."

"That's very kind, Mr. Mears."

Outside the air had warmed with the sun. The blossoms of the crocuses were open. I had started for the cottage gate when I heard the front door behind me.

"Mr. Mears!" Mrs. Wright called from the stoop. "You forgot your cap. Here, Sadie, take it."

The girl scampered down the steps and ran to me. She held up the cap.

"Thank you," I said. Her eyes were blue as robins' eggs. She looked at me for a moment.

"Momma went to see the angels," she said. She smiled. Then she ran back inside the house.

By the time I got back into Hampton it was getting close to deadline. I still had time to swing by the jail before going to the paper. In the square between the courthouse fence and the jail there was a crowd. Except for a pack of colored boys running footraces at the edge of the square, the people were white. Clouds had gathered and were spitting sleet. The pellets stung my face.

I could see Deputy Chas Curtis speaking from the steps of the jail. His face was red. I wasn't close enough to make out what he was saying. When he paused, people in the crowd hooted and whistled.

"Just hang that nigger!" a man close to me shouted. I walked on till I was closer. Chas saw me and nodded. He turned back to the crowd and lifted his chin.

"The mayor has directed the court to move forward on this case as quickly as the laws of the Commonwealth allow," he shouted. "You folks need to disperse."

"We don't need Commonwealth law!" a man yelled from beside the steps. "We need God's law!"

A murmur rose through the crowd like a swell in rough weather. There was quiet, then an eruption of sound.

"Send the nigger girl out!"

"We'll take care of her. Save the sheriff the trouble!"

The deputy raised his hands for quiet, but the shouting grew louder. The sleet fell harder, bouncing off the brick pavers. The crowd's anger seemed to rise.

"Send her out!"

The jail door opened and Sheriff Curtis stepped through. He was wearing his Stetson with the brim pulled low and an oilcloth slicker that reached to his boots. One side of the slicker was tucked behind a holstered Owlshead pistol on his hip. Slung over a forearm was a double-barreled Remington with the bore broken open. The brass shell casings shone in the dull light. Officer Hope and Constable Hicks stepped out behind the sheriff. Each man was wearing a holstered Colt. The constable closed the door and stood in front of it with his hands hooked in his holster belt. The big man was about as wide as the door. The crowd fell silent.

The sheriff looked from face to face. "I see people out here I know voted for me," he said. "And I appreciate it. You voted for me to uphold the laws of the Commonwealth of Virginia and Elizabeth City County in your behalf. I aim to do that." He gestured with his free arm. "These men standing here, they aim to do that."

He snapped shut the bore of the shotgun. "This ten-gauge is loaded with double-ought. At this distance I reckon it'd pert near cut a man in two. Now I'm asking you people to disperse. I know you want justice served and that's what we aim to do. But I'm damned if I'm gone stand out here in this cold and wet. Now do what Chas says, and get on home."

"She's just a nigger, sheriff!" a woman shouted.

"I understand that, ma'am, but under the law, she's a citizen of Elizabeth City County, same as you. Now move on. A grand jury is set to hear this case on the first of April."

"Well I never," the woman muttered.

The crowd began to break up. Officer Hope adjusted the globes and lit the gaslights on the façade of the jail. Sheriff Curtis removed his Stetson and shook the sleet pellets from the brim. He put his hand on Chas' shoulder.

"You did all right," he said. The sheriff replaced his hat and looked at me. "My cousin did all right, didn't he, Charlie?"

"Yes, sir, he did."

Just beyond the glow of the gaslights a small group of white men stood, murmuring like birds on a roost in the shadows. The sheriff and deputies watched them for a while, until the men began—by ones and twos—to walk away. The officers went back inside the jail. A colored girl raced across the square, brandishing a long switch. The pack of colored boys, huddled by a cistern where they'd listened to the sheriff's speech, sprang up laughing. They ran along the courthouse fence and scattered in the streets.

"I'm gone tell Momma where I found you!" the colored girl screamed, chasing after the smallest boy.

5.

Maebelle's Biscuits

There were wrought-iron stairs up to the little porch I had overlooking Lincoln Street. On the porch I kept a three-legged stool where I sat to smoke. There was a cuspidor by the stool where I put my cigarette butts. Mrs. Wingate, the landlady, forbade smoking in her rooms, and flipping butts into her boxwoods would have been an even higher crime. Mrs. Wingate lived in a handsome brick house with white columns on the other side of a boxwood garden from my rooms in the carriage house.

Maebelle told me Mrs. Wingate's late husband had been quite a cigar smoker. He was one of "them no-count rich folks in Richmond, think they all high-and-mighty," she said.

Maebelle was Mrs. Wingate's house maid and she came with the rooms. She was a tall woman with a big bosom and she was as strong as a man. Her face was youthful, but she was born before the war to the house servants of a family in Portsmouth. She remembered her father loading her mother and her sisters into a dinghy one night and rowing down the Elizabeth River across Hampton Roads. They landed at Point Comfort. She remembered the Federal troops' brass buttons shining in the firelight at Fort Monroe. The troops told them they were safe because they were now Confederate "cummerbund." I told her she meant "contraband." Maebelle was bundling my laundry. She said no, she knew what she remembered, since she was the one remembering, and was I one of them uppity white folks from Richmond, too? We left it at that.

Maebelle told me when Mr. Wingate wasn't smoking cigars, he was fishing. When he wasn't fishing, he was duck hunting. He left behind two Chesapeake Bay retrievers when he died. Mrs. Wingate moved the retrievers inside the house from the back porch where her husband had kept them "because them dogs was a sight easier to clean up after and better company than Mr. Wingate ever was, him tramping round in muddy boots and smoking them cigars in every room of the house," Maebelle said. The dogs were old and slept in their beds in the entrance hall most of the time, but they followed Mrs. Wingate to whichever room in the house she was occupying. When she left the house for errands or church, the dogs peered out the front windows of the sitting room until she returned.

From my porch in the evenings I liked to watch the sparks of the trolleys dance along the lines at the stop. The sparks threw crazy shadows from the figures of people walking. A man would come by and light the gas streetlight. The light pooled from the last step of the iron stairs across the sidewalk into the street. A screen door opened into the kitchen and when the weather was good I left the inner door open for the breeze. Behind the kitchen was a good-sized room with a bed and dresser and a couple of chairs, and beyond that was the toilet with a sink and claw-foot tub.

"Mr. Charlie, that smoking ain't good for you and it stinks up your clothes, too," Maebelle said. She was standing at the foot of the steps. She had a cherry basket in her hand. "Come on down here and get you something to eat," she said.

I put the cigarette in the cuspidor and trotted down the steps. She held out the basket. "Ham biscuits," she said. She pulled back the cloth, then tucked it down. "They still warm. You didn't eat a thing this morning, did you?"

I shook my head.

"Bony's you is, ain't no girl ever gone look at you twice. Lord!"
She stuck the basket handle in my hand.

"Thank you, Maebelle," I said.

"You welcome, Mr. Charlie. I got to get over to the house. Mrs.
Wingate wanting to clean her curtains," she said. "Mr. Charlie?"

"Yes?"

"What you think gone happen with this Christian girl? Used
to work with her momma over at the hotel, years back."

"Well, there's a good bit of evidence against her. She had Mrs.
Belote's purse, with some money."

She shook her head. "It's a bad thing, Mr. Charlie," she said.
"Colored folks got to be able to work in people's houses. You take
Mrs. Wingate, living here all by herself. What she gone think?"

"I wouldn't worry, Maebelle. The law will follow its course."

"I seen all kinds of laws, Mr. Charlie. I seen laws come and I seen
them go. Whatever gone happen, it best happen quick."

Maebelle headed for the front of Mrs. Wingate's house. The
wind had shifted to the southwest and the sky had cleared. The air
was beginning to warm. I came up to the porch and ate a biscuit.
Maebelle had sprinkled a little brown sugar and black peppercorns
on her ham when she fried it. I thought I could eat the whole basket.
I found a handkerchief and wrapped a biscuit in it for later in the
day. I tucked the cover cloth back in the basket and set it on the
table in the kitchen.

The cabinet above the sink in the bathroom was open, and from
the doorway I could see my reflection in the mirror. I did look thin.
And wan. When warm weather came on, I would go down to the
Roads more, get out in the sunlight. Smoke fewer cigarettes. Maybe
by fall I would be ready to go back to school. But now I needed to
go by the newspaper.

Mr. Hobgood tossed back a glass as I walked in and placed it on
his desk pad. He looked terrible. The circles around his eyes were

always dark and this morning they looked like bruises.

"People are stirred up, Mears," he said. "They want blood."

"Yes, sir."

"Good job reporting on the inquest."

"Thank you, sir."

"What was the name of that colored lawyer? The one the father went to on Wine Street?"

"George Washington Fields."

"Fields, that's right. Better see what you can find out from him. Make sure he's representing the girl before the grand jury."

"Yes, sir."

"And Mrs. Belote's brother. Hobbs." He rummaged around on his desk. "Where's that infernal note? Oh, here. Lewter F. Hobbs. Hobbs-Newby Equipment Co., Inc. Norfolk. Supposedly he's friends with Montague. They went to school together or some damn thing. See what you can find out there."

"He's friends with the Commonwealth's attorney?"

"Yes, yes, Edgar Montague. No need to shout, Mears!" Mr. Hobgood pressed his hand to his forehead.

"No, sir." I leaned forward. "Would you like some water, Mr. Hobgood?"

"No, Mears, I'm fine. Oh, be sure to check with Sheriff Curtis. Heard a Negro assaulted a white girl on Buckroe Beach."

"Yes, sir."

"Do you have a cigarette, Mears?"

"Yes, sir." I handed him my Luckies. He shook a cigarette out and returned the pack.

"I owe you," he said. He took a wooden match from his desk drawer and scratched it on his shoe. After he lit the cigarette, he blew the match out. He studied the white smoke purling from the tip.

"I need to explain something, Mears," he said. "This business. It's about the truth, right?"

"Yes, sir," I said.

"Indeed it is, Mears." He puffed at the cigarette and leaned back in his chair. "It's about the truth. When the truth sells papers. Do you understand?"

WHEN I ASKED SHERIFF Curtis about the assault, he sighed and shook his head. He was slumped in his chair. He looked tired. "About the last thing we needed right now, Charlie. We had a couple folks outside again last night. What I'm worried about is a deputy going off half-cocked and shooting somebody." He poured coffee from the pot on the stove.

"Well, the assault," he said. "Lawyer's daughter in Phoebus. Colored boy's in the house. Turns out he's the gardener. Neighbor lady decides to bring over some cornbread right out of the oven for supper. There he is, inside with the lawyer's fifteen-year-old girl. Girl starts screaming, says he broke open the door, intending to have his way. Course he's a good-looking young buck. Now you know and I know, Charlie."

He looked at me sternly.

"Hell, maybe you don't know." He sighed. "Deputy said there wasn't a scratch on the door. Hardware like new. Girl swore an affidavit, so that's all there is for it. He's there in a cell next to your girl. Name's John Wesley." He nodded. "That's right, like the preacher." He sipped his coffee and leaned back in the chair. "So we might get even more folks coming round, hollering. Colored girl's scared half to death as it is. She asked for you, by the way."

I looked at the jail door. "Go on, go on," he said. "It ain't locked. Just be quick."

"Mr. Charlie!" Virgie spoke before I was to her cell. "You was right. I has me a lawyer. Mr. Fields, got his office right down the street from us. Mr. George *Washington* Fields."

The colored boy stood in his cell and stared, but did not speak.

"That Johnny," Virgie said, nodding toward his cell.

"Miss Hattie ask me come into the house," Wesley said. "I ain't breaking down no door."

"Don't talk, Johnny," Virgie said. "That what Mr. Charlie told me, and he right." Wesley slumped onto his cot.

"Can you read, Virgie?" I said.

"Miss Price taught me some," she said. "But it been a while."

"All right," I said. "I have to go. I'll be back soon."

"See you then, Mr. Charlie. You ain't talked to my daddy, has you?"

I shook my head.

Sheriff Curtis had the deputy's report ready. I took down the full names of the individuals and the address for my story on the assault. Then I confirmed with the clerk of court that George Fields was representing Virginia Christian. Fields had named a second attorney, James Thomas Newsome. I had covered one of Newsome's cases in Newport News. He was an excellent advocate. I could follow up on the attorneys later. For Lewter Hobbs and Montague, the Commonwealth's attorney, I'd have to catch the ferry over to Sewell's Point. I decided to head to the shipyards instead.

While I waited outside the dry docks, I took Maebelle's biscuit from my pocket and ate it. Then I smoked a cigarette. As soon as the shift whistle blew, men began to emerge. Cahill was not nearly as tall as the others walking down the steel ramp, but somehow he took up space. The denim cap he wore flopped back on his head. A man walking next to him said something and Cahill laughed heartily, throwing his chin up. His white teeth flashed under his thick moustache. He put his hand on the man's shoulder and laughed again. His forearm was thick and pocked with burns. A red bandanna was tied around his neck. His denim overalls were dirty with oil and grease below the line where his welder's apron would fall.

"Mr. Cahill? May I speak with you?" Cahill paused and studied me.

"Well, Jack, it seems you're quite the celebrity," the big man next to him said. He slapped Cahill on the back and walked on.

"Sure, son, it's a free country," Cahill said. He grinned and started walking. "This about the widow woman?"

"Yes, sir."

"Well, come on then. I'll buy you a beer. Talked to one of your buddies yesterday. Young fellow, about your age."

"Was his name Pace?"

"Yes, that's it. Pace. Real go-getter. Here we are." The entrance to the saloon was level with the street. Men in greasy overalls lined the bar. Two made room immediately.

"Belly up, Jack," they said.

"Draft?" the bartender asked.

"Yes, and for my friend—what'll you have, friend?"

"A soda."

"A draft and a soda it is," the bartender said. He drew the beer and a sarsaparilla and set the mugs on the bar. Cahill gave him some coins. "Let's go over here where it's quieter," he said. We went to a small table by the entrance. "What's your name, son?"

"Charlie Mears."

"What do you want to know, Charlie? I didn't kill the widow woman, if that's what you're inquiring about. The deputies had quite a few questions for me about it." He took a deep swallow from the mug and wiped his moustache. The muscles rippled in his arm.

"About your neck cloth?" I took a sip of the sarsaparilla. It was bitter.

"Yes, the neck cloth. The finger marks on her throat. The cuts and bruises on her face and head. The broken spittoon. She was a tiny woman, Charlie, and frail. I could've crushed her skull with one hand." I knew he wasn't bragging.

"They wanted a man around the house, Charlie," he said. "The widow flirted like a girl. They wore my neck cloths, they wore my navy blouse, danced around, teasing each other. They wanted a little romance in their lives, Charlie."

"Do you think the Negro girl did it, then?"

"I don't know. She's little, too. But stout. I've seen her lift a kettle of wash water it would make a man grunt to do. She could've killed the widow. But it don't seem likely. If she did, something must've happened. The widow could be hard on that girl. But the girl always took it."

"I appreciate your time, Mr. Cahill."

"Sure thing, Charlie." He lifted the mug and drank it dry.

"Did you find a new place to live?"

"A room," he said. "Just down the street. Expect I'll shove off soon. I saved up a little money."

"Where do you think you'll go?"

"Subic Bay," he said. "Man can live like a king. I have a wife there."

"Why didn't you bring her with you?"

"She's Filipino," he said. "Colored. We got a little boy. He'd be colored too, way the damn government sees it."

I went to the paper and wrote up the story about the assault in Phoebus. Then I wrote a sidebar story about Cahill and suggested the headline, "Navy Veteran Unsure About Killer." On the way to my rooms I saw a bookshop with the lights on. Inside I found an illustrated edition of *The Pilgrim's Progress* for Harriet and *A Tale of Jemima Puddle-Duck,* a picture book I thought Virgie and John Wesley could share.

When I got back to Lincoln Street it was past hours for the trolley. From the porch I could hear frogs calling in the marsh near the church. The air was still. Then I heard what sounded like a chain jangling on the cobblestones. In the twilight I couldn't make out a thing. At the edge of the pool of light from the street lamp, a shadow seemed to move. It could have just been the darkness. With the unrest on the streets, I felt anxious. The shadow was low, not upright like a man.

I put my cigarette in the cuspidor. I opened the screen door quietly and went to the kitchen table. If Maebelle knew my intent I would never hear the end of it. I took one of the biscuits from the basket. I closed the screen door carefully and walked down the iron steps as quietly as I could. I set the biscuit on the far curb, just at the edge of the light from the street lamp. I came back up the steps and sat down on the stool.

The sound of the frogs grew louder. I thought I heard the chain. I focused on the biscuit. In the dim light my eyes were playing tricks. The biscuit vanished, reappeared. I thought of wiping the lenses of my glasses, but I might miss something. My eyes were getting heavy. I took a Lucky from the pack and struck a match. A snout as broad as a gator's snapped up the biscuit from the curb. A shadow merged into the darkness. I listened to the sound of a chain jangling in the distance until the match burned my fingers.

6.

Only Brother

That morning I saw Pace's story in the *Daily Press* before I saw my own. Mr. Hobgood was reading a copy at the office. He tapped the front page with a finger.

"That Pace has a nose for the news," he said. "And he makes fantasy sound more credible than fact. That's why people read gossip, Mears. They want something better than the truth. Now don't forget to follow up with the victim's brother, this Hobbs fellow, all right?" He folded the paper and threw it in the trash can on the way to his office.

"Yes, sir," I said.

I retrieved the paper. Pace had had the same hunch as mine about Cahill. Whatever conversation they'd had convinced him to go with a story. "SUSPICIONS ABOUT BOARDER'S ROLE IN MRS. BELOTE'S MURDER" was the front-page headline, over a second line reading, "White Man Questioned In Case." The article cited Cahill's navy scarf being found at the neck of Mrs. Belote's body at the murder scene, and that he had been questioned both by Deputy Chas Curtis and Dr. Vanderslice. The article quoted Cahill's testimony that he recognized Mrs. Belote's purse when it was shown to him at the inquest, and that he would have knowledge of its contents as well as other valuables that might be in the household.

"Authorities suspect the boarder Cahill may have encouraged

57

or colluded with the Negress to perpetrate the crime," the article stated, "robbery being the motive. There is also speculation that Cahill may have acted alone in the commission of the murder, given the violent disarray at the crime scene, and the brutality of the wounds inflicted on the helpless widow. Possibly the colored washwoman appeared on the scene only in order to spirit away the stolen articles later discovered on her person when she was searched by Sheriff Curtis' officers at the Hampton jail."

Pure fancy. Pace was a dogged reporter. He could have confirmed Cahill's whereabouts the day of the murder as easily as I did. I tossed the copy of the *Press* back into the trash.

My two stories made the front page of the *Times-Herald*. Mr. Hobgood had agreed with my headline for the Cahill story. He headlined the John Wesley piece, "NEGRO HELD FOR ASSAULT ON GIRL."

Straightforward; but he edited the lead, making it biased and wordy. "This entire section is highly wrought up and indignant on account of an attempted assault by J. Wesley, a Negro man, upon fifteen-year-old Hattie Power, daughter of W. H. Power, a prominent citizen and Town Attorney of Phoebus, in her home at Buckroe Beach last night."

Sheriff Curtis would be upset when he saw the Wesley article. I'd have to explain to him again that I could not control Mr. Hobgood's edits. And I'd have to remind Mr. Hobgood how helpful the sheriff had always been to me. I knew Mr. Hobgood would respond the way he always did.

"My job is to sell newspapers, Mears. I can't help it if the old rooster gets his feathers ruffled once in a while."

I decided to put off stopping by the sheriff's office until later in the day.

The offices of the Hobbs-Newby Equipment Co., Inc., were in the Seaboard Bank Building in Norfolk. I smoked a cigarette in the lobby and took the elevator to the fifth floor. When I opened the door into the Hobbs-Newby offices, I was surprised to see the Commonwealth's attorney, Edgar Montague, talking to a short, balding man. They were sitting in leather chairs beside a small lamp table across from a secretary's desk. The secretary had her hair arranged in combs atop her head. She sat erect as she typed, her back and wrists gracefully arched.

"Well, Mears," Montague said. He was a heavyset man rumored to be in poor health. He had a bright, florid complexion and thick, sandy hair. He wheezed when he spoke. "I see you're hard at work. On the Christian matter?"

"Yes, sir. Any news about the trial?"

"I'll tell you the same thing I told Pace when he came by the office. The grand jury convenes Monday morning. Evidence from the coroner's inquest suggests a heinous crime has been committed. While it is up to the grand jury to make the determination to move forward, I will tell you—and you may put this in your story, Mears—that the office of the Commonwealth's attorney is aware of the consternation aroused in the community by this brutal act and is absolutely certain of its ability to prosecute the case successfully and see justice done if and when a trial is set."

Montague leaned forward in the chair. He was wearing a brown tweed suit and vest that bulged with his paunch. A brown fedora sat on the table by his chair. From a vest pocket hung a gold watch fob. Montague touched the chain for a moment when he finished speaking. Then he pulled out the watch and checked the time. His hand trembled slightly. The secretary stopped typing and scrolled out her sheet from the platen.

"I'd better get back to the office," Montague said. There were tiny beads of sweat on his upper lip and his face looked clammy.

"I'm so sorry, Mr. Montague," the small man said. "I know Lewter was expecting you. I can't imagine what's keeping him."

Montague stood and the small man rose, too. Montague picked up the hat and smoothed the brim.

"It's quite all right, Howard. No doubt I'll see him this afternoon at the club. I'll see you at the courthouse Monday, Mears."

"Thank you, Mr. Montague. Any other comments?"

"Each individual must understand his place under the law, colored and white alike," Montague said. "That understanding represents the pediment and harmony and endurance of our culture. We have endured assaults on that understanding, Mears, especially of late, but the rule of law has always prevailed. As it will in this case."

The secretary sat at her typewriter, rapt. The small man cleared his throat and adjusted one of the garters on his sleeves. Montague placed the fedora carefully on his head and tipped the brim. He strode from the office.

"Who are you again, son?" the small man asked.

"Charlie Mears," I said. "I work for the *Times-Herald*. I wanted to see Mr. Hobbs."

"Well, sit here. Perhaps he'll see you when he comes in. I don't know how any of us can get any business done with all this commotion. We have to make a living, after all. Rose, will you take care of Mr. Mears?"

"Of course, Mr. Newby." The secretary scrolled another sheet of letterhead into the typewriter.

Newby walked quickly back to an office with a window overlooking the room where I sat with the secretary and closed the door.

"Would you like to look at some catalogs?" the secretary asked. "Why don't you sit down?"

"Yes," I said. "Thank you."

For the next hour I looked through pages of rebuilt locomotive steam boilers and train cars mounted with cranes, massive steam shovels on caterpillar tracks, concrete mixers powered by Lambert engines with dual flywheels so big they looked like side-paddle

Mississippi steamboats, and enormous steam hoists powered by coal-fired boilers the size of a house. I added another catalog to the stack on the table.

"I'll try to catch Mr. Hobbs another time," I said. "Thank you for your hospitality." I stood to leave.

The secretary touched her hair. "Do you have a card? I'll see that Mr. Hobbs gets it."

"Yes."

She studied the card I gave her. "Have you worked at the paper long?"

"Almost a year now."

"This is hard to read. I think I need glasses. Have you worn yours a long time?"

"Since grade school."

"Do you think glasses would make me look old?" she asked.

"No," I said. "I think you would look very attractive. I mean, you are very attractive." I could feel myself blushing. She dropped her eyes, then shot a glance back.

"That's sweet," she said.

"Yes, ma'am."

In the lobby I smoked a cigarette and made notes of Montague's comments.

I had carried *The Pilgrim's Progress* with me in the breast pocket of my coat. I decided to stop by Mrs. Wright's to leave it for Harriet.

The steam ferry to Newport News was right on time. The day had turned sunny. I took off my cap and put my feet up on the rail. There was a slight chop and the breeze freshened over the Roads. On a tall piling ospreys were building a nest. At the landing I caught the trolley to the Wrights' neighborhood and started walking.

Approaching on the sidewalk was a man in his thirties. He was not wearing a hat. His black hair was slicked back straight from a broad forehead. His moustache was black and curled at the ends. He was wearing a dark blue suit and he handled the umbrella he carried like a cane. His stride was brusque and powerful. He looked as fit as a wrestler.

"Mr. Hobbs?" I said. "I'm with the *Times-Herald.*" It was a lucky guess.

"Not now, boy," he said. "I don't have time." He brushed past me and turned the corner. I looked after him for a moment and continued on my way.

As soon as I got to the street, I recognized the cottage. I opened the gate and stepped up the walk to the stoop. I removed the volume from my pocket and knocked at the door.

Mrs. Wright opened the door immediately. She looked at me and smiled faintly. She seemed distracted.

"Mr. Mears," she said. "This is a pleasant surprise."

"I won't keep you, Mrs. Wright," I said. "I brought this book for Harriet." I held it out to her.

She started to take it but hesitated. She folded her hands together as if to pray.

"Wouldn't you like to give it to her yourself?" she asked. "Sadie's back in school, but Harriet's not quite feeling up to it. Why don't you go round back to the garden, and I'll bring her out. A little sunlight might brighten her up. Just follow the path." She closed the door before I could speak.

I followed a stone path around the cottage. At the back I passed through a trellis with climbing roses. Daffodils nodded in a bed of periwinkle. There was a small patio of flat stones and a bench.

The back door opened and Mrs. Wright led Harriet out by the hand. Harriet blinked her eyes against the sunlight. The breeze lifted her long black hair about her face. She brushed it back with her fingers.

"Here she is," Mrs. Wright said. Her voice was bright. Harriet took a step down onto the patio. Mrs. Wright put her hands on the girl's shoulders. "You know, Mr. Mears, we had a very nice thing happen," she said.

"Yes, ma'am?"

"The afternoon Momma was laid to rest, some colored people came over from the Ebenezer Baptist Church. They stood outside the gate on the street and sang hymns. Just for a few minutes. It was nice," she said. "I'm afraid Uncle Lewter put a stop to it. He was having tea with us and told them to move on. That evening my husband took a donation over to the church. Did you see Uncle Lewter on your way? He was just here."

"Was he carrying an umbrella?"

"Yes," she said.

"Then I did see him," I said.

"Harriet, you're shivering!" Mrs. Wright said. "Do you want a sweater?"

Harriet moved free of her sister's hands. "No, I'll be all right."

"I'll leave you two, then," Mrs. Wright said. "Look, Mr. Mears brought you a present, Harriet."

She raised her eyes to look at me. I held out the book. She took it.

"Thank you," she said.

Mrs. Wright fidgeted with the door latch until it opened. She went inside.

"Is Mrs. Wright all right?" I asked.

"She's just nervous," Harriet said. "Uncle Lewter makes everybody nervous."

"Oh," I said.

"Have you seen the Delectable Mountains?" she asked.

"So you've read it," I said.

"Not an illustrated edition," she said.

"I've seen something like," I said. "The Blue Ridge. Near Charlottesville. A friend lived there."

She smiled. "I haven't seen the mountains," she said. "I've only been to Richmond."

"Someday," I said.

"Would you like to sit down?" she asked.

"Thank you," I said.

We sat on the bench. There was a sweet fragrance. I noticed white clematis blooming against the wall.

"Have you seen Virgie?" she asked.

"Yes," I said. "I got a book for her."

"She can't read, you know."

"A picture book," I said.

"She likes to have someone read to her," she said. "I used to afternoons, when she was hanging wash. Maybe you could read to her. Is she scared?"

"Yes," I said.

"People want to kill her, don't they?"

"Yes."

She studied the bed of daffodils. "We have the same birthday. August fifteenth. Did you know that?"

"You and Virgie?"

"Yes," she said. She began to leaf through the book, stopping at each illustration. "This is pretty," she said.

"Do you mind if I smoke? Would Mrs. Wright mind?"

"Pauline? No, George smokes out here all the time. She won't let him in the house, though."

I lit a cigarette with a match cupped in my hands and held the match till it cooled. I tucked it into my pocket. She watched my face as I inhaled and exhaled the smoke. "I think I would like to smoke," she said. "But Pauline says it isn't ladylike."

"No," I said. "I suppose it isn't."

"I think I'd like to drink whiskey, too," she said. "Do you drink?"

"No," I said. "It isn't godly."

"Godly?" she said. She turned away. I saw her chin tremble. She shut the pages of the volume. "No," she said. "I suppose it isn't."

"I'm sorry," I said. "I meant no offense. It's just what I believe."

She nodded, and wiped her face with the back of her hand.

"Pauline says Sadie and I must live with Uncle Lewter and his family," she said. "He's Momma's only brother."

"I visited his offices," I said. "He must be very successful."

"Oh, yes," she said. "He has buckets of money. Have you seen his house?"

"No," I said.

"I guess you'd call it a mansion," she said. "Room after room." She lifted the little book to her breast and began to rock gently from the hips. "I won't stay there," she said. "I'll run away."

I took a long drag on the cigarette. Then I crushed it on the side of my shoe heel and tucked the butt in my pocket with the match.

"It's a big change," I said. "Maybe after a while it will feel like home."

"That's not likely," she said.

"I was sent away when my mother died, but it turned out all right," I said.

She stopped rocking. "Did they send you into a viper's pit?"

"No," I said. "Not anything like that."

Her eyes gleamed, like a bird's trapped on a limned twig.

"Do you mind if I call you Charlie?" she asked.

"No," I said. "Do you mind if I call you Harriet?"

"No," she said. She began to rock again, faster, clutching the book. Then she stopped.

"Charlie, my uncle uses me," she said. "For his pleasure. Whenever he has the chance. I won't live in his house."

I had never seen someone shudder. It was like something was shaking the breath from her body. I looked away, out into the garden. Purple hyacinths bloomed along the stone path. I wanted to look Harriet in the face but my courage failed me.

"Pauline doesn't believe me," she whispered. "She doesn't want to." She touched my hand. Hers was so cold I flinched. Then I held her fingers in mine.

I tried to think of a passage of scripture, some meditation or prayer. I turned and saw her lips pursed, like a schoolgirl puzzling over a question. Then her chin quivered and she stifled a sob. How had I never noticed her eyes were green as emeralds?

"I believe you, Harriet." I said.

She searched my face. Then she removed her hand and stood. Erect, shoulders back.

"Thank you for the book, Charlie," she said. She bowed from her waist. She opened the back door and disappeared inside the cottage. I realized the fragrance had been her hair, not the clematis.

When I got back to Hampton I stopped by my rooms to retrieve *A Tale of Jemima Puddle-Duck*. By the time I reached the jail, Sheriff Curtis was putting on his hat and coat.

"The constable'll have to give that to the Negro, Charlie," the sheriff said. "Any item received by the prisoners, you know. Got to be inspected. I'll make sure he takes care of it for you."

I looked down the corridor.

"Not this evening, son. Missus said she'd have supper on the table at five o'clock. I'm late as it is."

If Sheriff Curtis was upset about the John Wesley article, he never let on. No more crowds had gathered at the jail, even with the improving weather. Maybe seeing it wasn't likely a riot was in the offing put the sheriff in a good mood. For that matter, maybe he hadn't even seen the paper.

I asked the sheriff to give my regards to Mrs. Curtis and walked over to the *Times-Herald* offices. I typed up my article about Edgar Montague and turned it in.

Mr. Hobgood ran it the next morning on the second page. "COMMONWEALTH'S ATTORNEY CONFIDENT OF OUTCOME," the headline read. I hoped Sheriff Curtis would see that story. It might reassure him the town would remain quiet as we headed into the weekend.

Quiet it was. Still, Sheriff Curtis kept the constable on duty all weekend, along with Chas and another deputy.

On Monday, April 1, a grand jury returned an indictment against Virginia Christian for the felony murder of Ida V. Belote. The trial was set for 10 o'clock on the morning of April 8. There were front-page headlines in every newspaper in the region. At a hearing on Wednesday, April 3, the circuit court of Elizabeth City County awarded guardianship of the orphaned female children Harriet Martha Belote and Sarah Elizabeth Belote to Lewter F. Hobbs. All that appeared in the papers was the court record.

The evening of the guardianship hearing I sat for a long time on the iron steps to my rooms. Miller moths spun about the gaslight. The blue spark of the last trolley lit the new leaves on the limbs hanging over the line. After the last shriek of metal wheels on the tracks, I heard a sound I recognized as the chain. I moved up the steps as quietly as I could. In the icebox Maebelle had left potato cakes fried in bacon. I retrieved a couple and went across the sidewalk to the street. This time I placed the cakes in the middle of the pool of light and went back up on the porch to watch. I lit a cigarette and waited.

I finished my cigarette, lit another, finished it. I nodded off, then stirred myself.

Just then a gaunt creature dragging about three feet of chain from its neck crept into the pool of light. Its big head was connected to a frail body. It was a pit bull terrier, a male. His coat was black as pitch. His ears were clipped tight to his head and his left ear was torn. His paws looked like each had been dipped in white paint.

There was a big white mark on his chest the shape of a crushed cigarette packet.

"I'll call you 'Lucky,'" I whispered. The dog lifted his head at the sound, then snatched Maebelle's potato cake and wolfed it down. He disappeared into the twilight.

7.

Red

I stared into the darkness where Lucky had vanished. I wanted to help Harriet but I had no idea how. I understood little about intimacy, less about the danger Harriet had described. The men I worked with seemed to be versed in such matters. But their views were coarse.

Did I know how to befriend her? Friendship had been hurtful to me. I had retreated into despair when my friend Fitz died. Loneliness had become my shepherd.

I lit another cigarette and blew out the match, watching white vapor curl from the head. I dropped the match in the cuspidor. The first friendship of my life had been hurtful, too.

Red and I met at school in 1902. He sat on the bench next to me in Miss Quesinberry's one-room school on Flag Run. His hair was the color of copper wire and his eyes were green. He carried with him a little edition of *Aesop's Fables.*

"Mind if I try them spectacles?" he asked. His canvas trousers were patched with a variety of fabrics and held up with a length of sisal.

"No," I said. "I don't mind."

I loosed the wire rims from my ears and handed the glasses to Red.

"Them's like fish hooks," he said.

"Put the frame on your nose, then run your fingers round your ears," I said. "It's easy." He hooked the temples over his ears.

"Don't work worth a damn," he said. "Everything's blurry."

"They have to be made special," I said. "What's your name?"

"Red," he said. "What's yours?"

"Charles," I said.

"That your last name?"

"First name."

"Oh, then you mean Charlie," he said.

"No, Mother calls me Charles."

"That ain't no kind of name."

"How about Red? That's not a real name."

"Course it is."

"An old man I know has a dog named Red. That can't be your real name."

"Why, I reckon it is," he said.

"Would you boys be so gracious as to share your conversation with the rest of the class?" Miss Quesinberry asked. She stood over us, cradling the handle of a leather strop in her hand. "Franklin! Give Charles his eyeglasses immediately! Go to the bench in the back. I don't want to hear you two talking anymore today."

The next day at school when Red slid in on the bench next to me, he sighed.

"Well," he said. "You heard. Franklin my name. But everybody call me Red. Momma say the day I was born my hair so bright all the people call me that. She say even my skin was red day she showed me to people."

"That's all right," I said. "That's a nickname. I'd say Red is about as good a nickname as somebody could have."

"You mind I call you Charlie?" he asked.

"Just don't do it in front of my mother."

"They ain't no danger in that," he said.

That fall Red and I became friends. Not once do I remember my mother being in earshot of Red, although we often spent time in the company of his. Red lived with his mother, Sarah, in a one-room wooden shack by the railroad tracks just outside Jerusalem. The shack was roofed with tin. Red and I would sit on the little front porch and listen to the rain drum on the tin. Sometimes the wind would blow the rain spilling from the roof onto our faces, and it felt cold as ice. If we had found a toad in the shade under the house, we'd turn it loose and watch it hop down the steps, big drops spattering its back, until it made its way under the house to shelter.

Red's mother was a tall woman, tall as a man. Her eyes were queer, the eyes of a being who could cast spells over creatures or men. They were large, set far apart, the color of amber. Sometimes she caught me staring at her but she never scolded. She would smile faintly and look away. Her hair was always wrapped in brightly colored scarves, and she would carry water to the house balancing it in big jugs on her head. She was thin, so thin her ebony skin looked drawn over her bones.

"People say she been bony ever since I was born," Red said. "Course, I ain't got no way of knowing, cause I flat out don't remember. People say she got some kind of blood flux. Say that's why she don't have no more children than me."

"Where's your daddy?" I asked.

"Don't rightly know," he said. "Ain't never seen him. Some people say he got killed. Momma don't seem to know."

"People say my daddy was killed, too," I said. "Out west. By an Irishman."

"What's that?"

"A foreigner. They about starved out. So they came here. You can tell them by their red hair."

"Well, I ain't no Irishman."

"Course you're not. Not everybody has red hair is an Irishman."

"Humph," he said. "I'd whole lot rather be a red-headed nigger than some foreigner."

"Me, too."

Red's mother cooked hoecakes right in the coals of the hearth. She grew little green peppers in her garden she would hang from the rafters of the shack in the winter. She seasoned her batter with the peppers and they made your tongue burn and your eyes water. Red loved her hoecakes and I learned to love them, too. One time we tried seeing who could hold one of those dried peppers in his mouth the longest. I spit mine out right off but Red held his until his face turned red and his freckles were black as peppercorns. Tears were running down his cheeks, and still he held the pepper. Then his mother came in and caught us. She laughed out loud when she saw Red's puckered face. Then she quit laughing and switched Red good.

Sometimes Sarah would sit with us on the porch as we listened to the crickets and katydids. She would smoke a corncob pipe to help drive off the mosquitoes. She stretched her long legs down the steps, and the skin of her legs glistened. One evening a colored girl in a faded dress ambled along the road. She was barefoot, and a strap of her dress had fallen from her shoulder. She paused and plucked a stem of marsh grass and placed it in her teeth. She was older than Red and me, with fascinating curves and shapes. We leaned forward, studying every motion.

"Get on there, girl," Sarah said. "Don't you be lollygagging here front of my porch!" The girl said nothing and moved on. She looked back over her shoulder.

"What you two gawking at?" Red's mother said. "I'm gone tan your hide, boy, you don't act like you got some sense. Mister Charlie, that go for you, too. Don't you reckon your momma be missing you? Best get on home. I make you some more hoecakes tomorrow."

"Yes, ma'am," I said.

The next week, after a thunderstorm, Red and I caught some fat night crawlers in the grass behind the shack. We put them with sand and grass in an old bucket and tucked them in the shade of the house pilings. The next afternoon, we carried the bucket to a little pool on Flag Run, near the school, with our cane poles and a burlap sack.

The bullheads were biting, and each of us was bringing one in with nearly every cast. We hoisted them up, gasping and sucking, their bellies yellow in the sunlight, onto the bank. We unhooked them as quickly as we could, put them in the sack in the stream, weighted the mouth of the sack with a big rock, and baited our hooks. When we ran out of night crawlers, we started to search the marsh grass along the stream for crickets.

"What you two doing?" the colored girl asked. Her hair was tied in braids. I recognized her. She was the girl we had studied from Red's mother's porch.

"Who spying?" Red asked.

"Alreda," she said. "I ain't spying. What you doing?"

She looked pretty in a flowered smock made from a flour sack.

"Fishing," I said.

"We catching crickets," Red said.

"You a cute white boy," she said. "I seen you at Red's. What your name?"

"Charlie," I said.

"Charlie," she said. She closed her eyes. "Mr. Charlie."

"Don't you be studying about no name," Red said. "We trying to do us some fishing. Why don't you get on?"

"Mr. Charlie, you want to see my titties?" she asked.

"I mean it, girl!" Red said. He picked up a clump of sod.

Alreda lowered the front of her smock. She let me look, then pulled it back over her shoulders.

"I show you my jellyroll for a penny, Mr. Charlie," she said.

"He ain't got no penny!" Red said. He threw the sod. It landed with a smack on her ankle.

"You little nigger!" she said.

Red picked up another clump. "You get on!" he said.

Alreda scurried up the bank and out of sight.

"Look here, Charlie," he said. "Look the size of the damn cricket was under that sod."

Red and I gathered a few more crickets in my handkerchief. We baited our hooks and caught more bullheads and slid them in the burlap sack. Then we gathered our poles and headed to Red's house.

"Look here, Momma," he said, hefting the sack.

Sarah smiled. "I got some corn meal. Clean them and I'll cook them up for supper."

Red found a bowl and a knife in the kitchen. We carried them and the sack to the marsh grass on the other side of the road. Red pulled a bullhead from the sack.

"Them spines, see, you don't want one to poke your hand, Charlie. Sting like hell." He cradled the bullhead between his fingers and cut the skin around its head. He cut the skin around the spikes and pulled it back, pinching with his thumb against the knife blade. He threw the skin in the grass. Then he ran the blade down the backbone to cut the fillets. He tossed the head and spine into the grass. He held the fillets up.

"See yonder?" he said. He put the fillets in the bowl. "Now you try one."

I pulled a bullhead from the sack and rested its belly between my fingers.

Red nodded. "That's fine," he said. I began to cut the skin.

"Don't you be giving Alreda no pennies," Red said. "She show you that jellyroll for free." I looked up. He was grinning.

"Well," I said.

Red was right. Alreda would display her charms for nothing.

But we also discovered the wonders a penny could buy. Alreda would sway and shimmy before us, bare as the day she was born. For another penny she allowed us to touch. With her eyes she guided us to touch in ways she liked. At these moments I could feel my heart beating to the tips of my fingers, and my hand trembled.

"Don't you be skittish, Mr. Charlie, you doing good," she crooned. Her voice washed over me like warm rain. I closed my eyes. I could hear her breathing. I felt I was floating, nudged by wind like a leaf on water.

That fall, I didn't see Red at Miss Quesinberry's one-room school. When I asked Miss Quesinberry about it, she told me he was attending a special school just for Negroes.

"Well, what's wrong with this school? Why doesn't Red come here, like before?"

"He's colored, Charles. The district had overlooked it. But the new constitution strictly forbids the races going to school together. That's all. There's nothing wrong with anything."

A tall boy on the bench behind me snickered. "Aw, he misses his little nigger friend," he said. He tweaked at one of the temples of my wire rims.

"Mason Davis, you hush this instant!" Miss Quesinberry said. "You are never to utter that word inside these walls. Do you understand me?"

The boy slouched behind his desk.

"Well, do you?" Miss Quesinberry leaned over my desk. The wattles of her neck trembled. Her hand clenched the strop.

"Yes, ma'am," the boy said.

"All right, then. Open your books. We'll start our lesson," Miss Quesinberry said. The books were brand new. The ink smelled like enamel paint when I turned a page. "Commonwealth of Virginia" was stamped on the fly leaf. When the school superintendent visited, he said we had new books so we wouldn't have to use old ones that had been touched by colored children.

After school I walked to Red's house. He was sitting on the porch, holding the *Aesop's Fables*. He didn't smile when he looked up.

"You like this one?" Red asked. "About the mouse, chewed the ropes and saved that lion?"

"Uh-huh," I said. "You want to go down to the creek?"

"Naw," he said. "Momma had to see somebody. She say I got to stay right here, keep her fire banked. She cooking beans."

"Well," I said. "I'll be seeing you."

"My daddy a white man, Charlie. That what Momma say."

"Well," I said.

Red nodded and went back to his book.

The next day after school I walked to Red's house again. This time he was in the road in front of the shack. He and two colored boys I'd never seen before were kicking around a sock stuffed with corn shucks. Red saw me, but he kept right on playing. The other boys looked at me and frowned. They were silent. I watched them kick the sock. Their bare feet whispered in the dust. Sometimes they would try to steal the sock with their feet, bumping each other and laughing. I watched for a good while, and then I walked home. I didn't go over to Red's house after that. Sometimes I would see him at a distance in Jerusalem, and I would wave, but he didn't wave back.

One Saturday in spring two colored girls came to do the washing for Mother. I was reading on the porch as they hung sheets to dry. One of the girls said to the other that her cousin Alreda had moved to Newport News to live with her grandmother.

"Say she done got work cleaning houses," the girl said. "Be the last we sees of her round here." And it was. I remember looking across the fields, where my father's wagons bleached in the sun.

The last week of school that year, just after the tobacco sets had been planted, my mother died. The doctor said it was cancer. The final weeks, I read the Scriptures to her in her bed. Her maiden aunt rode the train down from Williamsburg and arranged my mother's affairs. She was buried in a small plot on the farm near the road. The stone her aunt had erected was carved with flowers.

I could remember my mother receiving her aunt's letters from time to time, but I had never seen her a day in my life. After the funeral I packed a suitcase and boarded the train in Jerusalem with her, bound for Williamsburg. I thought I spotted Red running with a pack of colored boys from the depot. But they were gone in an instant.

The house and land sold right away. My great-aunt told me I seemed to be a nice young man but she did not have the energy to raise me.

That fall she took some of the money from the sale of the farm and enrolled me at the Sulgrave Military Academy. I had not seen Jerusalem or Southampton County since, not even passing through.

8.

Syms-Eaton Academy

Harriet and Sadie stayed with Mrs. Wright. She had convinced her uncle it would be better for the girls if they remained with her until after the trial. And she felt it was important the girls remain at Syms-Eaton Academy, so there would be some anchor from their previous lives. From Washington Street they'd walked to school, but now they'd have to take the trolley from the Wrights' home in Newport News. The girls could ride together in the mornings, and Mrs. Wright would pick up Sadie when her classes ended at noon, but she didn't want Harriet riding home by herself. The girl was so fragile.

"I could meet Harriet after school," I said. "I'd be happy to."

"That's very kind, Mr. Mears," she said. "Uncle Lewter's putting them in Norfolk Academy as soon as they move in with him. He thinks a completely new situation will help. Bank Street's not far from his office. So he can drive them to and from school himself. I just hope it won't be too much of a change. Sadie's already excited about riding in an automobile every day!"

I arrived at Syms-Eaton at noon. The original academy building had burned during the war, and the new one was an attractive brick building with white pediments and Ionic columns. A white picket fence ran along the street. Harriet's teacher, Miss Hickman, walked out with Harriet, holding her hand until they reached the gate.

"Are you Mr. Mears?" Miss Hickman asked.

"He is," Harriet said. She smiled.

"Take good care of her, young man," Miss Hickman said. "She's one of Syms' best students."

"Yes, ma'am."

Harriet gave me her book strap and took my hand. I was surprised. But I felt happy. Her hand was cold as ice. The sun was bright and white clouds billowed low. A towhee was working in the litter under a pink azalea and called loudly.

"They always seem to be so mad when they're scratching in the leaves, don't they?" Harriet said.

I nodded. She was wearing a dark blue dress with a sailor collar and white piping. Her straw boater shaded her eyes. There was a long blue ribbon on the boater and it fluttered with her hair in the breeze.

"Do you feel like walking for a while?" I asked.

"Yes," she said. "The weather's so nice."

At the corner she turned on Washington Street, toward the C&O depot. I hesitated.

"I'll be all right," she said. "I want to see the house."

One of the hinges had been broken, so the front gate hung askew. It was latched shut. A "For Sale" sign was posted in the yard. Harriet looked at the façade of the house for a long time, studying each aspect, the chimneys, the dormers, the front door. She pointed to a window.

"That was our room," she said. "Sadie and me. And there, at the end of the house, that was the room Mr. Cahill rented." The curtains in both the windows were drawn shut.

"We'd better go, Harriet," I said. "You don't want your sister to worry."

"All right," she said.

We walked past the depot. Poindexter waved from the platform, grinning. I realized Harriet was still holding my hand. It felt warm now.

"Fine day, Charlie!" he said. I waved to him and lifted the book strap over my shoulder.

On the trolley Harriet folded her hands in her lap.

"Did you go to college?" she asked. "I think I would want to. I think I would want to be a teacher, like Miss Hickman."

"To William & Mary," I said. "But I left."

"Didn't you like it?" she asked.

"No, I liked it," I said. "But something happened. So I left."

She looked at my face. Then she looked out the window.

"Well," she said. "If you don't feel like telling me, that's all right."

"A friend of mine," I said. "He died. He was in classes with me." I didn't want to tell her, but the words leapt out. My throat grew tight. I hadn't thought of Fitz Scott in months.

"I'm sorry about your friend," she said. She looked down at her folded hands. "I try not to think about Momma, either. We have that in common, don't we? Somebody special suddenly taken away."

I nodded. We didn't speak anymore during the ride. She took my hand again after we got off the trolley. Mrs. Wright was pruning dead branches off the climbing rose at the trellis in front of the cottage. She pricked her finger when she saw us.

"Heavens!" she said, sucking her finger. "Harriet, you must come and eat something. It's nearly time for supper! What kept you? Mr. Mears, will you join us?"

"No ma'am, I'd better get to work. But thank you."

I gave Harriet her book strap. She leaned toward me and kissed me on the cheek. The brim of her boater caught the brim of my cap and the boater went flying. She scurried to pick it up, gathering the long ribbon. Her cheeks were pink. She trotted up the sidewalk to the trellis.

"Thank you, Mr. Mears," her sister called. "We'll see you tomorrow."

"Yes, ma'am." I watched the two of them enter the front door. Harriet peeked out, then shut the door.

When I walked into the offices of the *Times-Herald*, Mr. Hobgood was looking very pleased with himself. "Playing nursemaid or beau, Mears?" he asked, leaning back in his chair. "The Belote girl's a little young for you, I'd say, but pretty. Very pretty, in a delicate kind of way. Like an orchid."

I could feel myself blushing.

"Mears, I don't care. You can pack a picnic and make a day of it, as long as you keep your beats covered."

"Yes, sir, Mr. Hobgood."

"Maybe you'll even get an exclusive interview," he said. "She fascinates people. Everybody commented on her testimony at the inquest."

"Well," I said.

I was reading my daily scripture at the kitchen table when I heard Maebelle call from the foot of the steps. "Mr. Charlie, is you home?"

I stuck my head out the door. "Yes, Maebelle."

She grabbed the railing with one hand and started up the steps. In the other hand atop a big white bowl she was balancing a small cast-iron frying pan covered with a dishcloth.

"Here, let me help you," I said.

I took the bowl and frying pan. She followed me up the steps. I set the bowl on the kitchen table, moved my Bible, and placed the frying pan next to the bowl.

"I made you some chickpeas with ham and stewed tomatoes, with fresh cornbread in the skillet," she said. "You need to put meat on them bones, Mr. Charlie. You gone need your strength chasing after them news stories and walking a pretty little gal up and down town the same time." She put her hands on her hips and smiled broadly.

"I better look for another job," I said. "Who needs a reporter, fast as news travels in this town?"

"Oh, I was just teasing you, Mr. Charlie. Somebody heard Mr. Poindexter talking at the depot, that's all." She bent toward me. "What's the matter, child? You feeling poorly?"

I put my bookmark in the Bible and closed the pages. "Oh, I'm fine, Maebelle. I'm just, well, I'm . . ."

"Well, is you or ain't you?" she asked.

"Maebelle, I need your help. About the girl."

Her face beamed. "I knowed it," she said. "I knowed you didn't understand the first thing about courting no girl. You don't take care of yourself, don't pay no attention to your clothes . . ."

"Not about courting," I said.

Her face darkened. "Well, what then? Mr. Charlie, you ain't got yourself in no kind of trouble, has you?"

"No! It's just that Harriet says, well, she says someone is taking advantage of her."

"She got her another beau?" she asked. "Is that who?"

"No," I said. "Someone in her family. Someone powerful."

"Mr. Charlie, what you mean exactly, you say, 'take advantage of her'?"

"I mean, touch her. Have carnal knowledge." My ears were burning; they must have been beet red.

Maebelle's eyebrows shot up.

"Mr. Charlie, you mean some big shot want to stir that girl's jellyroll? Is that what you trying to say?"

"Yes."

"Lord God," Maebelle said. "Some man in her own family?" She cocked her head. "Maybe that girl just saying so to get your attention. Maybe she a little sweet on you, Mr. Charlie, and she scared to be by herself, cause of her momma being killed right in her own house."

"No," I said. "I mean, yes, she is a little sweet on me, but I think she's telling the truth."

Maebelle sat down in the chair next to me, clucking like a hen. She shook her head and looked at the floor.

"I want to help her," I said. "Because soon she'll be in even more danger."

She raised her eyes. "She done told any of her people?" she asked.

"Her older sister."

"Her sister don't believe her?"

"Harriet says no."

She sighed and leaned back in the chair. "Ain't nobody gone believe you, then," she said.

"I know."

"Well, you ain't gone marry her, Mr. Charlie, cause she too young by law. Was that what you was thinking? She ain't but thirteen, newspapers say."

"That's right, thirteen."

She stood and walked to the sink cabinet. "I don't see no way through right now, Mr. Charlie. I surely don't." She wiped her hands with her apron. "You been praying on it?"

"Yes."

"Well, you go on praying, and I'll commence praying about it, too, and maybe something good will come to us. Now I'm gone spoon you out some chickpeas and ham and cut a big piece of cornbread, and you gone sit right here at this table till you eat every crumb, you hear me?"

"Yes, ma'am," I said.

From the pocket of her big apron Maebelle produced a newspaper parcel dark with grease. "I got something for that dog you been feeding," she said. "I seen him slinking round. Mrs. Wingate seen him, too. What on earth that hanging from his neck?"

"I think it's a chain," I said.

"People do anything to a dog," she said. She folded back the edges of the newspaper. "Look here. Corn fritters fried in bacon." She smiled so wide, I could have counted every tooth in her head.

After supper I moved out to the porch to smoke. The street lamp threw light into the cemetery, where the grass was greening for spring. I smiled, remembering how Fitz used to chide me for smoking as we sat on the steps of our boarding house.

"You know, Preacher, tobacco ruins men just as readily as it ruins soil," he said.

"Well," I said, flicking ash from the cigarette.

He clapped me on the back. "Oh, don't look so solemn! A man's entitled to one vice, I suppose. Besides, the gospel is conveniently silent on the matter." He grinned and turned back to his book. "Now where was I? Right. 'We hold the wolf by the ear,' Mr. Jefferson wrote a friend regarding the Missouri Compromise, 'and we can neither hold him, nor safely let him go. Justice is in one scale, and self-preservation is in the other.'" He closed the text.

"Of course, our modern remedy is simple," Fitz said. "Have a mob tie a noose round the wolf's neck and let go the ear. Of course, the remedy of lynching only makes sense if the wolf has no value as property. A luxury Mr. Jefferson did not enjoy in his time."

"That's so cynical, it's grotesque," I said.

"You're right, Preacher. I admire Mr. Jefferson. But he was burdened by debt. He couldn't release any chattel, not for his own account, nor for his estate's."

"Granted," I said.

"So we've been left with the sins of our fathers. And our remedy is the hangman's noose. Or electric chair, now that Virginia's become one of the leading Progressive states in the South."

I sometimes felt that Fitz was everything I could not be. He had read Latin with his father since he was a boy. I still struggled with my declensions. His eyes were clear as a blue mountain spring, where mine were dull gray obscured by eyeglasses. He was straight, square-shouldered, and muscular. I was scrawny and slouched. In conversation he was fluid as a swimmer. Accompanying him to gatherings I felt flat-footed and dull.

It seemed so unlikely we could ever be friends. But friends we were.

His letter arrived in my box the day after I had read the news of his death in the Williamsburg paper. I ran my fingertip over the fine vellum envelope before I opened it and unfolded the letter. My sight blurred as I began to read his hand's steady, elegant script.

Dear Preacher, We have become comrades of the strongest sort, and I have found in my heart a love for you unlike anything I have known. That as a man you should find such love repulsive is no disappointment, for I find it repulsive in myself. But this is my nature, I see now, and I embrace it. For running alongside the passion I feel is likewise the deepest friendship I have known, in mind, heart, and soul. I have come to understand what the poet meant when he wrote of "comrades," for as such in my soul are you and I joined. I beg your forgiveness and the forgiveness of my family for following a course that must seem cowardly and shameful. But I go forward, believing that what awaits is "different from what anyone thought, and luckier." In the end, I am proud of who I am. I mean no rebuke to anyone. I love you all. Fitz

For a moment I hoped this was all a hoax Fitz had planned, like Tom Sawyer secretly attending his own funeral. Then my hope faded. I carefully refolded the letter and replaced it in the envelope. I placed the envelope in the breast pocket of my vest. Somehow its shape against my ribs consoled me, as if Fitz had draped an arm over my shoulder and smiled.

After I left school, I carried the envelope with me every day for weeks. It was in my breast pocket when I trotted from Mr. Hobgood's office out onto the street my first day running a beat for the paper. I have it now, along with a photograph of Fitz, in the top drawer of my bureau.

When I finished my cigarette, I went into the kitchen and opened Maebelle's parcel. I removed two of the fritters and nibbled at one. There were bits of bacon inside. I carried the fritters downstairs and set one of them on the curb in the pool of light. I sat on the bottom step and waited.

In a moment I heard the jangle of the chain. The dog crept into the light, flattening himself as he got closer to the food. He snatched it and retreated to the edge of the light.

"Here Lucky, here Lucky," I whispered. I held the other fritter in my hand. He laid his ears back, as if he would bolt.

"Here boy, good dog."

His face was full of doubt. There were gray scars on his muzzle and jowls. Slowly, he seemed to feel resolve. He kept flat and crept a step toward me. Then another. Another.

"Good dog, Lucky," I whispered. He was just an arm's length from the fritter in my hand. I didn't move. I didn't look in his eyes. He began to whimper, then crept another step closer.

"Good dog," I said. He snatched the fritter and crouched, devouring it in an instant. He sniffed my hand and licked the bacon grease from my fingers. I could see that someone had fixed the chain he dragged to a collar fashioned from barbed wire. Who would do such a thing? The smell of his flesh where the barbs festered was putrid. He backed away from me on his haunches, then turned and slunk into the darkness.

The Virginia Christian trial would begin in three days. I needed to visit her attorney.

9.

Inez

George Washington Fields' house sat on a big lot, with a brick walkway and wide lawn in the front. Near the house was a branch of Hampton Creek. Cattails grew on its banks. Toward the back of the house was a vegetable garden. Peas and lettuce were growing. The peas climbed willow branches cut and stuck in the earth for the purpose. There were three steps up to a screened front porch. I walked onto the porch and knocked at the door with a brass knocker shaped like a gavel.

A tall girl answered the door. She had high cheekbones and thick, expressive lips. Her skin was smooth, the color of coffee with cream. Her eyes were the shape of almonds and sparkled brightly. Her hair was straight, styled to hang partway down her neck. She had thick black bangs that glistened. I removed my cap.

"Yes?" she said.

She was beautiful. It took me a moment to collect my thoughts.

"My name is Charlie Mears. I'm with the *Times-Herald*. Is Mr. Fields available?"

"No," she said. "My father's with Mr. Newsome at his office. They're working."

"Mr. Thomas Newsome?"

"Yes," she said.

"They're working on the Virginia Christian case?"

"I couldn't say," she said.

"Will your father return soon? I'd like to speak with him."

"No," she said. "I don't expect we'll see him before supper."

"May I ask you some questions?"

"Why would you want to ask me anything?"

"To get background on your father. For my article about the Virginia Christian trial. May I?"

"I suppose I can tell you what I know."

"May we sit?" I gestured toward the porch swing.

"Yes," she said.

We sat side by side. I took my pencil and pad from my jacket pocket.

"Miss Fields, your name is?"

"Inez."

"Your family is very prominent in the Negro community of Hampton, aren't they?"

"Yes, I suppose. They came here in 1863. My father and all his family were slaves." She smiled. "Daddy says none of them even knew how to read."

"And now your father is a successful attorney."

"Yes."

"How did that happen?"

"Daddy says it's because of his mother. She brought her children here from a plantation near Richmond. Two of her sons had been sold to other farms in Virginia, and after the war they were also able to join her. With the help of an officer at Fort Monroe, she was able to get my Aunt Louise back, too. She'd been sold down to Georgia. When my grandfather was freed from the plantation where he lived, he made his way here, too. He worked as a blacksmith at the fort. They all stuck together, worked together, because of my grandmother, Daddy says. He says she held them all together. The first house on this property they built themselves of rough boards sawed from logs they cut right on the property. Daddy learned to read and studied at Hampton Institute, and then he went north and worked. Then he studied at Cornell Law School in New York. They say he was the first black man to earn a law degree there. Then he came back to Hampton to help his mother."

"Is your grandmother still living?"

"No," she said. "She passed away before I was born."

"What was her name?"

"Martha Ann."

"Does your father speak of the past? About his time on the plantation?"

"No," she said.

"Have you asked him about it?"

"Yes," she said. "But he doesn't like to speak of it. He says he doesn't want me to think of those times, especially while I'm young."

"I'm told your father is blind."

"Yes," she said.

"How did he lose his sight?"

"I don't know. He tells me he went blind before I was born. He says he thinks it's funny he only knows me by touch and sound." She smiled. "He says I sound a lot better than I used to. I had the colic when I was a baby so I cried a lot."

"Do you know Virginia Christian?"

"Goodness, no."

"But the Christian house is close by."

"Yes, but they're not people we would know." She bit her lip. "I don't want to be rude, but I should work on my studies now."

"Where are you a student?"

"At Hampton. I take my degree next year. You look like you would be in college."

"I was."

"Where?"

"William & Mary."

"Why did you leave? Didn't you like your classes?"

"No, I liked my classes."

"Then why did you leave?"

"Something happened. It just seemed like my life stopped."

She pondered this for a moment. She was forming another question, but reconsidered. Her brow furrowed. "How did you pick newspaper work? Were you a writer?"

"No."

"Well, what then?"

"I thought life would be all around me. Reporting the news."

"And it is?"

"Yes," I said. "Sometimes it's overwhelming."

"Will you return to school?"

"Maybe someday." I stood. The swing rocked slightly and settled. "Thank you for the information, Miss Fields."

"You're welcome," she said.

She watched as I walked to the porch door.

"I didn't ask you about you," I said.

"What do you mean?"

"After Hampton. What will you do?"

"I think I'll study the law," she said. "So one day I can help my father."

"I know you would do well."

"Thank you."

"I mean it. You got more out of me than I got out of you. And I'm supposed to be the one asking the questions."

She smiled and lowered her chin.

What a feature Mr. Fields would make. A former slave who had risen to become one of the most successful attorneys in all Hampton Roads, with clients of both races. And blind to boot. But only a colored paper would run such a story.

I walked up the street past the Christian house. The doors and windows were shut tight, though I saw a figure move past a window inside. Then I walked to the Belote place. The "For Sale" sign was still posted in the yard. I leaned against the picket fence and smoked a cigarette. Harriet hadn't asked to walk by after the one time we stopped on our way from Syms-Eaton.

Three girls living within blocks of each other. Teenagers. Yet how different were their worlds. Mr. Hobgood might go for a feature written around that theme. A white audience would read it. One girl white as paper. Another dark as pitch. The third the color of coffee with cream. How had Hampton kept good relations between the races before whatever happened with Virgie and Mrs. Belote? How would Hampton keep good relations after?

I thought of the passage in Hebrews. "All things are by the law purged with blood; and without shedding of blood is no forgiveness." I studied the empty house where the widow had lived with her two young daughters and the boarder, Cahill. Someone thinking about buying must have looked the place over; the window curtains to the bedroom Harriet said she shared with Sadie were open. Inside was darkness. In the twilight it seemed Mrs. Belote's soul lingered.

I walked down the street and passed by the C&O depot. Poindexter was sitting at his desk. He waved when he saw me passing. I waved back and crossed the street. I stopped at Sam Howard's store to buy a chocolate bar and a pack of Lucky Strikes. There was a small counter for hardware, hammers and the like. I noticed a small pair of tin snips. I asked Mr. Howard if he thought they would cut wire.

"Oh, yes," he said, "those blades are keen." I bought the snips and tucked them in my jacket pocket with the chocolate and cigarettes.

The streetlights were burning by the time I reached the jail. Deputy Chas Curtis was talking on the telephone when I opened the door. The earpiece looked like a chess pawn in his big hand.

"Evening, Charlie," he said, hanging up the earpiece.

"How's Sheriff Curtis?"

"Still feeling poorly," he said. He leaned back in the chair. "He come downstairs for a little while, but mostly he's been upstairs with the missus, which ain't like him. Coughing and snuffling the livelong day."

"I bought Virgie a chocolate bar," I said.

"Let me have a look, Charlie. Sheriff's orders."

I handed him the candy.

"That's quite a bulge," he said, gesturing at my pocket.

I pulled out the cigarettes and tin snips.

"All right, then," he said. "Don't reckon you could cut any bars with them puny things." I slipped the cigarettes and snips back in my pocket. He gave me the chocolate bar and took the key ring from a hook on the side of the desk. He paused at the jail door. "Don't stay long, now," he said. "I was fixing to get home pretty quick."

"I won't keep you long," I said.

He unlocked the door. "Her cell door is just pulled to, Charlie. It ain't locked." The door clanged shut behind me. I could see Virgie's hands gripping the bars of her cell.

"That you, Mr. Charlie?"

"Yes, Virgie."

"I'm mighty glad you here. It lonely."

I looked in the cell facing hers. "Where's John Wesley?"

"Deputies let him go. Got him to sign some paper. I been looking at pictures in that book you left. That Jemima one persnickety duck. Johnny read me some the things she say."

"Look here," I said.

"Why, Mr. Charlie," she said.

"Go on, take it."

"How you know I likes chocolate? Don't reckon I had it more than twice." She reached through the bars of the cell.

"How about a piece for me?" I asked.

She started to hand the chocolate back. "No, you do it," I said.

She carefully peeled the paper and foil and broke off a chunk. She held it delicately between her fingers.

"There you is," she said.

I took the chocolate and put it in my mouth.

"Pretty good," I said.

She broke another piece off and put it in her mouth. She smiled broadly.

"Sure is," she said. She broke off another piece.

"Better save some," I said.

"I will," she said. She put the piece in her mouth and rewrapped the bar. "Mr. Newsome come by today," she said. "He asked me a passel of questions. Say my trial coming up day after tomorrow."

"Yes," I said.

"You gone be there?"

"Yes."

"Mrs. Belote don't hit me with that chamber pot," she said, "don't reckon I'd got so mad. Then when she commenced to hollering so loud, felt like I had a knife sticking inside my head."

"Mr. Fields and Mr. Newsome are excellent attorneys," I said.

"Mr. Charlie, they ain't gone let me . . . what is it, when you tells what happened?"

"Testify?"

"That it. Testify. They say they ain't gone let me testify. How people gone hear what Mrs. Belote done to me?"

"I'm sure your attorneys know what's best, Virgie. I don't think you could find better men."

"That what people say. My daddy proud about it. He come to see me. He say Momma miss me something awful."

"I'm sure she does."

The door to the cells opened.

"Reckon I better lock up, Charlie," Chas said.

"All right," I said. He walked to the cell.

"Got to lock your cell for the night, Virgie," he said.

I stepped back from her cell door. He locked it and we came out to the office. He locked the metal jail door. I asked him what became of John Wesley.

"Girl changed her testimony," he said. "Said the boy just come in the house for a drink of water, and that's what scared her. Sheriff had an affidavit drawn up saying the boy trespassed. The boy claimed the girl asked him into the house. Sheriff told him he was gone have to forget all about that, and just sign what he told him to sign. So the boy did." He tossed the key ring on the top of the desk. "I'll be seeing you, Charlie," he said.

"Thanks, Chas," I said.

The pit bull terrier was crouched on his haunches by the steps when I got to Mrs. Wingate's. I stopped. He sidled away, still crouched, lifting his head to get my scent.

"Lucky," I whispered. "Here, Lucky." He sprang up and trotted to the corner of the carriage house, the chain dragging through the azaleas. He looked back at me.

I eased up the steps and opened the door. Sure enough, on the kitchen table Maebelle had left a fresh batch of fritters in a basket covered with a checked cloth. I tucked a handful of the fritters in my pocket with the snips and cigarettes.

The dog was waiting for me at the base of the stairs. I came down a slow step at a time. He backed away, shifting his weight nervously. I sat down on the bottom step. I took a fritter from my pocket, leaned forward as far as I could, and placed it on the ground. I leaned back.

He edged toward it, eyeing me closely. He crouched on his haunches and whimpered. I kept as still as possible.

He snatched the fritter, retreated a step, crouched, and gobbled it down.

"Good boy," I said. I reached slowly into my pocket and took out another fritter. I placed it on the ground at my feet.

He cocked his head, gazing at the fritter, then at me. He sidled at it from one angle, then another. He looked at my face. He crept forward and bolted the fritter down. He didn't retreat.

"Good boy," I said. I held out my hand. He licked at the bacon grease on my fingers. I reached into my pocket and took out another fritter. He sniffed it, looked at my face, sniffed the fritter again, then took it from my hand.

There were crumbs in my pocket, and two more fritters. I rubbed the tin snips against the crumbs. I held them out to him. He sniffed the metal and licked at the grease. I reached toward the wire collar. He stiffened. I cut a strand of wire. He started at the sound, and stood up. I put the snips back in my pocket and held out a fritter. We were face-to-face now. He wolfed it down.

"Good boy," I said. Again I took out the snips and let him lick the handles. When he finished, I reached forward and cut another strand. The end of the wire sprang away from his neck and the chain drooped a bit from his chest. The stench was dreadful. His lip curled, showing his canines. He growled. His breath was rapid.

"Good boy," I whispered. "Good Lucky."

He whimpered. I kept hold of the snips and took the last fritter from my pocket. As he leaned to take it, I cut the last strand of wire. The weight of the chain pulled the wire nearly free of his neck, but the barbs caught in his flesh. He yelped and snapped at my hand, but missed. With his tail tucked between his legs, he ran off into the night. I heard the chain rattle and fall on the cobblestones in the street.

My hands were shaking. I wiped the tin snips in the grass and put them in my pocket. I opened the pack and lit a cigarette. I listened to the rumble of wheels and crackle of electricity as a trolley passed on Lincoln Street.

When my nerves steadied, I walked out to the street and found the chain. Three strands of barbed wire were attached. I crushed out the cigarette butt and picked up the chain. I carried it to the alley by Mrs. Wingate's, with the barbed wire dragging, and dropped it in a garbage can.

10.

Day One

The evening before the trial was warm. A couple of newsboys sat on the back steps at the *Times-Herald*. They were nipping from a flask. I sat down for a smoke.

"Why, there's our ace reporter, one who's courting that little nigger," one said. "Chocolate can be mighty sweet, right Charlie?"

"Charlie likes them short and thick, like a stick of firewood," the other said. "Else they ain't worth pulling out his big wedge to split."

They both guffawed. I could feel my face getting red. I lit a cigarette. I had never been clever with a retort, not like Fitz.

"Why don't you two wisecracks lay off him?" It was Pace, standing on the sidewalk.

"Who asked your opinion, Scarecrow?" one boy said. He was big for his age. His father was a stevedore.

"Step on over here," Pace said. "I'll show you my opinion."

"Aw, knock it off," the smaller boy said. "Heck, Pace, he ain't gone fight you. We was just having some fun with Charlie."

"Cause he works at his job and all, unlike you two?"

"Come on, Pace, let's take us a drink," the big boy said. "Here, Charlie, you take you a drink." He held out the flask. "I was only teasing."

"No, thanks," I said. I took a deep drag and blew the smoke upward.

"You know he don't drink," Pace said. "But I'll oblige you." He took the flask from the big boy's hand, drank deeply, and handed it back. "Be seeing you," he said.

"Not if we see you first," the big boy said.

"Gee, what a hothead," the smaller boy said.

Pace trotted out of sight down the sidewalk.

"Think they gone convict the nigger girl, Charlie?"

The big boy winked at his friend. "Don't be calling Charlie's girl no nigger." He handed the flask to the smaller boy.

"I expect, if the jury's as ignorant as you two." I stood and flipped my cigarette butt against the base of the steps.

"Heck, Charlie," the smaller boy said. "Why don't you just go to church or something, you're so dang much better than everybody else?"

It was a good question. I hadn't been to a Sunday service since I left William & Mary.

"I'm sorry," I said. "I reckon things are just what they are."

"What do you mean?" the boy with the flask asked.

"I mean I'm sorry," I said.

"Oh, forget it, Charlie," the big boy said. "It ain't worth squabbling about."

I hoped to find Lucky at the base of the steps again but he was nowhere to be seen. I called, "Here Lucky, here Lucky."

I heard rustling in the azaleas. He poked his head from his hiding place.

"Good boy!" I said.

I walked slowly up the steps. The dog crawled from the bushes, watching. His tail beat in the leaf litter. On the porch in front of the screen door was a canvas pallet. Next to the pallet was a pint metal can. There was a note fixed to the screen door frame with a push-pin. It was in Mrs. Wingate's hand.

"Maebelle sewed the bed for Lucky and got Mr. Barlow over

at his carpentry shop to fill it with cedar shavings," Mrs. Wingate had written. "We brought the turpentine for his neck. There are white cotton flannel cloths on your table. He won't let us come near him." I moved the pallet aside, picked up the turpentine can, and took down the note. I walked into the kitchen. Next to the flannel cloths was another basket of Maebelle's fritters.

I set the turpentine on the cabinet counter and got a bowl from inside. I put a handful of fritters in the bowl.

When I turned to the door, Lucky was looking inside through the screen, waiting. His tail beat against the cuspidor. I set the bowl outside and watched him eat.

The next morning, Monday, was fair and cool. I arrived at the courthouse two hours before the trial was scheduled to begin. A big crowd had gathered, filling the square between the sheriff's office and the courthouse. Every face in the crowd was white, with the exception of the pack of colored boys who always congregated around the cistern. A lilac bloomed at the corner of the courthouse where I stood facing the square. The fragrance made me think of Harriet. Honeybees droned in the blossoms.

On the porch of the jail were the Curtises, along with Officer Hope and Constable Hicks. I saw Pace on the porch, too. He was talking to a deputy I didn't recognize. It was clear the deputies would have to fan out to open a path through the crowd when it was time to escort Virgie into the courtroom. The people in the crowd were calm, even jovial, exchanging handshakes and greetings. Some of the women carried picnic baskets and parasols. The mood reminded me of a religious camp meeting, or a river baptism, where people were happy, yet mindful of the solemnity of the gathering.

I smoked a cigarette. Deputy Chas Curtis opened the door and went inside the office. He was gone for a few minutes. When he came out on the porch, the officers huddled around him. I figured he was relaying orders from the sheriff. The officers kept their places in front of the jail. I decided to see if I could find a seat in the courthouse.

The court was segregated, of course. The left-hand side of the aisle was the colored section. The women wore brightly colored shirtwaists or dresses. Some even wore flowered hats. But they looked somber. There was little conversation. Here and there children, scrubbed and ribboned and groomed, sat squirming and wriggling between their parents. Many men wore overalls, washed and pressed. Some wore suits and collars. On the white side of the courtroom, the shrill laughter of a woman broke the quiet, and then died. There was a constant murmur of conversation. The white women were wearing hats, too, swirling and fluttering with long feathers and bows. With all the bodies in the courtroom, the temperature was rising. White men fanned themselves with their hats, faces pink and moist with sweat.

I walked down the aisle to the front of the room. On both sides every bench was packed, except for the front row on the colored side behind the table for the defense, marked "reserved for family." A couple of reporters from Chesapeake and Norfolk were sitting against the wall by the Commonwealth's attorney's desk, so I hunkered down with them. There was quite a stir when Chas and R. D. Hope finally brought Virgie into the courtroom.

One of the reporters leaned to the other. "They gone fry this girl like chicken in a skillet," he said. The other reporter grinned and clucked his tongue.

Virgie's hair was close-cropped, shorter than I remembered. Her head just reached the shoulders of the attorneys seated on either side of her. The chocolate-colored skin of her face and arms glistened. Her eyes were vacant and dull. She stared straight ahead.

Still, as she sat motionless with her attorneys, there was something in the set of her chin that said she believed she would live, that the jurors would hear her story and she would be spared.

Why, she might even be washing clothes in a few days. I realized she was the only person in the courtroom at that moment, white or black, who thought she might walk away from here, right back into her life of drudgery. She was an ignorant black child who had killed a white woman. Whether she did so in violent defense of her person or in larceny with malice aforethought, would it matter? I began where I thought a newspaperman should, with the facts. I scribbled furiously.

Elizabeth City County Courthouse, April 8.—The courtroom was packed with spectators today as the Commonwealth opened its murder trial against Virginia Christian, a Negro washwoman charged with the brutal murder of Ida Belote, a prominent white widow living in Hampton.

Judge Clarence Robinson, his voice raspy from a wound sustained at the Battle of Seven Pines during his service to the Confederacy, leaned forward at the bench.

Before him stood the defendant, Virginia Christian, wearing a white shirtwaist and a lavender skirt. She was a short, squat Negress of dark color and blotchy complexion.

"How do you plead to the charge of murder in the first degree?"

"Not guilty, your Honor," the defendant replied.

"Will the court clerk read the four-count indictment by the jurors of the grand jury?"

After Christian took her place between her Negro attorneys, Circuit Court Clerk Harry Holt stepped forward and read the counts.

Each of the first three—the assault upon the victim with an earthen cuspidor, the beating about the victim's head and shoulders with that weapon, the choking of the victim's neck by hand—was met with murmurs in the courtroom.

Judge Robinson pounded his gavel and warned against such

outbursts. Then the final charge was read by Clerk Holt.

"Count Number Four. We the Jurors further contend that Virginia Christian did on March 18, 1912, make an assault upon said Ida V. Belote and with her hands did push and shove with great force a large towel down the mouth of the said Ida V. Belote. The said Ida V. Belote was then and there suffocated and smothered of which said suffocation and smothering said Ida V. Belote then and there instantly died. And so, the Grand Jurors aforesaid upon their oaths aforesaid do say, that the said Virginia Christian, her the aforesaid Ida V. Belote did kill in the manner and forcibly by the means aforesaid. Did feloniously, willfully, and of her malice aforethought, kill and murder against the peace and dignity of the Commonwealth of Virginia."

The courtroom was silent.

"The Commonwealth vs. Virginia Christian," Judge Robinson said. "For the record, who represents the Commonwealth?"

"I will, Your Honor, Edgar E. Montague."

"Who will defend the accused?"

"We do, Your Honor. I am George W. Fields and my co-counsel is Joseph Thomas Newsome."

"Are both sides ready to proceed?"

"We are."

"Mr. Commonwealth's Attorney, call your first witness."

Before Mr. Montague could speak Mr. Fields rose and moved on behalf of his client for a change of venue.

"Motion denied," Judge Robinson said.

I couldn't keep up and started making notes. Commonwealth's Attorney Montague called seventeen witnesses in the course of the morning: George K. Vanderslice, coroner, who testified as to the state of the crime scene and of the victim's body; Constable R. D. Hope, who corroborated the crime scene testimony of Dr.

Vanderslice, who with a warrant from Mayor Thornton Jones searched the home of Virginia Christian in the company of officers Roy Sinclair and Leslie Curtis, and there arrested her, delivering her to the office of Sheriff R. K. Curtis, where she was searched; Leslie Curtis, Jr., who corroborated Constable Hope's testimony, adding that the shoes Virginia Christian was wearing were spotted with blood, as was the apron she was wearing; Constable Leroy Sinclair, who corroborated the testimony of the other officers and confirmed that while searching Virginia Christian at the sheriff's office with the sheriff and Constable Hicks, they discovered in her undergarments a purse other than the one she had previously surrendered to the sheriff; B. L. Poindexter, who testified as to seeing Virginia Christian on the morning of the murder approaching Mrs. Belote's house wearing a black skirt with a tear in the hem; John T. Cahill, the boarder at Mrs. Belote's, who testified that the purse introduced as evidence was the one the widow used to accept weekly cash payments of his rent; and ten others, white and colored, who testified as to seeing Virginia Christian approach or leave the Belote home on the day of the murder; who testified with wide disparity on how she was dressed that day, what the distance was from the Belote house to the C&O depot, where some of the witnesses had noted Virginia Christian's comings and goings, whether she was in a state of agitation or not, whether she was in fact a grown girl or not; and finally, Harry B. Sutton, who testified that he collected weekly payments for the *Daily Press* from Mrs. Belote, who used the purse introduced as evidence to pay him for the newspaper.

Judge Robinson called an hour recess. People in the courtroom kept their places, only leaving to heed the call of nature. I went outside to do the same, then smoked a cigarette. I hadn't seen Pace in the courtroom but noticed him standing in the crowd in front of the jail. There was a ladle at the cistern. I got a drink of water and went back to my place along the wall in the courtroom. I used the time to start working the notes I'd made into copy and to fill in biographical information on Mr. Fields and Mr. Newsome.

When Judge Robinson called the court back into session, Montague brought in Mrs. Belote's daughters. The first to testify was Pauline; then, little Sadie; and finally, Harriet. When Harriet described seeing her mother's hair combs and false teeth on the floor, along with the blood on the floor and walls, and running outside to call to the neighbor boys, it was so quiet in the court-room I could hear the honeybees in the lilac outside. She testified she also recognized the purse, and the ring that her mother had kept in it that was taken from Virginia Christian when she was searched at the jail. Other officers testified, including Chas, who had investigated the crime scene and corroborated the other of-ficers' testimony; Luther Belote, Mrs. Belote's son who lived in Philadelphia and had been friends with John Cahill in the navy, who testified that he had given the ring introduced as evidence as a gift to his mother; and finally, Professor George W. Guy, principal of Hampton High School and husband of Mrs. Guy, who had looked after Sadie on the day of the murder, who corroborated the testimony that the distance from the Belote house to the C&O depot was about a hundred yards.

Montague then rested the prosecution's case, and Judge Robin-son recessed the court until ten o'clock the following morning. If Harriet had seen me in the courtroom when she testified, I couldn't tell. She looked at Montague when he asked her a question. She looked at Judge Robinson when she responded. She kept her eyes downcast otherwise. I never saw her cast a glance at Virgie, or at anyone else, for that matter. She seemed to have folded tightly in on herself.

I crept down the wall and got out of the courtroom before the deputies entered to take Virgie back to her jail cell. The crowd had pressed close to the doorway. When I started to make my way through, a few of the men pushed back, so I nearly fell. Some of them reeked of whiskey.

When I was nearly free of the crowd on the other side of the square, a sound rushed over them, like the soughing of wind in willows. I turned and saw Chas Curtis and R. D. Hope emerge from the courthouse with Virgie between them, each man steadying her at the elbow. As the three walked toward the jail, the crowd opened and swelled and closed behind them, like a snake passing a bird through its gullet.

I turned and caught a shoulder in the jaw. It was Pace.

"Sorry, Charlie," he said, disappearing in the confusion. I pushed my way through and trotted toward the office. I knew Mr. Hobgood would be waiting. He was sitting in my chair with his coffee mug placed on my desk.

"Well?" he said.

"Five minutes and I'll have the copy. Mr. Fields and Mr. Newsome open for the defense tomorrow morning."

"And?"

"Silent as a tomb when the Belote girls took the stand. When Harriet testified, I don't think a man in the jury box even blinked, let alone moved."

"All right, then, Mears," he said. "Finish today's story. When the jury returns its verdict tomorrow, you get over here like a shot off a shovel." He gulped down the contents of the mug and made room for me to sit at the typewriter.

"How do you know the jury will return a verdict?" I asked, sitting at the typewriter.

"This is a Virginia jury of white men," he said. "They know what must be done."

I hung around for a while as the pressmen prepared the issue. Then I walked the streets. Things were quiet. On my way home I bought a copy of the *Times-Herald*. I read the headline, "MRS.

BELOTE'S DEATH IS DEPICTED IN THE COURTROOM," but I didn't read my story. I folded the paper and stuffed it in my pocket.

I hadn't eaten all day. I had smoked so many cigarettes my fingertips were stained yellow and my nerves sizzled like naked electric wires. I mounted the steps two at a time. When I saw Lucky peering down at me from the porch, I stopped.

"Good boy," I said. I moved slowly so I wouldn't startle him.

He wagged his tail and whimpered. Then he stretched. I stepped onto the porch and put my hand on his head. I scratched behind his torn ear. He butted my hand with his broad head. I could see he had been sleeping on Maebelle's pallet. I opened the door and went inside the kitchen.

There was a bowl of scraps and dog meal in a big bowl on the floor. At the center of the table was a porcelain bowl covered with gingham. I lifted the cloth. The bowl was filled with biscuits. I opened the icebox. There was a plate of fried chicken and green beans wrapped in wax paper. Beside the plate was a quart jar of buttermilk.

"God bless you, Maebelle," I said.

I ran some water into a bowl and took it with the bowl of food out on the porch. When I set the bowls down, Lucky feinted once or twice, then began to eat. I went back in the kitchen and pulled the wax paper off the plate and added two biscuits. I took the plate and the buttermilk out on the porch. I sat down on the top step.

Lucky had finished his meal. He stretched out and watched as I devoured mine. I offered him a piece of chicken skin. He sniffed gingerly, then wolfed it down. I gave him a piece of biscuit. When I finished eating the chicken and beans, I unscrewed the top of the buttermilk and drank half the quart.

I took the plate and jar inside. I picked a couple of white cloths from the pile and grabbed the turpentine can. I walked out on the porch. Lucky was resting in the sphinx position.

"Well then," I said. I let him sniff the cloth. I unscrewed the cap on the can and held it out to him. He sniffed at the metal and sneezed when he got the fumes. The gashes on the back of his neck were crusted with blood and the wider gash under his neck oozed pus. I soaked the cloth with turpentine and daubed at the cuts on the back of his neck. I felt muscles quiver under his skin. I pressed the cloth into the cuts, so the turpentine could soak in. A rumble started in his chest, and he bared his teeth. I pressed the cloth firm and held still. Finally he stopped growling. I knew I had to work on the big gash. Slowly I lifted the cloth. I soaked in more turpentine. I pressed the cloth into the pus under his neck.

He got my hand with his teeth and held it to his chest an instant before letting go. He'd brought blood. I reached for the cloth. He laid his ears back and started to growl again. I poured turpentine on the back of my hand where I was bleeding. I soaked more turpentine in the cloth. He sniffed at my hand and licked. Then he sneezed again. I pressed the cloth gently as I could against his neck. He didn't move. I pressed more firmly to get the turpentine in the wound. He stood it for a moment, then snapped again and slunk to the corner of the porch.

"Good boy," I said. "That's a start. Good Lucky."

11.

Sentencing

M r. Wright?" I called. I had been waiting on the sidewalk in front of the cottage since a little before sunup. The air was chilly.

"Charlie?" he said. "You all right? You look kind of peaked." George Wright was wearing his overalls and steel-toed brogans. A thick leather work glove was tucked in each hip pocket of his overalls. He carried a metal lunch pail.

"Yes, sir, I'm fine. Just couldn't sleep."

"Want to walk with me up to the trolley?"

"Sure," I said. I fell in beside him. His gait was brisk. The handle of the pail rattled as he swung his arms.

"You're wondering about Harriet, I'm thinking," he said.

"Yes, sir."

"She's fine, Charlie. She was a little shook yesterday. Pauline's not taking the girls to court today. Testimony was enough. She thinks it's better they not hear the end of it."

"Yes, sir."

"You should come see her, Charlie. Pauline says she liked it when you met her after school. Sadie asks after you, too. Has a new doll she wants to show you."

"I'll call on Harriet, Mr. Wright, once the trial's behind us. It seems to take up every minute."

"Call me George, Charlie."

"George."

"You know Lewter is taking the girls next week."

"Yes, sir."

"Well, I'd best get moving. See you, Charlie!" He broke into a run and reached the stop just as the trolley pulled up. I watched from the sidewalk. He waved as the trolley started off.

The sun had cleared the courthouse by the time I reached the square. Gulls were picking at food scraps from the crowd the day before. They shrieked and scuffled when one found a crust of bread or a chicken bone. Then the victor flew off with the prize. Here and there a gull rested on a leg, basking in the sun. People were walking into the square from each side. Two lines, colored and white, waited at the courthouse door, the lines snaking around opposite corners of the façade. Gulls waddled about, fluttering or cackling when somebody kicked at them. Finally they gathered and flew off toward the Roads.

Chas Curtis emerged from the jail and surveyed the crowd, his big thumbs hooked in his holster belt. I walked up to the steps of the porch.

"Morning, Charlie," he said.

"Morning, Deputy," I said. "How's Sheriff Curtis feeling?"

"Poorly," he said. "Still keeping to his bed. The missus fixed him some sassafras tea with a little whiskey yesterday evening, and he seemed to rest better. I reckon he's gone come round."

"Who's the new man?" I asked.

"Oh, that's Win. Second cousin. Sheriff sent to Nags Head for him to help till all the brouhaha with the trial quiets down. You want to get in the courthouse? I can sneak you in the side door."

"Thanks," I said.

After Chas left, I opened the door a crack and lit a cigarette. I blew my smoke out through the crack. I was nearly finished with the cigarette when I heard a voice outside.

"Hey there." An eyeball appeared in the crack. It was Pace. "Hey, Charlie. How about letting me in?"

I pushed the door open and crushed the butt on the stoop. Pace passed in.

"Thanks Charlie," he said.

I closed the door and turned the bolt.

"Guess today's the big day and all," he said.

"Yes," I said.

"Well then," he said. "Be seeing you." He disappeared down the hall.

The defense opened its case by claiming the evidence suggested a spontaneous altercation rather than a premeditated act; by undermining the credibility of the eyewitnesses because of the inconsistencies in their testimony about the accused's manner of dress, comportment, and time of day; by introducing expert testimony, including that of Dr. Vanderslice, that the physical condition of Mrs. Belote's body postmortem was insufficient to establish strangulation as the cause of death; by the testimony of Miss Fannie Price, Virgie's teacher at the Whittier School, who testified that school records transcribed three years earlier showed the girl's birth date as August 15, 1895, making her a female juvenile, aged sixteen, at the time of the crime; and with the character witness testimony of her father, Henry Christian, who testified that his daughter had never caused any trouble, although when casually asked by her attorney Mr. Fields at the beginning of his testimony, could not recall the year or day of Virgie's birth. There were whispers and puzzled glances on the colored side of the courtroom. Closing arguments were made.

"Elizabeth City County Courthouse, April 9.—After retiring with their charge from Judge Clarence Robinson, the jury in the murder trial of Virginia Christian returned to the courtroom in less than one hour's time.

'Have you reached a verdict?' Judge Robinson asked.

'Yes, we have, Your Honor,' the foreman of the jury replied.

Judge Robinson directed the accused to stand. Christian rose between the Negro attorneys representing her. Her face was without emotion.

'Ladies and gentlemen, I advise you again that no outbursts in the court when the verdict is read will be tolerated,' Judge Robinson said. 'Mr. Foreman, read your verdict.'

'We the jury, find the accused, Virginia Christian, guilty of murder in the first degree, as charged in the fourth count of the indictment.'

The jury was then polled individually by Judge Robinson. Each juror confirmed that the verdict as read was correct.

'Virginia Christian, is there anything further to be said, or anything new to be said, as to why the court should not proceed to pronounce judgment against you, according to the law?' Judge Robinson asked.

The Negro girl fumbled at her shirtwaist and looked up at the attorneys on either side of her. Neither of the men returned her gaze.

'And nothing being offered or alleged in delay thereof,' Judge Robinson said, 'It is considered by the court that the said Virginia Christian be electrocuted until she is dead, in the death chamber provided for that purpose within the confines of the penitentiary of this Commonwealth on the 21st day of June A.D. 1912, between the hours of 6 o'clock in the afore noon and 6 o'clock in the afternoon of that day.'

Judge Robinson again warned the court against outbursts. The murmuring of the crowd ceased.

'And the clerk of this Court is directed as soon as practicable after this judgment is entered,' Judge Robinson said, 'to deliver a certified copy hereof to the said superintendent of the penitentiary in Richmond, who shall cause the said Virginia Christian to be conveyed to the said penitentiary, there to be treated, dealt with, and executed in the manner prescribed by law in accordance with this judgment.'

'Your Honor,' attorney Thomas Newsome declared, 'counsel for the Defendant move that the Court set aside the jury verdict because it is contrary to the law. Evidence failed to disclose that the Defendant is more than seventeen years of age. It is improper to sentence a person to death when not seventeen years of age, until the Court is satisfied that there is no institution that will receive her as provided by Chapter 289 of the Act of the General Assembly of Virginia, Session of 1910, approved March 16, 1910.'

'Motion denied,' Judge Robinson responded.

'Excepted,' Newsome said. 'Counsel requests to file bills of exception on behalf of the Defendant.'

'Granted,' Judge Robinson said.

Christian stood stunned and silent before the bench. Then Deputy Sheriff Charles Curtis took the convicted murderess into custody and escorted her from the courtroom."

I noted at the end of the article that I thought the headline should read, "Death in the Electric Chair for Christian." I tucked my pencil into my jacket along with my notebook and stood to go.

The white side of the courtroom had emptied. But many people remained seated on the benches on the colored side. I nodded to Mr. Christian, who was sitting in the front row. He didn't notice me. He was staring toward the bench where Judge Robinson had pronounced his sentence. Two light-skinned colored boys were sitting beside him. The younger-looking one sobbed as I passed and covered his face with his hand. About a third of the way back, I saw Maebelle. Like Mr. Christian, she was staring straight ahead at the bench. There was no expression on her face. She pressed her lips with a kerchief. I nodded to her as I passed, but I don't think she saw me. At the door to the courthouse I replaced my cap.

The crowd outside had dispersed, though a few white people stood around in groups, talking. The colored boys looked to be playing a game of tag around the cistern. There wasn't a cloud in the sky. The sun shone so brightly in the dogwood blossoms it hurt my eyes. I squinted and looked about.

I saw Lewter Hobbs laugh and throw his head back. He was hatless. Hobbs' suit was deep blue, wool, with a vest, and wide pinstripes. A gold watch fob and chain sparkled at his waist. He tucked a cigar in his mouth and clapped Edgar Montague on the back so hard it toppled Montague's fedora. Hobbs quickly retrieved the hat and helped Montague resettle it on his head. Montague was smoking a cigar, too. His florid face glowed in the bright sunlight. Other men, all dressed in suits, were laughing with them. I walked toward them. As I drew closer, I recognized the jury foreman.

"On the first ballot," the foreman said. "Less than twenty minutes. We sat around for a while, killing time, before we sent a message to the judge."

Hobbs laughed again, and elbowed Montague in the ribs.

"Now here's a Commonwealth's attorney," he said. "Montague, we ought to run you for governor."

"President," another man said.

"What's up, Smith? That stenographer's case coming up on the docket?" Hobbs roared with laughter again, and the man's face reddened.

I pulled out my notebook and pencil.

"Mr. Hobbs, do you have a statement regarding the verdict?"

He rocked back on his heels for a moment, then jutted out his jaw. He took the cigar from his mouth.

"Yes, lad, yes, I do," he said. He tucked a thumb in his vest pocket. "As the only brother of the late Mrs. Ida Virginia Belote, I wish to commend the work of the Commonwealth's attorney, this honest Virginia jury, and the honorable judge at the bench, who have returned justice in my sister's memory. We all are aware of the strong feelings this case created, the large number of Negroes in this town, and the great significance the outcome of this trial held." He paused as I scribbled and puffed at the cigar. "When my friends and I learned of my sister's murder, and saw with certainty that the Negress was responsible for the crime, many felt that our only course was a lynching, but I restrained myself and my friends to allow the laws of the Commonwealth to follow their course. And they have. My sister's orphaned daughters have seen the life of their mother vindicated. Justice has been served. How's that, lad?"

"Thank you, Mr. Hobbs."

"My first name is spelled 'l-e-w-t-e-r.' Middle initial, 'f.' Got that?"

"Yes, sir."

"Well, I'd best be off to the office, boys," Hobbs said, looking at Montague and the other men. "The admiral of the fleet is stopping by this afternoon."

A newsboy started walking the square in front of the courthouse, waving a paper, the canvas bag slung over his shoulder filled. "Get your *Times-Herald*!" he shouted. "Get your *Times-Herald* right here! Death in the electric chair for Christian!"

Mr. Hobgood hadn't said a word to me about his plans. He'd decided to gamble on the verdict, which, as he'd implied, wasn't much of a gamble at all, and on the sentence, too. He'd won. Copies of the *Times-Herald* were on the streets, hours before any other paper would have the story. Mr. Hobgood had even used the headline I was going to recommend.

"Here, boy!" the man named Smith called.

Each man in the group gave the boy a nickel. The boy handed

out the papers. Hobbs gave him a dime and handed the extra copy to me. I tucked my notebook and pencil in my pocket.

"Thank you, Mr. Hobbs."

He leaned toward me, holding the paper at the fold. He pulled the cigar from his mouth and held it in his fingers.

"You're the one Harriet's so keen for, aren't you? The one brings her poems and such?" He nodded at me. Then he stuck the cigar in his mouth, turned on his heel, and was gone.

Mr. Hobgood wasn't at the office. One of the pressmen said he'd been at the office since the break of day fiddling with the layout of the front page. He'd gone home early. I edited what I'd written about the courtroom proceedings to use as background for the statement from Hobbs.

That night Lucky and I had supper on the porch. Afterwards, I treated his wounds with the turpentine. He growled a time or two but didn't snap. The edges of the gashes were pink and starting to mend. The pus in the gash under his neck was drying up. But even when his coat filled in, it would never hide the scars.

12.

Haunted

He scooped you, Mears," Mr. Hobgood said. "Pace is cunning. Now we have to make the best of it. Today you'll write human interest. Use the lead the way I wrote it. Put the girl's speech in dialect. Write it so it sounds like she's talking to you."

"Mr. Hobgood, I don't even know what 'squashy' means," I said.

"Damn it, Mears, I don't know, either. It just sounds right. Like combining 'squishy' and 'squat.' Now get on that typewriter and work with your notes. We have a deadline."

"Yes, sir."

That Pace. His article featuring Virgie's confession appeared on the front page of the *Daily Press* the day after the jury returned its verdict. Virgie had always wanted to tell her story in court. But Mr. Fields and Mr. Newsome decided against it. No doubt they considered what had happened with the Allens in Hillsville, and feared Virgie's description of her assault on Mrs. Belote might provoke violence in the courthouse or a lynch mob in the streets.

Rumor had it that Virgie soon after her arrest had confessed the murder to the colored preachers who visited her daily in her cell. Pace had decided to go to Virgie herself, rather than bird-dog the preachers for a statement. So he tried the new man. And Deputy

Edwin Curtis, cousin Win from Nags Head, had walked Pace straight into Virgie's cell.

As soon as Mr. Hobgood saw the *Daily Press*, he told me to head over to the jail. He said if I could to arrange an interview with Virgie and get back to the office pronto with my notes.

Sheriff Curtis must have been looking out the window onto the street. He opened the door to the office as I came up the steps.

"I'm right sorry, Charlie," he said. "I was gone leave Chas in charge, but his wife called and said his little girl had a bad fever, so I told him to head on home. I give plain word to Win for nobody to come in or out but the preachers." Sheriff Curtis seemed to be feeling better. His voice sounded strong but there were gray circles around his eyes. He coughed deeply and cleared his throat.

"I tell you, that colored girl was up all last night mumbling to herself, the springs on that cot squeaking when she sat down and squeaking again when she got up," he said. "And when she did quiet down for a minute, hell, about the time I was dozing off, she'd scream out loud like the devil himself had her by the hind leg. Good God almighty. I didn't sleep a wink.

"I'll be honest, Charlie. I'm looking forward to the day when I can cart her off to Richmond." We walked across the office to the metal door. The cell keys jangled when he pulled them from his belt.

"And I'll tell you what else, Charlie. I sent that Win packing. I told him to head to his boarding house and sit his ass there till he felt like he understood the English language, plain and simple, and when he felt like he did, to come on back here and clean the damn latrines, or light out for Nags Head, one of the two."

The metal door screeched when he pulled it back. We walked to Virgie's cell.

"Here he is, girl," he said. "Here's your Charlie." Virgie was standing with her hands on the bars. She watched as the sheriff unlocked the cell door. "I'm gone lock the other door behind me,

Charlie, and stretch out on the bed upstairs for a spell. Just give me a shout when you're done. I'll hear you."

"Are you all right, Sheriff?"

"A little light-headed is all. Reminds me of when I had the fever down in Mexico."

"I'll call out when we're finished."

"All right, son." He stepped down the hall and the door clanked shut. The key rattled in the lock.

Virgie's eyes were bloodshot and dull. Her hands still gripped the bars.

"Step back, Virgie," I said. "So I can come in."

"I'm right much worried, Mr. Charlie," she said. "Man outside the courthouse say getting in the electric chair like getting cooked alive."

"Oh, people who know the least always talk the most, Virgie."

"Humph," she said. She shook her head. She let go the bars and sat on the cot. "I told them I wanted to talk to Mr. Charlie. They knowed to bring you, since we was always talking. But this other boy walk in here, and the deputy say, 'Well, this here's Charlie, and you *said* Charlie . . .'"

"Pace," I said.

"Same one cook up the story about the white man, the boarder."

"Yes," I said.

"Since that reporter the one the deputy bring in, I talked to him. Like I told them attorneys, I say, 'I'm gone tell my side of the story, what Mrs. Belote done to me,' but them attorneys wasn't having none of it. Fore the reporter start asking questions, he say do I want a piece of candy first, like I a fool. But I took his damn candy."

"That's all right, Virgie. Now I need to ask you questions."

"Has you seen my daddy?"

"No," I said.

"Sure reckoned he'd come by this evening," she said.

"He'll come, Virgie."

Her eyes were wet. "Ask away, then," she said. Her voice cracked.

MR. HOBGOOD PLOPPED A copy of the newspaper on my type-writer. The paper was still warm from the rollers. He stood over my desk with a second copy. The confession story was headlined on page one, "VIRGINIA CHRISTIAN IS HAUNTED IN HER DREAMS."

I glanced up at Mr. Hobgood. He nodded. "Go on," he said. "Read."

Times-Herald Bureau, Hampton, Va., April 11.

Notwithstanding her confession to her spiritual adviser and to others that she killed Mrs. Ida Belote, and notwithstanding a clean bath and a good breakfast, Virginia Christian was a doleful little nigger gal, when seen in her cell in the Hampton jail this morning, and "wasn't feeling so mighty good." She had not slept very well and even when slumber came at fitful intervals, she had been haunted in her dreams by the ghost of the woman she slew. Her condition this morning was pitiful.

Virginia Christian is a full-blooded Negress, with kinky hair done up with threads, with dark lusterless eyes and with splotches on the skin of her face. Her color is dark brown, and her figure is short, dumpy and squashy.

She has had some schooling, but her speech does not betray it. Her language is the same as the unlettered members of her race. Her intelligence is below the average and her moral standard is evidently very low. She did not hesitate in her confession, and did not give the impression that she appreciated the enormity of her crime. She spoke of her "fight" with Mrs. Belote, as she called it, in a way that was almost flippant and her trouble today was due to the fact that she had been condemned to die in the electric chair.

"I'm right much worried," was her rather mild way of putting it.

She said she slept well the night after she killed Mrs. Belote and every night thereafter until the trial.

"But I didn't sleep well las' night," she said, "nor de night befo' nuther."

"Did you dream about Mrs. Belote?" she was asked.

"Yassir. I dremp she come in de coteroom an' wrote on a black bode."

"What did she write?"

"She always called me Virg an' she wrote on de bode, 'De reason I'm daid is because I made Virg mad.' Yassir, dats what she wrote, and dat was right. She made me mad an' I hit her wid de stick. I ain't had nuthin' against her. I laked her. She was good to me, an' I worked for her when she couldn't git no one else.

"She come to Mommer's house dat morning an' say she want me to come an' do some washin'. When I come home, Mommer say Miss Belote want me an' I went roun' to de house. I went in the back way an' when she see me she asked me about a gold locket she missed. I told her I ain't seen it an' don't know nuthin' about it. She also say somethin' about a skirt, but the main thing was de locket. She say, 'Yes you is got it, an' if you don't bring it back I'm goin' to have you put in jail.'

"I got mad an' I told her if I did have it, she wasn't goin' to git it back. Den she picked up de spittoon and hit me wid it an' it broke. They was two sticks in de room, broom handles. She run for one, an' I for de other. I got to my stick furst an' hit her wid it 'side de haid and she fell down. She kep' hollering so, I took a towel and stuffed it in her mouth. I helt it there twel she quit hollerin' an' jest groaned. I didn't mean to kill her an' I didn't know I had. I was mad when I hit her and I stuffed de towel in her mouth to keep her from hollerin'. I never meant to kill her. When I lef' her she was groanin' and layin' on her back."

When discovered the body of Mrs. Belote was lying face

downward. Virginia's attention was called to this, but she insisted that Mrs. Belote was "layin' on her back when I's left the house."

She says she was in the house about 11:30 o'clock in the morning and insists that she went there with a view to do some washing for Mrs. Belote, having no thought that she was to be taken to task and charged with theft.

Mrs. Belote fell on the floor near the stove and as Virginia went out of the house she saw Mrs. Belote's purse lying on the table and took it. The purse contained four dollars, but Virginia did not spend any of the money.

"Did you tell your mother about your trouble?" she was asked.

She replied in the negative and said that until her confession yesterday morning to the preachers, she had told no one except her lawyer, George W. Fields. She said she made a full confession to him and both her lawyers knew she had killed Mrs. Belote when they went into the case. Her confession to her lawyer was made on Sunday before the grand jury indicted her. She denies, however, that she had ever told her lawyer or anyone that a white man was mixed up in the case. She protests that no one had anything to do with the murder except herself.

She was asked if any man had suggested to her that Mrs. Belote had money and that she might be robbed. Virginia promptly and positively denied this. She repeated that she went to the Belote home to do some work, as she had been doing from time to time for two years, and had no thought that there would be trouble.

Her confession to the preachers was made yesterday morning. She told Sheriff Curtis she desired to see a spiritual adviser. He sent for Rev. T. H. Shorts, pastor of Queen Street Baptist church and Rev. Patterson, although her parents are members of the Zion church in Phoebus. To these she told the whole story as related above.

It was rumored during the day that the woman had confessed

to Rev. T. H. Shorts and a Times-Herald man endeavored to locate the preacher, but failed to find him until last night. Inquiry was then made at the jail, but the reporter was informed that they knew nothing about any confession.

Sheriff Curtis is sick and confined to his room upstairs in the jail. He said today that when the telephone message was brought to him upstairs, he told the man to say that he had no statement to give out. His explanation was that he wanted the statement to be given out by the preachers to whom the confession was made.

"You did a good job capturing the dialect, Mears. Well, what do you think?" Mr. Hobgood asked. The paper he was holding rattled in his trembling hands.

"She'll be angry it calls her nigger," I said. "She'll think I used her."

"I just added the word to paint a picture, Mears. Readers are so literal-minded. As for using her, it's the nature of our profession."

"Well," I said.

"Oh, for Christ's sake!" He slammed his paper down atop my copy and stalked to his desk. The drawer clattered as he opened it. He took out a full pint bottle and removed the cork. He drank a quarter of the contents and breathed deeply. "My mind's addled if I don't drink in the mornings," he said. "I don't know why I waste the effort trying not to." He took another swallow, replaced the cork, and returned the bottle to the desk drawer. "You don't see, do you?" he asked.

"Mr. Hobgood, I don't mean to upset you, but I don't understand what you're . . ."

"Spare me the delicate sensibility, Mears." He slid the drawer shut. He sat in his chair and put his feet up on the desk. He drummed his fingers on the chair arms. Then he stopped. He dropped his feet and leaned toward me, jutting his chin.

"Give me a cigarette," he said.

I took one from my pack and handed it to him. Then I lit it for him.

"Don't you want one?"

"No, sir, not at the moment."

He took a deep drag and exhaled loudly. "Now," he said. "You had the Fields and Newsome appeal statement in your earlier article, correct?"

"Yes, sir."

"In that article you state the basis of their argument for appeal is that the alleged confession shows there was no premeditation, correct? Wasn't that their argument in the courtroom? That the girl was provoked and reacted violently? That the appropriate charge was manslaughter, or at worst, second-degree murder?"

"Yes, sir."

"But the judge's orders to the jury called for a first-degree conviction, even if premeditation did not occur to the girl until right up to the very act of murder itself, correct?"

"Yes, sir."

"So it is likely that under the appeal the court will side with the presiding judge, correct?"

"Yes, sir."

"And did Fields and Newsome not attempt to establish the girl's age in the courtroom?"

"Yes, sir, they did."

"To prove that she was a juvenile, correct? So that even if the jury convicted her of first-degree murder, she could not be executed, correct?"

"Yes, sir."

"Didn't you write in your article that the death sentence was issued in direct contravention of Virginia constitutional law?"

"Yes," I said. I removed my glasses and began to wipe the lenses. "Article 289. Regarding juveniles."

He sat back in his chair. "Can it be that I'm finally seeing wheels turn somewhere in that earnest head of yours?"

"Yes, sir." I hooked the glasses over my ears.

"Virginia Christian described to you the simple dream of a child, Mears," he said. "She describes seeing a ghost appear in the courtroom and writing on a blackboard, for Christ's sake. A simple child's dream. Told in a simple child's words."

"Yes, sir."

"So maybe her confession to you as written will help her after all. In the court of public opinion. Anyone will tell you the attorneys' writs of exception will be denied. It was a quick trial, quick conviction, quick sentence to avoid a lynching. Mears, if mercy's to be found, it will be in Governor Mann's clemency for an ignorant child." He took another drag on the cigarette and tapped the ashes on the floor. "Now go home and pray or something."

"Yes, sir." I stood, picked up the paper, and folded it to carry with me.

"Mears," Mr. Hobgood said. "I apologize. I didn't mean that the way it sounded."

13.

Pride of the Line

A torrent of editorials followed. "GIRL MAKES CONFES-SION." "VIRGINIA JUSTICE." Paper upon paper. "JUSTICE MOVES SWIFTLY." "NEGRESS MUST DIE." Mr. Hobgood's was surprisingly balanced. "THE CHRISTIAN CASE."

I stopped by George Fields' home on Wine Street. His wife greeted me at the door. She said Mr. Fields was too busy to see me. He was working on the writs of exception with Mr. Newsome, and I was welcome to use the information in a story. I covered a meeting of the Newport News Rotary Club. I covered a fistfight between two white men at a saloon in Phoebus. The man who had broken his arm in the fight was taken to Dr. Vanderslice's office to have a cast built. It was a bad break and Dr. V had to get one of the deputies to hold the man while he reset the bone. The man hollered and swore, wanting to know who in hell was the quack sawbones working on him. Then he passed out.

"Quick verdict for the girl, wasn't it?" Dr. Vanderslice asked.

"Yes, sir."

"To be expected, I'm sad to say," he said.

The afternoon was stormy so Harriet and I sat in the parlor. Great flashes of lightning brightened the sky and thunder rattled the windows of the cottage. The wind was strong, flinging rain against the panes. Then the wind calmed and the rain was steady.

Mrs. Wright fixed us tea, and Harriet served it with cookies with lemon filling. Sadie showed me her new doll, Mrs. Betts. Then Mrs. Wright took Sadie into the bedroom for a nap. We sat on the sofa, listening to the rain. Harriet looked very pretty. She seemed to look prettier every time I saw her.

"They'll kill Virgie, won't they?" she asked.

"Maybe not. Mr. Fields and Mr. Newsome are filing appeals."

"Sometimes I wonder what Momma would want. I think she liked having Virgie around. So she would have somebody to stay mad at."

"I had a friend like that. Our teacher Miss Quesinberry liked having him around to stay mad at, too."

"I thought I would miss Momma. But I don't seem to. Sadie does."

"Maybe you haven't had the chance. With the inquest and trial. All the changes."

"I wish I could go away somewhere," she said. "Just go away." Her eyes started to fill with tears.

"Harriet, don't," I said. I reached for her hand and held it.

"I wanted you to read with me," I said. "I wanted to tell you something."

"What?" she said.

I had brought my Bible. I turned to the Acts. "I wanted to tell you about when my friend at college died. I was teaching in my Bible studies group and I couldn't finish. Another boy had to for me. Could we read it together?"

"Of course," she whispered.

"Our lesson is Acts 8: 26-39," I said. I began to read. "And the angel of the Lord spake unto Philip, saying, 'Arise, and go toward the south unto the way that goeth down from Jerusalem unto Gaza, which is desert.' And he arose and went: and, behold, a man of Ethiopia, an eunuch of great authority under Candace queen of the

Ethiopians, who had the charge of all her treasure, and had come to Jerusalem for to worship, was returning, and sitting in his chariot read Isaiah the prophet. Then the Spirit said unto Philip, 'Go near, and join thyself to this chariot.' And Philip ran thither to him, and heard him read the prophet Isaiah, and said, 'Understandest thou what thou readest?'"

We sat side by side on the sofa, our knees touching. I placed the book in Harriet's lap. "Now you read," I said.

"And he said, 'How can I, except some man should guide me?' And he desired Philip that he would come up and sit with him."

Harriet looked at me. "Go on," I said.

"The place of the scripture which he read was this, 'He was led as a sheep to the slaughter; and like a lamb dumb before his shearer, so opened he not his mouth: In his humiliation his judgment was taken away: and who shall declare his generation? for his life is taken from the earth.' And the eunuch answered Philip, and said, 'I pray thee, of whom speaketh the prophet this? of himself, or of some other man?'"

"That's where I stopped," I said. "Another boy read for me."

"Read now, Charlie," Harriet said. She gave me the Bible.

"Then Philip opened his mouth and began at the same scripture, and preached unto him Jesus. And as they went on *their* way, they came unto a certain water: and the eunuch said, 'See, *here is* water; what doth hinder me to be baptized?' And Philip said, 'If thou believest with all thine heart, thou mayest.' And he answered and said, 'I believe that Jesus Christ is the Son of God.' And he commanded the chariot to stand still: and they went down both into the water, both Philip and the eunuch; and he baptized him. And when they were come up out of the water, the Spirit of the Lord caught away Philip, that the eunuch saw him no more: and he went on his way rejoicing. Harriet, do you understand the significance?"

"No," she said.

"Because the eunuch had been castrated, he thought he was unclean, and would not be accepted by the Lord. But Philip preached that he could, if only he believed."

"I'm unclean," Harriet said.

"You're not unclean, Harriet," I said. "You're as beautiful as anything in creation."

"How I want to believe you," she said. Her eyes filled with tears. "You must get me away. You must. I can't live in the same house with that serpent."

"We'll find a way, Harriet. God will show us." I closed the Bible and set it by me on the sofa. I put my hands on hers.

"My friend had been castrated, Harriet. His family sent him to a clinic run by a doctor named Priddy because he was attracted to men. But the operation didn't work. He told me he had fallen in love with me. I didn't know what to do. I didn't know how to act. So I repulsed him. He went home to the estate where he grew up and shot himself. His name was Fitzhugh Scott. He was handsome and athletic and charming. He was everything I'm not. He was my dearest friend on earth. I've never told anyone, Harriet. I didn't know how to."

"Charlie, I'm so sorry," she said. She rubbed my hands.

"Tomorrow I have to do something," I said. "In Charlottesville."

"Please take me with you, Charlie. I could see the mountains with you. We could run away. Sunday Uncle Lewter is coming for us."

"They'd track us down, Harriet. They'd never let me see you again."

"Please, Charlie."

"Not tomorrow, Harriet."

IT WAS DARK THE next morning when I fed Lucky. I put a bowl of water by his pallet. There were hardly any passengers at the C&O depot. I had Fitz's letter tucked in the pocket of my coat. I changed trains in Richmond and arrived in Charlottesville a little before noon. From the station I caught the trolley to the foot of Monticello Mountain, and began walking from there.

Then I remembered. It was April 13, Mr. Jefferson's birthday. It was a beautiful spring day. Honeysuckle festooned the poplars and sycamores along the Rivanna River. I listened to the drone of honeybees in the honeysuckle. A mockingbird, Mr. Jefferson's favorite—he'd kept one in the White House—chortled from a wild rose. The climb was long. When I reached Monticello, I stopped to admire the west façade. The house was in bad shape, the shutters askew. It looked like the roof was being repaired. I'd read somewhere that a New York lawyer had bought the place.

The sun was warm. I loosened my collar and continued climbing. Beyond Monticello was Brown's Mountain. When he was a young man, Mr. Jefferson wanted to purchase the mountain so he could construct a waterfall guests could view from his lawn. From the west face of Brown's Mountain and beyond, down the eastern face into a wide valley below, lay the Scott estate. In a copse beyond the high meadow before me was the family graveyard.

I stood in the shade of the trees, catching my breath. A breeze stirred from the east, gently rocking the gate of an iron fence against its latch. Sunlight dappled the face of a white marble stone. It was modest in comparison to the grand vaults and obelisks nearby.

FITZHUGH TYLER SCOTT

AETATIS XX

AND WHAT I ASSUME YOU SHALL ASSUME,

FOR EVERY ATOM BELONGING TO ME AS GOOD BELONGS TO YOU.

I pushed open the gate and walked to the grave. I knelt in front of the stone and bowed my head. I asked Fitz to forgive me. I told him I loved him and would always love him. I told him he was not unclean and I was wrong to feel he was. I told him the world was hollow and dead without him and I had tried to fill it with life. I was trying to find the hope he had lost.

"Please forgive me, Fitz," I prayed, "but I have to stop now. I have to. I was too weak to help you and now I have found someone to help. Please forgive me Fitz if I do not help I will never know who I am. I will see you on the road someday Fitz I know I will and we will be comrades all of us. Amen."

I removed the letter from my pocket and unfolded it. The edges had begun to fray. I put the letter at the base of the stone and scattered litter and twigs to hold it in place. A wood thrush called from deep in the woods. I looked to the west and saw thunderheads building on the horizon.

I stood and folded my hands. "Good-bye, Fitz," I said. I walked to the gate and shut the latch behind me. The wind was picking up, and the white anvils of the thunderheads were beautiful in the blue sky. Swallows flashed and spun over the meadow. I made it to the trolley station before the storm hit. I arrived at the depot just in time to catch the Richmond train. When I took my seat, I caught myself checking my pocket for the letter. I smiled. Fitz would have laughed at that. On the seat was a copy of the Charlottesville *Daily Progress*. There was an editorial. "Virginia Christian Must Die."

It was after midnight when I reached Hampton. Lucky was waiting on his pallet. His water bowl was full, so I knew Mrs. Wingate had fed him. I barely got my shoes off before I fell to sleep on my bed.

SUNDAY MORNING I STOOD outside the Wrights' cottage. George came out with his hair slicked down and was wearing a collar and cuffs. He grinned when he saw me. Mrs. Wright said she would be delighted if I accompanied them to church. In the pew, George and I were the bookends, George, then Mrs. Wright, Sadie, Harriet, and me. I felt thankful to be there. I felt I was in the presence of God. I was too nervous to hold hands with Harriet in church, but walking home, we did. Mrs. Wright asked me to stay and have chicken salad sandwiches in the garden.

Even Sadie was quiet as we ate. Thunderstorms had cleared the air and there was a breeze. Shade from the trees dappled the tablecloth.

"We're so glad you came, Charlie," Mrs. Wright said.

"Yes, ma'am," I said.

"Uncle Lewter and Kate will be here for the girls this evening," she said. "I hope you'll still visit."

"Yes, ma'am. I'd better be going."

"Don't be a stranger, Charlie," George said.

"No, sir." We shook hands.

"Charlie, Mrs. Betts says she wants a kiss," Sadie said. "And I do, too."

I kissed the doll on the cheek and Sadie on the forehead.

"Good-bye, Charlie," Sadie said.

"Harriet," Mrs. Wright said, "why don't you walk Charlie out front?"

Harriet wore a pale dress the color of lilacs. It had a white collar and a white sash tied on the side of her waist. Her hair was pulled back and tied with a white ribbon. I tried to memorize everything about her, the way she set her heel when she stepped, the way the ribbons of her hair and sash fluttered in the breeze as we walked along the path by the cottage.

At the front stoop I took a step down and turned. We were face to face.

"I'll wait a week or so," I said. "Until you get into your new schedule. Then I'll look for you after school at the academy. All right?"

"Yes," she said. I kissed her on the cheek. "Charlie?"

"Yes?"

"How do you think this will end?"

"The way God intends," I said.

"God intended for Fitz to die?"

"Yes," I said. "For reasons we can't fathom."

"And what does God intend for me?" she asked.

"Happiness."

"Happiness? How can you think that? How can you know it?"

"I don't," I said. "It's what I have to believe."

LUCKY WAS ON HIS pallet on the porch. Beside him was a brown paper bag sitting on a stack of towels, and a galvanized pail. There was a note on the door. "Time for a Sunday bath," Mrs. Wingate had written. Inside the bag was Octagon soap and sprigs of rosemary and a new canvas collar. I took Lucky down the steps. He didn't like the hose much, but he stood. The soap foamed brown with dirt on his back and belly. When I rinsed him, his black coat shone and his white markings and socks were bright. I rubbed him down with the towels. He frolicked and gamboled in the yard. He rolled on his back in the grass. It was the first time I had ever seen him play. Then he lay in the evening sun, his big tongue hanging from his mouth. I went upstairs for the turpentine and treated his wounds. Then I put on his collar.

We went back up on the porch and I fed him. Then I ate supper myself. I hadn't looked at another newspaper since the morning on the train, and I didn't want to. I'd read enough about Virginia Christian.

The next morning Virginia Christian had disappeared from the headlines. Printed across the front page of the newspaper in two-inch letters were the words, "RMS TITANIC STRIKES ICEBERG—1,000 SOULS FEARED LOST." The pride of the White Star Line had slipped to the bottom of the Atlantic.

14.

George Jr.

Saturday morning two weeks later, Dr. Vanderslice sent his maid Cleopatra to the office with a handwritten note.

Charlie, here are the particulars. Our son, George K. Vanderslice, Jr., died at 1:30 o'clock this morning at our home. He was five years old. He had been ill for several months. Annie has a little portrait of him somewhere but we haven't been able to locate it for the paper. I didn't want to trouble her further before getting this to you. Funeral arrangements haven't been completed but we expect to hold burial services sometime Monday. Rev. J. J. Gravatt, D. D., former rector of St. John's Episcopal Church, and Rev. J. Martyn Neifert of the National Soldiers' Home have agreed to officiate. Burial will be made in St. John's cemetery. Thank you, Geo. Vanderslice, MD.

Mr. Hobgood rarely paid attention to death notices, but he looked a little misty-eyed as he read my brief account. He understood how admired Dr. Vanderslice was in the community and placed the story on the front page, at the bottom of a full column about the Mackay Company shipping the bodies of 189 Americans from Halifax, Nova Scotia, to the states. The bodies had been kept in storage at a curling rink because the morgues in

Halifax were already filled with victims from the *Titanic*.

Once again my porch overlooked a funeral. On Monday, April 29, the sun burned white in a pale sky, where gulls shrieked and dove. Lavender and white azaleas were blooming along the sidewalk. A dogwood tree, full of blossoms, stood close by the grave. I sat on my stool and smoked as people began to arrive for the service.

First came colored men and women, too old for work. They hobbled from the trolley stop to places far back from the arranged seating at the graveside. Then powdered and groomed white women in black dresses and black hats with feathers arrived. They took seats. Shortly they were joined by their husbands, some who drove up in cars, some who arrived by trolley, snatching time from banks and shops and law offices. I saw Mrs. Wright walking with Sadie. Groups of white children and black children, herded along by their teachers, began to file into the entrance. I recognized Miss Fannie Price leading a group of children from Public School No. 34 and Miss Hickman from Syms-Eaton Academy. Harriet was walking in line with the other children in that group. Then colored nurses and nannies and butlers and footmen, some accompanying their masters and mistresses, walked into the cemetery, heads lowered. Some had faces the color of mocha, some were as dark as bituminous coal. They wore uniforms and liveries, pure white, or gray with white lapels and cuffs, or black with white aprons. Embroidered apron strings undulated in the breeze. Colored washwomen and gardeners and colored and white men in canvas overalls from the shipyards joined the crowd. I saw George Wright. I saw John Cahill. Burly stevedores from the docks, some white, some colored, strode in and congregated near the old people at the back of the crowd. I heard a screen door clap and watched Mrs. Wingate and Maebelle cross the street and walk toward the cemetery entrance. Mayor Jones drove up, accompanied by Sheriff Curtis and his deputies. Commonwealth's attorney Montague was also in the group. I saw

Poindexter and Gus Stewart, and Pace, and Mr. Hobgood. There were nurses from the National Soldiers' Home, and teachers and officials from Hampton Institute. I had never seen so many people gathered in St. John's cemetery.

Then slowly up Lincoln Street came Mr. Rees' funeral caisson drawn by Dr. Vanderslice's Phoebe. Mr. Rees was driving. The black-spoked wheels dwarfed the small casket. Tied to the caisson was little George's paint pony, Cornwallis. The pony pranced on the cobblestones and whickered as the caisson turned into the cemetery. Behind the pony a black carriage carried Dr. Vanderslice and his wife and children. Members of the Vanderslice and Phoebus families followed. The men in the crowd removed their hats and caps and bandannas. It looked like a ripple moving on water.

I crushed out my cigarette and went inside. I brushed my hair. I made sure my cuffs and collar were clean. I tied my tie and put on a jacket. I looked at my cap, but decided to leave it on the bureau. I hurried down the steps and crossed Lincoln Street just ahead of the trolley. There was a bower of wisteria inside the cemetery wall. The fragrance was sweet. Bees droned among the blossoms.

The sound reminded me of the summer I met Dr. Vanderslice. It was my first week at the *Times-Herald*. I'd gone to the C&O depot to check with Poindexter about telegram traffic. There was nothing special, but he said he'd overheard some boys talking about a man at Hampton Institute not returning from his evening swim. One boy said a fisherman had seen a body floating near a pier.

The corpse had been pulled from the water when I came upon the scene. Dr. Vanderslice knelt, examining it. A small group of men and boys were gathered round him. I pushed my way through.

"Drowning?" I asked.

"No, I don't believe so," Dr. Vanderslice said, not turning from his work.

"Foul play?"

Dr. Vanderslice stood. "I'm George Vanderslice, coroner for Elizabeth City County. You are—?"

"I'm sorry, sir," I said. "I'm Charles Mears, *Times-Herald*. I just started."

"Very nice to meet you," Dr. Vanderslice said.

"Thank you, sir. You as well."

A boy who looked to be about my age ran up. He bent over to catch his breath. He had the big hands of a farm boy and his sleeves were a little short for his jacket.

"Drowning, Dr. V?" he said, still bent. "That's Dean Benbow, ain't it?"

"Charles Pace of the *Daily Press*, meet Charles Mears of the *Times-Herald*. I'll have a hard time keeping my Charleses straight."

The boy straightened and stuck out his hand. "Everybody calls me Pace," he said.

I shook his hand. "Everybody calls me Charlie," I said.

"How do," he said, nodding.

"How do," I said.

Pace let go my hand. "So it's a drowning, Dr. V?" he asked.

"Full fathom five thy father lies," Dr. Vanderslice said. "These are pearls that were his eyes."

"I'm not quite taking your meaning, Dr. V," Pace said.

"Ferdinand's father," I said. "Drowned. In *The Tempest*."

"Precisely," Dr. Vanderslice said. "And sank. But this man was found floating."

"Maybe he was dumped from the pier?" Pace said.

"No," Dr. Vanderslice said. "He's in his swim suit. I'm sure when the deputies go over to the institute they'll find a towel and personal effects where he set out. Appears he suffered a heart attack while he was swimming. Massive. There's no water in his lungs. Pace?"

"Yes, Dr. V?"

"You're right about the identification. It's Dean Benbow."

"Thanks, Dr. V. I got a file on him at the office."

"Charlie?"

"Yes, sir?"

"Where did you learn your Shakespeare?"

"The College of William & Mary."

"See you, Dr. V. See you, college boy," Pace said. He trotted off, licking the lead of a pencil.

"You'll have to come by the house some Sunday," Dr. Vanderslice said. "In the afternoon my children do short recitations from the plays. George Jr. was looking forward to the role of Henry the Fifth. Doesn't understand a word, of course, but he likes the sword. Now you'd better get going. Don't want Pace to have the scoop."

I PASSED THE GATE guard and entered the cemetery, trotting up the drive until I was in the crowd. The day was getting warm. Dr. Vanderslice sat with his wife and children under a green canvas canopy. George Jr.'s older brother Harrison stood at the foot of the grave, holding Cornwallis by the bridle. At his side he held a small pair of riding boots. The pony stood very still, flicking his tail at flies. From time to time, he snuffled at the raw earth of the grave. Reverend Neifert spoke the convocation and a prayer. Then Reverend Gravatt stepped forward.

"From the Gospel of Matthew: 'Take heed that ye despise not one of these little ones; for I say unto you, that in heaven their angels do always behold the face of my Father which is in heaven.'" He paused, still looking at the text.

"This is the word of the Lord," he said.

"Thanks be to God," the crowd responded.

Reverend Gravatt lifted his arms. "Little George Vanderslice Jr. now gazes on the face of his heavenly Father," he said. "How joyful the little angel must be! How radiant his smile! Yet how we here on earth long for the little boy who had to leave us so soon, so soon."

Mrs. Vanderslice sobbed. I saw a workman raise a coarse hand to his cheek. A young woman next to me was weeping. Dr. Vanderslice sat still as a statue. The reverend preached a good sermon, describing how there is nothing that moves us in such a way as the suffering of the innocent. There is nothing so difficult for us to comprehend. He spoke of redemption and the encompassing love of the Father.

The reverend closed with a prayer and greeted each of the seated family members. Then Dr. Vanderslice rose and with Mrs. Vanderslice holding little Emily on her hip they each placed a white rose on George Jr.'s casket, and then his sisters followed, placing white roses. The girls held the pony's bridle while Harrison placed the riding boots on the casket. Then Harrison began to cry. Dr. Vanderslice held out his arms, and Harrison ran to him. Dr. Vanderslice hugged him, then motioned for the boy to follow his mother and sisters. Then he stood alone by the grave, head bowed, lost in reverie. Men filed by, nodding and patting his back, and women from the church squeezed his hand. Some hugged him. The crowd moved out, too, some hurriedly, to get back to their places of work. Here and there a voice cried out, "God bless you, Dr. V!" That seemed to rouse him, and he raised his hand to wave at individuals in the crowd. "God bless you, Doc!" another person shouted.

I moved closer to the edge of the canopy, leaving room for others to greet him. I noticed a tall man with thick salt-and-pepper gray hair, eyebrows, and moustache moving toward Dr. Vanderslice. He was wearing a gray tweed three-piece suit. The thick lenses of his tortoise-shell glasses magnified his eyes. When Dr. Vanderslice saw him, he smiled broadly and took the man's hand in both of his.

"So good of you to come, Walt," Dr. Vanderslice said. He looked over the man's shoulder. "Is Kate here, too?"

"She sends her condolences," the man said. "She wasn't quite feeling up to the train. We're both so very sorry for your loss, V."

Dr. Vanderslice started to speak, but just nodded. "Thank

you," he whispered, releasing the man's hand. Then he noticed me. "Charlie, come over here and meet Dr. Walter Plecker. He's the man who delivered little George Jr. into the world. The two of us go back quite a few years. Walt, Charlie Mears, reporter for the *Times-Herald*."

Dr. Plecker extended his hand. His fingers were long and his grip strong as iron. "The *Times-Herald*," he said. "Didn't you print the confession of the Negress who murdered the Belote woman? The story with her dreaming about a blackboard?"

"Oh, Charlie's the man of the hour," Dr. Vanderslice said. "He conducted the interview."

"Unfortunate case, that," Dr. Plecker said. "Kate and I knew the woman's mother and father well. The Hobbses. Kate shopped at their grocery on King Street every week. The Negress is a sad example of the race. She's feeble-minded, isn't she, Mr. Mears? I seem to recall an article mentioning that."

"Well, she's had no education to speak of, sir," I said. "But I don't think she's feeble-minded. She just can't bring the moral perspective to what she's done. She's a child."

"No matter, young man," Dr. Plecker said. "It's the child-like nature of the race. Age and education can bring improvement in a very limited number of cases, but their abilities are sufficient only for other members of the race."

"But, sir . . ."

"Still have an apple for lunch, Walt?" Dr. Vanderslice asked, edging between us.

Dr. Plecker smiled. "That's right, V," he said. "And sometimes a cup of tea. No sugar, of course."

"I remember," Dr. Vanderslice said. He was smiling, too. "Could you come by the house, Walt? We're having people over for a meal. You could say hello to Annie and the children."

"No, V, I'd better get back to the depot. Tell Annie I'm sorry to have missed her. The two of you must come see us in Richmond."

"We will, Walt, we will in time."

The two men shook hands. Dr. Plecker held Dr. Vanderslice's.

"I'm sorry about little George," Dr. Plecker said. "Awful thing, that rheumatic fever." He held Dr. Vanderslice's hand a moment longer. Sunlight flashed in his eyeglasses as he looked down at the casket. "Little man howled like a catamount the night he was born, didn't he, though?"

"Yes, Walt, he surely did," Dr. Vanderslice said, nodding slowly.

Dr. Plecker released his hand and turned. He walked away in an instant.

Dr. Vanderslice noticed the white rose on his lapel. He began to fumble with the pin. His fingers were trembling.

"Here, Dr. V, let me help you," I said. I unpinned the rose, ran the pin into the stem, and placed the rose in his hand. He held it for a moment, studying the petals, and then dropped it onto the casket. It settled between the riding boots.

"Momentous times, aren't they, Charlie? Did you read what the morgue ship captain said? From the bridge the bodies looked like a flock of seagulls come to rest on the water, the white ends of the life-belts flapping like wings?"

"Yes, Dr. V, I saw the story."

"He said his ship was carrying every ounce of embalming fluid they could find in the town of Halifax. Enough for seventy corpses. Not enough by a thousand."

"No, sir."

"Little George made a drawing from an illustration in a magazine. I told him when he was hale and fit again, I'd take the whole family for a voyage on that ship. I told him the papers would run stories in the society section and he'd be the toast of all Hampton Roads. Oh, he was excited about sailing on the *Titanic*." His voice broke. "He was such a good little boy, Charlie."

I put my arm on his shoulder. There were two colored men standing at a distance with their shovels. They were bare-headed, their caps tucked in the back pockets of their overalls.

"Come on, Dr. V. We better get you home. I'm sure Cleopatra's fried more chicken than you or I've ever dreamed of."

BOTH ATTORNEY FIELDS AND attorney Newsome expressed publicly their outrage that the girl's appeals had been prejudiced by the confessions printed in the *Daily Press* and the *Times-Herald*. The black papers printed their full statements. The white papers printed notices. Mr. Newsome phoned me at the office one afternoon to chew me out personally. News of the *Titanic* continued to fill the papers day by day.

But what was done was done. Mr. Fields and Mr. Newsome filed their writs with the Supreme Court of Appeals in Wytheville. That area of the state was still preoccupied with the manhunt for the Allens, so there was little note of Virgie's case even being processed. Weeks passed.

On June 3, as scheduled, Virgie was moved by sheriff's van to the C&O depot, to be transferred by train into the custody of Warden J. B. Wood, the superintendent of the State Penitentiary in Richmond, where she was to be executed. The transfer seemed to be of little interest in Hampton, but Sheriff Curtis wasn't taking any chances. Deputy Chas Curtis was to accompany him to Richmond. Both men wore sidearms. Officer Hope and Constable Hicks followed the van in the sheriff's car. Hope was carrying a shotgun.

A handful of onlookers was at the depot. Most of them were white. They were quiet and orderly, but the officer and the constable made sure to keep them well back from the platform. Pace was there, and Mr. Christian, and of course, Poindexter. I stepped up to the side of the van. Sheriff Curtis let me hand Virgie a little chart

I'd made of the military telephony alphabet. I'd drawn pictures to help her memorize.

"I'll come help you with it in Richmond," I said.

"All right, Mr. Charlie," she said. "I's taking me a train ride. I ain't never rode on no train before."

"Well, then," I said.

Virgie looked excited, but when she saw her father, she began to cry.

"Don't you be doing that, Virgie," Mr. Christian said.

Sheriff Curtis let them hold hands through the bars of the van. Then the conductor stepped onto the platform. Sheriff Curtis touched Mr. Christian's shoulder.

"Reckon we got to get her on the train now," he said.

Mr. Christian was crying, too. He let go Virgie's hand, wiped his face, and stepped back. He stood with us as we watched the sheriff and Deputy Chas Curtis open the doors of the van and help Virgie down. She had shackles on her wrists and ankles. They clanked as she walked across the platform. Sheriff Curtis steadied her as she tried to step up onto the car. When Chas saw she was having trouble, he picked her up and carried her in. She had my alphabet chart in her hand when she disappeared. Sheriff Curtis followed.

Poindexter swallowed hard.

"I'd best get back to work," he said, and his voice cracked.

Pace swallowed hard, too. Then he took out his pencil and walked briskly from the platform.

15.

Cock Robin

The writs were denied, Charlie," Mr. Fields said. "I don't understand the confusion, though. First we received a written acceptance to hear the appeal from Wytheville, then a phone call from the clerk of court telling us to send the acceptance back. Maybe they're flustered by all the hoopla with the Allens. Anyway, I received written confirmation today. The Supreme Court of Appeals refuses to hear the case. So the matter of the printed confessions is moot. Newsome's forgiven you, by the way. I don't think he meant the things he said. Even if he did, you shouldn't take it to heart. Newsome is a good attorney and he likes to win. He felt bad because he argued against my putting the girl on the stand. Who knows, maybe the confessions will do some good, now that the matter's in the court of public opinion. The governor's a good Christian man. I'll draft a letter pleading for clemency. I'm sure Newsome will draft one, too."

"I'm sorry, Mr. Fields."

"The legal points were sound," he said. "But to hear an appeal on a case so inflammatory, well, it just wasn't going to happen."

A light-skinned boy appeared at the door to the library. "Momma said you and Mr. Mears might want some lemonade, Daddy," he said.

"Yes, thank you, Chester," Mr. Fields said. "Charlie, have you met my son?"

"No, sir."

"Chester, say hello to Mr. Mears. Mr. Mears is a reporter with the *Times-Herald*. Chester's only been with us a few months, Mr. Mears. He's here all the way from Detroit, Michigan. Chester, offer Mr. Mears some lemonade."

"Thank you," I said.

"You're welcome," Chester said. He took the tray to his father. Mr. Fields touched the edge and Chester guided his hand to the glass.

"Thank you, Chester," Mr. Fields said.

"You're welcome." The boy left the library. I sipped my lemonade.

"Sweet enough?" Mr. Fields said.

"Yes, sir."

"He's adopted," Mr. Fields said. "Just finalized the papers. He's ten years old. Mrs. Fields heard about him through our church. It's been a big change for him. But I think he's getting used to us. He's a good boy. Helps me with things. People say he looks like W. E. B. Du Bois. I couldn't say. Do you think so?"

"Why, yes, sir, from the pictures I've seen, I'd say he does."

Mr. Fields sipped his lemonade.

"Sir, may I ask you a personal question?"

"Of course, Charlie."

"How long have you been blind?"

He shook the glass and listened to the ice. "Well, in 1896 I had the great misfortune to lose my sight. It occurred five years after I was admitted to the Virginia Bar and four years after I married Miss Sallie, whom I'd met in New York. Quite a turn of events for a lawyer trying to build a practice." He shrugged.

"What happened?"

"I can't really say, Charlie. I woke up one morning and I couldn't see. Miss Sallie asked me why I was looking at her so funny, and I said I wasn't, I wasn't looking at anything. I remember being taken with a fit once, maybe twice, when I was working for Mr. Cornell up in New York, before I went to law school. Like lightning struck my head. But I don't know if that has anything to do with me losing my sight."

"It must have been hard to accept."

"Oh, yes," Mr. Fields said. "It seemed like such a cruel turn. After all the help people had given me, after getting my education and starting my career, after finding the love of my life, I woke up in darkness. I despaired, Charlie. I truly did. I had no idea what lay before me. I could not understand why I had been given this burden. I prayed, because that's what my mother always taught her children to do, but I could barely get myself out of bed in the mornings. I could hardly eat a bite. Miss Sallie sat with me for hours, reading aloud from the Bible, or from one of my law books. When she thought I was napping, I could hear her crying in the far end of the house.

"Then one evening, after Miss Sallie left me to sit on the back porch for a while after supper, I was listening to the bullfrogs booming in the swamp. Then, above that sound, I could just hear the flutter and squeaking of bats hunting in the marsh grass. I listened hard. Hard. Then, a simple thought came to me, Charlie."

"Yes, sir?"

"Justice is blind." He shook his head slowly. "Justice is blind. I was so excited, I called out to Miss Sallie. I think I scared her half to death. I asked her to help me into the library. I asked her to read to me some more. She read and read, and then I asked her to ask me questions. God bless her sweet soul, she stayed up past midnight, reading to me and quizzing me. The next morning she helped me hire a clerk to read a case I was scheduled to try, defending a man who was charged with assaulting his son with a gill hook.

"The case was tried the next day and the clerk helped me to the bar. I argued the case and put the defendant on the stand. Lo and behold, we won. In fact, the Commonwealth's attorney charged the son with assault and battery after his father's testimony was presented. Who would have thought? Like the hymn says, Charlie, 'God moves in a mysterious way His wonders to perform.'" He lifted the glass to his lips, drank, and then held the glass before his face.

"You know, Chester reminds me of myself at his age," he said. He turned the glass slowly in his hands. "I was slight like him, and nervous. Mr. Leary, the overseer on Miss Catherine's farm in Hanover County, gave me the nickname, 'Cock Robin.' And to tell you the truth, I was tied to my mother's apron strings. She was the house cook. I loved helping her in the kitchen. It was a hard day for me when Mr. Leary brought me a hoe and told me I needed to go out to the fields with the men. I cried and hollered and took on so, but he didn't relent. He just told me to go on with my brother James and do like James did. Do you have brothers and sisters, Charlie?"

"No, sir." The ice tinkled in his glass as he lowered it to his lap.

"I would be hard put to describe to you how much I looked up to my brother James," he said. "Do you see that picture there on the table?"

"Yes, sir."

"That's him. James Apostles Fields. When he served in the Virginia House of Delegates." The man in the picture had large eyes and a full beard. "He was in the very first graduating class at Hampton Normal. He taught school for a while, then went back to school to get his law degree at Howard. Achieved all that, and James was eighteen years old when he first started learning to read, Charlie. Contrary to Virginia law when we were at Miss Catherine's. Momma couldn't read herself, and never tried to. But she taught us when we were children to observe, to study the actions of the human heart, and to hold our own counsel.

"It was Mrs. Peake who taught James to read, before she got so sick. He sat there under that great big oak tree, the one they call the

'Emancipation Oak' now, grown boys and girls and little children, too, and Mrs. Peake taught them, each and every one. I learned to read under that selfsame tree. Mrs. Peake passed the winter before Momma got us to Old Point Comfort, so I never saw her. James said her eyes were so bright she looked like an angel. Said she always kept an extra lace kerchief in her sleeve for her cough. Tuberculosis. It was said she caught it before the war.

"It's odd how your mind goes back. My brother James passed, well, it's nearly ten years now, Charlie. When I think of him, I don't think of the man in the picture frame, the legislator. I think of my big brother, when we were on Miss Catherine's farm. I think about how tall and strong he was, how proud he was, how he looked after Momma and us children, like our father, since our own father could only visit from the neighboring farm every couple of weeks or so, and my other brothers had been sold to Richmond and King William County. Father was a blacksmith, and when James visited him, he worked with him at the forge, so his forearms rippled when he grasped a tool handle or shook a man's hand. For me, slight little Cock Robin, James seemed strong as Samson, the Bible story Momma told us.

"Maybe that was why Phil Winston was so hard on him, because he saw what a man James was becoming, how the other colored men admired him, too." Mr. Fields shook his head slowly. "Or maybe it was just because Phil Winston was a cruel son of a bitch, and was hard on most any living thing he happened to cross paths with.

"He was Miss Catherine's second husband, a good bit younger than her. He didn't come from any money, either, though Miss Catherine did. Momma said she never did see the connection. Maybe he got busy with Miss Catherine in a way she missed, who knows?

"The summer before James ran off, I saw my first soldiers, Confederates in butternut marching through a field of knee-high corn with bayonets glittering in the sun. They set up camp, white tents scattered across the field, their muskets stacked before the tents. They built campfires as evening came on, and you could smell coffee and fatback, and the long musket barrels shone in the firelight. The next morning Momma was on the porch of the cabin with her hand on a pole. There was a sound like thunder and the shakes of the roof rattled. There was not a cloud in the sky. Momma turned to me when I asked her was a storm coming and said no, it is the Yankees. Then the Confederates broke down the tents and loaded them on wagons, and there were big-wheeled carriages with artillery and skittish horses rearing and the soldiers shouldered their muskets with bayonets fixed and then they were gone.

"That selfsame summer I saw my first Yankee. He came busting on horseback out of the woods with his saber lifted in the air. He had a chin strap for his cap and a blue coat with brass buttons the color of the stripes on his pants. His horse was roan with a blaze face and his haunches shone like copper when he jumped the fence. The Yankee shouted something at the men hoeing at the edge of the cornfield, and the men looked at each other like they didn't know what to do, and the Yankee hollered at them again and pointed with his saber to the woods. The men gathered round him and then they threw down their hoes and climbed the fence and started running in the direction the Yankee had pointed. The Yankee reared his horse and turned a circle. Then he jumped the fence and disappeared with the men. I guess it was five or six men altogether. Miss Catherine had something like seventy-five slaves on the place at the time, counting the women and children.

"All evening long Phil Winston cussed about damned niggers running off with the blessed thieving Yankees, and everybody on the place gave him a wide berth. Miss Catherine finally got him to come into the big house for supper.

"I didn't see any more soldiers, Confederate or Yankee, that fall. It turned damp and cold. One day James was working with the other men clearing rotten rails from the fences around the place, which had to be done every year, so they could be replaced with new split rails. It had rained all day, a slow, cold rain, and James' clothes were soaked through. He carried one of the rotten rails home to saw it up for firewood, so he could dry out his clothes. Phil Winston saw him carrying the rail toward the cabins and called his two head men, Robert and Daniel, big colored men. They came up to Momma's cabin and took James to a hay pole by the barn and beat him bloody.

"When he staggered back to the cabin Momma was crying and she helped him take off his clothes. Then she washed him clean and put some jimson weed salve she made herself on his wounds. She put the salve on every day until he healed and got his strength back. Then one night he said to Momma, 'I am going to leave, and if I come across Phil Winston again, I am going to kill him.' I had never seen that look in my brother's eyes before and I never saw it again, thank God. Under the floorboards he had hidden a rusty bayonet and a little four-barrel pepperbox flint pistol. I don't know where he got either one of the weapons. He had them wrapped in an oily rag and he took them out from under the floorboards and tucked them in his coat. Then he threw the oily rag in Momma's cook stove to burn. He hugged Momma and kissed her on the cheek. He shook my hand and it hurt my fingers when he shook. I started to cry and little sister Catherine started to cry, too. I watched him make his way along the fence beyond the barn and then he disappeared into the woods.

"He came back one night to visit in the spring, and then he left again. We all missed him so, and wondered if we would ever see him again, Momma especially. She was worried sick, because she knew if Phil Winston caught him he would have the head men beat him again, or maybe hang him from a tree.

"It wasn't until Momma had gotten us children to Old Point

Comfort that we heard James' story. He told us our brother who had been sold to Richmond had been helping him hide out there, and that's how detectives tracked him down. When they caught him, they got hold of Mr. Leary, the overseer, who took a buckboard into Richmond to haul him back hog-tied.

"Mr. Leary stopped overnight at a tavern halfway back to Hanover County, and he brought James in to keep warm by the stove. When Mr. Leary turned in, James was able to convince a girl who worked in the tavern to loosen his ropes, and he waited until everybody was asleep to work them off. Snow was flying when he got outside. He ran for the river. He told us he could hear men hollering and dogs baying behind him when he scrambled down the bank and jumped into the Pamunkey. He heard a shot, and then another, but they didn't hit him. He floated along in the current for as long as he could stand the cold, till he could barely feel his arms and legs, and then he crawled up on the far bank. He made his way to a cabin and some people helped him. He said if they hadn't, he probably would have frozen in the cold before daybreak.

"I remember the look of calm in Momma's face as she listened to James telling his tale. When he finished, Momma nodded. 'I always told you children God was watching,' she said.

"Oh, my mind goes back, Charlie. I remember the morning sunlight in the fields, the dew on the blackberry bushes at woods edge. I remember the smell of Momma's cooking in the kitchen of the big house, and carrying in wood to keep the stove hot for her biscuits. I remember lambs in the spring, shaking their long tails and bleating, climbing on their mothers' sides as they rested in the pasture, pawing with little hooves into their mother's wool. I remember Uncle Sam playing the fiddle at corn shuckings after he got a snootful of applejack. I remember the pretty little colored girl who was a house servant helping me herd turkeys to a pen with a switch. I remember my brothers and sisters singing hymns Momma taught us on a Sunday morning."

Mr. Fields paused and took a swallow of lemonade. "You know, Charlie, it was a blessing James ran away when he did, because of what Phil Winston did to our mother before he died.

"In the summertime near dusk big bull bats flew over the fields, high up, so high when they shrieked it was hard to see them unless you had a sharp eye. One evening Phil Winston was sitting on the front porch of the big house, and called to one of the servants to bring out his rifle. He trotted down the steps and took a bead on one of the bull bats, and what do you know but he shot that bird down. This was something very rare, so he came down to our cabin carrying the rifle and the bird, and told Momma he wanted her to get up to the house to cook that bird for Miss Catherine. I know Momma was worn out from the day's work but of course there was no help for it but for her to go.

"I was on the pallet asleep but I roused a little when she came back to the cabin. She sighed and stretched out and quick as anything she was snoring.

"The next morning right at daybreak I heard somebody yelling at the door and Momma propped herself up on her elbow. Then Phil Winston kicked in the door and grabbed Momma by the arm and dragged her off the pallet. 'Nigger bitch, I'll teach you a lesson,' he said, and he dragged her out the door and down the steps. 'Stand up!' he said, still holding her arm and Momma got to her knees and then she stood. He ripped off her shirtwaist and she tried to cover herself with her free arm. 'You cooked that bird so dry Miss Catherine couldn't eat it,' he said. By then the field hands were out of their cabins, seeing what the ruckus was about, and women came out, too, pushing their children behind their skirts.

"Phil Winston was carrying a rope in his free hand and he had a riding crop tucked under the belt of his trousers. 'Hold out your hands,' he told Momma. She did and he tied her hands together. With the rope he pulled her toward an apple tree in front of the cabin. He threw the end of the rope over a limb and pulled the rope tight, so that Momma's hands were raised high above her head. He looped the end of the rope around a lower limb and tied a knot. My mother was sobbing. Her torn shirt hung from the waist of her skirt.

"I watched Phil Winston pull the crop from his belt. It was thick, the kind a man would use to ride a big horse, a hunter. He flicked it once against his boot and smiled when my mother started at the sound. Then he hit her, one-two-three, and paused. He hit her, one-two-three. My mother's face looked startled, and then she screamed. Her legs gave way, so she was dangling from the rope at her wrists. Phil Winston bent his knees to get a better angle. One-two-three. One-two-three. Blood was running down my mother's back. One. Two. Her eyes rolled white and her head fell back from her shoulders. Three.

"Phil Winston tucked the crop in his belt and untied the knot. The rope whirred as it slipped over the branch of the tree and my mother fell in a heap. Phil Winston spat on the ground. My mother started to moan. He untied the rope from her wrists and coiled it.

"'Reckon you'll remember how to cook a bird now,' he said. He started to walk up the row of cabins to the big house, looking from face to face. The men stared at the ground. A woman or two held his eye before they looked down, too. He went up the steps into the house and the screen door banged shut behind him.

"Momma was groaning, and a woman untied her apron and put it over her shoulders to hide Momma's nakedness. Another dipped a rag in a water bucket and touched it to Momma's lips. When Momma finally came to herself the women helped her stand, but she staggered when she tried to walk. The head man Robert took her in his arms and carried her back inside our cabin.

"To this day I thank Jesus my brother James wasn't there to

see Phil Winston beat Momma. She never spoke a word to him about it, nor did any of us children, not even when we started our new life in freedom. Momma was wise. I don't think James' mind could have stood it.

"Watching Phil Winston beat my mother was the only time I ever felt completely hopeless, Charlie. Waking up blind one morning was bad, but not nearly as bad as that morning at Miss Catherine's. I cried out, like the boy I was, but there was nothing I could do. I remembered Momma saying if God looked after the sparrow, surely he looked after us, even his little Cock Robin. But I didn't believe her that morning. I felt rage. I understood then it was what I had seen in James' face when he ran away. As I heard my mother moaning while Phil Winston walked away, rage was all there was in me, all there would be in me forever, I thought.

"That was the last time I saw Phil Winston standing. In a fortnight he came down with a fever and took to his bed. Near the end, Miss Catherine walked us slaves one by one by the foot of his bed, field hands and house servants alike, so we could bid him farewell. I don't think he recognized a soul as we passed. His chin drooped, and there was spit in the corners of his mouth. His eyes stared at the ceiling. Then he was gone, and Miss Catherine had him laid in the family cemetery overlooking the Pamunkey."

Mr. Fields lifted his glass and drained it. He cradled the empty glass in his lap.

"I haven't heard one tinkle of an ice cube, Charlie. Don't you like the lemonade?"

"Oh, no, sir. It's not that. It's just . . ."

"My mother never lost her faith, Charlie. Not ever. She prayed in the mornings, before any of us had risen. I remember the first morning I heard her, blinking myself awake, trying to find her in the dark. 'Deliver us,' I heard her praying. 'Oh Lord, will you deliver us?' She prayed when my brothers John and Robert were sold, when my sister Louisa was sold down to Georgia, when my brother James ran away. She prayed after Phil Winston whipped her. Every morning every day, Charlie, she prayed. My sisters treated her with the jimson weed salve the same way she had treated James, and in time her wounds healed.

"What's troubling you, Charlie? Is it the Christian girl?"

"Yes, sir. And other matters."

"Do you feel hopeless?"

"Yes, sir. And sad."

"Oh, sadness is easy, Charlie. It passes. You'll learn that. But rage. Rage is not easy."

16.

Golden Eagle

I heard the sound of the front door and girls' laughter. The door closed. Mr. Fields sat up straight and leaned forward in his chair. "Inez?" he called. "Inez, is that you, child?"

There were footfalls in the hall. Mr. Fields found the corner of the side table and placed his glass atop it. Then he stood and so did I.

Inez walked in and the room seemed to get brighter. Her smile was broad and her white teeth flashed.

"Hello, Daddy," she said.

"Hello, child. Give your old daddy a kiss." She pecked him on the cheek. "You met Mr. Mears, didn't you?"

"Yes. Hello, Mr. Mears."

"How was school?" he asked.

"Good," she said. "You know, summer session, we don't have to read so much. Then Benita and Jewel and I went to vespers. Has Momma started supper?"

"Is it that time?"

"Yes, Daddy. You've been talking again, haven't you? I'd better go help."

"All right, honey. Mr. Mears, would you stay and have a bite with us?"

"I'm afraid I'll have to go soon, Mr. Fields. Mr. Hobgood has me on the evening beat."

"All right, then."

"Good seeing you," Inez said.

"Yes," I said.

We took our seats.

"I wanted to tell you about the day I was born," Mr. Fields said. "I remember it clearly. Don't you think that's odd?"

"Well, yes, sir, I reckon I do. How is it you remember?"

"A lot of colored folk do. Because we've been born twice." Mr. Fields stretched his fingers and folded his hands in his lap. His fingers were long, curving back from the second joint.

"July 4, 1863, Charlie, it was hot as the blazes, not a cloud in the sky. A few field hands had fallen out from the heatstroke the day before. I rose early, even before Momma, and went outside to sit on the fence and see if I could cool off. I was on the top rail, listening to a mockingbird in the mulberry tree hanging over the fence. The colors of dawn were creeping across the field when I saw them. They came boiling out of the woods, Zouaves in their red trousers. They formed themselves into a rainbow, shouldered their muskets, and began to march across the field toward us. Then I heard the clank of metal and the sound of hooves, and I could see men on horseback on the south end of the rainbow, and men rolling up artillery on the north end. I saw fire and white smoke in the field and a cannonball whistled through the branches of the mulberry. I heard a boom and then another.

"I scurried off the fence and ran to the cabin. I flung the door open. 'Momma!' I shouted. 'It's the red men. It's the Yankees coming!'

"Momma ran to the fence with me and saw them. 'Thank the Lord!' she whispered. We rushed toward the cabin and saw Confederate troops running at us, taking cover behind the fence and along the row of cabins. We had made it to the porch when a cannonball knocked the support clean away and the roof sagged down, but it didn't hurt us. The Confederates started firing their muskets and men with a team of horses were bringing a cannon forward and then all hell seemed to break loose.

"I helped Momma roust the other children and we ran up to the big house. Miss Catherine was standing on the porch looking across the field. She was wearing her nightgown without a robe since the weather had been so hot. When she saw us coming she shrieked Momma's name, 'Martha Ann! What on earth is happening?' Momma ignored her and herded us into the kitchen. Those stone walls there were a good three feet thick. The kitchen door shook and banged open behind us. It was Madison Lewis, a field hand who had been courting my big sister.

"'Aunt Martha,' he said, 'Is you all right? Is Matilda all right?' 'Yes,' Momma said. 'Then I'm gone watch this,' he said, and ran back outside. Before Momma could say anything, I was right behind him. We ducked behind the stone foundation of the cow shed. 'Cock Robin,' he said. 'Your momma gone whip us both but she gone whip me the hardest, cause she be thinking I brung you.' But he let me stay.

"The Confederates held the line of cabins as long as they could, but the musket balls were zipping in the air like a hornet's nest stirred, and artillery shells had blown whole sections of the fence away. The Confederates began to fall back, until they were hunkered down behind the big house. Beyond the house was a stone wall and then the tavern and courthouse. Some of the Zouaves had made it to the cabins, and they were poking around the sides and firing. Then they were firing hot from behind what was left of the fence, and the Confederates fell back to the stone wall. The Zouaves had brought a cannon up, and were firing it on the wall, and the Confederates fell back again, behind the tavern and courthouse. Beyond the courthouse, where the slave stump was, the Confederates just turned and hightailed it.

"Zouaves and infantry boiled over the fence and around the big house, leaping over the stone wall. They went into the jail by the courthouse and started busting open the locks to the cells. There were slaves penned up, runaways who had been caught, and the runaways sprinted out into the courtyard, singing and hollering and dancing and jumping.

"The Yankee cavalry rode up and discovered Confederate grain stores and hay loaded on wagons, and set the wagons alight. Yankee troops spread out all along the cabins, getting into the shade wherever they could. Some of the field hands and house servants gathered up the Yankees' canteens to fill with water and brought them back. 'Here you are, uncle,' or 'Thank you, auntie,' the soldiers would say. They had little packets of sugar wrapped in cotton cloth they gave to the children. But many slaves stayed hid wherever they could, in the cabins, or in the cow shed, or in the woods, because Phil Winston had told us all manner of lies about the Yankees, about how the first thing the Yankees would do is cut off a slave's ears, and then they'd cut off our noses.

"Anyway, the shooting stopped and it got pretty quiet. Madison Lewis saw Momma poke her head outside the kitchen, and we both crouched low. She stepped outside.

"'Cock Robin,' she shouted, 'you within the sound of my voice, and you don't get in here right now, you gone find yourself in a heap of trouble. And Madison Lewis, that go for you, too.' She put her hands on her hips.

"'Told you,' Madison Lewis said, shaking his head. Then we heard the thunder of artillery beyond the fields where the Confederates had run off. Momma went back in the kitchen. Madison Lewis and I peered around the corner of the foundation and we could see ranks of men in butternut with muskets and bayonets, like a wave of steel moving across the fields.

"A Yankee officer was watching through a glass at the fence. He closed up the tube and turned. 'All right, men, we're falling back. Form on the colors!'

"There was all sorts of commotion, men hollering and whistling to each other. The supply wagons pulled away from the courthouse first, with the runaways who had been freed from the jail trotting alongside them. There were small colored children clinging to the sideboards and their parents shouting at them to hang on and not be scared.

"The troops followed in ranks and then came the artillery and cavalry. I saw my sisters Maria and Betty come out of the kitchen. Maria was carrying little Catherine, and they were running for the cabin. They saw me and told me to come help them pack what we had at the cabin. So I went with them and Madison Lewis headed for the kitchen to take his medicine from Momma, since Matilda was with her in the kitchen, too.

"'Momma said to get what clothes they was and to get that money she got wrapped under the floor boards,' Maria said. 'What you been doing, anyway, playing soldier?'

"Betty was carrying little Catherine, and little Catherine was cooing and laughing like she was watching the best thing she'd ever seen. We gathered the few clothes there were and wrapped them in two parcels, and I got the money from under the cabin that was wrapped in a rag and tucked it in a blanket roll. I carried the blanket roll and a parcel and Maria took little Catherine from Betty. Betty picked up the other parcel and we ran for the kitchen.

"Momma and Matilda had baked up four or five flour cakes and were tying them in paper. Madison Lewis was slicing pieces of fatback. Then he wrapped up a couple parcels in paper, too. Every time Momma said something he jumped like a deer, so I expect Momma had made herself pretty clear about letting me stay outside with him.

"'Did you get that money?'

"'Yes, Momma,' I said.

"'All right, then,' she said. 'You gone have to carry Catherine, cause she too small to walk herself.'

"'Where we going, Momma?' I said.

"'With the Yankees,' Madison Lewis said.

"'I don't need to hear a single word out your mouth this day,' Momma said.

"'Yes, ma'am,' Madison Lewis said.

"'We gone with the Yankees, Cock Robin,' Momma said. 'Quick as we can.'

"Momma distributed all the parcels and handed little Catherine to me. She retied the knot in her bandanna and picked up the iron pot with a handle she used for her stews. She turned it upside-down, with the handle back, placed the pot on her head, and tilted it back so she could see. Then we paraded out the door of the kitchen, Momma in front, then Matilda, Maria, William, Betty, me carrying little Catherine, and Madison Lewis bringing up the rear.

"Miss Catherine was standing out on the porch with Mr. Leary when we swung around the front of the house. Miss Catherine had put on one of her nice dresses but she still looked a mess, her hair down and stringing around her shoulders, her eyes red from crying.

"'Martha Ann!' she called. 'Are you going to leave me and take the children, too?'

"Momma stopped and tilted the pot back.

"'Yes, Miss Catherine, I am,' she said. Then she lowered the pot and continued walking past the picket fence in front of the house and out onto the road.

"After a while the sun was sinking low. We could see a glow in the sky to the northeast, the way the Yankees had marched toward the Pamunkey River. Along the edge of the woods, we would see a Yankee picket ride out of the woods and scan the road, then disappear back in the woods. When we rounded a bend, we saw the Yankees had burned Littlepage's bridge behind them. The last spar glowed red when the wind stirred and white ash drifted from it into the river. The timber caved just as we reached the bank and fell in the water with a hiss. Matilda sobbed out loud and Momma told her to hush. We all looked to Momma to know what to do and for a moment she looked bewildered.

"We could hear hoof beats and men shouting in the distance we had traveled. Momma removed the pot and set it on the ground. She knelt beside it, folded her hands, and bowed her head. I could see her making words with her lips but she didn't speak. Then she stood up and placed the pot back on her head.

"'Come on, children,' she said. 'We gone see my brother John.' She started downstream, pushing through a thicket of vines and saplings. There were brambles and greenbrier draped from the tree limbs, and they clutched at our clothing. Every time I heard a rustle in the leaves I was sure it was a snake. When a twig snapped I was sure it was a Confederate scout. But we stayed in file behind Momma, stubbing our toes on rocks and logs in the darkness. My feet were bleeding from the bramble thorns.

"She had told us about our Uncle John, but I couldn't remember having ever seen him. Momma said he was the master of hounds at the Wickham plantation, which was downriver. The moon was out by the time we were able to see house lights in the distance. Nearby was a hut at the edge of the woods. We could hear dogs whining and snuffling. My heart was in my throat because I had never been around dogs and had only heard stories about them hunting down runaways. I was terrified they would set on us and tear us to pieces.

"Momma set the pot down and told us to stay put. We watched her make her way through the high weeds. Then the hounds started to howl and bay. Little Catherine began to cry. I took a piece of bread from my pocket and gave it to her and she got quiet. The dogs kept baying and we could hear voices and then a man's voice said, 'Hush up, dogs!' and the hounds were quiet.

"Momma came back to us and said, 'Come on, children,' and we followed her to the hut. Hounds came boiling from underneath and from inside and I pressed Catherine to my chest and hunkered down. The dogs' noses were cold and they were licking us and whining and licking and snuffling. Then Uncle John said, 'They won't hurt a one of you. Stand up.' So we stood and Uncle John motioned us toward the river.

"'Water been high from the storms we had, Martha Ann. Might have washed away again.' We watched him scramble down the steep bank. Big snags littered the river. The water sucked and funneled among them. At the edge of the water Uncle John pulled away a pile of brush. There was the little boat he had hollowed out from a tree. It was flattened on one side.

"'Won't ferry more than one at a time, Martha Ann,' he said. 'You come on.'

"'No,' she said. 'I ain't going until my folks is safe across.'

"So Madison Lewis went first. Uncle John figured he'd have to be on the far side to hoist us up the bank. And he was the heaviest, so if the dugout didn't tip with the two of them, the rest of us should be fine. Momma and we children watched them make their way across the water, Uncle John paddling hard against the current, keeping the dugout clear of the snags. The far bank was muddy and rose straight up from the river. Madison Lewis was barely able to hoist himself up, holding onto saplings and roots. Finally he got to the top of the bank. Uncle John could see we children wouldn't be able to reach high enough to grab Madison Lewis' hand, so he took a spade he had in the boat and carved out a few steps in the bank for us to climb.

"Then Uncle John paddled back for Matilda, since she was big enough to help, too. I watched each crossing, until finally it was my turn with little Catherine. Momma remained. I strained to see her in the darkness as Uncle John paddled. 'Don't lean that way, boy,' Uncle John said, 'else you'll pitch us over.' I kept looking back for Momma, until she was like a shadow in the darkness, and for a moment I despaired of ever seeing her again. When Uncle John reached shore, he tied the boat to a sapling. Then he carried me and Catherine up the bank, holding us in one arm while he grabbed onto roots to pull himself up. Then Madison Lewis and Matilda were able to reach down and take us from him. Uncle John was breathing hard as he lowered himself down the bank and disappeared. I thought my lifetime passed before I could see Momma's form perched in the little boat, her iron pot tipped back on her head.

"Uncle John tied the boat and helped Momma up the bank. When he slumped down with us at the top, I could see he was all done in. An owl hooted and we all jumped, even Uncle John. Then he laughed out loud and put his hand on my mother's shoulder.

"'I gots to get that cook pot,' he said. He slid down the bank and crawled back up, carrying the pot by a handle.

"'You's in King William County, Martha Ann,' he said. 'Hush! Hear that? You hear that horn blow? That's where the Yankees is. You'll run into them fore long.'

"She roused Matilda and Betty, and loaded them with parcels. Catherine was sleeping in my lap. 'You children go over to that big tree and wait,' Momma said. 'Madison Lewis, you, too.' We walked to the tree and sat down, exhausted by the night's journey. I could hear the Yankee bugle clearly then. Momma and Uncle John hugged and then they held hands for a moment. I could see them talking. Then Momma turned for us and Uncle John turned for the river.

"Momma set the pot down when she got to the tree. 'You children stay here,' she said. 'Madison Lewis, you come with me.' Clouds hung low over the meadow and it started to rain. We watched Momma and Madison Lewis until they disappeared in the rain. The tree gave us some shelter, but it was hard to doze off with everything damp. Once and a while a big drop would drip from the tree and land with a thunk on Momma's iron pot, and startle me awake.

"When I opened my eyes again, the sky had started to lighten, and I could see Momma and Madison Lewis walking back in the rain. They were soaking wet, water dripping from the chins and fingertips, but they were both smiling.

"'Come on, children,' Momma said, and her face was brighter and happier than I'd ever remembered seeing it. We gathered our things, and I lifted little Catherine in my arms. We traipsed through the weeds, most of them taller than my head, and we were all soaked through. Then we reached the crest of a hill, and we looked down below, and there were campfires burning, and wagons and cannon, and tethered horses, and white canvas tents scattered before us.

"'Them's the Yankees,' Madison Lewis said. The rain let up as we made our way into camp. Men took us by a fire and added wood, and the flames licked up and danced and the heat felt wonderful. Then a cook brought us a bucket full of hardtack biscuits with slices of fried fatback, and tin mugs of corn coffee sweetened to taste. And we children were so hungry, we crouched and ate as fast as we could, and I saw Momma watching us eat, and she was smiling and crying at the same time. After we ate we stood by the fire, and turned when one side got hot, so our clothing was dried out in no time at all.

"The sun started to come out later and the rain had cleared the air, so it did not feel so hot and close. The Yankees fed their horses and oiled their muskets and some read from little devotionals, and some wrote letters. Then, in the afternoon, there was a great shout among them, and some flung their caps into the air. I heard Momma ask one what it was all about.

"'Victory at Gettysburg, auntie!' the Yankee shouted. 'Old

Bobby Lee turned tail!' A soldier broke out a fiddle and started to play and some of the Yankees danced, slipping and sliding and stomping in the mud. Then other slaves who were in the camp with us started to dance and sing and shout, and we joined in. Even little Catherine was hopping up and down, and there was laughter and dancing for a good while.

"Then an officer came into the middle of it and said the Confederates were flanking the position, and they would have to strike camp and fall back to the White House on the York River, and such a flurry of activity you have never seen. The tents were struck and packed on wagons, the stacks of muskets distributed to the men, their haversacks stuffed with their belongings and slung on their backs. Then the stampede began, us trailing along with the column of men and wagons, with the cavalry in the rear. Many slave women and children rode on wagons, but the teamsters said I was too big to ride. So I slipped on the back and Momma hid me under her skirt. We rode the whole way to the York, where we camped in a field by the river in front of the White House. Again we had a hot meal and sweetened coffee, and there were more and more slaves in our midst, folks who had escaped from plantations just as we had.

"The next morning we were fed breakfast and told to pack our belongings. We went down to the wharf and there were seven barges tied up with hawsers. We boarded the barges and took our places. I would imagine there were four thousand souls on the barges. That many. None of us knew where we were bound but Momma said we were headed to the place God intended, and wherever that was, would be all right.

"From across the wide river I saw a little tug steaming our way, and in its wake a white side-paddle steamboat. The steamboat gleamed in the water, black smoke curling from its stacks, and as it grew closer, I could hear the sound of its big pistons, and it blew its whistle, and the slaves on the barges shouted and began to sing, 'O freedom, O freedom, over me, over me, and before I would be a slave, I would be buried in my grave, and go home to my Lord and be free.'

"When the white boat drew nearer, I could see a golden eagle painted on the wheelhouse, shining in the sun, its beak so fierce and its talons so sharp, I knew it would protect me. And right then I looked at Momma, and she looked at me, and she said, 'Bless you, Cock Robin, God has set you free,' and I knew then I was born into a new life, the life that brought me here to Wine Street, in the company of my family, to sit here with you, Charlie, and drink lemonade, and talk about the law, talk about the past, talk about the day I remember being born."

"DADDY, MOMMA SAYS SHE'S ready for supper." It was Chester. We hadn't heard him enter the library. He was carrying a tray. He bent and held it before me. I put my glass on it. Then he went to his father, and helped him with his glass.

"How much did you hear, son?" Mr. Fields asked.

"I heard the part about the singing and the eagle, Daddy." Mr. Fields nodded.

"Sure you won't join us, Charlie?"

"Thank you, Mr. Fields, but I'd better be getting to work."

"Chester, you go on to the table. I'll show Mr. Mears out."

"All right, Daddy."

Mr. Fields rested his hand lightly on my forearm as we walked down the hall to the door. He reached for the latch, but then he dropped his hands by his sides.

"I feel you want to ask me something, Charlie."

"Yes, sir."

"Well?"

"Mr. Fields, when he was on the stand, why did you ask Mr. Christian about Virgie's birthday?"

He raised a hand and rubbed his chin.

"I see," he said. "You think maybe I slipped up? Violated the old rule: always know the witness' response before you ask the question?"

"No, sir," I said. "That doesn't seem possible. You slipping up."

"Oh," he said. He continued to stroke his chin. He stopped and raised a finger.

"What if I said to you I *had* to ask that question? That I knew Mr. Christian, like many fathers of my race, would not know the age of his own daughter? What if I said to you, Charlie, that in that courtroom I knew there was a black child counting on me for her life, and that at home, I knew there was another black child counting on me for hers?"

"Daddy?" A shadow blocked the light down the hall. Inez leaned in from the dining room doorway. "Are you coming?"

"Yes, child, I was just bidding Mr. Mears good evening. I'll be right along."

"All right, Daddy."

Mr. Fields placed both his hands around my right hand, his long fingers intertwined.

"Charlie," he said. "Do you know in the last decade how many colored men have been executed in Virginia for raping a white girl? The legal executions, not the lynchings?"

"No, sir."

"Nineteen," he said. "The most recent was this month. A black man from Chesapeake. Do you know in the last decade how many white men have been executed in Virginia for raping a colored girl?"

"No, sir."

"Do you know how many in the history of the Commonwealth?"

"No, sir."

"Not one," he said. He grasped my hand firmly. He was not

just saying good evening, he was bidding farewell. He released my hand and touched my elbow.

"Write a letter to the governor, Charlie. It's in his hands now. Maybe one day you'll forgive me."

"No, sir, Mr. Fields. There's nothing to forgive when a man does what he believes is right."

"God bless you, Charlie."

"God bless you, Mr. Fields."

I HEARD THE DOOR close behind me as I walked to the corner. I stopped to light a cigarette. A mockingbird sang in a tree by the streetlight. This time of year he might sing all night. I blew a cloud of smoke and started down the sidewalk. Bullfrogs boomed in the marsh behind Mr. Fields' house. I stopped and turned.

I could see Mr. Fields in the light of a window. He sat at his dining room table. Inez was at his shoulder, serving something from a dish onto his plate. I looked away, into the night.

I felt I would never meet another man like Mr. Fields. He had been a slave. Now he was free. He once had sight. Now he was blind. Was I feeling what he felt when he heard the whip on his mother's back? I flicked the cigarette into the street. I sat down on the curb. I was so angry it was hard to breathe. Who does Jim Crow leave free?

17.

So Long!

The morning air on the street was humid. I could feel beads of sweat on my upper lip. Ahead the Virginia State Penitentiary loomed dark and grotesque in the early light. I decided to have a smoke before I went inside.

At the entrance a Haxall Flour Mills freight wagon was parked, a pair of big mules standing in harness. The mules flicked their ears and switched their tails at flies. Two Negroes in floppy hats and overalls were unloading oak staves from the wagon onto a hand cart. Their shirts were stained with sweat. One man came forward to the wagon seat and pulled two burlap feed sacks from under it. He draped a sack over the face of each mule.

He paused as I struck a match.

"Morning, sir," he said. "Doggone flies about to eat the eyes plumb out of them mules' heads."

"Morning," the man at the cart said.

"Good morning," I said.

"Got one for a colored man, sir?" the first man asked.

"Sure," I said, tipping the pack.

The man took the Lucky and smelled it.

"That some fine Richmond tobacco right there," he said, tucking the cigarette between his lips. I struck another match. The man cupped my hand to his face.

"Will you have one?" I said to the man at the cart.

"Why, thank you, sir, I don't mind if I do. Hot already, ain't it?" He took the cigarette and placed it behind his ear. "I'm gone save mine," he said.

"Bet you here to see the colored girl they gone electrocute tomorrow. I seen you here before. Ain't that right?" the first man said. I realized I had the "Press" tag tucked above the bill of my cap.

"Yes," I said.

"Heard a white man say, back during the trial, say they gone burn that girl or they gone burn the town of Hampton, what that man say."

"Her attorneys did their best," I said. "Given the circumstances."

"Humph," the man smoking said. "Them attorneys don't matter. Jury, neither. That colored girl killed a white woman in her own house. Say her children even seen it."

"Well," I said. "Her daughters found her corpse."

"Don't matter—seen it, found it," the man at the cart said. "How old them girls, anyways?"

"One's eight. The older girl is thirteen."

"Lord," the first man said, puffing smoke. "It's a good thing they gone burn her. Else it'd be they gone burn *us*, is how it is. That colored girl don't amount to no more than a dog."

"The governor can change her sentence," I said. "Even today, he could grant clemency." The two men looked at me quizzically.

"How old you is, sir, you don't mind me asking?" the first man said.

"Eighteen."

"Well, then, sir," he said. "See, Governor Mann now, he done fought in the war. I just don't see him, being the governor—what you call that, sir, what the governor gone grant?"

"Clemency," I said.

"You two gone jawbone all morning or you gone unload this

wagon?" Another colored man was walking briskly from the prison entrance. He wore the same floppy hat as the other men. His face was stern. "Them trustees got hoops waiting on the shop line," he said. "You niggers best get the move on."

"Yes, sir, boss, we working," the man at the cart said. "Just stopped to catch us a breath." The two men fell back to unloading the staves.

"Morning," I said to the third colored man, flipping my cigarette butt beyond the curb.

"Morning, sir," he said, and nodded.

"Your wagon?" I asked.

"Yes, sir, and they expecting me to show with a load of finished barrels at the mill today. Course, these niggers here, they ain't studying none of that."

"I hope you make it before the rain," I said.

"You right about that, sir. Hot as it is, I expect we get us some storms before noon." He took off his hat and wiped his brow.

"I better get inside," I said.

"Good day to you, sir," he said.

"Good day to you."

I signed in at the guard station at the main gate and started down the walk. I stopped before I was in sight of the next station. Maebelle had made a little lemon cake about the size of my hand and iced it with chocolate. It was wrapped in wax paper. I removed it from my breast pocket and tucked it under my cap.

"Here to see the little nigger girl, Charlie?" the guard said. "Reckon this'll be the last." He grinned. He had a pinched face and pasty skin. His hair was black and so were his eyes. The ends of his mouth turned down. "Stand by the cage." He patted the pockets of my jacket and trousers and ran his hands down my legs to my ankles. "All right, then," he said.

He led me up the flight of stairs to a corridor. At the end was Virginia Christian's cell. The cell door swung open and Mrs. Bradley, the matron, emerged. She was holding a tray. "I'll check with you later, Virgie," she said, looking back in the cell. She had a big ring of keys at her waist. The keys rattled as she reached for the ring. Then she saw me.

"Why, good morning," she said. "Virgie, look who's here."

"Ain't them preachers again, is it?" Virgie asked.

"Lord child, no. They won't be here till evening. It's your friend Charlie, the newspaperman, come to see you."

Mrs. Bradley was a big woman and her skirts about filled the corridor. Her face was heavy and dull but her gray eyes were kind. She had her hair braided and set in a tight bun atop her head. Her big skirts rustled as she moved back to let me in the cell. She closed the door and locked it. "Just an hour, Charlie. That's all today," she said.

The springs on the cot squeaked as Virgie moved to make room for me. They squeaked again when I sat down. We listened to the footfalls as the matron and guard made their way down the corridor. The door at the end of the hall clanged shut.

Virgie's cell was dark but the death chamber across the hall was lit. A man wearing a blue cap and mechanic's overalls was working on an electrical connection on the chair. His elbow hit the enamel chamber pot underneath. It clanked against one of the legs. Virgie started at the sound and so did I. The man moved the pot back in place and continued with his work. The arms and back of the chair were oak and they looked golden in the light. I looked at Virgie as she watched. Her face did not move. Her breathing was steady. When the workman finished what he was attending to, he picked up his carpenter's tray and went out the opposite door of the chamber. He cut off the light.

"Maebelle made you something," I said. "For your birthday."

Virgie stirred. "Miss Harriet's, too," she said. "You remember to get her a present, Mr. Charlie?"

"Yes," I said.

I lifted my cap, exposing the flat parcel atop my head. I put my cap on the cot.

"Well?" I said.

"Well, what?" she said.

I nodded and the parcel fell into my hand.

"Birthday cake." I handed the parcel to her.

"More like birthday pie," she said. She folded back the wax paper. The chocolate icing had stuck and the lemon cake was mush. She grinned. "Looks awful good, Mr. Charlie!" She laughed out loud, then dipped a finger.

I laughed and dipped a finger, too. Maebelle was a genius. The cake was delicious, even wilted.

"What you get Miss Harriet?" she asked.

"A book of poems," I said.

"Mr. Charlie, you got to give up on them books. You get her some flowers or candy, something nice."

"All right," I said. "I'll get some flowers, too."

She dipped in the cake again and licked icing from her finger.

"My momma liked her chocolate. She make her a cake, chocolate through and through, chocolate icing, too. Momma sure could make her a cake, fore she got paralyzed." She paused. "Momma a high-tone woman. You said you seen her. Daddy the dark one. You seen him, too. Seen I take after my daddy. He gone come by this evening, matron say."

She dipped her finger in the cake. "I ain't thought about that. I ain't gone see my momma no more." She smacked her lips and licked a finger. "Tell you the truth, I kind of forgets what she look like. Momma sit in the light just right, though, her eyes turn green. Funny what you remember," she said.

I took another dip of cake, then licked icing from my fingers. I wanted a cigarette. I looked across the hall into the darkened room. "I don't think I really remember Fitz," I said. "I have a picture, and

I take it out and look. I reckon it's the picture I remember now. I brought it here for you, Virgie. It's a present. I wanted something special."

I pulled the photograph from my pocket. "This is Fitzhugh Scott. We called him Fitz."

She lifted a fold of her skirt and carefully wiped each of her fingers. Then she took the picture from my hand. It was curled with the humidity. She cradled it in her palm.

"Why, he look like he gone be President of the United States," she said.

"Yes," I said. "He did."

"I'm gone put this in the Bible them preachers brung me," she said. "Thank you, Mr. Charlie." She reached under the cot, slid out the Bible, and placed the photograph under the front cover. She closed the cover and slid the Bible back.

"Are you afraid?" I asked.

She shook her head.

"You're brave."

She began to fold the wax paper. "I ain't brave. I just ain't afraid."

"I was afraid," I said.

"You mean, with your friend?"

"Yes," I said. "Things might've been different."

"Things just is, Mr. Charlie. That's all I know." She folded the wax paper into a lumpy square. "Your birthday coming up too, ain't it?"

"Yes. The twenty-first."

"Humph," she said. "Me, and Harriet, and you. Guess folks get mighty busy, cold weather coming on." She grinned.

"Oh," I said.

"Mr. Charlie, I believe you blushing. You knows what I'm talking about, don't you?" She giggled. "Is you blushing?"

"I reckon I am," I said. She giggled again. We sat quiet for a while.

"Do you want to pray, Virgie?"

She shook her head slowly. "No, Mr. Charlie, I don't, to tell you the truth. Them preachers gone come back this evening and pray me straight up to heaven and back again, just like they been doing ever night this week."

"All right," I said.

The wax paper rattled as she folded it once more and handed it to me. I placed it in my cap.

"It's not just the preachers, Virgie," I said. "Think of the people who care about you. People who've written the governor, traveled to meet with him, people from all over Virginia, from Atlanta, and Boston, and Chicago. Lawyers and editors, businessmen and teachers, schoolchildren. They've all asked the governor to spare your life. Even Mrs. Terrell took the train straight from the meeting of the National Association of Colored Women's Clubs. Delivered their petition to the governor's hand. And visited you right here in this cell. She's one of the most prominent colored women in the country, Virgie, one of the most prominent women in the world, and she came right here to see you."

"Humph," Virgie said. "That high-tone woman come waltzing in here in her button shoes and ruffles and feathers, wouldn't even sit down, afraid she'd get her dress dirty. She pass for white any day she wanted, Mr. Charlie. She ain't no 'Negress,' like me. I's black as coal!"

"She helped, Virgie. Because of her the governor granted the reprieve. Maybe he'll grant another. There's still time."

"I don't wants no more time, Mr. Charlie," she said. "I wants to go. What girl'd want to live a life in here?"

"Maybe one day you'd be paroled, Virgie. It happens. You can't give up."

"Oh, Mr. Charlie. You always so good. But for a educated white boy, you don't know much." She folded her hands in her lap. "Let's just pass time, Mr. Charlie, like we do. Let's do the alphabet you taught me. Able, Boy, Cast, Dog, Easy, Fox."

I cleared my throat. "George, Have, Item, Jig."

"King, Love, Mike, Nan, Oboe. What 'Oboe' again, Mr. Charlie?"

"A musical instrument."

"These is my favorites," she said, "Pup, Quack, Rush, Sail."

"Tare, Unit, Vice, Watch."

"X-ray, Yoke, Zed. What 'Zed' again?"

"The Greek letter for 'Z.'"

"Dog, Able, Dog Dog, Yoke. 'Daddy.' He say he coming one more time, Mr. Charlie. Say he got the money for the train." She turned and looked out into the hall. "Stop that, Mr. Charlie, else you gone get me to crying, too."

I wiped my face with my hands. A door clanged at the far end of the hall. We listened to the footfalls. I picked up my cap and snugged it to my head with the folded wax paper inside.

"Fitz thought it was like this, Virgie. He said after this life you are on a road, traveling, and sometimes you stop and wait for your friends to catch up."

She grinned. "That why you brung me that picture, Mr. Charlie? So I know Mr. Fitz when I sees him?"

"I hadn't thought that, Virgie. I just wanted you to have it."

"Well, me and Mr. Fitz, we gone hide by that road, Mr. Charlie. And when we sees you coming, we gone jump out and scare the sweet Jesus out of you!" She laughed, bending forward. Her black eyes shone. She laughed again and shook her head, catching her breath. "That's what we gone do!"

"It's time, Charlie," Mrs. Bradley said. She put the key in the cell door and pushed it open. I stood up from the cot. Virgie looked at me. Her face was beaming. She held out her hand.

"So long, Mr. Charlie," she said. "I'll be seeing you."

I took her hand and shook it. Her fingers were warm.

"Virgie, so long!" I said.

I turned and pushed through the cell door. I started to trot down the hall. Behind me I heard the keys rattling. I trotted faster.

"Charlie!" Mrs. Bradley called. "Wait! I have to unlock that one."

I slammed into the steel door and pressed my cheek against it. I clutched at the latch. My throat clenched tight. I felt Mrs. Bradley's hand on my shoulder. I stepped back and saw tears running down her face.

"We've done all we can do, Charlie," she whispered. She banged her key into the lock. She opened the door and closed it after me. I turned and looked back through the grate.

"Thank you," I said. She nodded and wiped her cheek. Then she was gone.

OUTSIDE THE AIR HAD become hotter and even more oppressive. The men with the freight wagon were gone. I pulled off my cap and threw the wax paper by the curb. I put the cap on and pulled it down to shield my eyes. I looked up at the three big cupolas of the penitentiary. There wasn't a cloud in the sky. I looked at the curb. Next to the wax paper were cigarette butts and a pile of dung the mule had left. There were splinters from the oak staves. I started for the trolley stop.

I had already taken a seat before I realized I'd boarded the blackball car. There were two passengers. A lithe, pretty, high-tone girl dressed in a prim black uniform stared at me, annoyed. Then she looked out the window. She was carrying a white, crisply starched apron and cap with ties that fluttered in the air from the window. The other passenger was a grizzled black man in a wide straw hat. He dozed, nodding with the motion of the trolley. His patched denim overalls were clean and freshly ironed.

I looked out a window, too. Not much had been left standing in this part of Richmond after the Union shelling. President Lincoln

himself came to see the city the day after it fell. When they heard
the news, colored people lined his passage, pressing forward to
touch his coat.

Well, it was the Progressive South now. Governor Mann was
a Democrat, and he'd helped his fellow Virginian Wilson to the
Democratic nomination for the presidency. There were factories
and trains. There were mills and forges. There were bridges and
mines. There was scientific agriculture. The new constitution had
cut the voting population of the Commonwealth by half, nearly all
of those removed colored. Jim Crow danced in polling places, courts
civil and criminal, restaurants and diners, trolley cars and passenger
trains. He would dance at the penitentiary tomorrow morning.

The maid and gardener moved toward the door as the trolley
slowed. I kept my seat, pushing my glasses up my nose. I smiled
as they passed. The young woman averted her eyes, while the old
man smiled and nodded.

"A good day, sir," the gardener said. I nodded in return. I stood
and followed them down the steps. I was at the Main Street station.
The boarding call for the Tidewater train echoed from the platform.

Governor Mann had asked Commonwealth's Attorney Montague to review Virgie's case for error. He had ordered Warden Wood
to give the girl a physical examination to determine she was of adult
age. He had denied petitions for clemency from the girl's attorneys,
Newsome and Fields. He had rejected appeals for mercy in letters
from colored and white politicians, schoolteachers, businessmen,
suffragettes, children's welfare groups, pastors, temperance society
leaders, Chicago newspaper editors. He had informed the National
Association for the Advancement of Colored People that he did
not object to their hiring a private investigator to turn up new
facts in the case. He notified a group of concerned physicians in
Chicago that while they were free to send an alienist to determine
the girl's mental competency, he was satisfied of her intelligence.

He had met with William "Habeas Corpus" Anderson, attorney for prizefighter Jack Johnson, at the governor's mansion. He had listened politely to the colored attorney's points, but advised Anderson he was not sufficiently informed of the facts of the case. He had dismissed a notarized plea from the girl's father, signed with an "X," saying that his child had never been a problem to anyone. He had responded by letter to a note penciled on floral notepaper from her crippled mother, begging him to spare her daughter's life. "I am always sorry to see anybody get into trouble," the governor wrote to Mrs. Christian. He dismissed my letters, where I argued Virgie's confession clearly showed the murder was not premeditated, and that life in prison was a harsh and sufficient punishment. Having once been a sitting judge, Governor Mann had reviewed the case himself in point of law. A minister, he prayed fervently about the morality of the sentence. In the end, I believe he felt her execution was inevitable.

I watched the fields and towns and streams pass outside the train window. The sun bleached everything. When the cars pulled into Hampton, Poindexter spotted me from the platform. He pumped me with questions about my visit. I told him I couldn't talk because I had a deadline.

At the trolley stop on Lincoln Street, a colored woman was selling dahlias, ones with big faces painted the colors you would see on carnival clowns. I asked her to pick out the best ones for a birthday present.

"Now is they for your momma or for a pretty young girl?" she asked. "Cause that make a difference."

"A pretty young girl," I said.

She smiled. Her teeth showed white with big gaps in the front. Her face was jet black, and her head was tied in a bright yellow scarf. She reminded me of Red's mother. I had not thought of her in a long time.

I fetched the book of verse from my dresser. I wondered about checking on Lucky with Mrs. Wingate, but decided to wait till morning. She spoiled him so, why not let him enjoy it?

A maid answered the door when I rang at Lewter Hobbs' house. I held the book of verse and the bouquet of dahlias.

"I'm sorry, young man," the maid said. "They went for a drive in the country after Miss Harriet's party. I don't expect them back for a good while. Here, let me take the book, and I'll put those in water for you. Aren't they pretty!" She was fair-skinned and her features were delicate. She looked like a white woman. But there were no white maids in Norfolk.

I walked down to the dock to catch the water ferry back to Hampton. I smoked a cigarette. A brown pelican was perched on one of the pilings. A couple of boys had baitfish in a bucket. They threw a fish in the pelican's direction. It snatched it from the air without losing its perch. The boys laughed and threw another.

18.

Coming Home

That night the preachers prayed with Virgie for two hours. After they left, Mrs. Bradley sat in a rocking chair in the hall by her cell until the girl fell asleep. Although he had promised, Virgie's father did not visit. He did not have money for the train fare.

Friday morning Virgie was awakened at 4:00 a.m. She was given a breakfast of rolls, eggs, and coffee. She ate little. The Reverends S. C. Burrell and William Stokes were with her in her cell. They prayed and read from the scriptures. When Warden J. B. Wood arrived at the penitentiary he came straight to Virgie's cell. A keeper unlocked the door. Mrs. Bradley was overcome with emotion and had not come to work that morning. The warden stepped inside the cell.

"Virginia, it's time," he said. Virgie stood up from her cot. The warden unfolded a paper from his pocket and began to read. "Virginia Christian, you have been found guilty of murder in the first degree by a jury of your peers. It was the consideration of the court dated April 9, 1912, that you are to be electrocuted until you are dead, in the death chamber provided for that purpose within the confines of the penitentiary of this Commonwealth on the 21st day of June 1912, between the hours of six o'clock in the forenoon and six o'clock in the afternoon of that day, which order was suspended by the Governor until July 19, 1912, and August 2, 1912, and again until August 16, 1912, and that execution of the judgment be made and done by the superintendent of the said penitentiary or some assistant or assistants designated by him according to law, on this, the 16th day of August A.D. 1912. May God have mercy on your soul." He folded the paper and replaced it in his pocket. "Do you have any final words?"

She shook her head.

One of the preachers offered her a Bible. She refused it. The warden stepped through the cell door and Virgie followed. The preachers fell in behind, but she turned and motioned for them to stay. She walked into the death chamber behind the warden, alone. After she sat down in the chair, she watched her attendants as they fixed leather straps to her legs and arms. A witness said she showed "small concern." When the straps were in place, the witness said she looked up and "smiled, really smiled." Then an attendant whispered to her. She turned, and he showed her a black hood. She nodded, and he placed the hood over her face. The attendant stepped back. The warden raised his hand.

When the warden dropped his hand, an attendant threw the switch. At 7:26 a.m. and thirty seconds, 1,750 volts of electricity at ten amperes coursed through her body. As the electricity convulsed her arms and legs and contorted her torso, she shrieked. Witnesses said the attendants stepped back in horror. Virgie had inhaled just as the switch was thrown. Heated air in her lungs was exploding over her vocal cords. The shriek gave way to a moan.

Residents in the Fan district near the Tredegar Iron Works complained their lights dimmed and flickered. After thirty seconds the charge was turned off. Virgie was gone.

Witnesses said there was an odor, and one of the penitentiary surgeons hesitated by the death chamber door, covering his nose and mouth with his hand. That was Dr. Herbert Mann, the governor's son. The surgeons examined Virgie's body. She was pronounced dead four and a half minutes later. Warden Wood sent word to the governor's mansion.

A handwritten note was discovered in Virgie's cell after the execution. It read, "I know that I am getting no more than I deserve. I'm prepared to answer for my sins. I believe the Lord has forgiven me." Of course this was an invention of the preachers. Yet the papers reported it, including the *Times-Herald*.

A Chicago newspaper described a chamber of horrors. The *Evening World* claimed Virgie's "pitiful cries for aid filled the hardened guards with sorrow" as she was escorted to the death chamber. When the current was applied, "Virginia's hair sizzled and soon her head was a mass of flames."

Mayor Jones was worried about "rabble-rousing" and had asked Sheriff Curtis to post extra deputies on the streets of Hampton and Phoebus the evening of the execution. Despite the mayor's concerns, there were no disturbances.

Henry Christian did not have money to transport his daughter's remains from Richmond back to Hampton. Warden Wood's orders were to release the body to the Medical College of Virginia, but A. D. Price, a Negro undertaker in Richmond, intervened. George Fields may have requested his services. Price knew Fields. Both were born into slavery in Hanover County.

Price told a Richmond paper that when his morticians removed the winding sheet from Virgie's body there was slight bruising on her right temple, probably from the electrode. He said her hair "may have been trimmed"—he wasn't certain. He said the expression on her face was peaceful. In a cloth bag of her personal effects was a Bible with a photograph of an unidentified white man, a picture book, a telephony chart with drawings, some candy, and toiletries. After her body had been prepared, Price had his men take her to the Main Street station in Richmond. Poindexter was on duty when her remains arrived on a freight car at the C&O depot Saturday evening. He sent a boy over to my rooms with a message.

Poindexter said the Negro undertaker in Hampton had loaded the casket in a wagon hearse at the depot but Frank Rees signed and paid for the transport from Richmond out of his own pocket.

"Heard him say he's paying for the burial, too," Poindexter said.

I DECIDED TO VISIT Mr. Rees at his establishment. He was clipping blooms from a bed of dahlias on the north side of his building. He shook his head slowly as he saw me coming.

"I ought to've remembered you talk with Poindexter a good bit," he said. "Look at this one, Charlie." He held a scarlet dahlia with white points toward me. It was the size of a pie plate.

"I just bought dahlias as a present, Mr. Rees," I said. "They were pretty, but not as pretty as these."

"North side. A little sun in the morning, shade in the afternoon. Otherwise, the heat gets them." He added the blossom to others in a half-gallon Mason jar. "I reckon you're wondering why I'm paying that colored girl's expenses. Well, we both know her parents don't have the money. Heard Mr. Christian offered the deed to his house to the lawyers for their services, but they refused. Anyway, the girl deserves a place of rest, same as anybody, colored or white. That's all. I'd appreciate it if you'd keep my part out of the record, though. Gets out, the bereaved of every Tom, Dick, and Harry in Hampton Roads will want a cheap rate to plant their dear departed in the ground." He cocked his head. "Seems like this girl's weighing on your mind, Charlie."

"Yes, sir."

"Then I'll give you my two cents," he said. "Head on over to your office and write up your story. Go home tonight and say your prayers. I'd tell you to take you a nip before you turn in, but I know you ain't a drinking man. Then get up tomorrow morning and go to work. Do your job, same as always. That colored girl's life didn't amount to much and when you consider it, neither will yours nor mine. We all end up the same way. First Baptist Church cemetery. That's where I found her a plot. Service is graveside at two o'clock tomorrow. I'd bring an umbrella. It'll storm for sure, hot as it's been."

I jotted a couple of notes for the Sunday *Times-Herald* walking home. I had supper with Lucky. Then we went for a walk. When we got back to my rooms, I drank a glass of buttermilk Maebelle had left in the icebox and went to bed.

THAT SUNDAY I ATTENDED church services again. When I came home, Lucky was lying in front of the door in the last sliver of shade on the porch. His tail thumped the floorboards. I took him inside and gave him one of Maebelle's bacon biscuits and some water. Then I took him downstairs under the stoop where he would have shade all afternoon and shelter if it stormed. He scratched a shallow bowl in the earth and curled up. I thought about eating something but didn't have the appetite. I sat at the foot of the stairs and smoked.

A pair of blue jays snarled and fussed in the magnolia tree in front of Mrs. Wingate's house. The electric lines for the trolley sizzled in the heat. White clouds billowed over the Roads. My umbrella was inside the kitchen door, but I felt too lazy to walk back upstairs to retrieve it.

"Stay, Lucky," I said. He was already snoozing. I set out for King Street.

I had forgotten the old yew tree. It towered behind the Negro church near the entrance to the graveyard and its shade was a blessing. Virgie's grave lay at the edge of its shadow. The gravediggers had covered the earth with a green tarpaulin. They were leaning with their shovels against the trunk of the tree. Near them was Mrs. Wright. She was holding hands with Sadie and Harriet on either side. Mrs. Wright smiled when she saw me and so did Harriet. Sadie called, "Charlie!" Mrs. Wright raised a finger to her lips to shush her and retook Sadie's hand. I took a few steps into the graveyard from the street.

The hearse was pulled up at the narrow gate behind the church. The harness jangled when the mule shook its head and stamped at flies. Four pallbearers in suits were carrying the pine casket toward the grave. It looked small, even when I remembered how small Virgie had been. Behind the casket shuffled two young men, so light-skinned they could pass for white, one whose close-cropped head glistened gold in the light. They strained against the wood handles of what looked to be an old military hospital litter. Lying on her elbow on the litter was a big woman, olive-skinned, like the boys. She must have weighed three hundred pounds. She was wearing a green dress with big yellow flowers like birds of paradise. She was crying, and when she sobbed, the boys staggered to keep the load balanced. This was Charlotte Christian, Virgie's mother. I'd caught a glimpse of her inside the house on Wine Street as the deputies brought Virgie out to the street.

"Oh my baby," she wailed. A dark little girl, who looked to be about Sadie's age, was stroking Mrs. Christian's hand. Behind the litter two small dark-skinned boys followed, holding hands, their heads bowed. At the end of the procession was Virgie's father, Henry Christian. He wore a suit jacket over pressed dungarees and a white shirt, his black face twisted and gleaming. He hesitated when he saw Mrs. Wright and the Belote girls, and then he nodded toward them, nodding again as he approached the grave.

The Baptist preacher from the church waited at the graveside. He wore a black robe and purple mantle. He tucked the Bible under his arm and helped the pallbearers straighten the casket on sawhorses spanning the grave. Then he waited for the boys to lower Mrs. Christian's litter to the ground. The family lined up by the grave. Mrs. Christian sobbed loudly and then was quiet. The preacher began to speak. He said that God's plan was beyond our understanding, as was His grace and mercy, and that the angels were young and beautiful, and now Virgie was a child among them, young and beautiful and bright-shining as the angels themselves. Then he enjoined everyone in prayer. He asked Jesus to forgive our sins just as He had forgiven Virgie her sins, and to receive our souls into heaven just as He had received Virgie's. Then he said, "Amen."

I did not expect him to be so brief. No one did. We all blinked our eyes against the light. Maybe the nature of the thing and the heat had dampened the preacher's spirits, too.

Or maybe it was the growl of thunder I heard to the east. The white clouds had billowed higher, their towers flattened into anvils at the base. The sun was bright. I waited until the preacher had shaken hands with all the members of the Christian family. The two small boys started to cry. Mrs. Wright took the girls from the tree to the Christians, and they bent and shook hands, and nodded, and the girls kissed Mrs. Christian on the cheek, first Harriet, then Sadie. I started to walk toward the group, glad to be in the shade.

Sadie ran to me and hugged me and I took her hand and walked on.

"I had the girls for church today," Mrs. Wright said. "I decided to bring them. I don't think Uncle Lewter needs to know." She took my hand, then embraced me. Harriet hugged me, too.

"Mr. Charlie, I appreciate you coming," Mr. Christian said. "These tall boys is Charlotte's," he said. "From fore we was married. Thomas the oldest, he helps me with my work. And Chester, here, why he a streetcar driver. Then Irena, here, is mine, and Purcell, and Henry—he five year old now? Yes, five. Henry, you got to stop that crying now. Hush, son. You got to act big." Mr. Christian picked the boy up and held him against his chest. "Then, of course, Virgie's the oldest, of the ones that's mine." He looked off toward the church. "I mean, she was." He rubbed the back of Henry's head.

"And this my wife Charlotte," Mr. Christian said. "Virgie's

momma." He bent at the waist, the boy's legs dangling from his arms. "Charlotte, this here's Mr. Charlie. He a friend of Virgie's, when she in jail."

Mrs. Christian smiled. She was a pretty woman, with smooth skin and white teeth. Virgie had been right. When her mother turned in the light, her eyes were green.

"I'm sorry for you to see me like this," she said. "I don't get out of the house."

"I'm very sorry for your loss, Mrs. Christian," I said.

"Mr. Charlie the man writes for the newspaper," Mr. Christian said. "The one Virgie always was talking to."

Mrs. Christian's eyes narrowed. "The one wrote she was a nigger?" she asked. "After my little girl told him how Mrs. Belote hit her with the chamber pot and made her mad, my little girl telling him the truth, trying to get him to help her? I didn't raise my children to be struck by nobody, white or colored, less it was their father or me. Call my child 'nigger.'" She glared up at me from the litter. Her face was red.

"Mr. Charlie don't have nothing to do with that, Charlotte," Mr. Christian said. "Was his boss. Man can't do nothing about his boss. Why, Mr. Charlie wrote letters to the governor himself, trying to help Virgie."

"What you wrote, ain't that what you think of all of us? Niggers!" she screamed.

"Charlotte!" Mr. Christian said. Little Henry started to wail.

"I'm very sorry for your loss, Mrs. Christian," I said. I began to back away. I felt lightheaded. I turned and walked toward the street.

"Charlie!" I heard Harriet call. "Charlie!"

I WALKED TO KING Street and crossed, then turned at the corner. The wind gusted ahead of the storm. I loosened my collar. The cool air felt good.

A bolt of lightning lit up the sky as I reached the iron steps at Mrs. Wingate's. The steps rattled with thunder. Lucky scurried out from under the stoop, squinting against the rain. He trotted up the steps with me. As soon as I opened the door, he ran into the far room and crawled under the bed. His back legs splayed out under the edge of the cover. His tail was still.

My jacket was soaked through. I took it off and hung it on a kitchen chair. I took a cigarette from the pack in my jacket pocket. The pack was damp. I put it on the table to dry. I lit the cigarette with a match from a can on the stove and drew hard. The paper stuck to my fingertips. I walked out to the porch.

The storm was blowing from Mrs. Wingate's side of the building. Looking across the yard was like looking through a window of rain. The wind swirled onto the porch in the lee, lifting the water plummeting from the edge of the roof into flimsy, glittering chains. I huddled against the brick wall. A man ran along the sidewalk, the tails of his jacket fluttering. The wind blew off his hat. He stooped to retrieve it, then ran on.

In the time I smoked the damp cigarette, the wind stopped, and then the rain. Mist rose from the sidewalk. Mrs. Wingate's lawn was littered with twigs and magnolia leaves. Presently I heard the belling call of a wood thrush, then saw him scratching among the azaleas at the foundations of the house. The clouds began to break. Light gilded the rooftops along Lincoln Street.

I went inside. I could see Lucky's feet still splayed out under the bed, but I could hear his tail thumping.

"Here boy, here boy," I said.

He backed slowly out from under the bed, rose and shook himself, then walked into the kitchen. I fixed him a bowl of food and freshened his water. When he finished his meal, I let him outside. He trotted down the steps, waiting at the stoop. I fixed his leash to his collar. Mrs. Wingate was inspecting her garden. One of her rose trellises had blown over. She raised her hand and waved.

"Do you want any help with that, Mrs. Wingate?" I called.

"No, Charlie, thank you. Marcellus will take care of it in the morning."

I nodded to her. Lucky smiled and pranced, laying his ears back. I decided we would see if the gravediggers had beat the storm.

We set out for King Street at a good pace, though Lucky stopped to mark every mailbox or gate post and clump of debris clotting the street sewers. A chickadee was perched on a wisteria arbor by the street, its feathers ruffled and wet. It shrugged its wings and called, "Dee dee, dee dee," then flew.

The air was washed clean. The sky was curved and blue, cirrus clouds catching the golden light of the sun. I heard nighthawks and stopped Lucky to watch their silhouettes spin against the dome of the sky. We moved on. Two colored boys carrying cane poles and a shiny bait can were walking toward us. When they saw Lucky, one of them clucked his lips. They got off the sidewalk, watching from the trolley tracks until we had passed. I stayed on King Street until we reached the church. I wanted to go into the cemetery through the gate by the yew.

Lucky snuffled at the ground where the mule had stood. Fat drops of water dripped from the tree when the breeze stirred its limbs. We walked to Virgie's grave. The men had done their work. A mound of sandy earth rose just above the clipped grass of the graveyard. At the head of the grave a little wooden cross had tipped over in the storm. I shortened my purchase on the leash, so Lucky couldn't track the bare earth. I knelt and set the cross upright and smoothed with my hand the rivulets the rain had cut. Lucky lowered his head and lifted his ears to watch. Mr. Rees was right. Nobody's life amounted to much.

19.

Changes

Monday mornings were hard for Mr. Hobgood. Usually he'd tied a good one on, sometimes one that had lasted the weekend. His eyes looked like someone had pulled them from the sockets and stuck them back in his head. His mug was straight hair of the dog, not a hint of coffee.

"Sit down, Mears, sit down," he said.

"Thank you, Mr. Hobgood," I said.

"So that's it, then?" he said, rubbing a cheek to see if he'd shaved.

"Yes, sir."

"Buried and in the ground?"

"Yes, sir."

"You did a good job, Mears. Except for Pace scooping you on the confession."

"Yes, sir."

"You did the kind of job can make a young fellow's career."

"Yes, sir."

He emptied the mug, his hand shaking. He set the mug down on his desk, harder than he meant to.

"Now it's back to nigger knife fights and the occasional drowning," he said.

"Yes, sir."

"To wrap up, I'd say start at the mayor's office. No doubt he'll have a statement. Dignity and honor of the community. Peace in the streets. Good relations between the races. You know, the usual."

"Yes, sir." I stood. "Mr. Hobgood? After today, I wondered if I might take a couple of days off. Say till Saturday. I could cover the weekend."

He looked startled. He rubbed the stubble of his chin.

"It's been a while, hasn't it, Mears? Need some time to piece things together?"

"Yes, sir."

"Well, go on, then," he said. "Turn in your work this afternoon, and we'll see you Saturday morning."

"Thank you, Mr. Hobgood."

I decided I would take the train to Jerusalem. I wanted to visit Mother's grave. I had been part of a vile injustice. I longed to feel clean. And free.

Mrs. Wingate said she would be happy to look after Lucky for a couple of days.

"Thank you, ma'am," I said. "I'll bring him over in the morning, if that will be all right."

"Of course, Charlie," she said.

I packed a satchel with two shirts and a change of underwear and socks. I had a supper of cold fried ham and slaw Maebelle had left in the icebox. Then I fed Lucky. It was hot in my rooms, so I sat with him on the porch reading until daylight was gone. There was a light breeze. I closed my book. I watched passersby on Lincoln Street, the coming and going of the trolleys. I scratched Lucky's chest. He stretched and yawned. In a while he began to snore. I listened, stroking his neck. I smoked one more cigarette before waking him to go inside. I latched the screen door.

I stretched out atop the sheets. A little air moved. It was still hot. I closed my eyes and tried to remember Virgie's face. The details were fading. The memory of her voice was fading, too. I thought of

Harriet's face. It too was fading. I wondered when I would see her again. Her uncle's pretense for not allowing it was that I reminded her of the murder, so it was better for me not to call on her.

In the morning I got an early start so I could walk to the depot. I fed Lucky and left him with Mrs. Wingate. She had a boiled ham hock wrapped in butcher's paper. She held it open. He took the hock, trotted to the garden, and lay down. He started to gnaw. Mr. Wingate's retrievers whimpered from the porch, watching.

"Hush, you two," Mrs. Wingate said, crinkling the paper. "You've had yours. Where are you headed, Charlie?"

"Southampton County," I said.

"When shall we expect you?"

"Friday evening, ma'am."

"You mustn't brood, Charlie. When Mr. Wingate passed, I sometimes found my mind turning dark. You're too young."

"Yes, ma'am."

THE LAND FLATTENED AND spread to the horizon beyond the track. From the window of the passenger car I could see fields full of cotton and flax and tobacco and peanuts. I saw ink-black Negroes clothed in bright colors resting in the shade of paradise trees in the fencerows. Others worked in the sun, trimming tobacco suckers, stopping to wipe the sweat from their faces. Light glinted on the blades of their hawk's bill knives. Big houses hulked in the fields, shimmering in the heat as telegraph poles whipped past the window.

Jerusalem was as I remembered it, though I did not recognize many faces. I slung my satchel over my shoulder and stepped down to the platform. Some white men were sitting on a bench in the shade with their backs to the brick wall of the depot, chewing tobacco and swatting at flies. They nodded in greeting. One spat in a paper cup. I stood in the shade with them and smoked a cigarette. Then I went next door to the drugstore and had a chicken salad sandwich and a Coca-Cola at the counter. I bought a pack of Lucky Strikes. The proprietor gave me a book of matches with the address of the drugstore stamped on the back. There were silk poppies with wire stems in a jar on the counter by the register. I picked out six, two each in red, pink, and yellow. The proprietor had dark green wrapping paper. He arranged the poppies carefully in a spray with the paper. I tucked it in my satchel.

A "Rooms To Let" shingle was hanging in the yard of a house across the street from the drugstore. I rented a room with a dry sink for the night. The room was on the corner of the house so the windows gave a good cross breeze. I took out the silk flowers and left the satchel on the chair by the bed.

My shoes were coated with white dust from the road. Dog flies had tormented me whenever I stopped in the shade. I scratched at a welt they had left on the back of my neck. I stepped on stones to cross Flag Run. The windows of Miss Quesinberry's schoolhouse were boarded up. A support at the far corner of the porch was missing and the shingled roof sagged. A fat brown snake slithered through the tall grass where I stood into the shade under the porch.

I smiled. Miss Quesinberry was deathly afraid of snakes. One morning a blacksnake dropped from a roof beam onto the floor of the classroom as Miss Quesinberry was showing us long division at the black board. She shrieked and clambered atop her desk, revealing a fair amount of her undergarments. At first there was a stunned silence. Then the girls began to giggle and the boys snickered and slapped each other on the back.

Miss Quesinberry's face was purple with screaming. She had her eyes covered with her hands. Red got out of his desk and pinched his finger and thumb behind the blacksnake's head. He grabbed its tail with his other hand. Then he carried the snake outside and took his place back at his desk.

"All that hollering, snake done made it far as Georgia, Miss Quesinberry," he said. "I reckon you safe."

I walked to the back of the building. The elbow of a stovepipe hung from a wire; the tin pipe had long since corroded away. There was a little shade, so I smoked a cigarette. The smoke seemed to bother the dog flies.

When I finished the cigarette, I started for the cluster of shacks where Red lived with his mother. Bees droned in the chicory and daisies along the path. A breeze stirred. The sun glared in the sky. I wiped my brow with a sleeve.

Sarah's little shack stood just as I remembered it, across from the railroad tracks. Flames licked the bottom of a black, steaming kettle behind the shack. Bright white sheets and flowered pillowcases hung from a long clothesline tied between two trees. A tall woman was gathering a sheet from the line. She carefully folded it into a basket. Though she wore no brightly colored headscarf, for a moment I thought it was Sarah. But this woman was young. When she spotted me, she stiffened and stood still. She studied me, then shrugged and started to take another sheet from the line.

"Rose Ella!" she called. "You gets to ironing these here sheets. Miss Effie gone be looking for them in no time."

A door clapped shut and a colored girl about ten years old trotted toward the woman. Her hair was tied up in braids. She picked up the basket and went inside the shack. The woman raised a hand to shield her eyes from the sun. She studied me a minute longer.

"Sir?" she said. "You want you some water? You looking mighty dry."

"Yes, I would," I said. "Thank you."

She went into the house and returned with a big ladle. "Got spring water just this morning," she said. "For the washing." She handed me the ladle. I tilted it and drank, trying not to spill. She motioned at the flowers I was holding. "Those for your girlfriend?" she asked.

I finished the water and handed her the ladle. "Oh, no," I said. "For my mother."

"She live round here?"

"For her grave," I said. She nodded solemnly. "You know, I visited this house many times when I was a boy. A woman named Sarah lived here. Her boy Red was my friend."

I heard a child giggle and looked at the back door. The girl who had retrieved the basket was holding a little boy. A little girl peeked around her hip.

"You get back to that ironing, Rose Ella," the woman said. "You take them children, too." They scampered back inside. "I don't know no Sarah," she said. "But then, I ain't lived here that long."

"Thank you for the water," I said.

I tucked the silk flowers in my pocket and walked around the front of Sarah's shack to the narrow road that ran parallel to the railroad tracks. On the other side a colored boy was leading a fyce tied with a string. He stopped to let some other boys admire it. They dropped to their haunches and held out their hands. The dog yapped and snarled and bit one boy's finger. The boy howled and ran away. Then the other boys scattered.

"Told you niggers not to be poking no fingers at Goliath," the boy with the fyce said. "He don't like it." He tugged at the string. "Come on, boy," he said. The fyce pranced along at his heels.

Walking toward me on the road was a buxom black woman. She was barefoot and her feet were coated with dust. She wore a red bandanna knotted at her forehead. A strap on her dress had fallen onto the arm she had wrapped around a little girl riding on her hip. The woman staggered a little. Walking by her was a skinny boy, tall enough to reach her shoulder. He steadied her, and they continued walking. A cigarette dangled from the woman's lip. She was staring at me. Her eyes were glassy. I could smell the alcohol on her breath. Her face was empty and dull.

"You looking for something?" she asked. "White man, you need you something?"

"Momma, hush!" the skinny boy hissed. I kept walking. She stopped and stared. The boy took her arm, trying to get her moving. After I passed, I heard a shout.

"I know who you is!" she called. "You Red's Charlie."

I stopped and turned.

"You Red's Charlie," she said. The cigarette fell from her lip.

"Alreda?" I asked.

"Come on, Momma," the boy said.

"Yes, Alreda," she said.

"Momma," the boy said.

"You the one need to hush," she said. "This here man a friend of mine." The boy released her arm. The little girl on her hip blinked her watery eyes and puckered her lips.

"You ain't got no whiskey, has you, Mr. Charlie?"

"No, Alreda, I don't. I thought you moved away."

"Did. But Daddy got sick, so I come back to help Momma take care of him. He gone now, though."

"What about Red?"

"Stay in trouble after his momma die," she said. "Something won't right in his head, you ask me. Last time the sheriff come, we ain't seen no Red since."

"Handsome children," I said.

She nodded at the boy. "This here Marcus, and this Jasmine." She bounced the little girl. The girl cooed and blinked.

"And your husband?"

"Husband," she said. "I ain't studying no husband. Has you got a cigarette, Mr. Charlie?"

"Yes, Alreda, I do. I have nearly a pack. I have matches, too." I took the cigarettes from my pocket and pressed the match book against the pack. I held them out to her. She cupped her hand over mine and lifted her chin. She closed her eyes.

"You one sweet white man," she said. She took the pack and matches and tucked them in her bosom. She looked at her son. Her eyes seemed not to focus. "Marcus say he gone help his momma find something to drink, ain't that right, Marcus?"

"You don't need nothing more to drink, Momma," the boy said.

"Let's go, then," she said. "I see you, Mr. Charlie."

"See you, Alreda."

BY THE TIME I reached the farmhouse the sky was lavender. Mist was rising over the fields. The house was painted and in good repair. A neat picket fence separated the yard from the road. At the side of the house two white boys were having a game of catch. A woman came out on the porch, drying her hands on her apron, and called them inside. The porch door clapped shut. Someone lit an oil lamp in the window. I thought of the summer evenings I had sat with my mother on that porch.

"Hear the katydids, Charles?" she would say. "They're whispering, 'Autumn's here, winter, too; autumn's here, winter, too.'" She smiled and ran her fingers through my hair.

I passed by the house and stopped at the graveyard at the edge of the field. The cotton bolls were just beginning to open. My mother's stone was smaller than I remembered. Cut in white granite, it shone bright as the cotton in the gloaming. I took the silk poppies from my pocket. The flowers and the paper were flattened. I spruced them a little with my fingertips and placed them at the base of her headstone. I bowed my head and said a prayer. I thanked my mother for her love and for teaching me God's love. I thanked her for the life she and the creator had given me. I asked God to bless her soul and comfort her. I asked her to know I would never forget her as I knew she would never forget me. Amen.

I looked out across the fields, blue deepening in the east.

"Mother, I feel lost," I whispered. I sat down by her grave and wept. I could feel the white dust of the road on my face. I saw it on my shoes, the cuffs of my trousers. I watched a great blue heron beat its wings across the field, heading for its roost in a far grove. I put my hand on her stone. It was warm from the sun. In the trees and grass, the katydids ratcheted.

BY THE TIME I reached Jerusalem, my legs and feet were aching. I took the pitcher from the dry sink down the hall for water. I brought the pitcher back to my room and poured two big glassfuls and drank them down, one after the other. I wiped the dust from my eyeglasses and placed them atop the bureau. I poured water in the basin and washed my face and hands. I took off my shirt and rinsed my torso. I took my coat and trousers to an open window and shook them out. I cut off the light and flopped on the bed. The pillow smelled of rosemary. I said a prayer for the soul of Virginia Christian. A prayer for Harriet. And for Lucky. Then I was asleep.

The nattering of sparrows woke me. I went to the window. The flock flew from a trumpet vine bower by the gate. I looked at the clock on the bureau. It was eight. I'd slept for more than twelve hours! I splashed water on my face and shaved. I took the fresh shirt and underwear from the satchel and put them on. I wiped the dust from my shoes with the old underwear and stuffed it and the shirt in the satchel. I rinsed my glasses and put them on. I'd forgotten a comb. My cowlick spread up to the top of my head. I tamed it as best I could with water.

The landlady had corn muffins and bacon on the dining room table. There was coffee in a pot on a trivet. I put my satchel by a chair and poured coffee into a cup and drank. Then I wolfed down a muffin.

"Well, young man, you must've had a long day," the landlady said, pushing through the kitchen door.

"Yes, ma'am," I said.

"Sit down, sit down," she said. "Is that enough bacon?"

"Oh, yes, ma'am."

"Well, I'm off to market, then. Would you stay another night?"

"No ma'am, my train for Hampton's at one."

"Safe journey, then."

"Thank you, ma'am."

I finished my breakfast and went back to the drugstore for a pack of cigarettes. I had time for a brisk walk back out near the farm. I wanted to see if I could find the old man's cabin before I left Jerusalem.

I was sure I was near the right spot on the road so I doubled back. This time I saw one of the foundation stones. Everything was grown over with honeysuckle vine and greenbriers. A mockingbird scolded and flew from its perch. I walked to the back side of the tangle. I could see the charred remains of a log. There were a few pieces of rusted tin scattered about. I found a big stick and beat on the tin to scare any snakes. Then I turned it over. There was ash underneath, a rusted tin can or two. I turned another. There was a rusty cook pot. Something glinted. A shard of mirror. I turned over the last section of tin. A copperhead. The snake coiled, then retreated. I poked around in the ashes, certain I would find the bone. After a while, I threw the stick down. Maybe I had imagined it, after all. Maybe I had even imagined the old man.

I bought a newspaper at the depot and read it waiting for the train. On the trip back I dozed, smoking a cigarette between naps. It was near nightfall by the time I got to Mrs. Wingate's. Lucky made over me like I was the second coming, whimpering and gamboling and butting his thick head against my knees.

"Welcome home, Charlie," Mrs. Wingate said. "He's been fed."

"I'm sure he has, ma'am. Thank you."

She smiled and nodded. "Good night, Charlie."

"Good night, Mrs. Wingate."

I climbed the iron stairs and dropped my satchel in front of the screen door and listened. The katydids hadn't yet started in Hampton. There was just the drone of the cicadas. A fat moth whacked against the screen. Lucky looked up at me and whined.

"All right, boy," I said. When I opened the screen door a flat parcel tumbled onto the porch. I picked it up. The parcel had the heft of a book and I could feel an envelope taped to the side. I picked up the satchel and opened the door. Lucky trotted in and sat in front of the icebox. I flipped the light switch.

"Don't you think Mrs. Wingate's spoiled you enough?" I asked. Lucky looked at the icebox, then at me, then at the icebox. I laid the parcel on the table.

"All right," I said. "I'm sure Maebelle's left you something." There were two pieces of fried fatback on a plate. I set the plate on the floor. Lucky scarfed down the fatback. I sat at the table and pulled the envelope free. There was a little card printed with violets.

"Happy Birthday, Charlie!" the note read. "Pauline promised she'd deliver this for me, since the ferry takes far more time than I could get away from the house. A man at the bookstore said everybody's reading this. He's a new author. I hope you like it. Perhaps one day you and I will find the Surprise Valley, too. Love, Harriet."

I unfolded the brown paper wrapping. On the dust jacket of the book a woman and a man were riding horseback in high brush. The woman wore a long coat and thick leather gloves, but her head was bare. "Riders of the Purple Sage" was the title. "By Zane Grey."

SATURDAY MORNING I WALKED into the *Times-Herald* office. There was a wood table pushed up next to my desk and Pace was sitting in a ladder-back chair at the table, typing on the Remington Mr. Hobgood usually kept at his desk.

"Charlie?" Pace said. "Where've you been?"

"I took some time off," I said. "What are you doing here?"

"I work here," Pace said.

"That's funny," I said. I plucked a pencil from behind his ear. "Is this mine?"

"It was in the drawer," he said.

"Then it's mine," I said. "Where's Mr. Hobgood?"

He looked over at Mr. Hobgood's big rolltop, then out the window into the street.

"Well?"

He put his hands on the desk on either side of the Remington.

"I would've thought you'd heard, Charlie," he said.

"Heard what?"

"About Mr. Hobgood and all. Drowning in his bathtub."

It was like a punch to the gut. I must've taken a step back, because Pace rose and put a hand on my elbow. When my mind cleared, I ran for the door, flung it open, and ran down the street toward Sheriff Curtis' office.

He was sitting at his desk with his feet up as I burst through the door. He looked me over top to bottom.

"It's so, Charlie," he said. He put his feet down. "Landlady called over here, complaining about water running. Couldn't get nobody to answer the door. I sent Chas over. He's the one found him. Whiskey bottle right by the tub. Near as Chas could tell, he just passed out drunk. That's what Dr. V thought, too. Accidental drowning. Chas sent R. D. looking for you, so you'd have the straight story, and Mrs. Wingate told R. D. you was out of town. Come on in here, son, and sit down. You look all done in."

20.

These Truths

"We hold these truths to be self-evident, that all men are created equal, that they are endowed by their Creator with certain unalienable Rights, that among these are Life, Liberty and the pursuit of Happiness." Plummer Bernard Young, owner and editor of the *Norfolk Journal and Guide,* paused from reading aloud to adjust his glasses. He was a young man, but his hair receded nearly to the crown of his head, a widow's peak barely holding its own.

"How difficult it is for any Negro in Virginia to hear those words today," he continued. "Some may listen stoically, but each day I fear, many will react with despair or rage. This is especially true for any person of color who reflects on the case of Virginia Christian . . . Didn't your paper publish her confession?" Mr. Young asked. He pursed his lips. His moustache was neatly groomed.

"Yes, sir. I interviewed her at the Elizabeth City County jail."

"In violation of her rights, as her appeal was in process?" He looked at me over the frames of his glasses. His eyes were keen as a hawk's.

"Yes, sir." I shifted in my chair and the arm squeaked.

He shook his head slowly. Then he continued. "Certainly, her pursuit of happiness was short-lived. When her mother became an invalid and could work no longer, the girl was removed from school.

At the age of thirteen, she took a position as the washerwoman for the employer her mother had served for ten years. The money she could earn was necessary to help her father feed her family. The labor was dull and her employer abusive. Though the Commonwealth was charged with this girl's education and welfare, the lack of opportunity for the members of her family, their grinding need for mere food and shelter, overwhelmed the state's obligations. So much for Virginia Christian's right to pursue happiness.

"As for her unalienable right to liberty, the Commonwealth failed her there, too. She was arrested little more than an hour after her employer had been murdered, with the officers making no mention of the reason she was being taken into custody. She was charged with a capital offense by a grand jury within days, tried in a superior court of the Commonwealth less than a month after the crime, found guilty by a jury of her 'peers,' white male voters, in thirty minutes' time, after a trial lasting just over one day. Justice is surely swift in Virginia, especially for the Negro. Immediately upon her conviction, the Commonwealth's sitting judge pronounced the sentence of death by electrocution at the state penitentiary in Richmond, where the girl was remanded. So much for Virginia Christian's right to liberty.

"Now we are left with her primary unalienable right, the right to life. After a failed appeal by her attorneys in the courts and numerous pleas from the public, the governor of the Commonwealth, the man squarely responsible for her welfare, who after granting stays of execution, ultimately denied her right to life. Less than five months after her crime was committed, the day after her seventeenth birthday, she was electrocuted in a chair modified to accommodate her small size. Her execution was directly countermanded under Section 289 of the constitution of the Commonwealth, which states that no child under the age of eighteen shall suffer such a fate. So much for Virginia Christian's unalienable right to life.

"What ideal demanded this life, the life of a lonely, abused, illiterate Negro child? What system of government demanded its citizens stand silently by while this 'justice' was perpetrated? Is this the system of government Mr. Jefferson described nearly seven score years ago, a government where all men are created equal?

"In God's love, let us answer, black and white alike, 'No!' Let us bridge the divide between races and restore our souls and the souls of our children. Let us show Virginia Christian that her life accounted for something more beautiful and precious than she could ever imagine."

Mr. Young removed his glasses and rubbed the bridge of his nose.

"Well, you can write," he said. "Have you shown this to your new editor?"

"No. They brought in another reporter to cover my beat. I don't know why. Maybe the publisher thought they needed to clean house. Anyway, you know, Mr. Young, better than I, the *Times-Herald* would never run this piece."

"Thacker's the owner, isn't he?"

"Yes, sir."

"Financial problems, from what I hear. And Hobgood . . ." He tapped his fingers on the desk. "A sad case. He was a good enough man, in his way."

"Yes, sir."

"No, Mr. Mears, you're right. Thacker's interest is selling papers, not causes. Certainly not Negro causes."

"No, sir."

He put his glasses on and looked out the window. "So you want me to hire you here? To work for the *Journal and Guide*?"

"Yes, sir."

"How could I justify that? To hire you ahead of a colored reporter? On a newspaper owned by a colored man, written for a colored readership? That's not reasonable, Mr. Mears." He picked up the typed pages, carefully tapping the edges square, and held them out to me.

"Mr. Young," I said. "Every black person in the Tidewater looks up to you. Someone has to start building bridges. And not just in the white community."

He laid the typed pages on his desk pad and leaned back in his chair. He rubbed his right temple with two fingers. "I didn't get much sleep last night. My wife delivered another son."

"God's blessings, Mr. Young."

He sighed. "Call me P. B. Everybody does. I'm not that much older than you anyway. Makes me feel like a relic. I'll call you Charlie, if that's all right."

"Yes, sir, that's all right. But I wouldn't feel comfortable calling you P. B. I'll have to call you Mr. Young."

"You're an earnest young man."

"Yes, sir."

He rubbed his chin, then moved back to the temple. "I'm bone-tired from last night, Charlie, but honestly, me hiring you is about as crazy an idea as I've ever heard."

"Yes, sir."

"You want to write news and opinion?"

"Yes, sir. News and a weekly column."

"Pseudonym?"

"No, sir, I'd like the byline to read Charles Mears."

"A white man writing opinions for the colored. Don't we have enough of that in the legislature?"

"Yes, sir. But the people must be heard. All the people. I believe Virgie talked to me because she wanted a voice. I don't want to let her down."

He closed his eyes and rubbed both temples. "My God," he said. "A true idealist. How old are you, Charlie?"

"Nineteen."

"Nineteen," he said. "At your age I was helping set hot type and running messages for my father at *The True Reformer*. Littleton, North Carolina. Ever heard of the place?"

"No, sir."

He opened his eyes and gazed out the window. I could hear children laughing on the sidewalk. School must have let out. I thought about Harriet. He began to tap his fingers on the edge of the desk again. He turned and pushed the pages toward me.

"All right," he said. "Add some background. Let readers know why you're writing about the Christian case. We'll run it next week. And your salary won't be a penny more than my youngest reporter. I'm sorry, Charlie, but we have to run a tight ship around here."

"Thank you, Mr. Young."

"Maybe we should make a side deal, Charlie. If one of my employees asks you, or any member of my family asks you, or anybody anywhere asks you, you say you were passing when you worked at the *Times-Herald*. Understood?"

"Sir?"

"Don't look so flummoxed, Charlie. You think you're the only sandy-haired, blue-eyed Negro in the Tidewater?"

"Well, no, sir. I mean—"

His grin was impish. "I'm pulling your leg, Charlie. But I'd rather tell my wife you were passing than be around when she tells her mother I just hired a white boy to report for the *Journal and Guide*. My mother-in-law is a woman quite free with her opinions, Charlie. My employees aren't going to be pleased about it, either."

I picked up the sheets. "I'll add the background tonight, sir. And I'll do my best to make sure you never regret your decision."

"I know you will," he said. "But I'll be honest, Charlie. I regret it already."

THAT AFTERNOON I WAITED across the street from the portico

of the Norfolk Academy. I watched Harriet come down the steps. She didn't stop at the curb, but started walking. I walked along the sidewalk on the other side of the street. When she crossed the street a block from the school, I called, "Like someone to carry your book strap?"

She turned and looked across the street. "Charlie!" she said. She started out into traffic.

"Wait!" I said. I trotted over behind a car. The buggy driver following snapped his whip.

"Watch where you're going!" the driver shouted.

"Charlie," Harriet said. I wanted to hold her. She kissed me on the cheek. "Did you like your present?" she asked.

"Yes," I said.

"Have you read it?"

"Twice through. And I started again last night."

"Oh, Charlie," she said. "You're sweet." She handed me the strap. I turned the books spine up to read a title.

"*History of the Decline and Fall of the Roman Empire.*"

"Lustful tyrants," she said. "I could cite a modern example." Her voice had an edge I had not heard before.

"I feel filthy," she said. I tucked the books under my arm.

"We'll think of something," I said. "Keep praying."

"I can't pray anymore, Charlie. No one is listening and I don't know why." Blotches appeared on her throat and her eyes began to fill.

"Then I'll pray for us both," I said. I touched her hand. "I have good news, Harriet."

Her face brightened.

"What?" she asked.

"P. B. Young hired me at the *Norfolk Journal and Guide.*"

"The colored paper?"

"Yes," I said. "Just like I wanted. News and opinion."

She searched my face. Then she smiled.

"That's wonderful, Charlie!" She hugged me tight. The book strap slipped but I caught it. She stood back.

"I have good news, too," she said.

"Yes?"

"Drusilla showed me where she keeps the key to the side porch," she whispered. "She promises not to tell. You've seen the rose bower in the yard. We can meet there."

"Are you sure?"

"She won't tell, Charlie. Yes."

"That *is* good news," I said. "Even better than mine. You see? We've had a good day. We'll have better days, too."

"I hope so, Charlie." She stopped at the corner. "I'd better go on from here. Give Lucky a pat for me. When's the last ferry?"

"Ten o'clock," I said.

"He stays up till then," she said. "It's not safe till midnight. You won't have any way home."

"That's all right," I said. "I can sleep at the office."

"It may be a while before I leave word. He watches all the time," she said.

"You can call at the office," I said.

"I will."

I handed her the book strap. "I'll keep praying," I said. "I'll pray for the both of us. Maebelle is praying, too."

She gave me a kiss on the cheek and hurried down the street, the book strap over her shoulder. Her long black hair shone in the light. Her dress hung loose from the waist. She looked as delicate as a maiden in a poem by Edgar Poe.

WORK WAS WORSE THAN I expected. Pressmen and reporters acknowledged me only if I greeted them first. They would mumble some response, eyes downcast or darting away from my face. If someone looked me in the eye it was to express seething anger. It was like looking into the colored versions of the eyes of the white mob who had wanted to lynch Virginia Christian. I kept to myself. I made a point of meeting every deadline early if I could. I double-checked every story to make sure it was formatted correctly for the typesetters. I ate the lunches Maebelle packed for me alone at my desk.

I felt no regret. "Blessed are ye, when men shall hate you," the apostle Luke wrote, "and when they shall separate you from their company, and shall reproach you, and cast out your name as evil, for the Son of man's sake. Rejoice ye in that day, and leap for joy: for, behold, your reward is great in heaven: for in the like manner did their fathers unto the prophets." I knew I was no prophet. I was suffering. But for the first time in a long time, I felt there might be meaning to my life.

That feeling grew stronger on the streets. When I was covering a story, I was first met with doubt. But when black folk saw I was there to report the truth, the community supported me. Old and young offered information. They gave me the history of bad blood if there was such a history. They cautioned me about old wrongs, and new threats. My stories were full of punch. They were accurate. Sometimes they were scoops.

Mr. Young was supportive and genial. But he understood the reality of his situation, and mine. He made a show of disciplining me for the slightest error. As the weeks passed, I sometimes saw a friendly glance or even the hint of a smile at work. I even became a favorite of the typesetters, because they always got my stories early, written and punctuated to their specifications.

My columns were received well from the start. Since my work at the *Times-Herald* always appeared under Hampton bureau, few people in the white community and no one in the colored community knew who I was. I expect most of the *Journal and Guide* readers thought I was colored. Whenever Mr. Young received a letter from a leader in the Negro community lauding the quality of the opinion columns, he made a point of reading it to me aloud in his office after hours.

"Maybe you *were* passing, Charlie," he said with a chuckle. "You just didn't know it. You're gaining quite a following."

I grinned. "George Fields says justice is blind, Mr. Young."

"Maybe in the Justice with a capital J world," he said, "but not ours. And nobody knows that better than George Fields. I suppose in his own way, he's more of an idealist than you or me. His daughter graduates from Hampton soon. I hear she wants to study the law. Talk about her with Mr. Fields and he stands about two inches taller. He has big dreams for his daughter's world."

"Yes, sir."

"He's a great man, George Fields."

"Yes, sir," I said.

I smoked a cigarette on the front deck of the ferry. The wind was calm and moonlight rested on the smooth waters of the Roads. The weather had cooled. Maebelle claimed we would have an early fall. Something had stirred a flock of snow geese in the darkness. I could hear them honking high up in the sky, even louder than the ferry's engine. Their shapes were black against the silver night. When they turned, the moonlight shimmered on their wings.

As I climbed the steps to my rooms, I could hear Lucky whining inside. The porch light was out. I looked up and saw the bulb was shattered. I struck a match to help light the key slot. The wire of the screen door was ripped open and the spring was twisted. The cuspidor was turned over. Ashes and cigarette butts were scattered everywhere. My three-legged stool was smashed to splinters. Scrawled in white paint on the wooden inner door were the words, "We See All."

21.

Nickel Baby

D r. Vanderslice rang the office that afternoon and said he had some information, could I come out to his house for supper? I told him I was sorry, I had the evening beat.

"Just come ahead when you can, Charlie," he said. "I really need to speak with you. Annie will have something cold set out. Maybe some of Cleopatra's potato salad. And her duck jerky. How's that sound?"

"I should be there around seven, Dr. V," I said. "Unless there's a story. I'll send a note if I'm delayed."

"That'll be fine, Charlie. Splendid. We'll look for you at seven."

The sun was setting when I got off the trolley in Phoebus. I happened to look up as I walked from the stop and saw a line of pelicans, high up, headed east. There must have been twenty-five.

Dr. Vanderslice met me at the door. He was holding one of his daughters in his arms. I heard a child shriek from the top of the stairway behind him.

"Come in, come in, Charlie," he said. "It's the usual pandemonium here. All right, Miss Emily. It's time for your bath." The little girl beamed and put her hands on her father's cheeks.

"All right, Daddy," she said, nodding solemnly. She tugged at his Vandyke.

"Hello, Charlie," Mrs. Vanderslice called from the landing. She had a baby on her hip. Three girls scurried by her, followed by two boys, the younger one naked as the day he was born, followed by the Vanderslices' maid Cleopatra, carrying a load of towels.

"Don't you be trying me, Mr. Ellis," Cleopatra called after the boys. "You gone put them pajamas on right now!"

"Good evening, Mrs. Vanderslice," I said.

"Charlie, your supper's on the table. V, could you bring her up? The bathwater's ready."

"Yes, Annie," Dr. Vanderslice said, closing the door. "Charlie, make yourself comfortable on the back porch. It's such a fine evening, I thought you and I would dine *al fresco*. I'll bring your buttermilk in a moment."

On one side of the porch was a trellis clotted with vines. I sat down in front of the place set for me. A wood thrush called from the garden and fell silent. A mockingbird perched on a low branch of a willow oak by the porch and cocked its head. It flitted to a higher branch and began to sing.

Dr. Vanderslice came out carrying two glasses of buttermilk. He set them on the table.

"Go ahead, go ahead, Charlie," he said. "I've already eaten." He began to roll down the sleeves of his shirt. "Emily is a darling about her bath. Ellis, however, well, he is *not*. I see my shirt front is wet, too." He took a sip of his buttermilk.

"Hard to believe this house was ever quiet, but I assure you, once it was. Before the children. But we enjoy the racket. Annie grew up here. The town was called Mill Creek back then. Federal troops at Fort Monroe were withdrawn the year before she was born. With the occupation over, new people continued to stream in. The local businessmen were sure they'd all become millionaires. And some did.

"Annie's father, Harrison Phoebus, was quite the entrepreneur. Owned the Chamberlin and the Hygeia hotels. Ran a luxury charter boat line to Old Point Comfort. Built commercial buildings with his brother Frank, then put up a number of little houses for the hotel help. The government owned much of the land in the town, and a former slave could select a piece of property and claim it. The houses were well-built and each had a tiny side room. This was in case the village ever got running water, homeowners could install indoor plumbing. Mr. Phoebus dropped dead of a heart ailment when he was only forty-five, long before Annie and I met. He'd served in the Union army in the war. That's what had brought him to this part of the world. The buttermilk's not too sour for you?"

I shook my head.

"Good, then. I met Annie at cotillion while I was in the medical department at the University of Virginia. Dr. Barringer was head of faculty, before he left to become president of Virginia Polytechnic. What a clinician that man was. Insisted on a microscope for every student. They wouldn't have the hospital in Charlottesville were it not for Dr. Barringer's vision. And a philosopher. I'm sure you've read his essay, 'The Southern Negro.' Made quite a name for him, even on the national stage. Probably you don't hold with his conclusions, Charlie, nor do I, though you'd agree he considered the issue in a thorough and original way. But I digress.

"Annie and I were married and settled into a cottage on Rosalind Manor, Mr. Phoebus' estate. It was comfortable, and Annie was close by her mother. Invaluable when the children started to come. Later, we built the residence here on Mellen Street, so I could have my office right in town. The cold duck's quite good with Cleopatra's potato salad, isn't it, Charlie?"

"Delicious, sir," I said.

"Cleopatra's people are Jamaican. Absolute magicians with spices," he said. He finished his buttermilk and set the glass on the table. "It was April 1, 1900, when the town was renamed Phoebus to honor Annie's father. The date's easy to remember, because my mother-in-law always got a good laugh from it. 'How hilarious Harry would find it!' she'd say. 'To have the town named for him on April Fool's Day!'

"Even with the fancy hotels, Phoebus was a pretty tough place. The Hampton Normal and Industrial Institute was a real boon. It brought in educators, serious-minded people. There was Benthall's grocery, Wagner's photography and bookstore, Mugler's clothing store for men, and Heinickel's bakery. Most of the streets were paved with shells hauled in from the oyster house in Hampton.

"There were open ditches along the streets that carried rainwater and sewage. They bred mosquitoes the size of butterflies. And Annie said she would sit with her brothers and sisters on the edge of the ditches in summer, catching fireflies as they rose from the grass. They'd carry half-gallon jars home, filled with so many fireflies they could set the jars on the porch and read by their light.

"I purchased my old buggy from Washington Diggs' livery. He was a freeman. I had a little blaze-face roan filly named Rose. Wash used to say he gave up on brushing her and just polished instead. 'She so slick, air don't move when she passes, Dr. V! Shiniest filly I ever *did* see,' he'd say. I had Mrs. Baker, the nurse who assisted me at the office, and Hester, a colored midwife. Each woman was a paragon of ability. I charged one dollar for a house call. If someone had the dollar, well, that was all right, Mrs. Baker would record the payment, and if they didn't, that was all right, too. People settled up as best they could. I can assure you I never wanted for country ham or fresh eggs or boiled peanuts in season. I don't remember ever paying a cent for repairs at the cottage or weeding the gardens and lawn.

"Rarely could a Negro family pay for my services, Charlie. Most families had started with nothing, literally nothing. They'd been slaves. They were illiterate. They built shacks and lean-tos from what they could scavenge at Fort Monroe or the shipyards.

You know how I forget to set the buggy brake when I call at a house, and the roan filly liked to wander even more than Phoebe. Sometimes I'd have a devil of a time locating her. Soon enough, whenever I pulled up for a call, a colored child would appear with a few grains of oats or a teaspoon of sugar. The child would hold Rose's bridle and pet her face until I'd finished my call. So I'd give the child a penny.

"If the call was a birth, I charged two dollars, and sometimes the filly had to be minded for quite a spell. Brothers and sisters relieved each other. So I'd give them a nickel. 'Dr. V bought us another nickel baby, Mrs. Baker,' Hester would say when we returned to the office. Mrs. Baker would enter the call in the ledger—two dollars invoiced for services rendered, five cents paid for horse feed. Of course I'd never be paid the two dollars, so I was down a nickel on the call. Mrs. Baker said if folks kept breeding, I'd wind up carrying my family to the poor house.

"There was little talk about race in those days. Edgar Tennis, president of the bank, a white man, and Fred Robinson, a freed slave, made a fortune in the land business, working together hand in glove. That's not to say there wasn't trouble. There was too much whiskey around. In the old days there was a barroom on every corner and a whorehouse on every block. I'd often have a gentleman to patch up after a fistfight, and sometimes somebody was killed. A white man bled to death as I was treating him at the corner of Mallory Street by Wash's livery. He'd been stabbed in a dispute with another patron over one of Victor Sheets' whores. Femoral artery.

"Now *there* was another man who was quite the entrepreneur. Victor Sheets. He owned four brothels at the far end of our street, red lanterns glowing on the porches all hours of the night and day, except Sundays. The ladies had Pastor Fuller at the Zion Church to thank for that. Somehow the pastor convinced Sheets even whores needed a day of rest. And Sheets believed in full integration. White or colored was no distinction to him. All a customer needed was coin of the realm."

Dr. Vanderslice paused. He seemed to be listening to the mockingbird's variations in the willow oak. "Would you like more potato salad, Charlie?" he asked.

"No, thank you, Dr. V."

He cleared his throat. "Annie was none too happy when I told her I had started examining the women in Sheets' employ. She was concerned about the impropriety, of course. I never mentioned Sheets hadn't offered to pay me a penny. But it was an issue of the public health, Charlie.

"There were the usual maladies—chlamydia, gonorrhea, sores. Sometimes worse. Syphilis, tuberculosis. After a few weeks, Sheets began to see the salutary effects my examinations were having on his profits. 'A Sheets whore is a healthy whore,' he trumpeted to his patrons. He began to pay me for my visits, professing great concern for the welfare of his women and their guests."

Behind me I heard the tinkling of glass. Mrs. Vanderslice stepped out on the porch and set a silver tray on the table.

"I brought you port," she said, nodding to her husband. "And Charlie, I had a Lemon-Kola in the icebox. I brought a glass of ice, too."

"Thank you, ma'am," I said.

She appeared to be studying my head closely.

"Well, I see V hasn't quite managed to talk your ears off. Don't let him. I'm sure you both have work in the morning. I know my husband does."

"All right, Annie," Dr. Vanderslice said.

She gathered our buttermilk glasses. A pearl necklace set with emeralds drooped from her bodice.

"There are sweet biscuits here, too," she said. She straightened.

"Gentlemen, I bid you good night. The children are done in and so am I. Cleopatra's about to leave, V."

Dr. Vanderslice stood and kissed her cheek. "Good night, Annie. I promise I'll only keep Charlie a bit longer."

He sat down and sipped his port. The mockingbird had moved to a yard farther down the street. Beyond the thicket of roses and the longleaf pines at the end of Dr. Vanderslice's lot I heard a whippoor-will call. I poured the Lemon-Kola over the ice and watched it fizz. I could hear the rattle of dishes in the kitchen, and women's voices, then footfalls on the steps. Dr. Vanderslice was listening, too. I heard a door close upstairs.

"Charlie, I need to speak to you about matters of some . . . delicacy," he said.

I nodded and leaned forward in my chair.

"Phoebus was like a world unto itself," Dr. Vanderslice said. "The conventions of society and morality seemed insufficient to the place. One day I might treat a Negro broken by years of slavery whose family would starve if I couldn't restore his strength so he could work. Or at the Soldiers' Home I might fight to keep a veteran whose lungs were filling with fluid alive for one more wretched day. It was difficult to find the line between what was merciful and what was cruel."

Dr. Vanderslice sipped his port. "Some of Sheets' women weren't women at all, Charlie, they were mere girls, who sometimes ran into . . . difficulty." His eyes deepened with sadness. "You take my meaning, don't you?"

"I do, sir."

"I assisted them. Beyond the ethics of my profession. Beyond the statutes of the Commonwealth. Beyond the laws of my faith." He touched his beard. "If the girls couldn't earn money, Sheets would turn them out. He made that clear. If I didn't treat them or send them to a midwife who did, they might try their own methods. The risk of infection or hemorrhage was too great. So I helped them. I convinced myself I was acting in the interest of public health. That I was being merciful. In fact, I was an agent of their corruption."

"I think you're being hard on yourself, Dr. V," I said.

"Am I?" His jaw clenched. "I wonder why George Jr. was taken. A blameless, innocent boy. You know, my father holds a doctor of divinity degree, Charlie. He's the pastor of a Methodist church in Henrico County. I grew up in that church. It lies less than two hours' journey from here. Yet not once, Charlie, not once before I performed an abortion on those girls did I ask my own father's advice." Despair etched his face.

"Dr. V, think of all the people who attended little George's funeral. Think of all the good you've done in Hampton."

"I suppose," he said. "But when George Jr. died, I felt so angry. I thought my mind would explode with anger. All my training and all my prayer, and I couldn't save my own little boy. I came to the point where I couldn't bear to see his pony. So I sold him. Can you imagine? Little George hadn't been in the ground a fortnight. He loved that creature. Annie was frantic. I thought she never would forgive me. But she has. She has, God bless her."

Dr. Vanderslice's eyes were glazed. He cupped his brow in his hand.

"I've resigned myself," he whispered. "I must ask you to also, Charlie. Resign yourself to fate."

"Sir?"

"About the colored girl." He lifted the port to his lips and drained the glass.

"What do you mean, Dr V?"

He stared at the empty glass, turning the stem slowly between his fingers. "I seem to have gone dry," he said. He leaned toward the table, lifted the decanter from the tray, and refilled his glass.

22

Lorelei

C rickets chirruped loudly in the grass. I could hear my own breathing. I watched Dr. Vanderslice rub his eyelids with his fingertips. Then he sat up straight and looked me in the eye.

"I mean your safety," he said. "The world for us, Charlie, is rife with ambiguity, but for some men, the world is simple. Persons are either white or colored. The distinction is clear. One drop of blood makes the difference. These men believe the white race, the Anglo-Saxon race, is fighting for its very existence, and the races must be kept absolutely separate, to avoid polluting white blood. Remember Walt Plecker? At the funeral?"

"Yes," I said.

"He's the registrar of a new agency in Richmond, the Bureau of Vital Statistics. You've heard of it?"

"Yes," I said. "They want to make sure every child born in Virginia receives a birth certificate."

"Yes," Dr. Vanderslice said. "And that certificate will identify every child by race. Now Walt and I go back a long way. We arrived in Hampton the same year, '92. I was fresh out of the medical department at Virginia, so I spent most of my time at the Norfolk hospital, still learning. But Walt's ten years older. When he got here, he set up a private obstetrics and gynecology practice right off. Stiff-backed, formal—well, you met him. Old Virginia through and through. His father was a slave owner in the Shenandoah Valley.

"I met Walt assisting him with an operation at the hospital. The patient was a bill collector who'd had the bad judgment to exchange words with a tenant just out of the military. Wound up with a fractured skull. The operation was fairly delicate. Bone fragments right next to the spinal cord, but the patient recovered fully. Anyway, after the operation our paths would cross from time to time. Walt and his wife Kate weren't much for the social circuit; they had no children and kept to themselves. But Annie got to know Kate through the women's suffrage club, and we were close enough to invite them to our wedding.

"I saw more of Walt after I set up practice in Phoebus. The same year I was named coroner, he was named public health director. He did a lot of good. Introduced silver nitrate drops to prevent infant syphilitic blindness. Improvised a little home incubator for premature babies, just a paper bag, a light bulb, a cotton blanket— only cost a penny or two, so any household could afford it. He got doctors and midwives to improve sanitation for themselves and new mothers. Why, the mortality rate for colored infants dropped by more than fifty percent! Oh, Walt Plecker did a lot of good, especially among the poor.

"But in spite of his service, he held complete antipathy for the Negro. I remember him saying to me, when we were speaking of the colored nurse who raised him as a child, that it would be un-Christian to think of that woman as an equal, since such thinking only created expectations that could never be fulfilled." Dr. Vanderslice shook his head slowly. He set the port glass he'd poured untouched on the table. The whip-poor-will calling at the edge of the lot was answered from deep in the pines.

"Walt helped me with the prostitutes, Charlie." He seemed to look at me for affirmation. I nodded. His voice fell to a whisper.

"As in my case, to serve the public health. There had come into Sheets' employ a very special girl. Lorelei. She claimed to be sixteen, but I expect she was younger. The first time I laid eyes on her she was waving a little American flag as Professor Moton's Hampton Institute Corps of Cadets passed in a Fourth of July parade. Lorelei stood out in a crowd. So beautiful, you'd think she'd been painted by an Old Master and stepped alive from the canvas, breathing the same air as you.

"She said her home was in Fredericksburg, overlooking the river. I'm told she walked into Phoebus with mud on her dress, carrying a worn leather valise. She made inquiries after an English woman who taught at the school, said the lady had been a friend of her father's. But the woman had long since returned to London.

"The girl was penniless and homeless, and Victor Sheets dashed to her rescue. He'd found the jewel in the dung heap. Bright, cerulean eyes, skin pale as alabaster. Golden hair that billowed like wheat in a field. A child with the figure of a grown woman. Sheets gave her a room with bath and three meals a day until she was able to find employment. He clothed her in silk dresses and fancy shoes. His women washed and dressed her hair. When he discovered she was skilled on the piano and had the voice of an angel, he had her perform in the parlor of his fanciest brothel. Finally, she was his altogether. Are we all right for time, Charlie?"

"Yes, Dr. V. Please go on."

"You can imagine how some of the whores teased us when they hiked their petticoats for an examination. Walt got quite the worst of it. He was badly near-sighted, and sometimes a woman would snatch the eyeglasses from his face and put them on her own. And, of course, there was sport in his name.

"'Can you see, Dr. *Pecker*? Let me hold a lantern while you explore that big hole.' 'Old dog of yours still hunt, Dr. *Pecker*?' One woman prided herself in breaking wind just as Walt began his examination. 'Hope you got an umbrella, Dr. *Pecker*, I believe it's fixing to rain!' 'Confound you, woman!' he'd blurt, his face beet red.

"Lorelei, of course, was different. She would speak in a whisper, in language that was never coarse. Walt seemed to take an interest in her, maybe because the Pleckers had no children of their own. He'd buy little illustrated books of verse and romance novels for her to read to pass the time. His wife sent sheet music, songs she and Walt had admired back in the day.

"Given the circumstances, Lorelei's life was comfortable enough, I suppose. Sheets guarded her jealously, and like Walt, catered to her whims.

"Then one of the most commonplace things in the world happened, Charlie. Lorelei fell in love with a dashing young man. The captain of the Hampton Institute Corps of Cadets."

I drew a breath.

"Right, Charlie. Not a paying customer, but a Negro boy from Scituate, Massachusetts. After taking his degree in engineering that spring, he was to be commissioned a lieutenant in the U.S. Army. Robert Shaw Thomas. Handsome. Well-spoken. Tall. Athletic. Snappy in his uniform. Admired by his peers and his commandant alike.

"During her examination, I asked if she had missed any monthlies.

"'Yes,' she said, in a firm voice.

"'Does anyone know?' I asked.

"'No one,' she said.

"I nodded slowly.

"'No,' she said. 'I don't want that. It's Robert's. I want to have this child.'

"I took one of her hands. Her fingers were tapered like a statue's.

"'Lorelei,' I said. 'You're a child yourself. You have to consider the circumstances for any child of Robert's you bring into this world.'

"'Robert will take us to Massachusetts. I know he will. Robert loves me. And I love him.'

"Only a child, of course, could voice such wild romance, drunk on the prattle of God knows what hack poet or dime-store novelist.

"'Sheets will turn you out,' I said.

"'I know,' she said."

Dr. Vanderslice picked up his port and drank it in a gulp. He put the glass on the table and folded his hands.

"If this dashing young officer had been white, then he and Lorelei could've played the parts of a knight and damsel in *Ivanhoe*. Yet in my mind, Charlie, my own mind, and you know I fancy myself an enlightened man, I could not blot a feeling of repugnance at the notion of that child coupling with a Negro. I'm ashamed, but I couldn't free myself.

"When I told Walt, his calm surprised me.

"'This is suicide,' he said.

"'I don't think the girl will harm herself,' I said.

"'Not that, not that,' he muttered. 'Racial suicide. This is how the white race destroys itself.'

"I think some part of me believed that Walt might help me because of his feelings for the girl. But I didn't trust him with my darkest thoughts. The risk of losing my license was too great. I begged Lorelei to let me abort the child. I contrived ways to perform the procedure against her will, administering morphine under some pretense, then remedying the matter while she slept. It's shameful to think I considered such acts.

"For his part Walt withdrew from the girl. There were no more gifts of verse or music. Thin as he was, he lost weight. His coat and vest hung from his shoulders like a scarecrow's in a field. As the girl's condition became obvious, he seemed hardly able to endure her presence.

"Victor Sheets turned her out, of course, valuable though she was. On the quiet, some of the whores helped her rent rooms on Tennis Lane. When Walt and I came to examine his women, Sheets heaped us with scorn.

"'I pay you good money, don't I?' he snarled. 'I could've talked sense into her, you'd've told me in time.'

"On a cold December morning, Lorelei delivered a healthy baby boy in her rooms on Tennis Lane. Hester and I attended. He was one of my nickel babies. A colored boy kept Phoebe close by with a handful of clover hay I expect he'd pilfered from Mr. Diggs' livery. I gave the boy his pay and drove home. I laid my greatcoat on a chair inside. Annie offered me a dram but my hands were shaking so, she had to hold the cup to my lips. I told her there had been no complications, and that Hester was staying the day with the new mother.

"'This is the special girl, isn't it?' Annie asked. 'Lorelei?'

"I nodded and started up the stairs. Then I stopped.

"'Thank you, Annie,' I said. 'Thank you for everything you are to me.'"

The whip-poor-wills had stopped calling. The only sound was a cricket chirping by the hearth.

"Lorelei named the baby Robert Shaw Jr. Except for a bout of colic early in his career, he was a most robust little man. And with all the whores about, the most doted upon."

Dr. Vanderslice sat for a moment in reverie. He tapped the arm of his chair with a finger.

"And now comes the final act of our drama, Charlie. That summer the young captain of cadets graduated and received his commission. Lorelei, with little Robert Shaw Jr. in her arms, boarded the train with Lieutenant Robert Shaw Thomas Sr., Ninth Cavalry, U.S. Army, bound for Massachusetts. I noticed Sheets watching from the depot platform. He spat on a rail and walked out onto the street.

"That was all there was to it. Time passed. Then, one September, coming home from a house call, I saw Lorelei walking on Mellen Street. She was holding the hand of a sturdy, nap-haired boy who looked to be about three. I called out to her and she came to the buggy. I could smell whiskey on her breath.

"'Can you believe it, Dr. V?' she said. 'Turned out by niggers because a white whore wasn't good enough for their son?' She put her hand to her mouth and giggled. The little boy smiled up at me.

"Sheets refused her work when she asked for it. 'I won't have that mongrel whelp distracting my whores no more,' he growled. As it turned out, he'd made another good decision for the public health. In plying her trade in Providence and later in Baltimore to earn the train fare to Hampton, Lorelei had contracted syphilis.

"Walt helped me with her treatments. All we could do was administer morphine for her pain. Hester took little Robert Shaw Jr. to stay with her family. As the disease ravaged her body, Lorelei's mind grew addled. 'Who are you, old man?' she would ask Walt. 'Did you bring gold?' She twisted the sheets in her fingers, her bedclothes soaked with sweat. Her eyes flashed with fire. Two of Sheets' whores were with her the afternoon she died.

"As coroner, I examined the body to establish cause of death. Walt attended. Lorelei was disfigured, but in death she was a child again. When I finished my examination, Walt removed his glasses. He gazed on her for a long while, absently wiping his lenses with a handkerchief. He put on his glasses and bowed his head. He prayed for a moment. Then he turned to me.

"'Ruin is what comes of this perversion,' he said. 'This miscegenation. The Negro is not one of us.'

"There were letters in Lorelei's personal effects. Through them we were able to get in touch with her grandmother, a Mrs. Crowell, Lorelei's next of kin. Mrs. Crowell rode the train from Fredericksburg to Hampton. I met her at the depot. She was a pleasant woman, in good health for her age, but by her appearance and manner, I'd say she possessed more pride than means. No doubt the boy represented a great burden. But she took little Robert Shaw Jr. away on the train, along with her granddaughter's remains. Hester was angry with me for weeks.

"'Dried-up old woman,' she muttered. 'That little boy need him a *mother*.' But there was nothing to be done—Mrs. Crowell was kin, and that was the law.

"Our paths—Walt's and mine—seemed to cross less frequently, though Annie and I would greet him with Kate at church every Sunday. One of Sheets' women said Walt had sent money to Mrs. Crowell to place little Robert Shaw Jr. with the superintendent of a colored orphanage near Richmond. She told me the superintendent was a personal friend of Walt's. I never tried to find out if what the whore said was true."

Dr. Vanderslice cleared his throat, then stirred himself. "I may've kept you past your trolley, Charlie."

"I'm all right, Dr. V."

He leaned forward in his chair. "About the Christian girl. I know you believe—under the law—she should not have been put to death because she was a juvenile. But had justice not been served in the court, Charlie, it would have been served in the street. These are the times we live in."

"But we're a nation of laws, Dr. V."

He lifted his hands with the palms outspread, his eyes full of shadow, then closed his hands on his lap. "I ask you as my friend, Charlie. Please stop writing your articles. What you write is eloquent, but it's dangerous. Deadly dangerous. There are cunning men, ruthless men, who despise what you write. They believe either you are colored and had been passing, which they abhor, or you are white and a traitor to your race, which they loathe. Walt Plecker is among the lawful, but some of these men will seek vengeance wherever they can find it, Charlie. Sheriff Curtis has heard talk. Men in high places have their eyes on you. Be careful."

Dr. Vanderslice stood and offered his hand. "Better get to the station," he said.

I took his hand and shook it. "Thank you, sir. You're a true friend."

He opened the front door. The night air was damp. I turned up my collar.

"Dr. V?"

"Yes, Charlie?"

"There's a matter I'd like to discuss with you someday. When there's time."

"Of course," he said.

"Well, good night, then."

"Please do what I'm asking, Charlie," he said.

THERE WERE A COUPLE of passengers when I boarded in Phoebus but the trolley was empty when it reached my stop. I stepped onto the sidewalk and looked about. Lincoln Street was deserted. As I started walking, I noticed a big man in a bowler standing alone under a street lamp. He was wearing a long overcoat. He moved away from the light when I glanced his way.

23.

The Bower

Lewter Hobbs' house sat on the Elizabeth River, so close I could smell the sea in the darkness. I breathed deeply. There was the odor of salt and marsh, acrid with diesel and pitch. At the corner I stayed out of the glow of the streetlamp, passing onto the cross street toward the river, where there was an alley. I cut down the alley and vaulted the white picket fence into the back yard. I crouched to clean the lenses of my glasses and let my eyes adjust to the darkness. My fingers touched dew in the grass. A distance down the alley a dog barked. I heard the murmur of a woman's voice, a door latching. Then all was quiet.

The fall air was crisp. Mist spread over the river, undulating in the moonlight. I checked my watch. It was nearly midnight. I crept toward the bower. The sawing of the crickets was impossibly loud. I made my way up the steps and peered around the edge of the lattice. The house was dark. The roses in the bower had started to bloom again with the cool evenings. Their fragrance was lovely. A sphinx moth whacked the lattice so loudly I caught my breath. I listened as it hovered and spun, whirring from rose to rose, until it flew off into the night.

I thought of the cigarettes in my pocket. Far too risky.

In the darkness Harriet appeared near the house, as if I were imagining her. Her bedclothes rippled from her legs and arms as she ran. Her shoulder was wrapped in a shawl, or blanket, I couldn't tell. She didn't make a sound, until she was close enough I could hear her breathing.

"I saw you by the moon," she said. "I was watching from the window."

"Yes," I said.

"Mrs. Wingate is taking care of Lucky?"

"Yes," I said. "Maebelle answered when I called. She feels very modern, now that Mrs. Wingate has a telephone."

Harriet stepped into the bower. The blanket on her shoulders draped to her feet.

"Aren't the roses wonderful?" she asked.

"Yes."

"Are you afraid?"

"Yes."

"Of me?"

"Yes. I don't know why. It seems like a long time."

"Thirty-seven days and . . . um . . . eight and a half hours," she said. "But who's counting?" She put her hands on my shoulders. Her eyes were dark and wide. "I had to wait to call," she said. "He watches me every minute. Makes excuses to drive me everywhere. Even Maggie's noticed it. But she won't say anything. She thinks her mother would scold her for being jealous. For her part, Mrs. Hobbs is good to me but she's dull as a cow."

She leaned against my chest and lifted her chin. I kissed her as best I knew how. Her lips were soft and wet. She snatched my hand. "Come down here," she said.

She pulled me down the steps and we crept under the bower. I stooped to keep from hitting my head. It was warm, protected from the chill night air. She peered through the lattice toward the river.

"Look, Charlie. Can you see?" she pointed.

"Venus?" I said.

"Yes," she said. "The evening star. Hanging like a Chinese lantern." She took the blanket from her shoulders and spread it on the earth. She stepped to the middle and turned to face me. I noticed her feet were bare.

"Harriet," I said. "Aren't you cold?"

"No," she said. She wiggled her toes. "Do you love me?"

I stepped back and banged my head on a joist. My cap went flying and settled on the blanket.

"Well, I . . ."

"Take off your glasses, Charlie," she said.

I removed my glasses and put them in my jacket pocket.

She bent and took hold of the hem of her nightgown. She straightened and lifted it over her head. Her hair caught in the neck of the gown. It cascaded over a shoulder as she pulled the gown free. Her breasts were pale. She took my hands and rested them on her hips. Her skin was warm. The points of bone under my hands felt as delicate as birds' eggs. I looked at the shadow between her legs. I looked into her face. I could hear my heart pounding.

"Do you love me, Charlie?" she asked.

"Harriet, yes," I said. "But I don't know the first thing . . ."

"It's all right," she whispered. She stood on tiptoe and pressed her waist against mine. "I can feel you," she said.

I buried my face in her hair. It was hard to breathe. I felt ignorant and clumsy. When I touched her, she winced. Her body was rigid as stone.

"I hurt you," I said.

"No," she said. "Go on." I could feel her warmth. She gasped.

"I'm sorry," I said. "I know I'm hurting you."

She pressed her face against my neck. Her cheeks wrinkled. Her tears felt hot on my skin. She sobbed and dug her fingers into my back.

"I thought I could but I can't," she gasped. "I want you to want me, Charlie. I want you to love me. I need for somebody to love me. But I can't, Charlie."

"I do love you, Harriet," I whispered.

She sobbed again and began to weep. Her body shook against me, so hard my ribs seemed to rattle with hers. She melted into me, her grief sweeping over us like a tide.

WHEN I CAME TO myself, Harriet was spooned against my chest. She was looking over my shoulder. "Oh no, oh no, oh no," she whispered.

THE CRICKETS WERE SILENT. The moon had started to descend. The yard between the bower and house was glowing with silver light, the shadows of trees and shrubs limned sharply as if they had been drawn with a pen. I turned to look in the direction Harriet was staring.

I recognized the gait of Lewter Hobbs. He was striding purposefully, the white legs of his pajamas fluttering beneath a dark robe. The wet grass squeaked with each step. He was making his way straight for the bower. I could see his broad forehead. His hair and moustache were groomed. Something in his hand glistened in the moonlight. Then abruptly he turned, striding toward the river. Near the fence he stopped. I could see he was carrying a brandy snifter. He raised it to his lips, tilting his head, and drank. On the river, two sailboats were anchored. Their masts rocked gently. He appeared to be studying them. Then he raised his eyes to look at the moon. The grasses in the marsh were still, like spikes of crystal. Far down the river toward the Roads, a tug sounded its whistle. He drank again, raising the snifter high to empty it. Then he turned and strode back to the house. He stopped once more to gaze at the moon. Then I heard the door.

"Thank God," Harriet said.

"That was close," I said.

"Thank God I locked the door," she said. "I locked it behind me and left the key. He won't suspect."

"Clever."

She kissed me. "Say it again."

"You're clever."

"No," she said.

"I love you," I said.

"Yes," she said.

"The blanket feels good," I said. "But I'd better get going."

"In a little," she said. "Mrs. Hobbs says some nights he has trouble sleeping. That's funny, isn't it, Charlie?"

"No," I said.

"The stupid cow. She should ask him why he has trouble. At least he doesn't come for me when she's in the house. I guess she scares him at least that much. He tells me what we have is so special we mustn't tell. He says if I do tell no one will believe it anyway, and he'd just have to send me away to an orphanage."

"I've been praying, Harriet."

"I want you to, Charlie. I want to believe in praying." She smiled. "Say it."

"I love you, Harriet." She pressed her back into my chest tightly.

"Again," she said. "Say it again."

AT THE OFFICE I slept for a couple of hours on the daybed by the door to Mr. Young's office. Golden light spilled in the windows. A key rattled in the lock and one of the old pressmen shuffled through the door. He was carrying his lunch in a red bandanna knotted at the top.

He bent to study me. "Well, look what the cat drug in," he said, and whistled. "And don't tell me you been working. I see them grass stains. You best clean yourself up, fore Mr. Young get here."

He shuffled into the press room and closed the door.

I went to the washroom and brushed the grass clippings from my trousers. I took off my glasses and rinsed my face, then ran my fingers through my hair. I polished my glasses and smoothed the front of my shirt. I decided to go down the street to get coffee and a sweet roll. Then I smoked a cigarette. By the time I returned, Mr. Young was sitting in his office. He raised his hand and motioned for me to enter.

"Word is somebody burned a cross over in Hampton last night. Did you notice anything on your way in?"

"No, sir." He studied me for a moment.

"I don't think your fly's buttoned," he said.

I looked down. "Excuse me, sir." I arranged myself.

"On Lincoln Street. Don't you live on Lincoln?"

"Yes, sir. But I didn't get home last night. I was working here, and then I just dozed off." The phone on his desk rang. He picked up the receiver.

"P. B. Young," he answered. He listened for a moment, turning to look at me. Then he looked at his desktop. "Yes, ma'am," he said. "I'm very sorry for your trouble. I'll tell him." He placed the receiver in the cradle.

"You need to get home, Charlie. Take the day off. Call me this evening when you can take the time."

I SPRINTED UP THE sidewalk from the trolley stop. Deputy Chas Curtis was kneeling by the gate at Mrs. Wingate's. He had his thumb on a surveyor's tape that stretched up the sidewalk. A young colored boy held the other end.

"Same measure?" Chas called to the boy.

"Yes, sir," the boy said.

"All right, then," Chas said. He let go the tape and the boy started cranking it into the reel. The deputy stood and adjusted his holster.

"Reckon they phoned you," he said.

"Yes," I said.

"I telegraphed the sheriff to let him know. He's fishing with cousin Win, lives down in Nags Head."

"I remember," I said.

"Sheriff says the blues been running to beat the band. Pulled in so many his arms is sore. You feeling all right, Charlie?"

"Yes," I said. "I worked late last night."

"That why you wasn't home this morning?"

"Yes," I said. I took a cigarette from the pack. "Care for one?"

"No, thanks. I take me a pinch of snuff from time to time."

I lit the cigarette and took a deep drag.

"Same old story," the deputy said. "Interviewed everybody at the trolley stop, white and colored. Interviewed the folks run them shops across the street. Even found out who the trolley operator was yesterday evening, interviewed him, too. Nobody seen a thing. Nobody heard a thing. Nobody remembered a thing." He motioned. "I'd got more if I'd went over to the graveyard yonder, questioned them headstones.

"Pace come by a while ago, interviewed everybody he could find for a piece in the paper. Said he found out about as much as I did, maybe a little less. I talked to Mrs. Wingate and her maid and gardener. They told me what they could. You'd best get on up there. They was worried sick about you. Anybody been bothering you, Charlie?"

"I've seen men following me."

"Anybody you could describe?"

"They're always at a distance. To tell you the truth, Chas, I don't know for sure they're following me at all."

"I tell you what, Charlie. You get time later today or maybe tomorrow morning, why don't you come by the office and I'll get a statement from you?"

"All right, Chas." I finished the cigarette and crushed out the butt. The colored boy trotted up to the deputy and held out the tape. The deputy reached in his pocket.

"Here's a nickel," he said.

"I thanks you, sir," the boy said. He ran toward the trolley stop.

"Be seeing you, Charlie," the deputy said.

"Be seeing you."

Behind the brick wall at the street, the lawn from Mrs. Wingate's drive up to her front door was scorched black. A charred cross still smoldered. It tilted toward the street. Mrs. Wingate's gardener Marcellus was poking at the cross with a shovel. Embers and ash tumbled onto the burned ground. He shook his head. His eyes were bloodshot and glassy.

"You see this, Mr. Charlie? Blaze from this caught in them leaves and pine tags under the trees. I thought that fire gone spread to Mrs. Wingate's house fore we got it turned. My Lord, Mr. Charlie." He poked again at the cross.

"Mr. Charlie?" Maebelle was standing on the front portico. She called again, "Mr. Charlie?"

"Yes?"

"Come on up here, Mr. Charlie, come quick!" she said. She was wringing her hands in her apron. When I reached the steps I could see she was crying. I had never seen Maebelle cry. The wisteria climbing the lattice by the columns was blackened.

"Is Mrs. Wingate all right?"

"Mrs. Wingate's madder'n hell, what Mrs. Wingate is," Maebelle said. "And I is, too. White trash near burning this house down. But it's worse'n that, Mr. Charlie." Her shoulders heaved. She buried her face in the apron.

"Maebelle? What's happened?"

"I don't want to tells you, Mr. Charlie. Surely I don't. Aw, Lord!"

"Maebelle?"

"They done killed Lucky, Mr. Charlie." Maebelle pulled her apron over her head and collapsed in a rocking chair.

I stepped back from the portico. Marcellus put his hand on my shoulder.

"You go on inside, Mr. Charlie," he said. "I know Mrs. Wingate been wanting you."

Mrs. Wingate sat reading by a lamp on the sofa in her parlor. The room was darkened by black bunting draped over the windows. Black bunting covered the mirror. Mr. Wingate's retrievers lay at her feet. One lifted his head to see me. He groaned and put his head down. At the center of the parlor was the pallet Maebelle had sewn for Lucky. He lay on it on his side, the way he liked to stretch out in the morning sun. A single candle was burning on a pedestal by his head.

"'And there was war again,'" Mrs. Wingate read, "'and David went out, and fought with the Philistines, and slew them with a great slaughter; and they fled from him.'" She closed the Bible and placed it on a table by the sofa arm. She removed her reading glasses and folded them atop the Bible.

"He was poisoned, Charlie. Marcellus found butcher's paper wadded up under the steps at the carriage house. He slept in the garden with the other dogs most of the afternoon. Then he wasn't comfortable, and began to pace. He was panting, so Maebelle brought him water. He lapped up every drop. He lay back down and seemed to sleep.

"Then I heard him yelp. I came to the back window and he was standing in the yard. Then he ran as hard as he could into the side of the house and fell. He couldn't get up. Maebelle and Marcellus carried him into the parlor. He seemed to rest for a while. Then his breathing grew shallow, and then it stopped, near nightfall. That's when Marcellus saw the cross alight and ran to get help with the fire. I called the fire department. By the time their wagon arrived, we'd stopped the flames from spreading to the house."

"I need to move away, Mrs. Wingate," I said.

"You'll not move away from here," she said. Her eyes flashed. "Not if I have any say in the matter. Vile, self-righteous Philistines. You'll not bow to them, Charles Mears!" Her voice broke. She took her kerchief from her lap and wiped her eyes.

"Tell him good-bye," she whispered. "He was so gentle, brutally as he'd been used. It was you who saved him, Charlie. Go on."

The candle flickered as I stepped toward Lucky. The blaze on his chest seemed to move in the light. I knelt and ran my hand over his broad head. The tips of his ears felt cold. The torn ear crinkled like rusted tin. I touched the thick edges of the scars on his neck.

"Marcellus says now that the weather's cooler, he could take up two of the big azaleas in the garden," Mrs. Wingate said. "And we could lay him there. Marcellus says he would dig the grave deep and mulch the azaleas thick when he replants them. He doesn't have a doubt they would live and bloom. Marcellus is very clever about these things. Do you think Lucky would like that, Charlie?" Mrs. Wingate asked. "To rest there in the garden?"

"Oh, yes, ma'am, he would," I said.

"Well, he shall till the trumpet sounds," she said.

I was crying and I couldn't stop. I pressed my face against the great dog's chest and dug my fingers into his coat.

24.

First Lady

W hen the pressmen came in one morning and found a window to the back door of the office shattered, they were jumpy. But inside was a baseball, and they realized it must have been boys playing in the alley. Still, Mr. Young wanted me to cover straight news for a while.

"Let the column lie fallow," he said. But I told him that was just what they wanted, and it didn't seem right if we were to give up.

"Thought this kind of thing had died out," he said. "But I reckon it never will. I'm not going to push you, Charlie. But if something else like Lincoln Street happens, we're shutting down the column for a while. Agreed?"

"Yes, sir," I said. Fortunately, nothing did. I still felt men were shadowing me, but if they were, they were good at it. I was never certain I was being watched.

Two weeks after the presidential election, Mr. Young received a press release from the governor's mansion. First Lady Etta Donnan Mann and Governor William Hodges Mann requested the honor of Mr. Young's or his representative's attendance at the governor's mansion for a harvest party the Saturday evening before Thanksgiving. Governor Mann would be discussing for members of the press the Progressive initiatives the Commonwealth might expect with native son Woodrow Wilson in the Oval Office. Mrs. Mann would announce her plans for the coming year-long celebration of the governor's mansion centennial. Finally, Richmond's own John Powell, an internationally renowned concert pianist and composer, would be the guest of honor. Powell was just returning from a tour in Europe for a performance at the Richmond Concert Hall.

Mrs. Young wasn't about to let Mr. Young escape weekend duty minding the children. So I found myself riding the train from Hampton to attend Powell's afternoon concert. The hall was in walking distance of the Main Street station.

According to the program, Powell had graduated from the University of Virginia at the age of nineteen and made his debut as a pianist in Berlin after studying in Vienna for two years. His compositions melded American folk song and Negro rhythms with classical structure. *Sonata Virginianesque* had been performed in Vienna to great acclaim, and Powell's next concert was scheduled in New York.

His first piece was Franz Liszt's *Concerto in A Flat Major.* When Powell finished, every person in my section rose, clapping. I stood, too. Some cheered loudly. When the house finally quieted, violinist Efrem Zimbalist strode onto the stage to play Powell's newest composition, *Violin Concerto in E, Opus 23,* accompanied by Powell at the piano. The performance brought down the house. Amid huzzahs from the audience, Zimbalist crowned Powell with the oak laurel from the Wednesday Club, the ladies' musical group sponsoring the event. Mrs. Mann served as chairwoman.

Even the wrought-iron fence outside the governor's mansion was decorated. Wheat sheaves, Indian corn, and garlands of autumn leaves were woven into the fence and railing up to the portico. There were baskets of Golden Delicious and Albemarle Pippin apples, and pumpkins and gourds of every shape and color in the foyer and hall.

Mrs. Mann was in high spirits. Her gown was beige. The bodice was embroidered in hues of red and brown. When I entered the foyer she was speaking with a group of men. A genteel Negro with hair as white as cotton bowed toward me. He was wearing black tie.

"Sir?" he asked.

"Charles Mears," I said. A colored girl passed carrying cups on a silver tray.

"Lavinia?" the Negro said. "Would you offer Mr. Mears some punch?"

"Thank you," I said. He escorted me toward Mrs. Mann's audience. She paused in her conversation as I approached.

"Mrs. Mann," the Negro said, "Mr. Charles Mears."

"Of the *Norfolk Journal and Guide*," I said.

Mrs. Mann extended a gloved hand.

"I'm so pleased you could join us, Mr. Mears. Thank you, Winston."

"Yes, ma'am," he said. He bowed and returned to the doorway.

"As I was saying, the punch bowl in the governor's mansion was broken by accident the day Hodges and I entered the house," Mrs. Mann said. "And I viewed that as a good omen. Not once have we served spirits or wine, nor will we, as long as Hodges is governor. My personal recipes for punch are renowned in Richmond. Not once in my life have I seen Hodges drink alcohol or use tobacco. His favorite beverage is buttermilk. Does this recipe meet with your approval, Mr. Mears?"

I sipped from my cup. "Yes, ma'am," I said. "It's delicious."

"There's a touch of tangerine juice. It takes the bitterness from the cranberries."

"It's wonderful, Mrs. Mann," I said.

"Have you met Mr. Louis Jaffé? I expect the two of you are about the same age. He's the pride of the Richmond press corps. Very Progressive, so of course Hodges is in love with him. It's rumored he might be a Socialist, though, isn't that right, Mr. Jaffé?"

Jaffé was a short, powerfully built man. He wore a bow tie and his thick moustache was closely trimmed. I had met him on one of my trips to Richmond to see Virgie. He was at the penitentiary to interview Warden Wood for a *Times-Dispatch* feature about the crime rate.

"Why, some have even called me a Marxist, Mrs. Mann," he said. There were big dimples in his cheeks when he smiled.

"Oh, for goodness' sake," Mrs. Mann said. "There are so many 'ists' these days, it's impossible to keep up. And this absurd women's suffrage movement. Hysterical females declaiming at every public meeting hall or parade. Why any person, male or female, could believe women should have the vote in a general election is beyond my poor powers of reason. Anyway, we're grateful for your support of Tom Wilson, Mr. Jaffé. After sixteen years of Republicans in the White House, we turned them out. It took good Southern Democrats to accomplish that, didn't it?"

Jaffé bowed and raised his punch cup. "Indeed, it did, Mrs. Mann. And a little help from Teddy Roosevelt."

"Oh, the Bull Moose, the Bull Moose. I'm so weary of hearing about the Bull Moose. I remember now, Mr. Mears," she said. "Your eyeglasses. You covered the governor's inauguration."

"No, ma'am. I'm afraid not. I was still at my studies."

"Oh?" she said.

"Yes, ma'am. William & Mary. I joined the Hampton *Times-Herald* the second year of your husband's term."

"Now I recall," she said. "You're the young man who wrote that excellent article about the Enabling Act when you were president of the Inter-Collegiate Prohibition Associates."

"Secretary," I said.

"A leader, regardless," she said. "Now, the *Journal and Guide*, that's a colored newspaper, isn't it?"

"Yes, ma'am."

She arched an eyebrow. "Interesting," she said. "Well, we pray

Hodges will see Prohibition state-wide before the end of his term. If only we can get the cooperation of the legislature. That would be something grand, wouldn't it, Mr. Mears?"

"Yes, ma'am."

"I'm so sorry the governor isn't here to meet you. I'm afraid the concert quite wore him out, so he turned in right after supper. His health is excellent, but as you know, he's not a young man, Mr. Mears. Well, I'd better visit with some of the other guests. The mayor's wife can be affronted by the slightest neglect. You simply must meet John Powell while you're here. A genius of our time. I understand that his father the headmaster is bringing some girls from the seminary. They're quite attractive and sing like birds, I'm told. They should liven up the party for handsome, intellectual young men like yourselves."

"Thank you, Mrs. Mann," I said.

She moved into another room and extended her hand to a man in a military uniform.

"Forgive me?" Jaffé said.

"Yes?"

"You're not colored, are you?"

"No."

"Then how on earth did you convince Plummer Young to hire you?"

"I'm not sure," I said.

"You're doing a fine job," he said. "Writing what needs to be written. But Young's an accommodationist, you know."

"I know," I said. "But he stands when there's standing to be done."

"Yes, I suppose he does," Jaffé said. "Anyway, good luck. Been reading about the mess in the Balkans?"

"Yes," I said.

"It's a bloodbath. We'll stay out of any war for sure, now that Wilson's taking office. They say ambulance drivers are needed."

"Well," I said.

"I may sign on," Jaffé said. "Anyway, keep up the good work." He moved into the crowd.

I finished my punch and decided to go out on the portico for a smoke. The evening was mild, and several men were outside, laughing and talking. A man reached inside his breast pocket and removed a silver flask. He unscrewed the top and offered it to his companion. He took the flask and drank, then returned it. The man drank and screwed on the top, placing the flask back at his breast.

In front of the mansion was a pea gravel drive. There were a few motorcars, but most of the vehicles were shiny carriages with fine horses. Liverymen had the horses' noses draped with feedbags. The horses' teeth squeaked as they ate their oats. A harvest moon hung low over the James River. I watched a handsomely dressed couple walk down the steps towards a phaeton. Their feet crunched in the gravel. The driver got out from under the wheel and opened a passenger door. I leaned against a column and lit a cigarette.

"Figured I'd find you amongst the tobacco fiends," a voice said from the shadow of a column. Pace stepped into the light. He tipped a finger to his brow. "Evening, Charlie," he said.

I lifted my chin and blew smoke. "Well, it's Judas," I said.

"You got me all wrong, you know," Pace said.

I looked him over. "How so?" I asked.

"You think I wanted your job and all," he said. "Maybe I did. But the owner, Mr. Thacker, come looking for me, Charlie, not the other way round. He was standing right outside the sheriff's office when I walked out with Dr. V's coroner's report on Mr. Hobgood in my hand. He offered me the job right on the spot, with a raise to boot. He didn't say one word about you. For all I knowed, he'd give you a promotion. You's in my place, Charlie, have a man show up to offer you a job at better money than you was making, you'd done the same thing. I don't rightly know why Mr. Thacker wanted me, but he did, Charlie."

I looked out toward the river. From inside the mansion I could hear the sound of a woman's voice, then a ripple of laughter, followed by loud applause. Mrs. Mann must have introduced her guest of honor.

"Truth is, Charlie, I'm better than you at bird-dogging the news," Pace said. "But any fool knows I can't think as good as you. There, I've said it."

That sentence had cost him a lot. I thought about that.

"Thank you," I said.

Pace nodded. "I'll tell you something else, Charlie," he said. "What I been hearing, you'd best watch your backside."

"What do you mean?"

"Oh, bunch of crackers getting into their liquor, spouting off and all. Probably nothing. But better safe than sorry. See you around."

"See you, Pace," I said. He disappeared behind the column. I crushed the cigarette with my shoe and dropped it in the cuspidor.

INSIDE THE CONVERSATION HAD grown louder. A courtly man with silver hair led a group of six young women onto a dais in the hall. They were very pretty. I saw Jaffé standing close to the front, along with some other young men. The courtly man clapped his gloved hands. When the crowd quieted, he announced that the young ladies from the Richmond Female Seminary would now sing James Bland's popular anthem, "Carry Me Back to Old Virginny." Mrs. Mann had been right. The girls' voices were lovely as birdsong. The people in the hall clapped and whistled. Some of the women were dabbing silk kerchiefs to their eyes.

I grinned to see Jaffé gazing up at the face of a songstress who had her blonde hair braided in a twist. He seemed to hang on her every note. Her throat was smooth and pale. I thought of Harriet. I decided I might try to find a quiet place to sit down for a moment.

Off the reception hall was a room with the door just ajar. I pushed it open. There were no guests. I stepped inside.

Atop the fireplace mantel were several daguerreotypes and photographs in silver frames. One was a portrait of the Manns with their children and grandchildren. Another showed the governor and Mrs. Mann in the front seat, and Governor Wilson and his wife in the rear seat of an open touring car. The ladies' bonnets were securely tied. By a window with floral drapes closed from ceiling to floor sat a Steinway & Sons piano with handsome mahogany inlays. I lifted the fallboard and touched middle-C.

There was a rustle at the door behind me. Mrs. Mann stood next to a tall young man with brown hair and eyes clear as springwater.

"My mother purchased that instrument just before the war," Mrs. Mann said. "She selected it herself at the Steinway offices on Varick Street in New York. Mr. Steinweg himself—he hadn't yet Anglicized his name—helped her. She waited until the piano was crated for shipment and brought it with her on the train to Petersburg. It's remarkable it wasn't chopped up for firewood during the siege. I'm not quite sure how Mother managed it—I never asked her. Oh, she had such a lovely singing voice. She taught me to play on this very instrument. We moved it to the governor's mansion just after she passed away. I'm afraid this parlor is a bit snug for it. Do you play, Mr. Mears?"

"No, ma'am," I said.

"I wanted to be sure you met Mr. Powell," she said. "*Et voila!* Mr. John Powell, this is Mr. Charles Mears of the *Norfolk Journal and Guide*."

"How do you do?" Powell said. He stepped over to the piano and extended his hand. I shook it.

"How do you do, sir?" I said. "Your music is magnificent."

"Thank you," he said.

"Come, gentleman, let's visit for a moment," Mrs. Mann said. She gestured to the sofa and chairs at the center of the room. Powell helped Mrs. Mann take her seat in a wingback chair facing the sofa, then sat by her in the other chair. I took a place on the sofa. The maid who had served me punch earlier stood in the doorway.

"Mr. Mears, you must try one of Lavinia's cheese biscuits," Mrs. Mann said. "They're envied in these parts." Lavinia smiled broadly and walked over to the sofa, extending a tray.

"Thank you," I said. I took a biscuit.

Powell also took a biscuit and tasted it. His brow rose. "Delicious, Mrs. Mann," he said. The maid smiled even more broadly.

Mrs. Mann took a biscuit and placed it in her napkin. "Thank you, Lavinia," she said. The maid left the room.

"Lavinia is one of Winston Edmunds' children," she said. "Do you recall Uncle Win, Mr. Mears? He announced you when you entered."

"Yes," I said.

"Uncle Win has served every governor of Virginia since Fitzhugh Lee," Mrs. Mann said.

Powell nodded. "Impressive," he said.

"He's simply superb," Mrs. Mann said. "One of those old-time darkies who knows his place. He anticipates the thing to be done at just the right moment in just the proper way. I never breathe a word or lift a finger. It can all be left to Uncle Win. He's a Negro who understands true Virginia hospitality."

"Yes, ma'am."

"Lavinia is Uncle Win's youngest child," she said. "I say 'child.' She'll soon be twenty-one years old."

Mrs. Mann took a bite of her biscuit. "They're remarkable, aren't they?"

"Oh, yes," I said.

She looked at the piano. "It's a shame how many of our childhood

memories are lost to us," she said. "I feel blessed in my own case. I
retain the most vivid memory of my uncle in his colonel's uniform
with sash. I was four years old. He was home for Christmas. To me
he looked like a European prince, his brown beard full and manly
and tinctured with witch hazel. He picked me up and kissed me
on the lips and I scrubbed my mouth with my hand because his
beard itched so. He laughed out loud and set me down. There was
a thin garland of pink roses and smilax draped on the mantel, and
a sparse little tree with presents wrapped in brown paper. He was
killed at Petersburg that spring, when the siege lines were broken.
Of course, it was over a few days after that.

"Those were dark years. Federal troops everywhere. Colored
freemen in Congress, even in the state legislature. It wasn't until
I was a student at Mary Baldwin Seminary that I saw some of the
old places in the Valley being restored to beauty and prosperity.
Mr. Mears, may I ask you a favor?"

"Of course, Mrs. Mann."

"Whenever you write about my husband," she said, "will you
always express what a good Christian man he is? Hodges is so
devout. Such a noble and gentle man. He cares so deeply about
what is good in the world, about what is good in the South. And
how to make it better. His mind is sharp as ever, but he's growing
frail. I'm forever reminding him to wipe his moustache. Men like
Hodges are not made every day, Mr. Mears. A man of such deep
faith. 'We shall not look upon his like again,' as the bard wrote."

"No, ma'am," I said.

"Indeed," Powell said.

"Sometimes I feel my faith—well, flags," I said.

"No, Mr. Mears, you mustn't say that," she said. "Faith is like
coal hidden in ashes; it will flame forth! You are a young man.
Your devotion has not left you. It is, perhaps, obscured, for now."

"Thank you, Mrs. Mann."

"Why would you say such a thing?"

"I lost a friend. A dear friend. And my mother. Not long ago. Everything changed."

"You see?" she said. "Even now, Mr. Mears, your speaking demonstrates faith dwells in your heart. Why else would you tell me?"

"I don't know, Mrs. Mann. I apologize for burdening you."

"Nonsense," she said. "Nonsense, Mr. Mears. You have burdened no one but yourself. If Hodges were here he would tell you the same thing. Only Hodges would be able to comfort you the way only a man can comfort another man. Your open heart makes you able to understand my husband's faith, Mr. Mears, makes it possible for you to write about him as the words *should* be written. I know you will do this."

"Yes, ma'am."

She touched her napkin to her lips. Her gaze came to rest on the piano. She mused for a moment.

"You know, Mr. Mears," she said. "This mansion has seen great men, brilliant men." She smiled. "And of course, here and there, a scoundrel. But it has also seen genius. A true genius. Tonight. This very night." She turned her gaze toward the other chair. "Mr. Powell," she said, "I beg you to play something on my mother's piano."

Powell leaned forward in his chair. "Mrs. Mann," he said. "It would be my honor."

25.

Anglo-Saxon

Powell stood. There was something majestic about him. A lock of hair had drooped to his forehead and he pushed it back calmly. His steps were measured. He sat at the piano. His hands, small for a pianist's, arched above the keys.

He turned and smiled. "Forgive me, Mrs. Mann, this is merely an idea, but a seductive one. I believe I have at least the leitmotif."

His fingers pounded the bass keys and Mrs. Mann gasped. Rhythms swirled over the drumming of the bass, fantastical, clamoring in the minor key, like shrieks. Mrs. Mann leaned forward, agitated. And then the melody of the Negro spiritual, "Swing Low, Sweet Chariot," began to emerge amid the shrieks and pounding, and its melody surged from the piano, filling the room. Mrs. Mann breathed a sigh.

Powell stopped. We applauded.

"Thrilling!" the first lady said.

"I warned you, Mrs. Mann, it's merely an idea. But the minor-thirds are fierce, are they not?"

"Frightening," Mrs. Mann said.

"God willing, when I'm able to complete it, I'll name it "Rhapsody Nègre," in tribute to my friend Joseph Conrad. We became friends in Vienna. Have you read his *Heart of Darkness*, Mrs. Mann?"

"Goodness, no," she said.

"I understand," Powell said.

"But perhaps our Wednesday Club might take it up," she said.

"In truth, Mrs. Mann," Powell said, "the novel is not appropriate to every sensibility. Certainly you and the ladies of your club have more suitable and entertaining books to read."

He closed the fallboard and pivoted on the bench. "And you, Mr. Mears, what is your opinion?"

"Well, Mr. Powell, I'm no musician."

"All the better," he said.

"The spiritual," I said, "the way it emerges, like redemption. It's beautiful."

"Thank you, Mr. Mears. You are far too modest about your powers of perception."

"Yes," Mrs. Mann said. "Like folk song in Stravinsky!"

"Oh, Mrs. Mann, now you really do flatter me. Thank you. Thank you both."

Mrs. Mann folded her hands in her lap and glanced up at the ceiling. Then she rested her gaze on me.

"Hodges showed me your letter, Mr. Mears," she said.

"Ma'am?"

"There were hundreds, of course. But he showed me yours, the day after he received it. He wanted to know what I thought. As a woman. No one truly understands how Hodges agonized over his decision about clemency for the Negress, Mr. Mears. How he prayed."

"Mrs. Mann, I didn't mean to trouble your husband. But the girl . . ."

"The girl!" she said. "Hodges did precisely what needed to be done. He had the prison superintendent examine the Negress to confirm her age. She was an adult. The warden so advised Hodges. She was convicted by a jury of her peers who weighed all the evidence. That Negress murdered a white woman in her own house.

She left the woman in a pool of blood and broken crockery to be discovered by her own daughters!"

"Her teacher testified according to school records Virgie was sixteen years old at the time of the crime, Mrs. Mann. A juvenile. Just one day past her seventeenth birthday when she was executed. Still a juvenile."

"Her own father couldn't confirm her birth date," she said.

"That's true, ma'am. And sad to say, not unusual."

"A moot point," Mrs. Mann said. "The Negroes are a race of children, Mr. Mears. At the beginning of his administration Hodges was able to have legislation passed denying them access to alcohol. Think of the violence and debauchery that law has subverted! Whether the Negress was sixteen or sixty, what does it matter? She would have no more capacity to understand. She would have no more ability to control her instincts. Yet all Hodges heard for weeks and months were cries for mercy. Where was the mercy for poor Mrs. Belote?"

"May I get you anything, Mrs. Mann?" Lavinia was standing at the door to the parlor. Mrs. Mann eased back in her chair and caught her breath. She touched her napkin to her lips.

"No, thank you, Lavinia."

"Yes, ma'am."

Mrs. Mann again turned to me. "Believe me, Mr. Mears," she said. "I know your intentions are good. You saw an ignorant Negress who had committed a brutal act, her mind so simple she could not even comprehend the significance of the crime. Good Lord! She bought penny candy at the local store with money stolen from the murdered woman's purse. This Negress was bereft of family, alone in her prison cell. She was terrorized by her dreams and God knows what demons. She confessed her crime to you, its manner and motive. She opened her heart, spoke of her fears, her desire to live. Like any good Christian, you wanted to help this Negress.

You told people her story, when she had not the words to tell it herself. You wrote a letter to another good Christian, my husband, a man of wisdom and position, and asked him to show mercy by sparing this Negress' life.

"You are a young man, Mr. Mears, full of ideals. So you can little imagine the violence and suffering that could have occurred in Hampton, in Virginia, maybe even beyond the borders of our state, if Hodges had listened to your plea for clemency, or the editorials of colored newspapermen, or the outcry of pastors and women's groups. You haven't seen what Hodges was trying so desperately to avoid, what happened so often in the past, what sadly still happens in these modern times. Innocent Negroes dragged from their homes and shops and lynched, Mr. Mears. Negroes could've been barred from working in white households. Little children through no fault of their own could have starved from their parents' lack of work.

"Hodges loves Virginia. He loves it to the very core of his soul. Think of the times he lived through, Mr. Mears. Think of him seeing gentility sullied, and jackanapes running the government he revered, all while sullen troops in blue, his conquerors, made sure the 'rule of law' they had imposed was kept?

"I cannot count the times he woke from his sleep, crying out, lost in his nightmares of men dying in agony about him where he lay in a field hospital. You have perceived what a delicate and caring man Hodges is, Mr. Mears. Surely you can imagine the condition of his mind. Such a gracious, Christian man, having seen Hell itself in the war?"

She began to fold her napkin edge-to-edge, undoing it, then folding again.

"Hodges had relented, Mr. Mears. After your letter. You remember how hot it was this July? He was sitting with me on the gallery overlooking the gravel drive at the mansion. The evening breeze from the river was a blessing. 'You know, Etta,' he said. 'I enjoy hearing the sound of hooves and carriage wheels on the drive. It makes me feel young.' He took my hand and held it. 'Blessed are the merciful,' he said, 'for they shall obtain mercy.' Our Savior taught us that, Etta. It's just one colored girl. You saw what the newsman wrote.'

"'I did, Hodges, but it's not just one life,' I said. I reminded him he had to be strong not only for himself but for all of us. I helped him write his response that very night. 'I know this woman's life is in my hands and it is a serious matter to me, but I also know that the lives of the innocent people of this Commonwealth have to be protected, and that in showing mercy to the guilty I always run the risk of being cruel to the innocent.'

"You remember reading those words, don't you, Mr. Mears? I'm sure they came as a deep disappointment. Don't look shocked! I merely helped my husband remember what he believed, though for a moment he had been overwhelmed by the onslaught of public opinion." She placed the folded napkin on the table beside her chair.

"Perhaps not this evening, but some day, you will understand my position, Mr. Mears." She rose, and Powell and I stood. "I'm afraid I've abandoned my guests," she said, "but I've so enjoyed conversing with you two gentlemen."

"Thank you, Mrs. Mann," I said. "You were kind to share your time."

She offered her hand. "Like most newspapermen, Mr. Mears," she said, "you make an excellent liar." I pressed her hand. She smiled and left the room.

Powell moved from the piano bench over to Mrs. Mann's chair.

"Shall we sit?" he asked.

"Yes," I said.

Mrs. Mann's napkin lay on the rug at his feet. He retrieved and carefully folded it. He placed it on the table between us. He sat back in the chair for a moment and studied the ceiling. Then he sat upright, leaning toward me.

"Would you grant, Mr. Mears, that a final solution for the Negro problem must be found?" he asked.

"The 'Negro problem' as defined by whites is quite different from the definition held by most blacks, Mr. Powell. Which one do you mean?"

He smiled and tapped a finger on the table.

"Mr. Mears, I know you are a Christian and I admire the enthusiasm of your faith. But history clearly shows that no white society has survived the taint of colored blood. Miscegenation corrupts society and defiles ideals. The Negroes are a race of brutes, Mr. Mears. This is not my verdict, but the verdict of history. Mixing with the colored represents nothing short of the suicide of the white race.

"Your crossing the color line, if in fact you *have* crossed the line, a subject I'm sure Dr. Plecker's office is looking into, has done nothing to better the good relations that exist between the races. Your writing has achieved nothing, except to stir up bad feelings. When passions are inflamed, the actions of the white race can be as brutish as those of the Negro. I know you are not the sort of man who subscribes to lynching and riot, but there are some men who do.

"Why not listen to the voices of enlightenment and science? Why not look at the bright future eugenics and racial purity offer the modern world? A world free of disease and hunger? Someday soon, Mr. Mears, the educated and successful will organize here in Virginia and across the South, even across America, to guard the sacred values of Anglo-Saxon civilization, and advance the cause of science, so that the Negro and all his infirmities are segregated and finally expunged from white society.

"That day is not yet here, Mr. Mears, but it is coming. I assure you."

"Mr. Powell, I can't come round to your way of thinking. It's not Christian."

"My God, man, talk to Plecker! He'll tell you yours is the un-Christian belief. He'll tell you stories about innocent children, the offspring of lust between the races, children whose lives are ruined forever, because they have no place in the white world or in the Negro world, for that matter."

Powell stood and tugged down the hem of his jacket.

"I apologize for the heat of my comments, Mr. Mears. I know you are a man of reason and ideals. I hope my enthusiasm in our conversation has not caused you to doubt I am such a man myself. But I must caution you, Mr. Mears, that there are others who share my beliefs, and they are *not* so reasonable as you and I."

"Who do you mean, Mr. Powell?"

"I mean no one," he said, smiling. "And everyone, Mr. Mears. Many are wanton criminals, no better than the Negro himself, in my opinion. I have no control over their actions. But many gentlemen of Virginia see science and medicine as the true path to salvation for the Anglo-Saxon race, Mr. Mears, not the violence of drunken louts."

"I was taught the Lord Jesus Christ was the true path to salvation."

"Of course you were," Powell said. "It's quite obvious. And now I must bid you a good evening, Mr. Mears. Thank you for your kind words about my music." He bent at the waist and turned to leave, pushing the lock of hair from his forehead. Then he stopped.

"I believe you have no family. Is that correct?"

"Yes, my parents are dead."

"Family are so important to one's development. And you were good friends with a young man, Fitzhugh Scott, also deceased?"

"Yes," I said. "Did you know Fitz?"

"The girls' school where my father is headmaster is always in need of money. Anyone in need of money knows the Scotts, Mr. Mears. Good night."

ONE OF THE PHAETONS I had noticed at the governor's mansion clopped by as I walked toward the Main Street station. I looked about for Pace, but he must have left the party before me. The night had grown chilly. The harvest moon was high in the firmament, white and cold, casting shadows on the roof tiles and façade of the station. The face of the clock in the tower shone silver in the moonlight.

Just a handful of people were waiting for the Tidewater train, the last eastbound of the day. I showed my ticket to the conductor as I boarded. I found a seat by the window, loosened my tie, and tucked my eyeglasses in my pocket. I leaned my head against the glass, and was asleep before the train departed the station.

Poindexter was working late. He must have spied me from the platform as the train pulled into the depot. He was standing by my seat, shaking my shoulder.

"Better roust yourself, Charlie," he said. "Train's about to head for the shed."

I felt groggy. I fumbled for my glasses and put them on.

"Hobnobbing with them bigwigs must've wore you out," he said. "Did you shake hands with the governor?"

We stepped down onto the platform. "No," I said. "But I spoke with Mrs. Mann."

"Ain't you the big cheese," he said. "Anybody else? Maybe a congressman or opera singer?"

"No," I said. "I saw Pace."

Steam gushed from the brakes as the train moved out. The rush nearly blew off my cap.

"Oh, yeah, he come through quite a while ago. Said he got some swell statement about the role the governor played in electing Wilson."

"Well," I said.

"Sorry about your dog, Charlie," he said. "Takes a mean son of a bitch to pull a stunt like that."

"Thanks, Poindexter. I'll be seeing you."

"Charlie?" he said.

"Yes?"

"I hear a lot of claptrap. Way I see it, a man's got the right to work for who he wants to, where he wants to."

"Thanks."

"Be seeing you, Charlie."

Thump, thump. I remembered the sound of Lucky's tail beating the floor when he heard me trotting up the steps. But now my rooms were silent. The lock seemed stiff when I turned the key. I stepped over the jamb and reached for the light. Then I noticed the sour odor of witch hazel.

"We been waiting for you, Charlie," a voice said.

I heard a thump. There was searing pain and light, as if I had fallen into the sun. Then everything went black.

26.

The Colony

When I woke I was adrift in darkness. There were voices and lights and darkness again. Then I saw a round hole with gray light. It seemed a universe away. I blinked and fell back to sleep.

I don't know how long it was before I awoke again. The light in the hole was brighter. I could feel broad, rough-sawn boards beneath me. I ached all over. My groin burned. I wanted to throw up. I lifted myself and leaned against a wall. My foot struck something metal. I heard a slosh, then smelled the stench of waste. I rubbed my finger over my lip and felt something warm. I ran my finger over my teeth and counted. They were in place.

I heard a rooster crow. Then I heard footfalls. The light in the round hole disappeared. Everything looked misty. I touched the bridge of my nose. My eyeglasses were gone. I heard keys and the tumblers of a lock. Light poured in and I raised my hand to shield my eyes.

"Is you awake, Charlie?" a voice whispered. "You *my* Charlie, ain't you?"

In the mist an orb moved close. I felt breath on my cheek. I could make out the shape of a face. It had no ears. Its eyes were green.

"Don't you know me, Charlie?" the voice said. "Where your glasses?"

I reached for the face and pulled it closer. The head glistened copper. My fingers touched the scar where an ear should be. The skin felt warm. I realized how cold I was. My fingers were stiff.

"Red?" I said.

"You damn right it's Red!" he said. "Doc done sterilized me and cut off my ears, too! What you think about that? Say they gone let me go, now folks can see I's a mongrel. Here, try to stand up. Look like somebody busted your lip good." He took hold of my arm and lifted. "Cold as a witch's titty," he said. "We got to find you a coat."

When I stood, pain licked up my groin like fire. I leaned against the wall and Red steadied me. I was shivering.

"Doc Priddy operated on you his own self," Red said. "Boss man. Heard him say he finally got that Mears the newspaperman and I figured that just had to be *my* Charlie Mears. You think about it, how many Mearses would they be running round, anyhow? And see? I's right." He took off his gray muslin jacket. "Stick out your arms and put this on," he said. He pulled the jacket onto my shoulders.

"What is this place?" I said. "Where am I?"

"Amherst," Red said. "The Colony."

"What's that?"

"I don't know. Just the Colony, is all." He buttoned the coat over my chest.

"Doc say cause my daddy a white man and got my momma, they say he sure to been a degenerate and I sure to be, too, being his son. Maybe even a moron. That's why I's here. Doc Priddy say you degenerate, too, things you been writing. What you been writing, anyways? Must been something damn aggravating, them putting you in the blind box straight after they got you fixed. Usual they keeps you in bed a couple days. Next thing I knows, long come this tall fellow, say he looking to fetch Charlie Mears out of here. So I figures he got to be looking for *my* Charlie, too."

"Who?"

"Pace."

"Charlie Pace?"

"He just say Pace. Got some girl with him."

"Harriet? Harriet's here?"

"Didn't say no name. I just seen her. Face white like a ghost. Funny, though. Most times when a new girl see me now, she scream her head off. But this one don't bat an eye. Come on, Charlie! I got to get you downstairs quick, fore them nurses come round. They gone fix me worse'n when they catches me choking my pecker. They don't like no masturbating, I tell you. That masturbating *degenerate*, what they say."

Red held my elbow as we moved down the hall. Dawn brightened the windows. From the balcony I could see Pace and Harriet crouched by the façade steps.

"This way, Charlie," Red said, opening a door to a stairway. I had to take the steps one-by-one. Each step down was a knife in my groin. We exited through a door by the front steps. Pace and Harriet sprang up and ran to us. Harriet buried her face in my chest and hugged me. Red pushed us all into a clump of rhododendrons by the building. The earth was frozen beneath the litter. It crunched under our feet.

Pace took wire rim eyeglasses from his coat pocket and handed them to me.

"Found these on the floor at your place," he said. "Thought you might be needing them, you being blind and all." He grinned.

"Well," I said.

Harriet was sobbing. "Charlie," she said. "I was so worried."

"It's all right, Harriet," I said. "Everything will be all right. We're in the hands of God."

"Brought you a pack of smokes, too," Pace said. I nodded, pulling the wire temple pieces behind my ears. The nose piece was bent, but it was all right.

"Now what?" I asked.

"First thing they gone do after they sees you is out the box is turn loose them dogs," Red said. "We got to get to the river. Crouch down when you runs."

Red took my hand and I took Harriet's. We pushed clear of the rhododendrons. Pace trotted behind us, then sprinted ahead, taking cover behind a fence beyond the main building. I did the best I could, but crouching, I could barely manage to walk. We joined Pace at the fence. I was breathing hard. I heard cows lowing from a barn beyond the fence, and a rooster crowed again. I heard pigs grunting. Ahead of us stood two brick gate guards with a sign marked "Virginia Colony for Epileptics and Feebleminded Cemetery." The plot was lined with an iron fence. Beyond the fence was a wide meadow with tufts of broom sedge and beyond the meadow, a dark line of trees.

"That way," Red said. "Don't quit running till you gets to the woods, no matter what. Skedaddle! I'll catch up."

Pace took my hand and I clung to Harriet's. We made it as far as the cemetery. I leaned against one of the gate guards and vomited. I wiped my mouth with my hand and looked into the cemetery. There was a lone marker. "John Doe," it read. "October 16, 1911. Aged sixteen." I could see Red waving us on from the fence. I couldn't get my breath.

"Charlie," Pace said. "Lock your hands round my chest and hop on." I let go Harriet's hand. She helped me onto Pace's back. I locked my hands as he cupped his hands under my thighs. He started at a trot and held it to the middle of the meadow. I could hear him breathing hard. He slowed to walk a few steps.

"Pace," I said. "I can make it from here."

"That's all right," he said. He moved his hands closer to my knees for better grip and took up his trot. "Harriet," he said. "Run ahead to the trees."

"No," she said. "I'm staying with you." Pace managed to keep going. Harriet steadied him at the elbow when he staggered. There was a thicket of blackberry vines and greenbriers at the edge of the woods. Pace stumbled through, thorns clutching at his trousers and jacket. In the woods we collapsed against a poplar trunk. I could hear the sound of water.

I looked back and saw Red jump the fence. He ran past the cemetery, sprinting across the meadow. He was smiling the broad smile of our boyhood days. He ran like a wild thing. His mutilation made him all the more feral, as if everything human had been taken away.

"Hey!" A man in a white coat was standing in front of the building. He pointed in Red's direction. "Hey," he shouted. "You stop!" I heard voices at the barn, and the clank of milk pails. By the pigpens there were boys in gray muslin jackets pointing toward the meadow.

Red collapsed on his knees next to us, his chest heaving. "Straight through the woods," he said. "Till you comes to the bluffs. Head right. You'll see a path. At the river, head downstream. You'll sees a big rock white as goose shit. Sight on it fifty feet straight up the bank. Stole me a little boat. Covered up with sticks. Ain't got no paddle. Fetch you a limb, maybe you can pole a ways. Stays to the bank. Don't gets in the current. They's sure to be looking on the river, though. You rides far as Scottsville, they ain't no way in hell sheriff won't pick you up. You got to get off the river fore Scottsville. You sinks that boat and head cross-country."

"What about you?" I said.

"I'm gone run up yonder," Red said. "Where all them morons is. Railroad spur come in behind the barn. One time hopped me a car far as Danville. Doc Priddy give me thirty days in the box for that one. Anyways, dogs'll run my scent. They knows it plenty good."

He looked at me. "Sorry I didn't play with you that time you come to see me, Charlie. I's just mad about school. Momma found out what I did, she tanned me good. I don't blames you for not coming back." He rose and helped me stand. "Alreda sure miss them pennies, though." He grinned.

"Franklin," I said.

"Told you don't never call me that!" he said. Then he ran, dodging gray tree trunks. I heard dogs baying. The man in the white coat in front of the building had vanished. Pace lifted my arm over his shoulder and we started for the bluffs. I heard something whiz and snap through the tree limbs above our heads. Then I heard the report of a rifle. Harriet gasped. I turned. She was balled up at the base of the tree, clutching her hands to her ears. Her face was pale and frozen. I thought if I touched it, her face might shatter in a thousand pieces.

"Harriet," I said. "We have to go. We have to go *now*."

Her eyes darted about the meadow. Then she calmed herself and stood, pressing her dress with her hands. Suddenly bits of bark splintered from the tree and settled in her hair. I saw a white crease like a scar across the trunk. Then I heard another report. With my free hand I grabbed hers and pushed her in front of us.

"Run!" I said. And she did, tumbling over a tree root but getting quickly up. We ran blindly, till we reached the bluffs. The river was a dizzying plunge below, dark water roiling with current, big white bubbles riding the chute. We turned to the right and found the path, Harriet leading us single file down the escarpment, with me following, and Pace behind to steady me. I felt no pain, though I seemed to move in a dream, my limbs responding so much more slowly than they should, my vision graying out. I felt Pace's hand press my elbow, and roused, moving forward. We clattered through dry stalks of marsh grass and thistles, till we reached the bend of the river. There was a broad sand shingle.

"Wait here," Pace said. Harriet leaned against me as we settled into the sand. Pace ran downstream. I studied the round river stones in the sand, then gazed up to the bluff where the sun shone on the trees. I dropped my gaze to the litter of twigs and gravel. Everything was beautiful, beautiful as anything I had ever seen. I tried to think of a prayer to celebrate such beauty.

"Charlie?" Harriet said. Her face was in mine and I could see her white hand on my brow. "Wake up," she said. "I'll help you stand."

I saw Pace downstream. He was dragging a rowboat through the alders by the water. He stopped and waved his arms broadly. I remember rising, and stumbling with Harriet to where Pace stood. I remember his tight grip on my arms, and the narrow boards of the bottom of the boat, and the sound of the boards scraping against stone. Then all was quiet and I was asleep again.

THERE WERE VOICES AND shapes, and light and dark. I saw ice and fire. I smelled forest loam. I heard singing, but not a song I remembered. I saw the dark face of a woman, leaning into me, her raven hair cluttered with feathers. Her hand was over my face. I watched her through her fingers. When she saw my eyes were open, she lifted her hand.

"I have seen your dream," she said. She folded her hands in her lap.

Next to her sat a dark man, his hair also raven. He was wearing a gray bowler.

"Listen to her," the man said. "She has medicine."

"There is a white deer running," the woman said. "When she runs, she makes a great light, like the sun. She has teeth like the bear. Wolves chase her, but her light blinds them and they cannot see to pursue her anymore. But one wolf can see through her light. When the wolf draws near, the white deer turns and tears him to pieces with her teeth. That is your dream."

I tried to speak but no words came out. I could see a fire burning in the hearth behind the woman, and I heard crackling. I thought it was the fire, but it was my teeth chattering.

"Oh, Charlie, you're so sick." I recognized Harriet's voice. I watched her pull the edge of a quilt close under my chin.

"Maybe a half mile, we turned a bend, couldn't hear the dogs," Pace said. "I reckon we covered maybe twelve, fifteen miles, altogether." His face was in the shadows, behind Harriet's. "The wind picked up. By nightfall my hands was so numb, I kept dropping the pole. Harriet said your fingers was blue, and you might get frostbite. It started to snow. We seen a light by the river. Reckoned we'd better take our chances, so we sunk Red's boat. This is Mr. Branham. He helped me haul you in here."

The dark man nodded.

"Help him sit," the dark woman said. "He must drink." She picked up a ladle and leaned toward the fire. There was a blackened pot hanging from the spit. She dipped the ladle in the pot and turned to me. Pace raised me by the shoulders. The quilt fell to my waist. I was naked. "Strong tea from the willow," she said. "Drink. To wrestle the fever." The tea was bitter. I winced and swallowed. "No," she said. "You must drink it all."

When I finished, Pace lowered me onto the pallet. I shivered all over and my teeth chattered more. Harriet started to cover me.

"No," the woman said. "Change the poultice. The other is full of poison now."

Harriet pulled the quilt below my groin. I grabbed at the edge to cover myself.

"Charlie," Harriet said. "Don't be so bashful." I had not seen her smile since I gave her *The Pilgrim's Progress*. She removed the poultice and handed it to the woman. She wrapped a new one in flannel. She dipped it in a basin and squeezed water from the flannel. She placed the poultice on my groin and covered me with the quilt.

"Infected," Pace said. "Not bad. Mr. Branham says we can stay here till you're stronger." He turned toward the woman. "Mrs. Branham, is it all right for Charlie to have him a smoke, him being laid up and all?"

The dark woman nodded. "Tobacco is good," she said. Pace pulled the pack from his pocket.

"Luckies," I said.

"Well, now he can talk," Pace said, smiling at Harriet. "We was kind of enjoying you being the strong, silent type and all." He lit the cigarette and held it to my mouth. My lip stung. I took a drag, and then another. The tobacco tasted wonderful. Pace leaned back in his chair, holding the cigarette between his thumb and finger. The butt was tinged with purple. I touched my lip.

"Pokeberry," Mrs. Branham said. I watched the white smoke from the cigarette curl toward the ceiling. Sweat beaded on my forehead. Mrs. Branham's tea had started its work.

"How'd you find me, Pace?"

He grinned. "Here," he said. He held the cigarette to my lips. I took another drag.

"You're asking the best damn bird-dog reporter in all Hampton Roads that question?"

"Well," I said. The room seemed to grow darker.

"And Harriet? How did she . . ."

"Shush, Charlie," she whispered. I felt her lips on my forehead. Then everything went black.

THE SNOW STOPPED THE next day. More than a foot had fallen, and the wind had drifted it over the Branhams' cabin porch. Mr. Branham said it would be better if we did not venture out. Mrs. Branham looked after me, and called Harriet to help her with some chore whenever she noticed her silent, staring into space. Staying cooped up was hard for Pace, active as he was and anxious as he was to get back to Hampton and the *Times-Herald*. There was a single window by the cabin door and from it we had a view of the river. The Branhams had a Bible, and Harriet read to me to help pass the time.

Mr. Braham kept catfish lines in the river. The morning after the snow stopped I watched him from the window as he rowed out to check his lines. The day was cloudy and the river looked black. I watched a canoe coming downstream, close to shore. There were two men paddling. They stopped paddling and Mr. Branham raised his head from his work. A big catfish was flapping at the end of the line and he dropped it into his boat. The man in the bow of the canoe back-paddled to hold it in the current. I could not make out if it was a rifle or shotgun propped against his knee. The man in the front of the canoe gestured with his arm. Mr. Branham had the brim of his bowler pulled low. He shook his head. The man gestured again and Mr. Branham nodded. Then he bent down in his boat. In a moment he dropped the line in the river and started to hoist his anchor.

"You come with me," Mrs. Branham said. She had been peering over my shoulder. I looked across the river and saw another canoe hugging the far shore. Mr. Branham was rowing his boat toward the cabin. The two men followed in the canoe.

"Be quick," Mrs. Branham said. Harriet and Pace were standing by the hearth. Mrs. Branham pulled a linoleum rug aside. There was a trap door. She lifted the door and guided Harriet by the elbow. "Down here," Mrs. Branham said. "Take the quilts covering the taters. Get behind the bins and cover yourselves."

The root cellar smelled of earth. We all crouched to make our way under the log joists. Mrs. Branham shut the trap door behind us. I heard her scoot the linoleum back in place. Then I heard the sound of sweeping. Dust filtered through the cracks in the floor-boards. I started to sneeze but held it. My foot bumped something and I heard the clunk of an earthenware jug against another.

"Here," Pace said. He put a damp quilt in my hand. I could smell sassafras root. Then everything smelled like potatoes. I could see better in the dim light. Pace and Harriet scooted under the potato bin. I followed.

My groin ached. The earth was damp, warmer than I expected. I spread the quilt over me and ducked under. Harriet clenched my fingers in her hand. She was trembling. I heard men's voices outside and then stamping on the boards of the porch. The door opened. Mrs. Branham stopped sweeping.

"Just you and the missus?" a man asked.

"Yes," Mr. Branham said.

"She looks like a squaw," a second man said.

"Yes," Mr. Branham said. "Monacan."

"Looks like a nigger," the first man said. "Ain't that what the bureau in Richmond says now, though? You's all niggers?"

"Yes," Mr. Branham said.

"Reckon you's a Monacan, too. Right, Chief? Till they made you a nigger?" the second man said. He chuckled.

"Yes," Mr. Branham said.

"Now I's to ask the woman what I asked you on the river, reckon she'd answer me the same?" the first man asked.

"Yes," Mr. Branham said.

"You don't talk much, do you, Chief?" the second man said.

"No," Mr. Branham said.

"Ma'am," the first man said. "You seen any travelers?"

"No," Mrs. Branham said.

"Not on the river nor by land?" the man asked.

"No," she said.

"You don't talk much either, do you?" the second man said. "Bet you's to have you a real man, that'd loosen your tongue."

The floorboards creaked.

"Hold on, now, Chief," the first man said. "I's to draw this piece,

I surely will pull the trigger. He didn't mean nothing. You didn't mean nothing, did you, Fred?"

"No, I didn't mean nothing," the second man said.

"All right, then," the first man said. "We had us some retardeds escape up at the colony. Two white boys and a white girl. Mongrel nigger tried to run off with them, too. But he ain't gone run no more. Chief, I don't recollect noticing no root cellar in the hillside when we was walking."

"No," Mr. Branham. "Under here."

"Got anything in there?" the man said.

"Apples. Taters. Whiskey," Mr. Branham said.

"Whiskey?" the man said. "Why, I like what you're saying, Chief."

"Reckon we ought to take us a look," the second man said. "Course, we understand you wouldn't be harboring no fugitives, would you?"

Harriet pinched my fingers together. I heard the scratch of the linoleum and the trap door open. There were footfalls on the steps.

"Dark as Hades," the second man said. "Where's that whiskey, Chief?"

"Steps," Mr. Branham said.

The second man grunted as he bent to pick up a jug.

"See anything else?" the first man asked.

"Tater bin. Apple barrel. Some kind of roots hanging."

"Well, then," the first man said.

There were steps and the trap door closed.

"Thanks for the whiskey, Chief," the second man said. "Cold on that river."

The door opened.

"Now, you was to see them retardeds," the first man said, "you be sure you notify authorities."

"Yes," Mr. Branham said.

"That sure was a nice fish, Chief," the second man said. "Mind if we fetch it out your boat?"

"No," Mr. Branham said.

"You ought to talk more, Chief," the man said. "You too, ma'am. Might stop by one day when I ain't so busy. We'll have us a regular confabulation."

The door closed. There were footfalls across the porch. Then laughter in the distance.

"Sons of bitches," Pace said.

I told myself not to think about Red. Harriet let go my fingers. When the blood started, it felt like needles pricking. I recited as fast as the words would come.

"Blessed is the man that walketh not in the counsel of the ungodly, nor sitteth in the seat of the scornful. His delight is in the law of the Lord, and in his law doth he meditate day and night." Selah. "He shall be like a tree planted by the rivers of water, that bringeth forth his fruit in his season; his leaf shall not wither. The ungodly are not so: but are like the chaff which the wind driveth away." Selah.

27.

Bear Mountain

My father's lodge was there," Mr. Branham said. "Where the schoolhouse stands." He pointed at a log building above the rock shelf where we stood. The logs had been sawed green. They were shriveled and warped. The mud chinking between the logs was nearly gone. There were two windows facing south and a pane in one was missing. It was patched with newspaper from the inside. Between the windows was a door with a stoop and rickety board steps.

He pointed beyond the little clapboard church next to the school. "Up this ridge, my father killed a bear with a knife when he was ten years old," he said. "He was small for his age and when he told the story he said the bear was small, too. But the people saw there was greatness in him and saved the skin for his mantle as chief. I remember standing by him with my mother holding my hand when he was chief and first wore the skin. The people sang songs and danced. The skin was not the skin of a small bear but hung down to his heels when he walked. The lodge he built with woven branches. It had a wood chimney and kept us warm many winters. Now the school covers the place it stood. Soon the white men will close the school because we are not Monacans anymore. Here, stand closer to the rock where there is shelter from the wind."

He pulled the bowler tight on his head. The moon was full and pressed against the treetops. The snow reflected its light. When the wind stirred the shadows of the tree limbs slithered like snakes over the snow.

"The white men are good at taking things away. This is the great strength the creator gave them. I do not understand but it is the gift the creator chose."

"Not for Christians," I said.

Mr. Branham studied my face for a moment. "The Episcopal built the church and the school," he said. "They are white men. They built the church for the people to be Episcopal, too." He looked off in the distance. "I listened to the Episcopal father. I turned from the ways of my father to the white father's teachings. Now the father in Richmond has a new teaching. The children will go to the school for the colored in the valley. My father was chief of the people. Now the people are leaving. The father gives them pieces of paper that say their children become colored when they are born and they are colored when they marry. It is a strange thing. The people came to Bear Mountain when the river was young. They were Monacans when they came here from the land west of the mountains and they have been Monacans until now. Now the father tells them they are not Monacans anymore. Who is the father who knows this?"

"A doctor. A man named Plecker. He used to practice in the city where I live. He helped many people."

"He must be strong medicine, to know what people are and they do not know?"

"Yes."

"It is hard to understand the ways of white men. I think I am too stupid for it."

He shook his head slowly. An owl hooted high up on the ridge top.

"Mr. Branham, did your wife say to you what the white deer is?"

"No," Mr. Branham said.

"Could it be a person?"

"Maybe," he said.

"Could it be Harriet?"

"The girl? My wife does not say. Is the girl strong medicine?"

"I suppose," I said.

"The white deer is always strong medicine," he said. "You must remember that." He pointed east. "We will go to Wingina Depot at midnight. Now we will smoke one of your cigarettes. Maybe we will not meet again. If we do, you will tell me if you learned if the girl has medicine."

I lit a cigarette and handed it to Mr. Branham. He took a long drag. The ember glowed in his eyes. He handed the cigarette to me. The wind had calmed and the woods were silent. The stars seemed close enough to reach. The owl hooted again, closer. I could make out its shape on the low limb of a tree. Then it flew.

"Where will you go?" Mr. Branham said.

"Hampton."

"This is your home?"

"Yes."

"By the big water?"

"Yes."

"Kecoughtan lands. My father's father traded there for shells. Big, rough shells, he said, good for scraping hides."

"Oysters."

"Yes, oysters. But the Kecoughtan are gone."

"Yes."

"At Wingina Depot the train stops for mail. You must be quick. There will be the man in the mail car and the man in the station."

"Thank you for the sweater, Mr. Branham. It's warm."

"I am sorry I did not have a coat. You are stronger now?"

"Yes." I crushed the cigarette butt on the stone and scattered the tobacco. "Do you ever go to the colony, Mr. Branham?"

"I have sold venison to the father there. Potatoes. Beets and corn." He stamped his feet and rubbed his elbows. "We must get your friend and the girl. Are you cold?"

"Yes," I said. I rubbed my hands together.

"The train will be cold. You must stay close together," he said.

We started walking. The snow crunched under our feet. In the moonlight I could see all the way down the ridge to the blackness of the river.

"I had a friend in college, Mr. Branham. He was my best friend. He was taken by his family to a clinic of the doctor who runs the colony now. He said the doctor castrated him."

Mr. Branham stopped and studied my face. "This grieves you," he said. He started walking.

"Yes." I fell in beside him.

"My wife says there are evil spirits at the colony. I cannot go there to trade unless she has put a spell on me. She says I must have the spell to protect me from the spirits. Maybe the family of your friend did not have a spell."

"He was sick. He had seizures. His family believed they caused the other thing."

"What thing?"

"He loved men."

Mr. Branham glanced at me. "I have seen this," he said. "But my people do not speak about it."

"No one does."

"This is the reason the doctor took his manhood?"

"To stop his urges."

Mr. Branham put his hand on my shoulder. "You should not grieve about this. The creator decides."

I wiped my face with my hands. My cheeks stung with the cold.

"When he came back to school, he was ashamed. But he told

me. He told me how he felt. I told him I couldn't love him the way he loved me. I told him I didn't know how to be his friend anymore. Now he's gone. He shot himself."

Mr. Branham stopped and put his hands on my shoulders.

"Do you believe your friend had no courage? Is that why you grieve?"

"No, no, he was brave."

"Then you must believe he chose to go to the spirit world. To have you remember him as he was, a young warrior. Maybe now I wish I had made his choice. Instead my people will remember me as an old man who was empty."

"No," I said. "They'll remember you as a chief, the son of a chief."

He lowered his eyes and nodded slowly. Then he raised his eyes and smiled.

"Maybe it is not the girl, Charlie," he said. "Maybe you are the white deer." He pressed my shoulders and dropped his hands. We started walking.

ON THE RAIL CAR we made a nest for ourselves among the hogsheads of tobacco, out of the wind. There were cloth sacks of buckwheat flour in the back. We carried a few sacks forward to sit on. We huddled together and soon Harriet was asleep between Pace and me. A sliver of moonlight entered through the gap under the sliding door of the car.

"That fellow got shot was a friend of yours?" Pace asked.

"When we were boys," I said.

"Mulatto?"

"Yes."

"Somebody sure carved him up," he said.

"Yes."

"You know, Charlie, I worked in Lynchburg at the *News* for a while," he said. "Anyway, one time the editor gets all pissed off

at me cause he caught me spitting on the floor of the office. So he
sends me out to cover a medical association meeting. Like anybody
would give a damn about what a bunch of doctors have to say.
Anyway, this doc goes up to the podium, bandy little fellow with
red hair and a goatee. Says he's practiced medicine in Roanoke for
twenty years and he's alarmed by the rise of lawlessness. Says he
knows the cure. Truck any nigger's committed a crime or winked
at a white woman off to a hospital. Clip his nuts, cut off his ears
so's everybody will know he's been treated, and turn him back in
society. Citizens will be safe and the state won't have to bear the
cost of incarceration.

"Them docs applaud like he'd just told them there was free
whiskey after the show. Then the red-headed doc at the podium
says for anybody, white or colored, who won't work for a living,
degenerates, he calls them—misfits, wayward girls, the mentally
deficient, morons, lunatics, idiots—sterilize them, and leave the ears,
since they ain't committed a crime exactly. Generation or two, this
doc figures, society's problems will be over. Some kind of science,
he said it was. Now, what the hell did he call it?"

"Eugenics?"

"That's it. Eugenics. Editor laughs his ass off at the way I'd
spelled it but turns out he don't know how to spell it, either. Had
a hell of a time finding it in the dictionary."

"Well," I said.

"Funny," he said. "I didn't give it much thought at the time.
Sounded like a big load of horseshit."

"Yes," I said.

"I'm sorry about your friend, Charlie. Took real guts to spring
you. I don't know how we'd ever got you without him."

"Yes."

"Sorry about what the doc did, too. Maybe they can fix it."

"Maybe. I don't know."

"No, I reckon not," he said. "Not now, anyways."

Harriet whimpered in her sleep. I looked at Pace and put a finger to my lips. He nodded. The train started down a grade. The couplings clanked and chattered. Harriet stirred but did not wake.

"Say, Charlie," Pace whispered. "Why you going back to Hampton and all?"

"I promised," I said.

"Wouldn't it be better just to light out somewheres?"

"Harriet needs to say good-bye."

"Reckon what she says is true? What she said her uncle did? Maybe she just imagined."

"I believe her."

"Well, that's it then," Pace whispered. "She seems plenty highstrung, though."

"Yes."

Pace studied for a minute. "Now what if we was to take down Mr. High-and-Mighty? You two hide out while I do me some bird-dogging?"

"Against his money? And what's to keep whoever came after me from coming after you?"

Pace looked at the moonlight. He blinked his eyes and sighed. "See us a lot in this line of work, don't we, Charlie?" he whispered.

"Yes."

"Anyway, my cousin in Richmond's a regular bigwig entrepreneur. Has him a Ford automobile and all. I'll wager he'll tote us all the way to Hampton when we tell him the situation."

Harriet cried out and her eyelids fluttered, but she settled back to sleep. Pace blew on his hands and tucked them into his coat.

"That's what we got us, ain't it, Charlie?" he whispered. "Got us one hell of a situation."

28.

Fugitives

When the train started to slow for the Main Street station in Richmond the light was just strong enough I could make out the shapes of trees through the cracks in the freight car. Pace crawled over and slid the car door back to get his head out. He scanned forward and aft.

"Don't see nobody," he said. I nodded. The wind bit my cheeks and hands. "Still a little too much speed."

"Harriet?" I said. She was huddled beside a hogshead, her head against a buckwheat sack. She raised her head. "Move over there with Pace. Watch what he does. Don't be afraid." I steadied her as she crawled toward Pace. Her hands felt like ice. Her face was white and stiff as a plaster mask.

"You go first," I said. "Show Harriet. I'll follow."

"Speed's about right, Charlie," Pace said.

"All right," I said. I helped him slide the door open wider.

Pace put his foot on a brace and swung out from the car, holding with one hand to the edge of the door. He looked at Harriet.

"See?" he said. "When you land, make sure to roll. Easier'n falling off a log." He grinned. Then he let go his grip and swung away from the car. He dropped and rolled a couple of times. There was plenty of snow covering the crossties. He sprang up and waved.

Harriet said nothing. She gripped the door, placed her foot on the brace, and swung out, just as she had seen Pace do. When she released her grip, she seemed to float like a feather, then dropped, rolled once, and stood. Pace trotted up the tracks and pulled her farther away from the passing cars.

I followed. I grunted when I hit and rolled, and pain stabbed my groin. I lay by the tracks in the snow, getting my breath. The big wheels of the cars rumbled as they passed, lifting the head of a loose spike against my knee. Pace and Harriet tugged at my jacket shoulders, pulling me away from the rails. They huddled over me.

"Charlie," Harriet said. "Are you hurt?"

The pang quickly passed. I pushed my eyeglasses up the bridge of my nose and rehooked the earpieces.

"Just knocked the wind out," I said. "Help me sit up."

They tugged at my arms until I was sitting. In a moment I was able to stand. We crouched and started to make our way across the tracks away from the depot platform. The train had stopped. The caboose was only a few cars away from where we crouched. The lamp was on, but we didn't see any movement in the windows. Steam from the locomotive boiled down the platform onto the tracks. A porter came out through swinging doors with a big handcart. I heard Pace whistle softly and turned his way. He nodded toward the depot. I looked. A thick boxwood wreath with a scarlet ribbon adorned the clock face of the station.

"I clean forgot, Charlie," Pace whispered. "It's Christmas morning!"

"Hey you!" The engineer in the caboose was hanging from the side of its deck. "You three!" He began to climb down the ladder. "You're trespassing!" he shouted.

Pace and I got hold of Harriet's hands and we began to run with her between us. The engineer was running in the snow now. The porter watched from the platform, craning his neck.

"Police!" the porter shouted. "Hey, police!" He didn't move from the handcart.

The engineer was heavyset and didn't run far. He stopped and bent, placing his hands on his knees. He tried to holler again but he couldn't get his breath. Clear of the rail yard, we began walking. We were fortunate it was a holiday. Hardly anyone was on the streets, and Pace's cousin would almost certainly be home.

"His place is way out on the West End," Pace said. "Too far to walk. I think I saw a phone box on the street when we was at the governor's, Charlie."

"Yes, I saw it."

"Let's mosey up that way, then," he said.

A block toward the mansion we found a Western Electric box. Pace had to whack the door with the ball of his fist to jar ice from the hinge. He dropped in a nickel and asked for the operator. I heard him give her a number.

"Are you all right, Harriet?" I asked.

"Cold," she said. "I'm so glad you're safe, Charlie."

"Just traveling with some friends back to Hampton," Pace said into the receiver.

"Well, we're not safe yet. They'll keep looking."

Pace hung up the earpiece and slammed the box door shut.

"Cousin says to head over by the river to the Hotel Rueger and keep a sharp eye out for him," he said. "Says he'll pick us up in front inside an hour. Says we can keep warm in the lobby. It's just him and the missus, so they'll feed us Christmas dinner." Pace shrugged. "Said he wouldn't hear otherwise."

There was a shed for carriages on the side of the Rueger Hotel. From it we could see the front clearly. As the sun rose clear of the building roofs, light pooled at the wall where we sat. The sunlight felt like a benediction. Pace took off his shoes to let it warm his toes. He wiggled them in his socks. Harriet closed her eyes and leaned into my shoulder. A little color had risen in her cheeks. There were brambles in her hair from the greenbriers. None of us spoke. We loafed in the sunlight. I smoked the last Lucky Strike in the pack Pace had brought me. My eyes were heavy, and I nodded, trying to keep awake. I dozed off.

"There he is!" Pace whispered. A Ford Model T coupe sat in front of the hotel. Pace jammed his feet in his shoes and scampered to the car. The driver rolled down the window.

"Cousin Pace," the driver said. He smiled broadly.

"Cousin Wade," Pace said. He turned and motioned to us. I roused myself and helped Harriet get up. We trotted to the car.

"Harriet, Charlie, this is my cousin, Wade Antrim. Cousin Wade, meet Harriet and Charlie."

"Jesus wept," Antrim said. "What happened to you three? Where's your overcoat, son?"

"Well, I just don't have it, sir," I said.

"He's a newspaperman, too, Cousin Wade. He don't need no sissy overcoat," Pace said.

"Well, pile in here out of the cold," Antrim said, rolling up his window. "We can all get on the seat. That girl ain't as thick as a pencil, anyway. Looks like you starved her half to death. Get in here."

We opened the door and slid in the passenger side. Harriet sat next to Antrim, then me, then Pace. There was plenty of room. The seat cushion felt luxurious.

Antrim looked us over before he began to drive. Like his voice, every move he made was charged with energy. His eyes were bright blue. He stared straight out the windshield as he drove. He wore a neat bowler the color of buckskin, a thick wool camel overcoat, and driving gloves with sleeves.

"So what you been up to these days, Cousin Wade?" Pace asked.

"I'll tell you what I been up to, Cousin," Antrim said, never taking his eyes from the road, "I believe I've sold a mimeograph machine to every bank, school, and business establishment in near every county east of the Blue Ridge Mountains. I'd sell west of the mountains, too, but I'd have to take the Ford up those grades in reverse; otherwise, the radiator overheats. Too hard on the transmission. Anyway, I got a whole new line, now. And we'll make us some real money there."

"What's that, Cousin Wade?"

"Radio," he said. "You can make you a crystal set for next to nothing, and they're only going to get better. Next thing you know, they'll be broadcasting music, news that's in the newspapers, vaudeville acts, advertising for every tonic, potion, and excuse me, Harriet, every feminine product, along with every geegaw you can think of and some you haven't, you name it, they'll be broadcasting it on radio into every household the livelong day. But selling radios ain't where the real money is."

"It ain't?"

"No, Cousin Pace. The real money's in licenses. Act of Congress this past summer. Every station's got to broadcast at one frequency and just that frequency so they don't overlap. I'm gone buy up every license I can. Already bought a couple down in Southside. Little towns, of course. I couldn't afford one for say, a city like Richmond. But anyway, that's where the real money will be. Licenses."

Pace whistled. "I always knowed you's gone have a mansion on the hill, Cousin Wade."

"Maybe so, Cousin," Antrim said. He mused for a minute, keeping his eyes straight out the windshield. "Cousin Pace," he said, "you know I'm not one to pry. But we're gone have to have a story for Mrs. Antrim. You three look like you been fighting cats the last month, and looks like the cats been getting the better of the contest by considerable. And looks like when you wasn't occupied with the cats, you was wallowing in the mud. So we need us a story for Mrs. Antrim."

"Well," I said.

"Charlie and me was on special assignment, Cousin Wade," Pace said. "Harriet come along to help us out."

"Special assignment?"

"It's hush-hush and all right now, Cousin Wade. Otherwise, we'd tell you and the missus the whole story. It's gone be one of them exclusives."

"Exclusive?"

"That's right," Pace said. "Has to do with politics. Charlie's been working on it for months and months, ain't you, Charlie?" Pace nudged my rib cage.

"That's right, Mr. Antrim," I said.

"We had to get in the backwoods to bird-dog some facts," Pace said. "And you know how some of them backwoods folks can be, Cousin Wade. Sometimes you got to clear out fast, they take a notion on something."

Antrim rubbed his chin with a gloved hand. "Yes," he said, "I'm sure Mrs. Antrim will understand that."

"WELL, THAT'S THE TRUTH of it, Iris," Antrim said. "The whole truth."

"I never in my life," Mrs. Antrim said. "Look at this girl! This child has been starved to death, when she wasn't being frozen!"

"We was amongst some pretty tough customers," Pace said.

"Oh you be quiet," Mrs. Antrim said. "Bringing a female child in on your misadventures."

"Yes, ma'am," Pace said.

The aroma of turkey and dressing filled the house. My mouth watered. Coals glowed on the grate in the room where we were standing. In the corner was a Christmas tree, festooned with red and white ribbons, and strung with popcorn.

"Husband, take these boys upstairs and see that they scrub

themselves from head to toe. Then go through your chifforobe and find them something decent to wear. That bird is going to be cooked in about an hour, Mr. Antrim, so don't fiddle-faddle. I'll tend to this child. Come along, my poor, dear thing. Oh my goodness, how you've been treated!" She flashed a look at Pace that could have peeled paint.

Antrim was a wiry man almost exactly my height. The suit, shirt, and collar he brought wouldn't have fit better if they'd been tailored. Pace's fit well, too, though his lanky frame was a tad too long for the sleeves and the trousers.

"Look like a fine pair of gentlemen and all, don't we, Charlie?" he said.

Mrs. Antrim had banked more coal on the grate. Harriet was sitting on the sofa with her back to the fire as Mrs. Antrim brushed her hair dry. The handle of the brush was silver and it glittered in the firelight. Mrs. Antrim's empty hand followed the hand with the brush, touching Harriet's hair with the tips of her fingers.

"Lovely," she murmured, shaking her head. "Just lovely." She heard us on the stairs and paused.

"Well, Mr. Antrim, do you remember this dress? Stand up, Harriet, let him see," she said.

Harriet rose. The dress was cream-colored, with a white lace bodice. There was white lace at her wrists. Her neck and cheeks were flush from the heat of the fire. My throat tightened when she smiled at me.

"I remember it, Iris," Antrim said. "Our first dance."

"It's a little full on her," Mrs. Antrim said. "Starved as she is. But doesn't she look pretty?" She pulled free a scarlet ribbon she had tucked at her waist. She tied Harriet's hair. She made a short bow, letting the tails of the ribbon hang down Harriet's back.

"For Christmas," Mrs. Antrim said. "The color of faith. Now let's get this meal served." She put her hands on Harriet's shoulder and kissed her on the cheek. "Will you help me, child?" she asked.

When we gathered at the table, Antrim remained standing while he asked the blessing. Then he carved the turkey. Mrs. Antrim filled our plates with dressing and gravy and sweet potatoes and collards and cranberry dressing from the sideboard. When the Antrims had finished their course, they sat and watched us. Mrs. Antrim served each of us seconds, and Pace thirds of everything. She reached for her husband's hand and held it. She smiled, nodding slowly. There was pecan pie with whipped cream for dessert.

After dinner, we sat in front of the fire. Pace and I sprawled in chairs. Mrs. Antrim sat on the sofa, holding Harriet's hand. Antrim sat in a Morris chair by the fire.

"Cousin Pace, I meant to tell you about something I saw in the *Times-Dispatch* a couple weeks ago," he said. "It was an article about some lunatics escaping from this asylum up near Lynchburg. Doctor who runs the place got authorization to hire Baldwin-Felts men to track them down. They must be pretty dangerous, these lunatics. There was three of them, I believe. There was another one, too. Shot dead before he could get away."

Mrs. Antrim pursed her lips and squeezed Harriet's hand. "Goodness me," she said. "What's this country coming to? This lawlessness."

Pace sat up straight in his chair. "Baldwin-Felts?" he asked.

"Uh-huh," Antrim said.

"Husband," Mrs. Antrim said. "This child is trembling all over. I knew she'd caught her death out there on that tundra."

"Oh no, Mrs. Antrim," Harriet said. "Though I'd like a glass of water, please. Would you go to the kitchen with me?"

"Why, of course, you poor, dear thing."

Mrs. Antrim and Harriet pushed through the swinging dining room doors.

"Got a good friend in the automobile parts business, boys,"

Antrim said. "Has him some delivery trucks. Metal sides, locked door in the back, so nobody'll happen to borrow a part or two if the driver stops off for a sandwich somewhere. Has one fellow makes a run all the way to Hampton. We'll just tuck you two and Harriet in the back with some blankets and you'll be there in no time. Course, you'll have to stay out of sight during stops. My friend is a man who don't ask a lot of questions. He'll just tell his driver he's helping out a cousin of mine. And that's the truth of it."

"That's cagey," Pace said.

"Think you can keep your tail out of the threshing machine for a while, cousin?" Antrim winked.

"I reckon so, Cousin Wade," Pace said. Antrim turned to me.

"Have you thought out the girl?"

"Yes, sir."

"And?"

"She wants to say good-bye to her family."

"That's the only course? To light out? Like Cousin Pace told me?"

"It seems so, sir. We've studied it every way. Prayed on it."

Antrim stood. "Don't tell me any more. I'm phoning my friend. You two and Harriet better turn in. We'll have to roust out good and quick to get over to the warehouse before dispatch." He started for the hallway. Pace and I stood. Antrim stopped at the door.

"Since it looks like you two've poked your privates straight in a hornet's nest," he said, "I don't suppose I need to tell you to keep a keen eye?"

"No, sir," we said.

"Merry Christmas, boys," Antrim said. "I'll see you bright and early."

29.

White Deer

I heard the key in the lock and roused myself. The driver opened the door wide.

"Here's your stop," he said.

Pace and Harriet had fallen asleep, too. They blinked their eyes. "Where are we?" I asked.

"C&O depot. Hampton," the driver said.

"Damn!" Pace said. He scrambled up and poked his head out the door. He ducked back inside.

"Hey!" the driver said. "I got to get these parts unloaded."

"Porter's coming with a cart and Poindexter's talking his ear off, Charlie," Pace said.

"Poindexter?"

Pace nodded. "Just as well run a banner headline on the front page," he said.

"See here," the driver said. "You kids got to clear out of the way."

The porter's head appeared on one side of the driver and Poindexter's on the other. Poindexter's brow lifted like he'd seen a ghost.

"Charlie," he whispered. "Is that you?" He took another look. His face went pale. "There's men looking all over for you, Charlie. Sheriff Curtis, too. James," he said to the porter. "Go fetch us a tarp, will you? I'll help the gentleman unload these parts."

"Yes, sir, Mr. Poindexter," the porter said.

"Will somebody tell me what the hell is going on?" the driver said.

"Oh, just a big holiday surprise party," Poindexter said. "We need to get these kids there without anybody seeing them. Here, let's get this cart loaded."

"Fine then," the driver said. He climbed inside. Harriet shifted to the side of the truck, out of his way. Pace and I helped the driver hand corrugated boxes out to Poindexter, who stacked them on the cart.

"That's it," the driver said. "The last one."

"James," Poindexter said. "Spread that tarp, will you?"

"We ain't expecting no weather, Mr. Poindexter," the porter said. "I know, I know."

The porter spread the canvas over the load on the cart. Poindexter motioned to Harriet. She stepped out of the truck and climbed under the tarp. Pace and I joined her. Poindexter lowered the edge to cover us. I peeked out.

"Don't forget the blankets," the driver said. He handed them to Poindexter, who tucked them under the canvas. "I need somebody to sign for the parts," he said. He slammed the rear door of the truck and held out a clipboard.

"Sure thing," Poindexter said. He signed and dropped the edge of the canvas over the side of the cart. "James, let's roll the cart into the office, so we can lock up. Don't want anything to happen to them parcels."

"Be seeing you," the driver said. He cranked the engine. I heard him drive away.

"Mr. Poindexter," the porter said, "we always leaves these out on the platform. Ain't nobody gone bother them."

"I know, I know," Poindexter said. The cart started moving and we heard the swinging freight door close behind us. "Thank you, James," Poindexter said.

I heard the porter cluck his tongue as he walked away. "Beat anything I ever seen," he said.

I heard a light switch. Poindexter pulled back the tarp. It was dark in the office.

"Charlie?" he said. "What have you been up to? Everybody's been worried. There's Baldwin-Felts detectives crawling all over town. Sheriff Curtis has been asking about you. And the girl, too."

"It's a long story," I said. "I need for you to keep it quiet."

"Oh, I'll keep it quiet, Charlie. Whatever you say. Them detectives can take on quite an attitude, if you know what I mean."

"We need to get Harriet over to her sister's, Poindexter. In Newport News."

"Near the shipyard?"

"Yes."

"Too far to walk. They'd spot you for sure."

"Yes."

"Gather up them blankets while I fetch a little tarp from the back," Poindexter said. "I got a dinghy down at the pier."

CLOUDS HAD MOVED IN, so the night was dark. We moved as quietly as we could. Poindexter started at every sound. The canvas of the tarp he carried whispered each step, and made even more noise when he tried to smooth it.

"Here, let me carry that," Pace said. Poindexter handed him the tarp. I heard a scratch and saw a flicker of light. A big man at the street corner was lighting a cigar. We crept slowly through the shadows, well away from him.

It was a little warmer by the water. Pace and I lowered the dinghy while Poindexter held a rope at the bow. We loaded Harriet with the blankets and tarp. Then Pace stepped in. Poindexter handed him the oars.

"There's a couple burlap sacks under the seat," Poindexter said.

"Stuff them in the locks. That'll keep the noise down." I stepped into the dinghy. "Stay close in," Poindexter said. "In case of a swell. Them dicks won't be looking on the water, anyway." He untied the rope and threw the end to me. "Tie her up at the pier where the ferry comes in. If you don't need her later, no matter, I got a friend'll fetch her out of the water come morning."

"Thanks, Poindexter," I said.

"Don't worry about me blabbing, Charlie," Poindexter said. "I wouldn't tell Saint Peter on Judgment Day."

"All right."

THERE WAS A SWELL, but not bad. It was so dark a wave would overtake us before we could see it coming. Even staying close to shore, it was difficult to keep oriented. Pace's eyes were much keener than mine, and he could make out landmarks as we rowed. Each of us took an oar, so we made good time. Harriet was wrapped in the blankets and covered by the tarp.

Pace bent toward me. "Cousin Wade's a piece of work, ain't he, Charlie?" he whispered.

"He's a good man," I said.

"You bet he is," Pace said.

"You're not so bad yourself."

Pace looked at me. We took another stroke, leaning into the oars.

"You know, Charlie, it's near been worthwhile moving heaven and earth for you these past few days, hearing you say that." He grinned broadly. We took a few more strokes in silence. "You know I ain't cutting with you, right?"

"I didn't think so," I said. "But you could."

"Could, hell. Somebody's got to stay round here, report the news and all. Them dicks ain't gone bother me." He looked over his shoulder. "There's the pier," he said.

The streets near the cottage were empty. There were no cars, no one on the sidewalks. I smelled wood smoke. We unlatched the front gate and listened. The cottage was silent. We stepped into the yard and went around the side of the house, looking in each window we passed. The lights were on in the parlor. I watched George Wright stand up from the sofa. He moved to the fireplace and worked the coals with a poker. He placed a log in the fire. I could see someone sitting on the sofa. It was Mrs. Wright. She looked up at her husband and said something. Then he joined her. They both looked down, as if they were listening to someone.

We crept to the back of the house. I tapped on the door. George came into the kitchen. He turned on the light. He looked uneasy. I tapped again. He walked over and opened the door.

"Charlie?" he said.

"George?" Mrs. Wright said. "What is it?"

I was holding Harriet's hand. I helped her to the stoop. She felt fragile as a bird. She was trembling. She blinked at the light spilling from the door. Mrs. Wright came to the door of the kitchen.

"Harriet!" she said. She opened her arms and Harriet rushed into them. Mrs. Wright sobbed and held her tight. Her sobs racked her body as the two sisters clung to each other.

"This is my friend Charlie Pace," I said to George.

"Get in here, boys, get inside," George said. He quickly shut the door behind us. Standing in the kitchen doorway was Sadie.

"Charlie!" she said. I knelt as she ran to me. She hugged me and stepped back. "Where've you been, Charlie? You had everybody worried. Mrs. Betts couldn't even sleep at night. But you know what, Charlie? Santa came to see me at Uncle Lewter's house and then he came to see me at Pauline's. I didn't know he could visit you in two different places. Isn't that something?" She stopped and studied Pace for a moment. "Your britches are short," she said.

"Sadie!" Mrs. Wright said.

"Mrs. Wright," I said. "We can't stay long. I'll have to take her. I'll have to take both of them."

Lights flashed in the windows from the street. I heard motors and car doors slamming and men's voices. I jumped up. Pace bolted for the front door. At the same moment it opened I heard the back door behind me.

"Evening, everybody," Sheriff Curtis said. He held the front door open by the knob. Behind him stood Deputy Chas Curtis, his hand resting on a holstered Owlshead.

Someone touched my shoulder. I smelled witch hazel. I turned and was face-to-face with Lewter Hobbs. He smiled broadly, showing his white teeth. The gold watch fob on his vest sparkled when he moved. Behind him stood a big man with a square jaw. He was wearing a bowler. His jacket was too tight for his chest. The big man turned and shut the door.

"Well, this is convenient, Sheriff Curtis," Hobbs said. "We weren't expecting you. Arrest this boy."

"Charlie?" Sheriff Curtis said. "Arrest him? On what charge?"

"Kidnapping my daughter," Hobbs said. "And transporting her for lewd purposes."

Harriet turned, still clinging to Mrs. Wright. "I'm not your daughter," she said.

"Oh yes you are," Hobbs said. "Under the law."

"And Charlie didn't kidnap me," she said. "I ran away. I ran away from *you*."

"I don't recollect no report of a kidnapping," Sheriff Curtis said.

"I filed a complaint with the Norfolk police," Hobbs said.

"Even so," the sheriff said. "It ain't on the wire."

"Oh, you fool! Why else would she be in his company? Detective, arrest him." The big man stepped forward, and so did the deputy.

"Now hold on, Mr. Hobbs," Sheriff Curtis said. "I'm charged with keeping the peace hereabouts."

The big man reached inside his jacket. Then he saw Chas' Owls-head leveled at his chest. Sadie began to cry.

"Come here, honey," Mrs. Wright said. "Come here." Sadie ran and hid herself in the folds of her sister's skirt.

"Detective," Sheriff Curtis said. "You's to draw down on a peace officer, I don't reckon neither Mr. Baldwin nor Mr. Felts would be much pleased." The big man dropped his hand to his side. "That's the spirit," the sheriff said. "Now as to kidnapping, Mr. Hobbs, report I got from this boy's landlady surely made it sound like he was spirited away against his will." He turned to me. "Is that about what happened, Charlie?"

"Yes, Sheriff."

"Well now, what do you reckon would make this girl run off from her new home, Mr. Hobbs?"

"Maybe she's wanton," Hobbs said. "Her upbringing wasn't the best."

"Wanton?" Mrs. Wright said. She searched her skirt for Sadie. When she found the little girl's hand, she pressed it into Harriet's. The light from the fire flashed in her eyes. Her first steps were small and tentative, but gained purpose. She stood before Hobbs, the top of her head just under his chin, her eyes raised to his face. Then she slapped him, so hard it sounded like a gunshot. Hobbs' face filled with disbelief. She slapped him again, and again. He staggered back to catch his balance. George caught her wrist as she tried to strike again.

"I know what you do to Harriet," Mrs. Wright said. "I know what you did to *me*. And I'll die before you do it to Sadie." She lunged at Hobbs. George held her back.

"Pauline," he whispered. He folded her arms together and pressed her small form against his chest. Her face twisted and she collapsed, like a rag doll that had been standing. She cried out and sobbed. Her sobs seemed to fill the room.

"I'll tell everyone!" she screamed at Hobbs. "Everyone!"

"Pauline," George whispered.

"Mrs. Wright, why don't you take your sisters upstairs for a spell, where you'll have some peace and quiet?" Sheriff Curtis said. "Us boys is gone have ourselves a little conversation down here, and then we'll be out of your way, ma'am."

George helped Mrs. Wright up the stairs. Harriet led Sadie by the hand. They went up the steps and shut the door.

"Well, I'm damned," Pace said.

"Thornton Jones will hear about this, Sheriff," Hobbs said.

"The mayor?" Sheriff Curtis said. "I's a man in your position, Mr. Hobbs, I'd sure hope to God he don't. Detective? What's your name anyhow, Detective?"

"Smith," the big man said. Sheriff Curtis grinned.

"Sure it ain't Jones? Anyway, come on over here, Detective Smith, and let Chas take a little weight out your pockets. Move easy, now."

The big man stepped to the middle of the room. Chas reached in his jacket and pulled out a Colt automatic pistol. He handed it to the sheriff. Sheriff Curtis shook his head.

"Well, now, we don't see many of them in these parts, Detective Smith. That's a mighty fine weapon. Got a nice heft to it. Chas, how about checking the detective's ankles?"

Chas bent down and patted down the man's legs. He stretched open the sock on the right and pulled out an over-under derringer.

"Nasty-looking, ain't it, Sheriff?" Chas said. He stood up, cradling the weapon in his hand.

"Sure is," the sheriff said. "Forty-four, Detective Smith?"

"Forty-five," the big man said.

"Use her much?"

"For shooting snakes and the like," the big man said.

"I tell you what, Detective Smith," the sheriff said. "You's a regular comedian. Ain't he, Chas?"

The deputy nodded.

"Pleasant as this all is, Sheriff Curtis," Hobbs said, "I can't stay here all night."

"You're right about that, Mr. Hobbs," the sheriff said. He turned to me. "Charlie, how much time you reckon you'd need?"

"Maybe a couple hours," I said.

"All right," Sheriff Curtis said. He reached over and shook my hand. "Okay, boys, here's what we're gone do. We're gone load up in them cars outside and head over to the office. Young Pace here is gone ride along to make sure the story gets writ up the way we want it in the paper. Ain't that right, Pace?"

"Yes, sir," Pace said.

"Hold on," Hobbs said. "You can't take me into custody."

"I ain't taking you into custody, Mr. Hobbs. I just need for you to answer some questions about the kidnapping. Need to get the facts straight for my report. And I got a few questions for Detective Smith here, too. Shouldn't take more than an hour or two." The sheriff winked at me. "Well, I reckon we'd best get started, so we don't lose any more of Mr. Hobbs' valuable time."

Pace came over and held out his hand.

"Reckon this is it," he said.

I grabbed him and held him tight. He hugged me back. Then we shook hands and he was gone. I walked upstairs and knocked on the door.

George opened it. Mrs. Wright was looking into her sister's face. She stroked her hair and cradled her cheek in her palm. Two small valises lay on the bed. Mrs. Wright knelt and embraced Sadie. She held her away from her and studied her face. Then she hugged her again.

"When I see them again, they'll be grown, won't they, Charlie?"

"Yes, ma'am," I said.

George pulled a roll of bills from his pocket and pressed it into my hand.

"For a rainy day," he said.

I nodded.

Mrs. Wright stood and took each of her sisters by the hand. Tears ran down her cheeks.

"Don't write," she said. "Not for a long while. So there's nothing for them to track."

"Yes, ma'am," I said.

Harriet's eyes were wide and dark. "You mustn't worry, Sister," she said.

Mrs. Wright pulled Harriet to her and kissed her face again and again. "Oh, how I failed you, child! Please, please forgive me."

"You didn't fail me, Sister," Harriet said. "You saved me."

George touched his wife's arm. "Pauline, we'd better let them go. Those men will be looking."

"Yes," Mrs. Wright said. She kissed Harriet once more on the cheek. She bent and kissed Sadie.

"Kiss Mrs. Betts, too," Sadie said. Mrs. Wright kissed the doll on the forehead. "Let me stay upstairs," she said. "It will be better."

George carried the valises. I helped Harriet and Sadie down the steps. I took the valises from George while he held the door. We looked up. Mrs. Wright waved from the window. Then she turned off the light. George closed the door behind us and we started for the pier.

30.

Mount Nebo

C oast is clear," Poindexter said. He had a porter's cart loaded with freight by the office door. Harriet stepped out holding Sadie's hand and I followed. Poindexter rolled the cart across the platform as we crept along beside it. At the passenger car, I helped Harriet and Sadie scurry up the steps.

"To the right," I whispered. Then I stepped up under the hood between cars. Poindexter handed me the valises. I took them into the car. Harriet and Sadie followed me. In our compartment I hoisted the luggage onto the overhead racks.

"Hang up your coats and I'll be right back," I said. "Pull down the blinds, too." I walked to the car door. From the hood I could see all the depot offices were closed, even Poindexter's. The platform lights were burning. Rime glistened in the cinders and crossties. Poindexter stood alone on the platform.

"Reckon we won't be seeing you in these parts?" Poindexter asked.

"Probably not."

"Say, Charlie, look yonder at them lights." I looked in the direction he pointed, about a hundred yards from the depot.

"That's the girls' old house," he said. "The Belote place. See? New family's moved in. Noticed it the other evening. Don't know who, though." He rubbed his chin. "See right there?" He pointed up the track just behind the tender. "That's where the colored girl liked to pick up her coal. See? When a locomotive pulls out, the couplings jerk, drops coal from the tail of the tender. Heard her family's done moved away."

"Well," I said. A whistle shrilled.

A conductor leaned out from the lead passenger car. "All aboard!" he shouted. He checked the front and the rear of the train and waved the all clear toward the engineer.

"You're a good man, Poindexter. Helped me many a time," I said. I leaned over the rail and held out my hand.

Poindexter shook it. "I'd help you many a time again, Charlie, you's ever to come back."

There was a hiss of steam. The couplings lurched and complained the length of the train.

"Good-bye, Poindexter," I said.

"Good-bye, Charlie." He stepped back from the track and started to wave. I waved back. The train began to accelerate. I dropped my hand and watched as he kept waving, until he fell out of sight in the bend of track.

I stood by the door. The night air was bracing. The train gathered speed. I could see the white winter moon over the water of the Roads. The water was calm, with gentle swells. It glistened like a river of steel. I could see moving lights, and columns of black smoke purling against the silver sky. A dreadnought, running in the darkness. Maybe the *Texas*. The moonlight glinted on its heavy guns. I slid up the window to the car passageway and locked it.

I stepped into the compartment and hung my coat on the hook. Sadie was studying my every move. She was holding Mrs. Betts on her lap.

"Harriet says you're our brother, Charlie. That for a while we didn't know but now we do. Is that true?"

I looked at Harriet, then back at Sadie.

"Yes, Sadie, that's true."

"Harriet said Momma said she lost you but then you came back and she told Harriet all about it before she went to see the angels."

"That's right."

"Well, how in the world did Momma lose you?"

"We don't know," Harriet said. "Momma never did say."

Sadie creased her forehead. "Well, how did you get back, Charlie?" she asked.

"I just traveled. People helped me along the way. I knew I had to get home."

"Was it scary, being all alone, traveling like that?"

"A little."

She nestled Mrs. Betts in the crook of her arm. "I like having a brother with me," she said. "You know, all my other brothers are grown up and moved away."

"I know."

"Harriet says if anybody asks, I'm to say you're my big brother."

"That's right, Sadie. And I'll always look out for you."

"Sadie, I think Mrs. Betts looks sleepy," Harriet said. "Here, I'll fluff your pillow, and you two get under the blanket." She arranged her sister and doll on the seat so their heads peeked over the blanket.

"Good-night, Harriet. Good-night, Charlie," Sadie said.

"Good-night, Sadie." She closed her eyes. The train was rocking gently. She was asleep in an instant.

I saw that Harriet had the Bible open to the gospel of Matthew. I leaned my head against the seat back and closed my eyes. She began to read.

"'Blessed are the poor in spirit: for theirs is the kingdom of heaven. Blessed are they that mourn: for they shall be comforted. Blessed are the meek: for they shall inherit the earth. Blessed are they which do hunger and thirst after righteousness: for they shall be filled. Blessed are the merciful: for they shall obtain mercy.

Blessed are the pure in heart: for they shall see God. Blessed are the peacemakers: for they shall be called the children of God. Blessed are they which are persecuted for righteousness' sake: for theirs is the kingdom of heaven.'" She stopped.

"Why didn't Christ remember the lonely?" she asked. I roused and looked at her.

"I don't reckon he understood," I said.

"How could he not understand? Don't you think he felt alone?"

"Not till he was dying."

"Charlie, sometimes I don't understand you."

"He knew God was inside him."

"Until he cried out?"

"Yes."

"And asked why he was forsaken?"

"Yes. It proved he was a man."

Harriet lifted her chin and looked at the ceiling of the compartment. A lock of hair had loosened. It touched the back of her ear.

"Do you think Christ believed everything could be fixed?"

"The God part did. Not the man part."

"I don't think either of us can be fixed, Charlie. Do you?"

"No, I reckon not."

WHEN SADIE SAW THE snow piled so deep it frightened her. The train we boarded for Provo had a plow mounted on the locomotive. The track through the passes was drifted, but the train slowed and plowed right through. We found rooms in a boarding house. Not long after, Harriet was employed as an assistant at the little school she and Sadie attended. I found work as a reporter for the *Provo Herald*. The paper wasn't around during my father's time. I rode the train north to Salt Lake City one afternoon and found an article in the morgue of the *Salt Lake Tribune*. It was sketchy, but the date was about right. A Mr. Henry Means, that was the spelling, was killed in a fight with a fellow worker. The weapon was a knife. Mr. Michael O'Rourke was charged with the murder. The case never came to trial. The Irishman, evidently desperate for drink, hanged himself in his jail cell the night of his arrest.

A train ride thirty miles south of Provo is Mount Nebo, the highest peak in the Wasatch Range. The mountain is an easy hike from a little station on the line. Harriet, Sadie, and I made the trip in late spring. We wore snowshoes. When Sadie grew tired I hoisted her and Mrs. Betts on my shoulders and we trekked on. Harriet likes the mountain air. She says it is like drinking pure water from a spring. We stopped at the base of the mountain on that trip. An ascent was too dangerous that time of year. The spring melt undercuts the snow pack. Sometimes hikers fall through and perish.

The peak is named for Mount Nebo in Pisgah. That was the peak where Moses caught his glimpse of the Promised Land. According to scripture he died on the mountain and was buried in a valley nearby.

Our Mount Nebo has three peaks. Sadie claimed the highest as her own. She said if you squinted you could see the light on the angels' wings as they flew up and down from there to heaven. I squinted and looked and told her she was right. She left the other peaks to Harriet and me.

Harriet calls these our Delectable Mountains. The pinnacles of Mount Nebo are covered with snow year-round. In the fall we returned on another hike. This time we skirted the peaks and descended into a valley with a green meadow. In the meadow is a lake. We spread a blanket on a rock promontory by the lake and had a picnic. Afterwards Sadie dangled her feet in the water. The water was so cold it looked like she was wearing little pink socks when she drew out her feet. We wiped them dry and rubbed them with our hands in the sunlight until she fell asleep. Mrs. Betts was cradled in her arm. Cow elk grazed in the meadow. Harriet and

I watched the reflected clouds drift across the surface of the lake. The reflected peaks were defined so sharply we could see individual rocks and crags. Blue shimmered in the water and sky. The aspen trees floated like spun gold.

"This is our Surprise Valley," Harriet said. "Even without the secret entrance."

I turned to her. A breeze lifted her hair. It glistened with silver, like water as it cascades from a fall.

"Yes," I said. "Who'd've reckoned we'd find it?"

"No one," she said. She lay back on the spread, perching on an elbow.

"Charlie?"

"Yes?"

"Did you mean to quit smoking?"

"No," I said.

"Well, you haven't smoked. Not in weeks."

"I haven't?"

"No," she said.

"Well," I said. "Who'd've reckoned that?"

"No one," she said. She sat up and kissed me on the cheek. "Look, Charlie. Yarrow." She plucked a flower head and tucked it behind her ear.

"Pretty," I said.

"It's funny," she said. "I don't hate him so much anymore. I used to carry it around with me, like a bottle of poison, but now it's gone."

"That's a blessing," I said.

"I just seemed to forget. It can't be that simple. It doesn't feel that simple."

"Maybe better not to think too much on it."

"Yes," she said. "Probably better." She settled back on an elbow. "Last night before prayers Sadie asked after Pauline."

"Yes," I said. "I heard her."

"Could we go back?"

"When she's of age. He'd have no claim then."

"Maybe he'll die soon. We'd be orphans again."

"Maybe."

"I don't think I want to go back. There's nothing for us there. Pauline will have her own family with George. It would help her forget if we don't go back."

She took the yarrow from her ear and held it between her fingertips on her breast. "Charlie, I think you did everything you could for Virgie."

"I want to believe so," I said.

"Maybe it was better she died. To spend her life in prison. To grow to be a woman and die there."

I looked out over the lake. A flock of gulls settled onto the water, shrieking and cackling. They began to bathe. They dipped their heads and bodies and popped back to the surface. I could hear the pinions as they beat their wings, splashing water. Their white heads gleamed in the sunlight. Their bills were bright yellow. As they preened their feathers, drops of water spun like scattered jewels. Ripples spread across the surface of the water, running faster and wider, until they vanished.

Acknowledgments

My journey finding this novel began in the stacks of the University of Iowa Libraries, where I read Derryn Moten's 1997 dissertation, "A Gruesome Warning to Black Girls: The August 16, 1912 Execution of Virginia Christian," between sessions at the 2011 Iowa Writers' Workshop Reunion. Of very special help as my search progressed was Ajena Cason Rogers, a descendant of the Fields family, who provided a copy of the manuscript, "Come On, Children: The Autobiography of George Washington Fields, Born a Slave in Hanover County, Virginia," Sis Evans Collection, Hampton History Museum. Fields's account is now included in *The Indomitable George Washington Fields: From Slave to Attorney,* by Kevin M. Clermont. Also helpful was *Grant Me to Live: The Execution of Virginia Christian, 'A Legal Homicide,'* by Charles Vaughan, and *Encyclopedia Virginia*, a publication of the Virginia Foundation for the Humanities, in partnership with the Library of Virginia. Special thanks to Christian Allison, A. K. Brinson, Becky and Jim DeHaven, Mary Ann Garcia, Marianne Gingher, Greg Hlavaty, Christopher Kerr, Suzanne La Rosa, Ginger Moran, Victoria Shropshire, Randall Williams, and the staff at the Library of Virginia and Belk Library, Elon University.